HOLIDAY Wedding

DR. MELISSA DYMOND

The story, all names, characters, and incidents portrayed in this production are fictitious. No identification with actual persons (living or deceased), places, buildings, and products is intended or should be inferred.

Book Cover by Qamber Designs

Character art by Hungrydamyart (Etsy), Lorena@Chocological.art, lulybot, and Sonia Garrigoux (artbysoniagx)

Formatting by KUHN Design Group | kuhndesigngroup.com

Copyediting by Dymond and Associates

TRIGGER WARNINGS (CONTAINS SPOILERS)

Death of a parent from cancer (happens 11 years before the story)
Gun violence (no one is shot)
Stalker
Kidnapping
Military trauma/PTSD
Remote history of alcoholism (mentioned)
Issues with body image

Please check trigger warnings.

Your mental health is more important to me than book sales.
XOXO, Melissa

Copyright © 2024 by Melissa Dymond, DO

All rights reserved. No part of this publication may be reproduced, distributed, or transmitted in any form or by any means, including photocopying, recording, or other electronic or mechanical methods, without the prior written permission of the author, except for the use of brief quotations in articles or book reviews and as permitted by U.S. copyright law. For permission requests, contact www.melissadymondauthor.com.

ISBN (eBook-spicy/open door) 979-8-9903958-3-1
ISBN (eBook-clean/closed door) 979-8-9903958-2-4
ISBN (Print-spicy/open door) 979-8-9903958-4-8
ISBN (Print-clean/closed door) 979-8-9903958-5-5
ISBN (Photo cover-spicy/open door) 979-8-9903958-6-2
ISBN (Photo cover-clean/closed door) 979-8-9903958-7-9

Please visit the author's website at

WWW.MELISSADYMONDAUTHOR.COM

for character art, book deals, writing updates, and more.

CONNECT ON SOCIAL MEDIA—LET'S BE FRIENDS!

INSTAGRAM: https://www.instagram.com/melissadymondauthor

FACEBOOK: https://www.facebook.com/melissadymondauthor

TIKTOK: https://www.tiktok.com/@melissadymond6

BOOKBUB: https://www.bookbub.com/authors/melissa-dymond

OTHER BOOKS BY DR. MELISSA DYMOND

Holiday Star—a holiday celebrity romance

Paging Dr. Hart—a medical romance with suspense

*This is for all the women who've been told you're too much.
Too emotional. Too opinionated. Too demanding.
And for the women who've been told you're not enough.
Not pretty enough. Smart enough. Funny enough.
Don't listen to those lies. You are enough.
You're perfect. Just the way you are.*

MUSICAL INSPIRATION
Love Never Felt Like This by Max

TUESDAY, DECEMBER 10
14 DAYS UNTIL THE WEDDING

GWEN

Caleb Lawson has about a million ways of kissing. Sometimes hard and fast. Sometimes sweet and slow. This is his teasing way, where he presses his mouth to mine in a series of firm kisses, then retreats. My lips chase his, and he returns to me this time with a gentle kiss, soft as butterfly wings. I sigh, content in his arms.

The world melts away.

There's only us.

Minutes, hours, an eternity passes where all I see is him. All I feel are his strong arms around me, holding tight. Finally, he pulls away. He tucks a strand of hair behind my ear with a soft, "I love you, Gwen."

How I adore that sound—the way he says my name.

GweN.

Round G, flat N.

I'll never grow tired of hearing him say it. Never tire of holding this priceless man in my arms, of sharing my life with him. Thank goodness I won't ever have to give it up because in two weeks' time we're getting married. I'll be his wife, and he'll be my husband, united forever.

"Love you, too." I nuzzle into his neck, inhaling his spicy cinnamon scent, and sigh mournfully. "I wish I didn't have to go."

"Me too." He cups the back of my head, threading his fingers into my hair.

"It's the worst timing with the wedding so soon." I pull away and throw my arm over my face, but not before I spy the mistletoe that hangs from the ceiling in his living room. It spins and swings, dangling on a long string right over our heads. Caleb put it there earlier today as a surprise for me. He knows I love the holidays. He said it was to "get us in a Christmas mood."

I slide my arm down and peek at him over the top of it. "I still can't believe we convinced our families to let us have the wedding on Christmas Eve."

Caleb laughs, sending the couch cushions shaking. "It didn't take much convincing. Once our moms proposed it as a way to have family reunions and to spend Christmas together, everyone got on board *real* quick."

I drop my arm and sigh. "That makes me leaving even worse. I want everything to be perfect for our families who are flying in. I should be here to help."

Caleb turns to face me. "I know you don't want to, but you have to go. I mean, it's huge. The American Cancer Society asks you, a *resident*, to come to its conference and give a talk about your colon cancer research. You can tell everyone how they're supposed to start screening at age 45."

That makes me grin. "Look at you, smarty pants," I tease. "You're getting an honorary medical degree just from hanging out with me."

Caleb smiles back. "I do listen to you, *Dr. Wright*." He tickles my ribs when he says my name, sending me into a fit of giggles. "Besides, you'll only be gone for a little over a week, and it's in L.A., so you can visit your mom and Teddy before the conference starts. It's perfect. When you get back, we'll still have a couple of days to finish any last-minute details before the wedding."

He's right. It's winter break, so my mother is off from her job teaching in Japan. She's spending the next couple of weeks here in the States. First, she'll stay in California, checking on her house there and on my younger brother, Teddy. After she's done in California, Mom will fly here to New York to meet up with my newly minted stepdad, Seth, who is also Caleb's uncle. Once she arrives, she can assist Caleb's mom, Marjorie, who's been making wedding arrangements.

With me working over 90 hours a week in the hospital and Caleb juggling acting on Broadway and managing his restaurants, we're too busy to plan the wedding on our own.

"My family will beat me back here. Mom, Brandon, and Teddy will all fly into New York before I'm done with the conference." I lean my cheek against the back of the couch.

Caleb chuckles. "Do you think we'll survive it? Both our mothers working together?"

I laugh with him. "We may end up with 500 people at the wedding and a dancing elephant, but I think we'll live."

"My mom would for sure be the one to order the elephant," he agrees.

"Yes, she would."

We've kept Marjorie on track so far, but we've had to shoot down some crazy ideas of hers, like releasing 100 doves over us as we say our vows. Caleb had shaken his head at that one. "Bird poop, Mom. No way do I want our guests ducking and covering."

Then there was the giant ice sculpture that she almost ordered. "Don't worry, kids," she'd told us, "we'll keep the room temperature at 55 degrees, so it won't melt too fast." Even though it's a winter wedding, I've chosen a sleeveless dress. A fact that I reminded her of, stating, "I'd rather not be covered in goosebumps all night."

The truth is, we need her help. We've only been engaged for six months, not a lot of time to plan a wedding, but once Caleb placed that diamond on my finger, we rushed to make it official. It felt right to celebrate our union during the holidays, my father's favorite season.

Caleb runs his thumb, rough with guitar string calluses, slowly over my cheek as I stare back. He's gorgeous, relaxed and happy. His bright aqua eyes shine. His golden hair has grown longer, curling over the tops of his ears. His muscles, all those gorgeous, sculpted muscles, shift as he runs his thumb down my jaw and then over my lips. Almost two years together and I still can't get enough.

I suck in a breath, overcome by it—my love for him. It's a deep, deep pool I could swim in forever.

"I love it when you look at me like that," he says softly.

"Like what?"

"Like I'm your favorite thing."

The curl of my smile brushes against his fingertip. "That's because you are." I lean forward to run my nose along his and then whisper in his ear, "My favorite."

When I pull back, I expect him to be happy, but he's not. There's a wrinkle between his eyes as he frowns.

"What if you stop feeling that way?" he asks, suddenly forlorn. "What if you change your mind? Love is fragile, and life is long. How many people have found love only to lose it?"

I move closer, pressing my body along his. I soak up his warmth and return it back to him. "Those people aren't us, Caleb. We won't lose this. It's you and me, forever and always. Remember? We promised."

Both of us are silent for a minute, recalling how we broke that promise once before, about how he left me. But then he returned, and my once-shattered heart was glued back together, stronger than ever.

That worried furrow in his brow remains. "But—"

I silence him with a kiss.

I know this Caleb. This is anxious Caleb. Insecure Caleb. He's told me before that it's times like this, when the what-ifs of life have overwhelmed him, when he's ended up with a bottle in his hand and alcohol on his tongue. That's not going to happen anymore. I'm here, and I'll soothe away those worries. I'll comfort him like he comforts me. Sometimes I think we take turns freaking out, with one of us spiraling into darkness and the other pulling us back into the light. Looks like it's my chance to be the savior today.

I kiss him breathless, until I feel his body relax under my touch, and only then do I stop. "There's no world where we aren't end game," I tell him. "With everything we've already been through, all the obstacles we've overcome, you're the one for me, and I can't wait—" I choke on my words, tears building in the back of my throat. "I can't wait to put on my white dress and walk down that aisle to you. Heck, I'll run down it if you're there at the end waiting for me."

He gives me my special smile, small and tender, brimming with love. "I'll be there. I'd wait for you for a million years and then a million more."

I melt, my body folding around him as my mouth seeks his. He kisses me like he's memorizing the shape of me, the sound of my sighs, the taste of my lips.

"I wish you'd take the jet," he murmurs into my mouth.

I push away with a huff. "We've already talked about this."

Caleb runs his hands through his hair, tugging at the ends. "Come on, Gwen. I own an airplane. This is what it's meant for. Use it."

"I don't want to be like that," I counter, frustrated that we're discussing this *again*.

"Like what?"

I push away and stare at the wall, refusing to meet his eyes. They say a storm is coming, but for now, the sky outside the window is clear. Dawn splashes rays of rosy pink, yellow, and orange across the room. Normally, the sight would send me scrambling for my paintbrush to capture those transient hues, but not with how aggravated this conversation makes me.

I answer his question. "You know that I want to travel in coach like a normal person, at least for now."

He tenses next to me. "How do you not understand? You can't be that way, not if you're going to be with me. There's nothing normal about my life."

I'm aware I'm frustrating him. That I'm full of contradictions. With one hand I cling to who I've always been, but with the other hand I eagerly grasp for who I'll be in the future, once I become his wife.

I can't have both.

I have to let one go, but it's hard.

I sigh, equally frustrated. "I get that, but for now I can still go out and not be recognized."

"That won't last," he argues. "After this wedding, everyone will know who you are and what you mean to me."

This isn't just an argument about the airplane. It's about where I end and he begins. It's about how to balance his fame and my day-to-day life. It's about fitting the discordant pieces of our lives together like the jigsaw puzzle we completed years ago.

Caleb says, "Already, the paparazzi are sending out their spies. Trying to figure out where the venue is and who's catering the wedding." He picks up my hand and presses a kiss to my palm, then curls my fingers over it, so I hold the sensation of his touch.

The corners of his mouth tug down. "I hate to think of you out there, where people might be mean to you or judge you or hurt your feelings, all because of me."

"I'll be fine. Besides, if someone recognizes me, I can handle it. I'm not scared of the press. Remember, I've dealt with them before. I need you to trust me, Caleb. Trust that I'm strong enough."

This is an old wound, a painful one. Fear of exposing me to the harsh realities of his fame was the main reason Caleb left me before. I'm determined to prove him wrong. Show him I can withstand the pressure that comes with being his wife. I'm tired of him underestimating me.

"It's not you I don't trust," he murmurs, refusing to look at me.

"I'll be okay," I reassure him once more. "Alvina will be with me. She'll visit with her cousins in L.A. while I go to my lectures."

"Well…," Caleb says, drawing out the word, trepidation written all over it. "I did a thing."

"What?" I whip my head up to him, immediately suspicious.

"I know *you're* not worried, my brave lion-hearted fiancée, but *I* am, so Wayne's coming with you. I booked him a ticket and got him a seat next to you." He says the last part as fast as he can and then squeezes his eyes shut, scared to see my reaction.

"What!" My voice echoes off the hand-laid bamboo floor of his penthouse apartment as I picture the thin-faced tabloid reporter turned friend.

One aqua eye cracks open and, not liking what it sees, closes again. "Wayne's going," he says in a tone that leaves no room for argument.

He's marrying the wrong woman if he thinks I'll give in that easily.

I hate giving in.

"No way," I insist. "It'll be fine. I love Wayne and all, but I don't need him."

Both his eyes fly open. Caleb sits up, his back ramrod straight, and glares down at me. "I wanted to send one of my bodyguards, like Dean, but I knew you would hate that, so Wayne's going instead. He'll be my eyes and ears out there. He can spot the press a mile away."

"Because he *is* the press." I throw my hands up, exasperated.

"Exactly." He nods like I just proved his point.

"Wayne will probably be on the job himself. I bet he's going so he can hang out at the airport and take pictures of other celebrities who're traveling. You know what he always says, 'Business is business.'"

"That may be true, but he'll still keep an eye on you."

"Caleb," I growl, my temper rising, "I'm a grown woman. I can look out for myself."

He sighs and hangs his head, shoulders slumping. For a moment, I flashback to when we were broken up. How he had sat like this a year and a half ago. When he had turned back to the bottle and let his alcoholism take over. It's hard, seeing him this way, so I force myself to calm down. He's trying to protect me. Sending Wayne to California is his way of saying he loves me. That he needs me safe.

"Fine." I relent. "Wayne can come, but he and Alvina are going to fight like cats and dogs, as usual. I'm warning you now. I'll call every night and complain about it."

Caleb's relief is instantaneous. "Thank goodness. I thought we were heading toward a huge argument." He settles back down next to me and mutters, "You can be so stubborn."

"Who?" I say with mock indignation, widening my eyes. "Me? I'll have you know I'm a *very* reasonable person."

We both laugh. He's right. Sometimes I can be incredibly stubborn. It's a trait that's gotten me through rough times. Medical school. My broken engagement. When my dad died. Once we've quieted, I tell him, "I don't want to fight with you. Not when I have to leave in an hour."

An ache, deep and piercing, gnaws at my chest as the reality of leaving him sinks in. This is the first time we'll be apart since we became engaged. Ever since we got back from Tokyo last summer, we've spent almost all our free time together. It had been easy, a seamless transition to us spending time together.

Probably because we'd done it once before, almost two years ago, when we spent a month in my mother and Seth's house in Los Angeles. Back then Caleb had hidden in that house, one I was already living in, on the run from his fame. That's when we first fell in love, only to break up a month later when the paparazzi found us. It had taken months apart and then months getting reacquainted until our relationship found solid ground. Now, I can't imagine not seeing him at least once a day.

Caleb throws his leg over mine, the weight heavy and familiar. He likes to cuddle like this, with one leg on me, like he's a human blanket pinning me down.

"I can think of more enjoyable ways to spend this time."

I inch closer and smirk. "What exactly did you have in mind? For things to do until I go?"

"Oh, future wife. I've got ideas." His voice lowers, all mysterious.

I giggle at the mischievous sparkle in his eyes.

His arm comes around, and he pulls me close. All my remaining tension seeps away. Attraction ignites, burning between us. It's always there, simmering, waiting like I'm kerosene and he's the spark.

"Future wife," I say, right before his lips meet mine. "I like the sound of that."

GWEN

CALEB

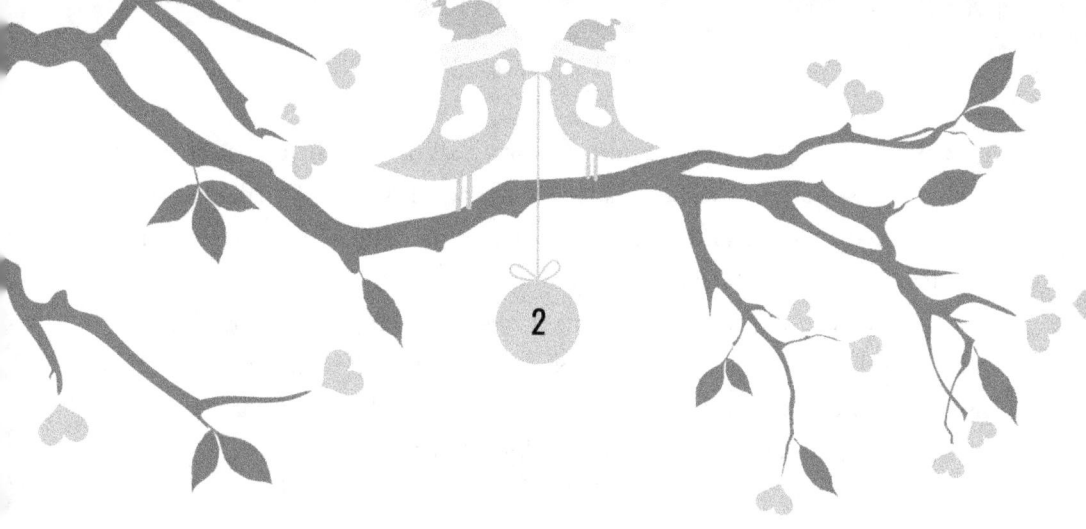

2

**TUESDAY, DECEMBER 10
14 DAYS UNTIL THE WEDDING**

—JENNY—

"Stop fidgeting," Dean hisses out of the side of his mouth. His lips are pursed in an angry scowl while his gaze remains firmly planted on Caleb's back.

Ignoring him, I twirl my curly dark-brown hair around one finger. I spent a long time this morning straightening and then curling it into my favorite style. My watch says it's 11:00 a.m. I get busy taking notes and shooting an occasional photo. The camera clicks as I capture the line of fans who stretch out the theater's double doors and onto the ice-slicked Manhattan sidewalk. They huddle in bulky jackets and fuzzy earmuffs as their breath clouds the air in little white puffs. Many of them have brightly wrapped presents tucked under their elbows.

Caleb's giving out autographs today, a publicity event put on by the Broadway theater where he performs several times a week. This signing is holiday-themed, with staff handing out complimentary scarves that come in one of three choices: a grinning Santa, a snowman with a black top hat, or a red-nosed reindeer. Caleb wears the Santa scarf. I straightened it for him earlier, making sure the rosy-cheeked St. Nick was clearly displayed.

I stand in the theater lobby and press my eye to the viewfinder to capture an older woman as she hands Caleb a large box with a big blue bow. He opens it to find a handmade quilt featuring all of his movie posters. I can't imagine how long it took to make something so beautiful. Caleb gives the fan a one-armed hug and grins while she grabs a selfie with her cell phone.

To everyone else, he looks happy, but I've spent enough time around him to know he's acting. Before the fans arrived and he plastered on that false grin, he'd been subdued, reserved. Not his normal self at all. He's been that way ever since he dropped Gwen off at the airport this morning. It's like he can't shine quite as bright without her light to channel.

I understand. Gwen's been my best friend since sixth grade. I love her just as much as he does.

My phone rings. I pull it out and peer at the tiny screen. My stomach lurches when I see the incoming call labeled "Butthead." Not in the mood to talk to him, I silence my cell and put it away. A quick glance around shows no one's paying attention to me. I reach into my pocket and retrieve a sugar-free butterscotch candy. The wrapper makes a crinkling sound when I untwist the ends. I pop it into my mouth and hum quietly as it melts on my tongue. When I bite into it, the candy makes a loud crunch, which earns me a glare from Dean.

The crowd continues to inch forward. Every time the doors open to allow the next person in, an icy breeze enters with them. Out on the street, people stomp frozen feet and blow breath-warmed air onto their hands. These fans must really adore Caleb to be out in weather like this. On the drive over, the radio said we've got a bad storm heading our way.

"Caleb," I call over and get his attention, "hold up that quilt."

He obliges. I take a photo using my heavy-duty professional camera and then another quick shot with my cell phone. The second picture I send to Gwen, who should still be at the airport.

Jenny: Check out what some lady made your fiancé.

Gwen: Wow. Amazing. What scarf is Caleb wearing?

Jenny: Santa. I got one, too.

Gwen: I want to see.

I shoot a selfie and check it to make sure my reindeer scarf is visible. My light-brown eyes stare back from the photo, tinged red from the flash. A couple of dark, springy curls hang over my forehead, and the rest of my long hair tumbles over my shoulders. I send it to Gwen.

Gwen: Cute scarf. I like it!

Jenny: Of course you do, you Christmas-loving freak.

Gwen: It's true. Plane's boarding. Tell Caleb I love him forever and always. Love ya, too.

Jenny: Love you. Travel safe.

I make a mental note to grab a scarf for Gwen before I leave. The snowman, so between her, Caleb, and me, we'll have the complete set. I smile, picturing how it'll complement her long, blonde hair and pretty, light-blue eyes. It was no surprise to me when Caleb fell for her. Gwen's got outer beauty, that effortless California girl look, but even more she has inner beauty with her kind heart, so loyal and caring.

The crowd moves forward. A kid, about six years old, standing in line, holds his mom's hand and stares blankly ahead, bored. When he glances my way, I cross my eyes and stick my tongue out the side of my mouth. A delighted smile spreads over the little boy's face. He imitates me. Next, I suck in my cheeks and blink comically, giving him my best fish impression. Soon, the boy and I are giggling, trading funny faces with each other.

Dean observes our exchange with a strange expression. Annoyance, I assume.

A gust of winter-chilled wind sweeps in, distracting me from Dean and the boy. I shiver and pull the cream-colored sleeves of my sweater down to cover my hands. I've always loved its fuzzy cashmere yarn, how the light color contrasts against the warm brown of my skin, a gift from my Nigerian ancestors. I sigh and adjust the hem of my sweater to make sure it covers my stomach.

My weight fluctuates based on a million different circumstances. It can depend on the weather, if I'm about to get my period, and, of course, on what food I put in my mouth. I work out every day, but still my body remains soft and curvy. I run my fingers over the fabric one more time, smoothing it out.

"You're doing it again," says Dean next to me. "Stop moving."

"I can't help it," I whisper back.

His tan cheeks flush red beneath his five o'clock shadow—ridiculously named since it's only a little after 11:00 a.m. His stubble matches his hair, both brown, so dark in color it's just shy of being black. He wears his usual attire, a navy-blue suit and white button-down shirt. The top buttons are undone, showing off well-defined collar bones and the beginning of a muscular chest. No tie for him, yet he manages to radiate professionalism with an edge of intimidation. Not the kind of guy you want to piss off. Too bad for me. I ticked him off two years ago, and he's still not over it. When his glower shifts my way, I avert my gaze, not wanting to get caught staring.

I try unsuccessfully to stop the twitching of my foot, the shifting of my weight, the plucking of my collar. I've always been like this. Unable to hold still. I'm too full of energy, with a constant need for motion. It's as if my mind and body are set to fast forward, speeding along twice as quick as everyone else.

"You're distracting me," Dean says. He stands motionless. Every limb in place, exactly where it should be. The very picture of control.

"So don't look," I counter. Irritation zings through my nervous system, which only makes me squirm more.

Although I'm annoyed by Dean's criticism, I do understand it. As Caleb's lead bodyguard, he has to stay focused to do his job. Unfortunately for him, his job and mine have overlapped a lot in the past month, ever since the newspaper I work for, the *Los Angeles Times*, sent me here to New York. I'm its primary reporter assigned to Caleb. Once a week, I write an article recapping all of his activities. As a famous actor, singer, songwriter, and restaurateur, everything he does is considered noteworthy.

"Do you have to come to *all* of Caleb's events?" Dean swings his head my way, his gaze unflinching. Sometimes, when he looks at me, his eyes are like laser beams, designed to burn a hole right through my center.

"Yes, *Dean*," I spit out, equally frustrated by our role as begrudging co-workers. "You know the drill. Don't make me explain it to you again."

He snorts. "All the newspaper really cares about is the wedding. They're using your friendship with Gwen to get exclusive access. It's no coincidence that you leave as soon as the ceremony's over."

He's right. I'm under no illusion that my reporting skills landed me this job. Before the newspaper learned of my connection to Gwen and Caleb, I spent most of my time fetching the senior reporters coffee and doing their online research. I was good at that, tracking down leads and then having my co-workers take credit for them.

I'd been surprised to be called into my editor-in-chief's office. I was even more surprised when they said I was getting a "promotion." For a fleeting moment, my heart had soared, thinking I was being transferred to the investigative journalism department where I so desperately wanted to work. But no, it was yet another assignment in the entertainment division, the last place I want to be.

"They ask you to spy for them, and you're totally okay with that." Dean gives me a disgusted glare.

"I am not," I protest. "Caleb gets approval on anything I write. He's in control. Not me." The newspaper editors hadn't liked it when I said I would take this job on that one condition, but, after weeks of heated negotiations, they'd given in.

A handsome man with dark blond hair comes over to Caleb's table. He stoops down and gathers a bunch of the gift boxes Caleb's accumulated into his arms. Carefully, he piles them on top of each other, stacking them as high as his chin. He walks toward me. I do a double-take as he gets close. The man looks eerily like Caleb. Same coloring, but his jaw is a little less square and his eyes are wider set.

"Need help, Justin?" Dean asks.

The man smiles pleasantly and says, "I got it." Using his shoulder, he pushes the heavy front door of the theater and walks outside, where a brisk wind makes the tower of presents sway dangerously. I hold my breath, waiting for them to topple, but the man shuffles his feet, balancing the stack until they steady.

"Where's he taking those?" I ask Dean.

He glances at the door. Justin is no longer visible, having walked farther down the sidewalk. "He's giving them to Janice. She'll load them in her van to take to Caleb's storage unit and sort them out later."

"Storage?" I tilt my head, peering up at him. I know who Janice is, Caleb's personal assistant. A nice grandmotherly type of woman who helps with Caleb's day-to-day tasks. But I've never heard of this storage unit.

"Caleb has an entire storage unit filled with gifts that fans have sent him. Most of it gets donated to charity. Janice figures out what goes where—" Dean's shiny dress shoe inches over to step lightly on my foot, which has been tapping the ground. With firm pressure, his shoe traps mine, halting the motion.

Darn it. I didn't realize I was doing that.

He lets out a frustrated huff, clearly displeased.

"So sorry, Mr. Roboto," I say sarcastically and roll my eyes. Dean does remind me of a robot, all stiff movements and very little change in his facial expressions. I've never seen him smile. Not once.

"Apology not accepted, *Jennifer*." He says my name like it's poison and he needs to spit it out before it kills him.

Jerk.

I turn toward him and ask, "Why do you despise me so much?"

His jaw ticks, the muscle jumping. Geez, even his cheek has muscles. What does this man do to get so strong? He's tall, at least six feet, and built like you would expect for a bodyguard, as if he works out 24/7. I picture him on his rare days off, shirtless and sweaty at the gym, deadlifting weights twice the size of my head. The mental image is startlingly vivid, each detail clear in my imagination. It's…disorienting. It takes me a minute to refocus on my surroundings.

Dean glares forward as he answers my question. "You know why, Jabber Mouth." Not a single glance in my direction.

He's dedicated. I'll give him that.

Shame rushes from my chest and over my cheeks, heating them. I drop my gaze to the ground, unable to come up with a retort for that. I *do* know why he detests me, and I hate myself for it, too. I'm the reason Gwen and

Caleb broke up last year. My thoughtless remarks led the paparazzi to their door and forced Caleb to walk out. If I'd kept quiet, they could have stayed together. Instead, I ran my big mouth and Gwen, who had already endured too much, had Caleb leave her.

When Gwen found out it was me who spilled her secrets, I almost lost our friendship forever. Somehow, by the grace of her enormous heart, she forgave me. Even though she's let that dreadful past go, I can't do the same. The knowledge of how I could have ruined their relationship haunts me. I don't need Dean to remind me of what I'd done. I remember every time I look in the mirror.

"*Dean.*" Caleb's voice, unnaturally high and strained, snaps me out of my thoughts. I glance up to see Caleb standing where he'd been signing autographs. He stares with a wide-eyed expression of horror at a large white box open on the table in front of him, with a discarded red bow next to it. A scruffy young man before him stammers, "I—I didn't know what it was. I swear! Some guy gave me $50 to bring it to you."

Dean strides over to Caleb and sweeps the box off the table, slamming the lid on it before I glimpse what's inside. His narrow-eyed gaze scans the crowd as he announces in a firm voice, "That's it, folks. Signing's done for today."

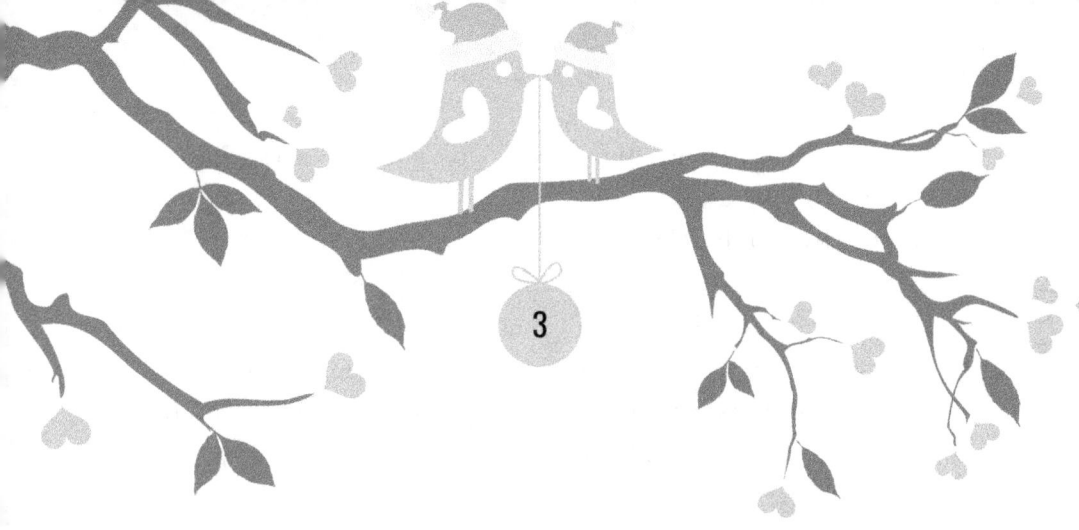

TUESDAY, DECEMBER 10
14 DAYS UNTIL THE WEDDING

—GWEN—

The airport is packed, filled with the frantic energy of thousands of people desperate to make it home for the holidays. Lines to check in and get through security snake down hallways and around corners. Piles of luggage wait to be loaded onto conveyor belts. Angry passengers argue with ticket agents over delayed flights.

"Geez," I tell Alvina, one of my best friends, raising my voice to be heard over the near-constant flight announcements and the noise of the crowd. "It's still a couple of weeks until Christmas. I didn't think it would be so busy yet."

She jumps back to avoid having her foot run over by a passing suitcase. "Me either. It's a madhouse."

"That's what you get for traveling during the holidays," says a gruff voice behind us. We spin around to find Wayne standing there, rumpled and frowning as usual. He points to the enormous Christmas tree in the center of the lobby. The illuminated star on top reaches toward the arched ceiling high over our heads. "They've had that thing up since September."

"Wayne!" I cry out and rush to give him a hug, which he begrudgingly accepts. I'd been angry when Caleb told me Wayne would join us, but now that he's here I'm happy to see my friend.

"Yeah, yeah." He pats my arm. "Good to see you." His eyes shift over my head to Alvina. "You too."

She nods back and smiles.

I step away and swing my gaze between them. "What? No snarky exchange? You two are being awfully civil to each other." Usually, they don't get along, exchanging barbs and snide comments like it's an Olympic sport.

Before they can answer, something strange catches my attention. I bring my nose to Wayne's jacket and inhale deeply. I shift closer, sniffing his shoulders and up his neck.

He freezes, eyeing me suspiciously. "Why are you smelling me like a dog?"

Baffled, I straighten and search him. Wayne's in his early fifties, just like Alvina. He's got sharp gray eyes and short brown hair, touched with silver at his temples. He looks the same as always, but something is different.

"You don't stink."

"Excuse me?" His eyebrows slash together, and his voice rises.

"I mean, you don't smell like usual—"

"Gwen…" He says my name as if I'm going down a dangerous path and he's giving me one last chance to turn around.

"You didn't let me finish. You don't smell like you usually do. Like cigarettes."

"Oh." He relaxes, his shoulders dropping to their normal position. "That's because I quit."

"You did?" I can't keep the shock off my face.

"Yeah." He lifts his chin. "A week ago. Haven't had a puff since."

"Wow." My eyebrows rise. "I did *not* see that coming." Wayne is distinctive for his dry wit and the cigarette that's always clutched in his hand.

"What? People change." He rises to his whole five feet, seven inches, indignation flashing in his eyes.

"People, yes. You, no." When a shadow of hurt crosses his face, I quickly amend to say, "At least I didn't think you could, but clearly I was wrong." I sigh a relieved breath, glad I won't have to worry about him getting emphysema.

"Wow. It's a Christmas miracle. You know I'm happy. I've been asking you to give it up for ages."

"I know. I know," he grumbles.

"How're you doing it?" Statistics from medical school pop up in my head, and they aren't good. Less than 10 percent of people who attempt to stop smoking are successful. "It might be hard." I don't want to rain on his parade, but maybe I can help? Offer some advice? "There are pills and other things—"

"No need." He holds up his hand, stopping me. "I've got this." Wayne opens his mouth and sticks out his tongue, showing off a piece of mint blue gum.

I wrinkle my nose at the sight. "First of all, eww. Second of all, what is that?"

He sucks it back into his mouth and proceeds to chew loudly, smacking his lips together. "Nicotine gum. It helps with the cravings."

"That's great. I'm proud of you." I beam at him, hopeful he'll beat the odds and stay off the cigarettes. If anyone can do it, it's Wayne. He's the most bull-headed person I know. "Isn't that wonderful, Alvina?"

She gives us a soft smile. "It is."

Sharp-eyed Wayne zeroes in on me. "Are you wearing a...fanny pack?" he asks incredulously. "Didn't those go out of style in the Eighties?"

Of all people, I'm not taking fashion criticism from him. Wayne wears jeans, a T-shirt, and a plain jacket most days. The one time he said he was going to "dress up" he had arrived in the same outfit as usual, except he traded the T-shirt for a button-down flannel shirt.

"No," I answer, clasping my newest purchase. My fingers dig into the brown imitation leather. I tighten the nylon strap that holds it close to my body. "It's a waist bag. My old purse was so worn that one of the straps broke. I got this to replace it. These are the new hot fashion item. I read *all* about it in a magazine." I lift my chin, proud to be ahead of a trend for once. Most of my life is spent in scrubs, so I rarely have reason to feel fancy, but this bag makes me walk a little taller, swish my hips a little more, just so it can sway with my movement.

"I don't care who wrote about it," declares Wayne, "that, my friend, is a fanny pack."

"It is not!" My voice gets louder as I argue with him. Sometimes hanging out with Wayne reminds me of being with my younger brother, Teddy. He brings out the angsty teenager in me.

Wayne addresses Alvina. "Back me up here. Is that or is it not a fanny pack?"

I beseech her with my eyes, begging her to agree with me.

She sweeps her gaze over me and declares, "It's a fanny pack."

"*Traitor*," I mouth silently to her, but she simply frowns in response, shaking her head like *I'm* the one who should be ashamed.

An announcement overhead calls our flight number. "We'd better get going," I tell the two of them, not minding the interruption. The security line takes twice as long as usual. Once we're through, I grab an iced coffee and sit down next to Alvina to wait for boarding while Wayne heads to the bookstore to pick up a magazine.

"Did I show you the sunglasses Caleb got me?" I fish them out of my waist bag, which by definition is *not* a fanny pack, and hold them up proudly.

She looks them over, nodding politely. "Very nice."

"Watch this," I tell her, working hard to suppress my smile. I slip on my glasses and say, "Glasses, text Caleb and tell him I love him."

I take them off with a flourish and hand them to Alvina. "They're smart glasses. See? You can make phone calls and send messages with them. There's a tiny computer screen up in the corner."

She takes the glasses and holds them up to her eyes. "Wow. They have a clock and the weather, but I can still see through them."

"I know! So cool, right? Caleb gave them to me for my birthday. I said they were too much, but he insisted. Now I use them everywhere. My favorite is how they have tiny speakers in the earpiece, so I can listen to music hands-free when I go for a run."

A faint pinging sound emanates from the glasses. Alvina squints to read the small screen. "It's a text from Caleb. He says he loves you more." She takes off the glasses and hands them back, rolling her eyes. "I swear you two give me a toothache. That's how sweet you are."

My smile breaks free. "We really are cute together, aren't we?" I bounce happily in my seat, picturing Caleb from this morning, the love in his eyes when he looked at me.

A woman's voice interrupts our conversation.

"Excuse me, are you Gwen Wright?"

Immediately, I tense, wondering if this is what Caleb warned me about. Random strangers accosting me in the airport.

A petite young woman about my age stands before me. She tucks shoulder-length, dark hair behind her ear and sends me a warm, shy smile.

"Yes?" I answer hesitantly. "That's me."

"I thought so." She sticks out her hand, and we shake. "Dr. Helen Chu. I think we're heading to the same conference. A minute ago, I was checking out the schedule. I saw your name and picture on it and then I looked up and, well, here you are."

"So nice to meet you." I let out a breath, allowing my chest to expand. Thank goodness. Not a Caleb fan. A colleague.

Helen laughs softly and says, "I bet you and I will be the only ER doctors there."

"You work in the Emergency Room too?" I ask, excited. I thought I'd be the only one.

She nods. "My father's an oncologist in California. When he takes time off, I cover for him, so I try to stay up to date on the latest cancer treatments and research. That's why I'm going."

"I grew up in California." I tell her, "Are you from there too?"

"Born and bred in Los Angeles. I did my training here in New York and stuck around to work since then. I'm moving back to California soon, though." Something troubled passes over her expression. "My family needs me." Then, Helen's gaze drops and lights with interest. "Is that a waist bag? I've been wanting one of these."

I flash a triumphant "told you so" look at Alvina. She sighs, like I'm already tiring her out with my shenanigans.

"Why, yes, it is." I unclip the bag and give it to Helen.

She examines it, running a finger over the silver zipper. "So cute." She hands it back. I attach it to my waist, reaching behind me to secure the clasp. I'm about to ask which hospital Helen works at when another voice, this one younger and shriller, breaks in.

"Did you say Gwen Wright?" asks a girl sitting on the other side of me. She's in her late teens or early twenties. She shoves light-brown hair out of her face, showing off chipped red nail polish and a tiny gold nose ring. Her hazel eyes are wide and fixed on me. Another girl with matching nail polish and hair dyed a startling shade of green leans around her friend to stare.

"Yes, that's right," I answer, already knowing where this is heading. It's the way these two stare at me, a mixture of curiosity and unwarranted disdain.

"As in Caleb Lawson's fiancée?" The first girl's voice is loud, pitched high with disbelief as her eyes roam over my faded jeans and plain white T-shirt. She stares extra-long at my earrings. They're Christmas light bulbs, one red and the other green, dangling from my ears. They have buttons on the side that make them light up and flash, but I have them turned off for now. Even I realize that might be too obnoxious. The thing that snags the girl's attention the most is the large diamond solitaire that adorns my left hand. I resist the urge to tuck it under my leg, hiding it.

Alvina leans closer, her elbow brushing mine, an unspoken vow of solidarity. The touch grounds me. Alvina can make you feel about one inch tall with just the twitch of her eyebrow. I've seen her reduce grown men to tears, doctors that acted rashly and not in the patient's best interest. As long as she has my back, I'll be fine.

"That's me." I give a friendly smile as I remind myself that these girls don't know me yet. That's why they're looking at me like I have three heads. Once they see what a nice person I am, I'm sure they'll like me.

Helen still stands before me, watching this exchange with interest. So much for keeping my identity as Caleb's fiancée low-key at the medical conference. Other passengers stare as well, their bodies angling my way, clearly eavesdropping. With all those eyes on me, it's like I'm suddenly onstage, playing a role, but I don't know my lines.

"What are your names?" I ask. Maybe if I win these girls over, it'll prove to Caleb that he has nothing to worry about.

"Skylar," the one with the nose ring answers.

"Hannah," says the green-haired girl as she cocks her head. "How'd you guys meet? I heard it was in rehab and you were his doctor—"

"No," interrupts Skylar. "It was from that movie Caleb did. Where he was a surgeon. They hired her to make sure everything was medically accurate. What was that like? Working on set with him?"

"Oh, yes." Hannah's eyes gleam. "What about when he kisses his co-star? Do you get so jealous, because if that was my boyfriend I would like *die*."

I reel backward, shocked by the misinformation spewing out of them, but the two girls continue with their barrage of questions before I get a chance to respond.

"Do you see all of his movies free?" asks Skylar.

"Is he a good kisser? Because he seems like a man who knows how to kiss," says Hannah.

"Where does he put all of his Academy Awards?"

"Is he paying for the wedding?"

"Are you really a doctor?"

"Did you make him stop acting in movies?"

"Are you giving up your career for him?"

The questions come so fast I can hardly keep track of which girl is asking. My head pivots between them. My palms sweat and my ears ring as they overwhelm me with their demands to know about the intimate details of my life.

"It is true you're already married?" asks Hannah. "Like you eloped because you're pregnant? That's what my roommate heard."

Whoa. Hold up.

My mouth drops open as two thoughts war in my head. On the one hand, I want to correct her and tell the truth. On the other hand, I want to tell her to buzz off since it's none of her business. Years of being the polite people pleaser wins out. "We're not married yet."

"When's the wedding, then?" Skylar demands.

Like I'd tell her. Fat chance.

"We're still selecting a date," I say diplomatically, hoping she won't pick up on the lie.

Her eyes narrow and she gives me a look like she can read my mind.

I shift in my seat, pressing harder against Alvina.

"What's he like?" Hannah asks, as if she has a right to know. "In real life?"

What's Caleb like? My brain supplies a million answers at once. He's funny, kind, loyal, so talented it's almost disgusting. He's a great cook, singer, and dancer. He still forgets to put the cap back on his toothpaste. His body temperature runs hot, but his feet are always cold—so chilly he sleeps with his socks on, those child-like white ankle socks I find oddly endearing. He's a big baby when he gets hurt or sick. Band-Aids for cuts. Ice packs for bruises. The king of the Man Cold bundled up on the couch, begging me to bring him one more glass of water.

What's Caleb like? He's the center of my world. The star on top of my tree. He's my everything.

I don't tell her any of that, of course. Instead, I say, "He's great."

"Great?" Hannah repeats.

"Great," I say more confidently, as if that word contains all the information she needs to know. "I'm very lucky," I add, to fill the silence that hangs uncomfortably between us.

"Lucky?" Skylar snorts, shaking her head slowly. "You get to marry Caleb Freaking Lawson. That's more than lucky. You won the whole lottery." Her lower lip sticks out in a pout. She stares me straight in the eye and, completely deadpan, says, "I hate you."

My mouth unhinges, all the air in my body escaping with a gasp. Alvina grabs onto my elbow and surges to her feet, dragging me up with her. Overhead, they announce boarding for our flight. Alvina gives me a shove toward the jetway, where I follow Helen Chu into the line of passengers waiting to board.

Right before we reach the ticket agent, Wayne walks up and, in a surprisingly jolly voice, says, "Got my magazine. What'd I miss?"

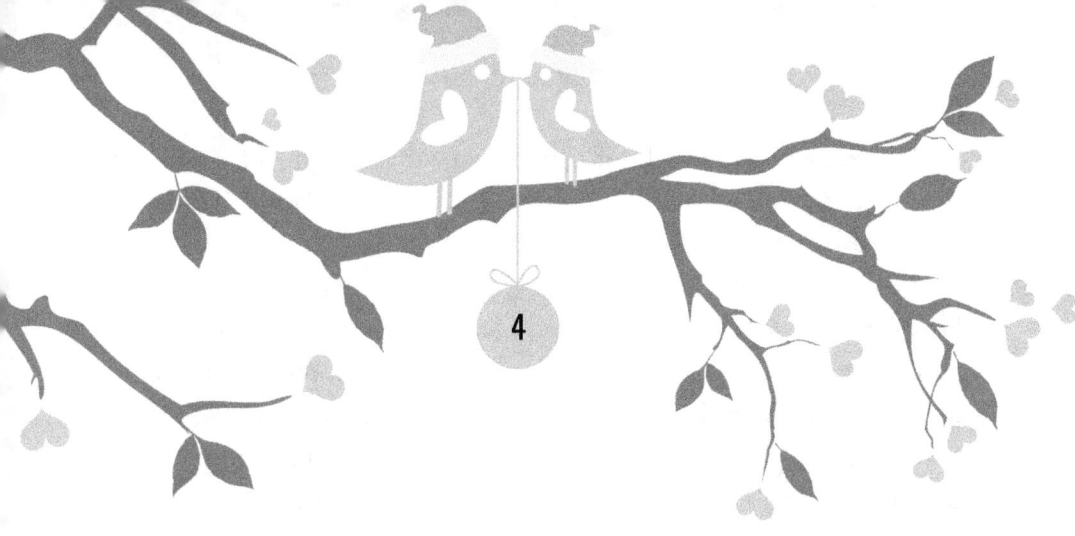

4

TUESDAY, DECEMBER 10
14 DAYS UNTIL THE WEDDING

—GWEN—

Hate me? How can she hate me? She doesn't even know *me.*

Besides Dr. Benson at the hospital, I can't think of anyone who actively dislikes me. I'm usually a very likable person. I'm cheerful, respectful, helpful…all the "-fuls." It makes me nauseous. The thought that there are a million Skylars out there, hating me simply because I'm the one Caleb chose.

My mind is in such a spin that I barely notice our seating assignment. It's not until I sink into the plush double-wide chair that I realize we're in first class.

"Hey," I protest. "There's been a mistake. I booked economy coach."

Alvina is on one side of me, and Wayne's on the other, like bookends.

"Caleb upgraded when he added me," Wayne answers. He stretches his legs out.

I open my mouth to protest our seating arrangement, my shoulders tensing with irritation. Caleb has the best of intentions—I understand that—but he knows this isn't what I want. We literally just talked about it.

Alvina joins the conversation. "You're marrying one of the most famous actors of his generation, Gwen. You'd better get used to first class and his fans."

I sigh, knowing she's right. It's just a bit of a shock, that interaction with Skylar and Hannah. All of Caleb's warnings, all of his fears, sound more reasonable now.

"You've been with Caleb for almost two years." Alvina digs in the backpack by her feet, pulling out a book and her reading glasses. "Haven't you had to deal with this before?"

"I mean, not really." I pick at a loose thread on my jeans. "We've been so busy with work that when Caleb and I are together we usually stay home."

I pause, remembering the few times we've been in public together, and it comes to me how Caleb always places himself between me and the press. How he steps up to the microphones and shuffles me behind him. I've never been to one of his premieres or theater openings or walked the red carpet with him. I thought it was because he hates that stuff and wants to spare me, but now I wonder. *Is it because he believes I can't do it? Stand next to him in front of those flashing cameras. Does he think I'm not up to the task? Is he worried I'll embarrass him?*

"I guess I didn't realize how much Caleb shields me when we're out," I admit. "This is the first time I've been on my own."

Overhead, the captain asks us to fasten our seat belts. We taxi down the runway with the plane's engine rumbling loudly and the floor vibrating under my feet.

"Are you ready?" I turn to Wayne, wanting to change the subject. "To officiate?" When we had announced our plans to get married on Christmas Eve, Wayne volunteered to preside over the ceremony. We'd been shocked to learn he has an officiant license, having gotten it years before to help marry some friends. "You got our vows, right? Also, remember I'm keeping my last name, so announce us as Mr. Caleb Lawson and Dr. Gwen Wright."

"Yes, Gwen." He slits his eyes at me. "I have it all under control, although I don't know what's wrong with the usual 'for better or for worse.'"

"We thought it would be fun to write our own vows, make it more personalized."

Wayne lets out a disapproving "*hmph*" as he returns his attention to his magazine, *Fishing Around the World*.

I cock my head, perplexed when I read the title. *Since when does Wayne fish?* As far as I know, all the man ever does is work.

I pivot back to Alvina. "Do you miss the hospital?"

"Yes," she answers, "but not enough to return."

Once Caleb and I had gotten back together, Alvina had given him one of her famous chocolate chip cookies. He'd immediately put them on the menu as the signature dessert in his restaurants, and they soon became a fan favorite. Customers plastered candid photos of the treat all over social media. That had caught the attention of a major cookie company, one with its products in grocery stores across the nation. They offered Alvina a hefty chunk of change to buy the recipe.

"Remember when you told me your cookie recipe was a family secret and that you'd *never* tell it to anyone?" I elbow her lightly with a grin, happy to move the conversation along to lighter topics. I like to tease her about how she's no longer an ICU nurse since she retired a month ago.

Alvina flips strands of curly black hair over her shoulder. Her eyes are a warm brown, the same as her skin. "I remember." She raises a brow, daring me to continue.

"Now look at you, on a permanent vacation. No more night shifts or overtime or bad cafeteria food. Must be nice." I clearly have no sense of self-preservation to goad her like this.

"Things change." She shrugs. "Life has seasons. You're in your getting married season. I'm in my retired and living off cookie money season. After working over 30 years in the hospital, I have no shame in that." Alvina closes her eyes, like she might take a nap. She adds, "Each phase of life has its highs and lows. Better embrace them all because none last. Always changing, Gwen, life's always changing."

Her words conjure an image of my dad. He's been on my mind a lot recently, partly because of the wedding coming up. I keep wanting him here. It seems wrong to walk down the aisle without holding onto his arm. "Do you ever wish it wasn't that way?" I whisper softly, a hollow sensation in my chest. My therapist, Dr. Jill, says this is normal. That grief comes in waves. She warned me it's triggered by the holidays or by big life events, like getting married. Since I've decided to combine my marriage and Christmas, it's been a double whammy of missing him.

Eyes still shut, Alvina says, "All the time. I used to wish my babies would never grow up. After my husband died, I wanted so much to have him back, but that's not how it works. The world keeps spinning. The clock keeps ticking. Try not to fight it, honey. This wedding is going to pass by like a whirlwind. Savor those moments."

Mulling over her words, I turn to stare past Wayne out the window as the plane takes off, the ground falling away. Once we level out, I get out a magazine and attempt to read. It's hard to concentrate, though. My thoughts keep returning to the incident at the airport.

I can't believe she hates *me.*

"Stop it." Alvina's voice brings my attention to her.

"What?"

"Thinking about that girl. She doesn't know you or Caleb. She doesn't have a right to worm her way into your brain and make you feel bad."

"I'm not," I lie, but Alvina has the best BS detector of anyone I know.

Immediately she counters, "You're upset. I can tell."

I stare glumly at the floor. "Nobody wants to hear me complain. I'm about to have the," I use my fingers to make air quotes, "'wedding of the century' to the 'sexiest man alive' according to *People* magazine. What right do I have to be unhappy about anything?"

"If you make air quotes one more time, I'm tying your wrists together," warns Alvina.

I drop my hands and rest them in my lap.

"Just because everything looks great from the outside doesn't mean you aren't allowed to have problems," she continues. "No one's life is perfect. No one is happy all the time. It's okay to be human, Gwen."

I needed that. Her permission to admit my feelings.

"It bothers me," I say, and it feels good to get those words out. "How can I not think about it?"

Her chestnut eyes pop wider to give me a pointed stare. "By reminding yourself that girl is jealous of someone who never existed. A Hollywood-generated image, a false idol. You know the *real* man. You get to go home to Caleb, the actual human being who loves you more than anything."

She's right. Intellectually, I understand that, but it takes Alvina's words to make it sink in. I do know Caleb better than anyone, except maybe his parents, and it occurs to me at that moment what a privilege it is—to know him so well—in a way that Skylar and the rest of the world doesn't. It's not special because he's rich or famous. It's special because that's the magic of a committed relationship, where you crack yourself wide open for another person. You let them into your heart, your mind, so they see all of you, the sparkly bits and the dull ones, too. I love all of him, even the parts he believes are unlovable. I do that because he sees and accepts me, this version of me who strives to improve but will always be flawed.

"Okay, I'll try." I sigh and wiggle deeper into my seat, determined to take Alvina's advice to heart. I need to develop better coping strategies to deal with the press and Caleb's fans. Otherwise, every encounter will leave me like this, shaken and insecure. It's time to get used to this.

After all, I am Caleb's future wife, and, even more importantly, I'm Gwen Freaking Wright.

TUESDAY, DECEMBER 10
14 DAYS UNTIL THE WEDDING

—JENNY—

Dean and Caleb took the box into the men's restroom to look it over. Much to my annoyance, they refuse to let me in. A few years ago, I would have pressed my ear to the door and listened as hard as I could. But now, in my continued effort to become someone worth trusting, I don't do that. Instead, I stand outside, shifting from foot to foot, getting angrier by the second, annoyed they're leaving me out.

When they emerge from the bathroom, I can tell they've been fighting. They have identical stiff shoulders and tight jaws and are shooting glares at each other.

"I'm serious, Dean. No police," Caleb says over his shoulder as he walks out. "They never help any—" He cuts off whatever he was about to say when he sees me.

"What's going on?" I demand for the tenth time.

"It's nothing," Dean says without a glance my way.

"Caleb!" A voice cries out. We all turn in unison to see Caleb's mom, Marjorie, standing by the theater entrance. She rearranges her windblown, dark blonde hair, running her fingers through it. "Are you ready for lunch?" She beams at us, her smile dimming as her question is met with a tense silence. "Everything okay?"

"Everything's fine," Caleb says quickly. He stares at Dean and me as if daring us to contradict him.

"We should leave. Our reservation is in 20 minutes." Dean checks the large watch he always wears on his left wrist. It's black and bulky. The kind with all the extra dials so he can go scuba diving, rock climbing, or walking on the moon. Whatever a guy like him does in his limited free time.

"We'll do the interview after lunch, right, Jenny?" Marjorie asks.

"Sounds great," I reply, excited for the chance to interview Caleb and his mom together.

The four of us make our way to the parking garage and climb into Caleb's Aston Martin DBX. With a roar of its engine, Caleb guides the car up the ramp and out onto the crowded city street.

This assignment is my first trip to New York. As a native Californian, I'm in awe of the bustling sidewalks and towering skyscrapers. I've seen the city many times in films or on TV so to be here now is exhilarating, if also slightly terrifying.

During the drive to the restaurant, it starts to snow. Fluffy white flakes drift down from the sky like confetti at the end of a concert. I chew on a butterscotch candy and press my nose to the chilled car window, watching with delight as New Yorkers spill into Central Park to build snowmen and ice skate.

Dean sits in the back seat next to me since Caleb drives and Marjorie rides shotgun. I pester him with questions. "What's that ice-skating place called?" I jab at the picturesque rink surrounded by windblown trees and the tallest buildings I'd ever seen. Dean grew up in the Bronx, so I figure he should know.

He flicks his gaze to see where I pointed. "Wollman Rink."

"How about over there? With all the snowmen?" My phone rings with "Butthead" flashing on the screen. I turn it to silent, making a mental note that I have to talk to him eventually. The window fogs from my breath. I trace a defiant smiley face into it that quickly fades away.

"Sheep Meadow." Dean answers my question.

"What about the area with the boats? Gwen told me she went on a date with Caleb there."

"Loeb's Boathouse."

"Oh! Oh!" I bounce in my seat and clap my hands with excitement. "The fountain from *Friends*? How about that one?"

He heaves a sigh. "How about you stop asking so many questions and use the map on your phone?"

"How about *you* stop being such a jerk?" I grip the door handle, so I don't throttle him.

Caleb overhears that last part. He glances over his shoulder and says, "Children, children. No fighting. Don't make me pull over the car."

Marjorie tells him, "This is why I only had one kid."

They laugh, the sound surprisingly amicable.

That shuts us up. Dean stares sullenly out his window, and I go back to looking out of mine for the rest of the trip.

We have a private room in the back of Tavern on the Green, the famous restaurant located in Central Park. We enter through a rear door, with Dean sweeping ahead like he's a Secret Service agent and Caleb's the president.

Garlands made of pine and colorful ornaments line the walls close to the ceiling. Holiday music plays overheard, an instrumental version of "Winter Wonderland." A server arrives and takes our order. Within minutes, he's back with drinks. Mine is an eggnog latte.

I marvel over how two years ago I had sat with Gwen sipping eggnog while she complained about how her family had abandoned her for Christmas. Little did we know that the same night an unexpected intruder, Caleb, would come into the house and she would knock him unconscious with a wrench. The memory stirs a soft laugh, which makes Dean glance sharply at me.

He frowns, cocks his head, and wrinkles his brow with a silent, *what?*

I glare back, trying to broadcast, *none of your business.*

Behind him, the curtained windows reveal the stark winter beauty of Central Park. The trees are bare, and the ponds are a glassy blue-gray, reflecting the cloudy sky above them.

Soon, our food is served. As I eat my grilled chicken sandwich, I listen to Caleb and his mom as they go over the guest list for the third time. Marjorie wants to add some old neighbors, but Caleb refuses. Gwen told me they're trying to keep the wedding to less than 100 people, only family and close friends like me.

Dean's silent, methodically chewing his salad, because of course he only eats healthy food. No candy for him. Must be how he maintains that Adonis physique. He acts like he's not listening to the conversation, but I don't buy it. He's way too observant for that.

"Please, Mom," Caleb says with a trace of impatience. "No more. We're done sending out invitations."

"Fine," Marjorie says, the word sharp with disappointment. There's a beat of silence, then she turns to me. "Jenny, do you want to start the interview? I have an appointment at 3:00."

"Sure. No problem." I reach for my bag, which I'd hung on the back of my chair. My brain is already humming with questions. This is the first chance I've had to question Marjorie. I'm curious about Caleb's early career. Since he started acting when he was five, he doesn't remember any of that time, but his mom will. After I've opened my laptop and selected a blank document, I place my phone on the table and press the record button.

"I'd like to discuss Caleb's younger years before he became famous. It's been covered before, but not in great depth." I angle my seat toward Marjorie. "Can you tell me a little about the city you're from? The one where Caleb was born?"

She takes the napkin from her lap and places it on the table, next to our dirty plates and the red spotted poinsettia centerpiece. "Marion. It's a small town in southern Illinois. Less than 20,000 people live there, nice folk, but I never quite fit it. I was always looking for a way out. I would spend weekends in the old theater downtown, watching movies up on that giant screen. Everything seemed so glamorous in Hollywood, like nothing bad could happen there. No girls got bullied for having their nose stuck in a book or for being too plain, too smart, too awkward."

She pauses, her eyes unfocused, remembering a past only she knows.

"I wanted to go away for college, but my father wouldn't hear about it. He said it was too dangerous. A girl like me off on her own. Who knew what could happen? Someone might take advantage." Her shoulders hunch, folding in. "After high school, I took a job at a hotel. I was the late-night front-desk clerk. It suited me. I liked that it was quiet in the evening, which gave me time to read."

Her eyes sharpen, and she looks at Caleb. "One hot summer night when the cicadas were so loud I thought I might lose my mind, your father walked in." She smiles at the memory. "He was in insurance and had to travel to Illinois once a week from St. Louis for a department meeting. He was so shy at first, quiet but always kind. It took six months for him to ask me out. The longest six months of my life. We were married six months later, the shortest six months of my life."

Marjorie tells Caleb, "We never told you because we didn't want you to dislike your grandparents, but they refused to come to our wedding."

Caleb's head jerks up at that, surprise widening his eyes. "Really?"

"They didn't approve—well, my father didn't, and my mother followed wherever he led." She sighs. "He said it was a mistake to marry your dad. I was so in love I wouldn't listen. When your dad suggested we elope, I agreed instantly."

Caleb's jaw drops.

I shift, guilty to be a part of this conversation. It's obviously personal. Not wanting to intrude, I half rise to leave, but Marjorie's hand shoots out and tugs me back down. "It's okay, Jenny. Stay."

I sit and lean in, secretly relieved because I want to hear more. I've always been drawn to a good story like it's my own gravity. My newspaper would gobble up these intimate details about Caleb's family, but I vow not to write about them. For this assignment, my loyalty lies with Gwen and Caleb. I won't sacrifice my relationship with them for the sake of my career.

"He was always disapproving of the things I did, my father," Marjorie continues, a mix of bitterness and sadness thickens her words. "He said nothing good would come of our union." Tears have filled her eyes, but she doesn't cry.

"Then we had you, Caleb, and I knew he was wrong. You're the best thing to come out of our marriage. When you started to be successful, I guess I saw that as further proof my decisions were right. Every role you booked, a little voice in the back of my head said, 'See, Dad. Told you so.'"

Caleb shifts impatiently. He's heard this part of the story before.

Marjorie continues, "It was a huge leap of faith, one I could never have made without your father's support, to come to California, but I never doubted what you would become. It was your destiny."

Caleb rubs the back of his neck. "I'm not sure that's how destiny works, Mom."

"It was," she insists. "I could feel it. It wasn't until you were an adult that I questioned my decisions. Once you started drinking, and especially after the car crash, I wondered if I'd been selfish. I was unhappy in my hometown, but maybe you wouldn't have been if we'd stayed."

She lets out a watery sigh and rests her hand on top of his. "It's a hard thing, being a parent. When you're in the middle of raising your child, there's no clear answer if you're doing it right and then, when time has passed and you see the outcome of your choices, it's too late. Whatever damage you've caused is already there. You can't take it back." Her eyes have filled again, making the blue in them, the same aqua as Caleb's eyes, seem like it's underwater. "I worry I haven't done the right things for you, darling, and I'm sorry for that."

Caleb's misty-eyed too. "You had good intentions and in so many ways you gave me an incredible, although not always easy, life. Now, I look at Gwen and know no matter how crooked the road was that led me here, I'm where I'm supposed to be." Caleb and his mother hug, their arms wrapping tightly around each other, then continue their conversation in hushed tones.

I scoot my chair back to give them privacy. My fingers itch to grab my phone and call Gwen. It's one thing not to share this moment with the newspaper, but another thing entirely to not share it with my best friend. I clasp my hands in my lap, resisting the urge. *You're not a gossip anymore*, I tell myself. As much as I would love to hear Gwen's reaction to Marjorie's confessions, it's not my story to tell.

It's Caleb's.

I look over at Dean, the only person unmoved by this touching display. "How can you sit there so stoic?" I hiss at him.

He sends back a tight-lipped glare. "It's not my job to eavesdrop, *Jennifer*. I'm here to protect Caleb."

"We're in a private room. Who could possibly threaten him right now?"

I'm frustrated by his single-mindedness. "What? Do you think someone's hiding behind the curtains or under the table?" I make a big show of leaning over and searching under the white tablecloth.

"Stop acting crazy." He scowls. "This isn't all fun and games. There are threats, real threats."

"Yeah? Like what?" I challenge.

He scrubs his hand over his face, more agitated than I've ever seen. "Like that present Caleb got today at the theater." He scrutinizes me. "You want to know what was in it?"

I nod, my curiosity piqued.

A long pause, like he's waging an internal battle, before he says, "You can't write about this. Do you understand?"

More nodding from me. "I promise. I won't tell a soul."

Another moment of silence while he stares at me, calculating, deciding his next move. Then a tiny nod, more to himself than to me. Dean's lips tighten, his expression troubled.

"Caleb's had his fair share of stalkers. Did you hear about Chrissy Sanfield? The woman who broke into his place in Malibu?"

I remember the story. It had been all over the Internet and on television. "She was barefoot, right? When the police arrested her?"

Dean gives a grim laugh. "She told us she didn't want to be a bad house guest and get Caleb's carpet dirty. Never mind that she smashed a window to enter the place."

"She's out of prison? Isn't she on probation?"

"No. She was, but now she's back in jail. She violated her parole, showed up here in New York, stood outside Caleb's building. Said she'd wait for Caleb out there forever. Police had to come and take her away. She's not his only stalker, though. He's got tons of them following him. There's another that scares me the most, though. The person who sent that gift today."

I lean forward, desperate to hear more. "What was it? What was in the box?"

"It was a bunch of Caleb's clothing stolen from his dry cleaner."

"Is that all?" I relax, relieved, since that doesn't sound too awful.

Dean's mouth sinks into a deep frown. "Whoever sent it had tampered with the clothing. There was a pattern. If it was an outfit he'd never worn around a woman, the stalker put lipstick kisses, bright red, all over it. If it was an outfit he'd worn when he was with a woman, any woman at all, the stalker had taken scissors to it and ripped it to shreds."

A chill runs through my body. "That's pretty bad."

He whips out his phone and thumbs through it quickly. "There's more. Here, look at this." He shoves it in my face. I take it from his hand, my fingers brushing against his. Good grief, his skin is warm, almost too burning hot to touch.

Dean's phone is set to a website called Caleb's Secret Santa. It has a Christmas theme with a red and green background. Animated GIFs of grinning Santas and reindeers dancing a jig are scattered around the page. The top of the screen shows three tabs, labeled Caleb's Sleigh, Naughty or Nice, and Find Caleb.

I select the first tab, Caleb's Sleigh, and am astonished to see pictures of his private jet, along with a detailed summary of Caleb's flight history, including departure and arrival times and miles flown.

"Holy cow!" I hold the phone up to Dean. "Can they publish this? Isn't it private?"

"Totally legal," he answers, his expression even more serious than usual. "All public information, although most people won't comb through the required data to track it. Each plane has a tail number registered with the FAA. That's how whoever is in charge of this site knows exactly where Caleb's jet is."

"You don't know who's doing this?" A chill settles low in my stomach.

"No clue. We've tried everything. The police. The FBI. Even Wayne hasn't been able to find anything. The airplane's not the worst of it." He leans over, his chest brushing against my shoulder. Again, that flare of heat transfers from his body to mine. A minute ago, I had been cold, but suddenly I'm flushed with warmth.

Dean hits the Find Caleb tab. A map pops up with a flashing red arrow pointing to the Tavern on the Green. Not only is it directed at the restaurant, it's aimed at the back half of the building, scarily close to the room where we now sit. The fine hairs on my arm rise.

"What the heck?" I look up to find Dean's face near mine as he peers over my shoulder. His eyes are brown, but for the first time I see tiny flecks of gold that cluster in a ring around his pupil. "Please tell me this is illegal. Isn't this stalking?"

He shrugs. "It's a gray area. It's not against the law to post where someone is located. The criminal part would be how they're getting the information. If they installed a tracking device without your knowledge, for example, they could get arrested for that."

"A tracking device? Have you checked Caleb for one?" I look over at Caleb, who's still talking with his mom, their blonde heads bent close together.

"We searched everywhere. Caleb even had a full body scan to make sure someone hadn't implanted one under his skin or in his teeth."

"What?" This situation is turning more science fiction by the minute.

Dean lowers his brows, his eyes serious. "A dentist in L.A. got caught putting trackers in his famous clients' teeth while they were under anesthesia."

He gestures to the phone in my hand. "Go on. Keep looking."

My mind reeling, I select the Naughty or Nice tab. It's a series of photos, each one stamped with a bold, red "Naughty" or "Nice." There's a picture from the event at the theater this morning. It's taken from outside, like the photographer was standing on the sidewalk. The image focuses on Caleb as he bends down to greet the young boy I'd been making faces with. I see myself in the background. I'm talking to Dean, or more likely fighting since I'm giving him a belligerent stare. This photo is labeled as "Nice."

Another picture causes my blood to freeze. It's one where I'm straightening Caleb's scarf. The image is zoomed in on us. I'm smiling up at Caleb, probably teasing him. There's a large "Naughty" stamped over the middle of that picture. Red ink bisects my face like I've been slashed with a knife. I scroll through more photos until I see a pattern emerge. Anytime Caleb interacts with a woman or girl, it gets the "Naughty" designation. If he interacts with a man or boy, it's labeled as "Nice."

Dean takes his phone back. "This website is password-protected. Users subscribe and pay $200 a year to have access to it. There are hundreds of thousands of subscribers. Whoever owns it is making millions selling Caleb's location."

I gasp. "Who would do that? Who pays that kind of money?"

"Fans," he says simply. "They want to know everything about Caleb, including where he is. It makes it easier for them to position themselves for photo ops, selfies, or autographs. I guarantee that when we walk out of here there will be a horde of people waiting outside that've been tipped off by this website."

"What!? Why are we sitting here, then? We should leave right now. Try to get away." I reach for my purse, but Dean puts up his hand in a calming gesture.

"It's always like this for Caleb," he explains, unfazed. "The fans and the paparazzi constantly chase him. If we ran every time, he would never have any peace. Besides, that's why we picked this place. This restaurant is used to having famous patrons. It has its own security staff patrolling."

"Oh, okay." Appeased, I settle back into my chair, my head spinning. "This whole situation is terrifying."

Dean nods solemnly. "What's even scarier is that the person who runs this website is escalating."

"What do you mean?" My hand clutches my chest, where my heart is racing.

He glances around like he's worried someone might overhear, which is ridiculous since we're in a private room. Dean leans closer and whispers, "I think the upcoming wedding is antagonizing the stalker. Making them bolder. That wasn't the first present they've sent to Caleb, but it's the worst one so far."

"You mean there've been others?"

"Boxes wrapped like they're Christmas presents with these huge red and green bows. Whoever the stalker is, they're obsessed with the holiday. The website looks like this all year long."

Foreboding stirs low in my gut. "How do you know the gifts are from them?"

"They include letters and sign them from 'your secret Santa.' They've referenced the website in their notes several times, using details only the person running it would know."

"What was in the earlier boxes?" I'm not sure when I started, but now I'm whispering too.

"Stuff Caleb left behind at restaurants or on movie sets." Dean shrugs. "A sweater, a note he jotted down on a napkin, things like that."

"This is terrible." My mouth goes dry. I think of Gwen. *Is this what she's* signed up for by marrying Caleb? A complete violation of privacy for the rest of her life? Followed by unhinged stalkers?

No wonder Caleb left her before.

When Dean glances away to put his phone in his jacket pocket, I fetch a candy from my purse, this one a spicy cinnamon disc, to bring some moisture back to my mouth.

"Does Gwen know?" I ask, wondering why she didn't tell me. *Maybe she doesn't want me to worry or maybe she doesn't trust me to keep the details to myself?*

"A little, mostly about the website and a couple of the gifts. Caleb doesn't want to scare her. I told him she needs to be warned more, but he's resistant." Dean lets out a gust of air. "He can't stand making her upset. I think it's left over from when they were apart. Some kind of guilt he still carries."

"He has to tell her everything," I insist. I glance over at Caleb, but he's not paying attention to us, too busy talking with his mom.

"I know." Dean lifts his shoulders. "I'm worried the stalker might target the wedding. Do something crazy to stop it. I told Caleb to quit being an ostrich, burying his head in the sand, but he doesn't want to alarm anyone, especially Gwen. He's lived this way his entire life. I don't think he understands how abnormal it is."

"What about me?" I shove curls off my forehead, only to have them bounce back into the same position. "Will Caleb be mad you told me?" When I was a teenager, I had a schoolgirl crush on Caleb. I even had a poster of him in my bedroom. Now, through Gwen, I've gotten to know him, to become friends with him—the *real* Caleb, not the movie star version. The last thing I want to do is threaten that relationship.

Dean waves a dismissive hand, like he's shooing away a gnat. "Nah. He leaves this stuff to me."

I square my shoulders as an idea comes to me. I turn to my computer and quickly type in the Caleb's Secret Santa website.

"Give me the info to login," I tell Dean, my fingers poised over the keyboard.

"Why?" he asks, brows lowered.

"Because I want to join," I say sarcastically, rolling my eyes. "I'm going to track down the location of their server."

Dean cocks his head. "You can do that?"

"Didn't Gwen mention I double majored in college?" I lift my chin. "Journalism *and* computer science."

Once he gives me the login and password, my fingers fly over the keyboard. I open window after window on my laptop as I attempt to unwind the convoluted series of servers that host the Secret Santa website. After 10 minutes, I give up, slamming the computer closed with a muffled curse. "It's no use. They're bouncing the origin of the website off so many international servers, most of them anonymous, that I can't narrow down where it's located."

Dean's been bent forward, watching over my shoulder as I worked. Now, he leans back, taking his warmth with him. He gives a satisfied nod. "That's exactly what the computer experts we hired said."

"What!" I half shout. "You already did this? You could have told me."

"Why would I do that?" He crosses his arms over his chest. "What if, by some miracle, you were the one to crack the code?"

"Well, I didn't." I don't miss how he said it would be a "miracle" for me to find the server. Of course, he doesn't believe I can do it. A glum feeling sinks into my stomach. After a beat of silence, I say, "What're you going to do?"

Dean taps his fingers on the table as he eyes me. Begrudgingly, he says, "Maybe you could help."

"Me?" I ask incredulously, gesturing to myself.

"Yeah. Desperate times and all that." His voice drops. "You must know some reporters in L.A., right? Investigative journalists?"

I nod slowly. "Yeah?"

"We need to find out who's targeting Caleb and how they're doing it. I'm rushing to solve this before the wedding, so Caleb doesn't have to worry on his big day. I think the person is based out of L.A., because when Caleb goes there, his location and candid photos are updated immediately. When he leaves Los Angeles, there's a slight delay. Like whoever it is needs to catch up with him. I've exhausted all the law-enforcement options. I was thinking that if you put your reporter friends on the job, they could help figure out who's behind this." Dean tilts his head and lowers his voice. "If they crack the case, I'd even arrange an exclusive with Caleb."

I note he doesn't ask *me* to discover the stalker's identity. Why would he? I'm just an entertainment reporter. "I might know some people," I say, thinking about his request. Immediately, a couple of names come to mind. I've worked long enough at the newspaper that I know all of its reporters and most of the staff on the rival papers as well. I'll have to ask them in a way that doesn't get back to my editor.

I'm about to answer when it hits me. This is the first conversation I've had with Dean that wasn't hostile. I ask, wide-eyed, "Did I just lose my mind? Because I could swear you said you need me?"

Dean heaves a heavy, soul-shuddering sigh. "Yes, I did," he mutters, staring down at the table.

Pretending like I'm hard of hearing, I cup my ear with my hand and say loudly, "I'm sorry. What was that?"

Another drawn-out sigh from Dean, this time with a side order of eye rolling. "I said I need help."

Unable to resist making the most of this moment, I keep my hand to my ear. "Sorry, still couldn't quite make that out. *Who* exactly do you need help from?"

His narrow-eyed glare tells me I'm pushing my luck, but in the end Dean humors me. In a satisfyingly loud voice, he admits, "You. I need you, Jennifer."

Even though I'm completely freaked out by that website and the idea of a stalker, seeing Dean's obvious discomfort causes a grin to stretch over my face.

He needs *my* help?

Oh, this is going to be fun.

JENNY

6

TUESDAY, DECEMBER 10

14 DAYS UNTIL THE WEDDING

—JENNY—

I finish my interview with Marjorie and Caleb, going over their move to L.A. and the first few years when they went to audition after audition. They answer honestly, and I get a couple of unique stories I haven't seen in articles before. Satisfaction expands my chest. Success!

It's nearing 3:00 p.m. Marjorie rises from her seat. Caleb gives her a kiss on the cheek, a gesture that warms my heart, thinking back to when I first met them, how tense their relationship had been before Caleb went to rehab. Marjorie says good-bye and ducks out the back door. She'll walk to her appointment since it's a few blocks away. I hope the paparazzi won't give her a hard time. They don't usually harass her unless she's with her megastar son.

My phone buzzes yet again with the word "Butthead" on the screen. Unable to avoid him any longer, I excuse myself and duck out into the narrow hallway, where I accept the call.

Eddie's voice, nasal and high-pitched, comes onto the line. "It's about time," he says. No "good afternoon" or "how ya doing." Nope. He skips straight past the pleasantries. "I've been calling you. You know, it's not a great idea to ignore your supervisor." He pauses, no doubt waiting for me to apologize.

I won't.

He continues, ignoring that I haven't spoken a word yet. "Just because we used to date doesn't mean you get special treatment, Jenny."

"I don't expect that," I protest, horrified by the idea. I've never asked for anything from him. Not when we were dating and definitely not after he dumped me.

"You have to keep me updated, like everyone else."

"We already talked this morning," I counter, exasperation shortening my words. I can't believe I dated this douche. *What was I thinking?* "I even emailed you Caleb's agenda for the day."

"I saw it." There's the creak of a chair. I can picture him leaning back in that old, putrid green office chair he loves. The hum of the press room in L.A. comes over the phone line. I used to love that sound, the noise of reporters talking into phones and tapping at computer keys. I loved the smell there, ink and burnt popcorn and weather man Al's cologne. For years, that place felt like home to me. I'd get a buzz of excitement whenever I stepped through the door.

Not now, though. After the disastrous relationship with Eddie and my inability to prove myself to the investigative team, I've started to dread going to the newsroom. I've found excuses to work remotely or go out on assignments. This New York trip has been a welcome distraction. A chance to escape all the mistakes I made back in L.A.

"Don't you think it's strange for Gwen to leave so close to the wedding?" Eddie asks.

I pull the phone away and glare at it, instantly defensive. Pressing it to my ear again, I tell him, "Caleb told her to go. He insisted."

Gwen had spent months debating whether she should leave. We talked about it dozens of times as she listed the pros and cons.

Pros: Once in a lifetime opportunity to showcase the colon cancer research Gwen had spent the last four years working on. Research that was especially poignant to her since she lost her own dad to that dreadful disease. Gwen was on a mission to spare other families from what she'd endured. This conference would be instrumental in achieving her goal.

Cons: Missing out on wedding planning. Guilt over leaving wedding preparations to Marjorie and the rest of us.

"What should I do?" Gwen had asked, so conflicted she was losing precious sleep over the decision.

"Go," I told her weeks ago. "You deserve to show off your hard work. Caleb wants you to go and so do I. Don't worry about the wedding. I'll personally make sure everything is ready when you get back. With your mom and Marjorie, we can get it all done. I promise."

I defend Gwen's choice to Eddie. "Gwen's slaved away for years on her research. This isn't just any conference. It's sponsored by the American Cancer Society and only happens once every four years. It's a huge opportunity. She cares about her job, Eddie. She's going to end colon cancer."

He makes a scoffing sound, which I ignore. I've always believed in Gwen. When she puts her mind to something, she doesn't fail. "Her work is as important as, if not more than, this wedding."

The chair creaks as Eddie shifts. "I don't know. If I were getting married, I'd want my fiancée to be around to make sure everything ran smoothly. That's all I'm saying."

That's because you're a selfish pig, I want to tell him, but I don't. As annoying as he is, Eddie *is* the head of the entertainment department and therefore my boss. I walk a fine line with him, being respectful but not letting him push me around. He'd been different when we first started dating. He'd blunted his bad behavior, but the longer we were together, the more it came out. The more he became the bully he is now.

"Well, they talked about it, and Caleb said she should go." I dodge a waiter carrying a large silver tray.

"What did you learn from his mom? Anything new? Something juicy?" Eddie fires out.

I fill him in on the stories Marjorie told at lunch, leaving out the more intimate details like her relationship with her father.

"That's it?" Eddie asks once I've finished. "That's all you got?"

An image of the Caleb's Secret Santa website flashes through my mind. Eddie would sell his own kidney to know about that, but there's no way I'm telling him. I'm still surprised Dean told *me* about it.

He must be desperate.

"That's it," I tell Eddie, wanting to be done with this conversation.

The door next to me swings open, and Caleb pokes his head out. His gaze scans around until he sees me. "You okay?" he silently mouths. I give him a thumbs-up, smiling weakly. His eyes narrow for a second, like he doesn't believe me. I make my grin wider, more convincing.

Finally, Caleb nods and goes back into the private room, closing the door softly behind him. He's been like this since I arrived in New York, always checking up on me, asking if I need anything. At first, I thought it was because Gwen told him to do it, to keep an eye on me, but when I asked her about it she just laughed.

"Caleb likes you, Jenny," she said. "Even separate from me, he thinks of you as his friend. That's what he does for the people he cares about. He's protective, nurturing. Why do you think I love him so much?"

Those words warmed me, because I like Caleb too. He's good to everyone around him, friends and strangers alike. I've never seen him be mean to his staff or to any of the fans who approach him looking for an autograph. You'd think he would be snotty, growing up famous like he has, but honestly, he's one of the most down-to-earth people I've ever met.

"What about the wedding? Any news there?" Eddie's still talking in my ear. He doesn't bother to hide his eagerness. He wants a promotion. When we dated, he once confessed he wanted to break a big story. Something to give him notoriety so he could move up to the editor-in-chief position.

"Nothing more than I already told you." I scuff my feet along the floor, pacing slowly. "Besides, if anything did happen with the wedding, I'd have to get Caleb's approval before I printed it."

"You don't really have to do that, you know." Eddie's voice drops low.

"Yes, I do. It's part of my contract." I gnaw on my lower lip. I'd been worried about this. The paper gave in too easily when I made that demand. I should have known they'd send Eddie to harass me, wanting to know more details. He's famous for finding the biggest scandals in Hollywood, so of course he'd want to see one involving the "wedding of the century."

"The newspaper would cover you if you breached the contract. We have lawyers for exactly that kind of situation."

"Lawyers wouldn't help me get my best friend back." A group of women brush past me, heading for the bathroom and talking loudly. I put my finger to my ear so I can hear Eddie better.

"Jenny, you know what you need to do if you want that investigative job—"

"I gotta go. They're done with lunch now." I cut him off, knowing this cajoling tone too well. That's the voice that talked me into staying, even though I thought about breaking up with him many times before he finally broke up with me.

"Okay," he says, his voice clipped. "I'll see you in two days. Hopefully, you'll have something more interesting to discuss by then."

I freeze at his words. "What do you mean, you'll see me? You're in L.A. and I'm in New York."

"Oh," he says with feigned nonchalance, as if he weren't delivering a bomb designed to blow up my serenity. "Didn't I tell you? I'll be in New York. Just for the day. I've got some meetings in the morning, but I'll make time for you. We can go to lunch at noon."

I should have anticipated this. When we were dating, Eddie would frequently travel to New York, often leaving L.A. abruptly. A couple of times, I didn't even know he'd left California until he called me from LaGuardia Airport in New York. My stomach twists at the thought of seeing him. I've been enjoying my Eddie-free existence here.

"I already have lunch plans," I say automatically.

"Break them," he says, his voice cold and commanding.

"What if they're with Caleb? Like to interview him? We're going to the flower market that morning with his mom," I say, lying through my teeth. We need to choose a bouquet for Gwen and boutonnières for the groomsmen, but there's no lunch planned.

"You see him practically every day. Do it at a different time."

He won't let this go. I know him. I give in to his demands like I have so many times before. "Fine."

Eddie chuckles, as if he knew my defeat was inevitable. "I'll make it easier for you," he says, like he's doing me a big favor. Like he's the good guy in this situation. "I can meet you at a restaurant close to the flower market, so you don't have to travel far."

A pause, where he waits for me to thank him for his generosity. I refuse. Instead, I sigh and repeat, "Fine." I stand with my hand on the door that leads to Dean and Caleb. "I'll see you then."

After he says good-bye, I slouch back into the room where servers are silently picking up our discarded silverware and napkins. One waiter piles dirty plates and bowls into a tall stack in his arms as we gather our things to leave. I bend over to shove my computer into my backpack. A loud crash from behind startles me, making my heart jackhammer against my sternum. Next to me, Dean jumps at the sound.

I twist around and find the server kneeling on the floor with an embarrassed blush. He's picking up the shattered pieces of a plate. When I glance up from the ruined porcelain, I see Dean frozen with his eyes squeezed shut. I wait for a minute, expecting him to relax so we can go, but he remains in that position, every muscle vibrating with nervous energy. I grew up in a noisy house with three rambunctious big brothers. I recover quickly from the racket of something breaking since I heard it so often in my youth.

Apparently, Dean isn't the same.

Caleb brushes past me and places a gentle hand on Dean's arm. He leans close to Dean and whispers something I can't hear. Whatever he says makes his bodyguard relax, the tension leaving his body as quickly as it came. Caleb ushers us out of the room and down the long hallway.

What was that all about?

Before I can give it further thought, we're outside. The courtyard is brightly lit with twinkling white lights everywhere. Strands wind up branches and extend over our heads, connecting to a large Christmas tree.

As Dean predicted, there's a crowd of paparazzi and fans waiting for Caleb. They're held back by a thin red velvet rope that sways precariously as the crowd surges forward. Security guards from the restaurant are stationed at regular intervals along the barrier. Local police have joined them, no doubt called in as reinforcements. With raised hands and shouting voices, the guards and cops hold everyone away, creating a narrow path that leads to Caleb's car, which a valet has left idling at the curb.

I glance back to gauge Dean's reaction to all the commotion, but he seems unshaken. Maybe he has a specific phobia that only involves broken dinnerware? The fans wave their hands and reach out, trying to get our attention. They scream for Caleb, but it's not just his name they chant. It's…Lola?

There she is, walking into the restaurant as we walk out. Lola Monroe with her long black hair, plump lips, and deep cleavage. Hot starlet, top model, current "IT" girl, and Caleb's ex-girlfriend.

Uh-oh.

She saunters up with a wide, red-lipped grin. Her voice is raised to project over the din of the crowd. "Caleb! I had no idea you'd be here."

Before I have time to blink, she takes his face between her hands and gives him a quick, hard kiss, leaving her lipstick smeared across his mouth. He pushes her away with a scowl, wiping his lips with the back of his hand, but it's too late. The fans go wild, screaming and clapping. The reporters' cameras click. I'm momentarily blinded by the flashes. Everything is too loud. Too bright. Too much. I rub my forehead with a trembling hand.

Oh, no.

That photo will be on every social media page within an hour. I'd better warn Gwen. I reach for my phone, but then hesitate. *What if I say the wrong thing? Maybe I should let Caleb handle it? Does this count as gossiping?*

"Lola," says Caleb stiffly. "We were just leaving."

"Oh, so soon?" Those red lips shape into an exaggerated pout, and I can't look away. The woman exudes sex appeal. Every curve, every expression is beguiling, but there's an iciness to her. She reminds me of a poisonous flower, beautiful on the outside so she can lure you close but toxic on the inside.

Caleb isn't charmed. He says a brusque, "Yeah. Gotta go," and strides off amid the shouting of the crowd. He stops a few feet away and goes down the line, signing autographs and taking selfies with star-struck fans.

"Nice to see you," Lola calls loudly after him. She turns back my way, and I get a good look at her. She's wearing a sparkly red sweater, a black leather miniskirt, knee-high black boots, and an unbuttoned trench coat.

Her eyes land on me, sweeping up and down with a quick assessment, similar to the one I just gave her. That button nose wrinkles like it smells something foul. "Who are you?"

"Jenny, Gwen's friend." I say Gwen's name extra loud in an attempt to remind the fans that Caleb is already taken. I don't like how enthusiastically they responded to the kiss. "You know, Gwen, Caleb's *fiancée*." I arch a brow, waiting for her reaction.

"Oh yeah, that," she says, waving her hand airily. With a conspiratorial air, she leans in and says, "It won't last."

I bristle with anger. No one insults Gwen in my presence. *No one.* I grit my teeth. "Gwen will be around a lot longer than you. I guarantee it."

Lola's mouth drops open in shock. I'd forgotten Dean was behind me, but I hear his amused snort. I get a glimpse of Lola's hate-filled glare. Then Dean's scorching hand is at the small of my back, pushing me forward, rushing us down the sidewalk to the car where Caleb waits, done with autographs. I turn to say another cutting remark, but Dean interrupts me.

"Calm down there, Tiger." He's chuckling, an entertained twinkle in his eye.

"Did you hear what she said?" I ask, outraged.

"I did. I also heard what *you* said." There's something close to respect in the way he looks at me. He lowers his voice. "I never liked her either, back when Caleb was dating her. She's an ugly piece of work."

My eyes widen. "I doubt anyone's ever called her ugly before."

He shrugs, nonchalant.

We've reached Caleb now. I can't help but ask, "How could you have dated her? She seems all wonderful on TV, but in real life . . ." I shudder.

Caleb scratches the back of his head. "Honestly, I was mostly looking for a drinking partner. I wish I had a deeper answer, but that was it."

I shoot him a disappointed stare and mutter under my breath, "Men!" Sometimes I think they really are from Mars.

We climb into the car and shut the doors against the clamor of shouting reporters and fans.

Caleb rubs his eyes with the heels of his hands. "Gwen's going to see that photo, isn't she?"

"Yes, she is." I won't sugarcoat it. It may be unfair to blame Caleb for things he did before he met Gwen, but I'm weirdly disgruntled right now. Somehow, I expected better from him.

He leans his head against the headrest with a quiet "Shoot."

The car fills with silence until Dean says, "Gwen's pretty reasonable. She'll probably understand…" The words die in his throat when he sees the doubtful looks on both Caleb's and my faces.

Outside the window, snow falls lightly to the ground.

TUESDAY, DECEMBER 10
14 DAYS UNTIL THE WEDDING

—GWEN—

"That flight took forever," Wayne grumbles as we exit the plane. He winces, rubbing his neck.

"I'm surprised you noticed, since you slept the entire time." Rising onto my toes, I peer over the crowd in front of me, searching for a bathroom. I spy one ahead. "Hang on. I've got to stop. I drank three iced teas back in New York."

"Me too," says Alvina.

Together, we duck into the restroom. After a few minutes, we come out.

Wayne's waiting right by the exit. "Okay, ladies," he says in an overly bright tone that immediately makes me suspicious. "Baggage claim is this way. Hurry up." He takes my elbow in one hand and Alvina's in the other and drags us along, which is odd because Wayne doesn't usually initiate touching.

"What's going on?" I ask, my feet stumbling over each other as I attempt to keep up with him.

"Nothing!" His voice is high and harried. He tightens his death grip on my arm and tugs me forward.

"Wayne." I pull back, wrenching my arm out of his grasp. "What are you doing? Why the rush?" I take in his agitated expression, wondering why he's acting so weird.

A television screen at Gate 11 catches my eye. It shows a photo of Caleb, a head shot from his movie-star days. Drawn like a magnet, I wander toward it.

"Gwen, wait," Wayne says from behind me, a warning in his tone. "I don't think you want to see that."

"What do you mean?" I ask over my shoulder, stepping closer to the TV. "They're talking about Caleb. Of course I want to see."

I can hear the announcer's voice now. He says, "These photos taken earlier today have the Internet buzzing." The image changes to a photo of Caleb. He's outside on a patio with twinkling Christmas lights strung from tree to tree until they make a canopy over his head. A light snow is falling. Snowflakes land in Caleb's hair. They dust his shoulders and gather on the collar of his jacket.

The man continues, "As we all know, Caleb Lawson is currently engaged to Dr. Gwen Wright, but now everyone's wondering if that couple will make it to the altar."

In the photo, Caleb's not alone. A woman with long black hair and curves for days stands before him, her hands on his cheeks. My mind stutters, unwilling to grasp what I'm seeing. My mouth falls open and an unintentional whimper comes out, the sound of an injured animal.

Alvina moves up next to me. "I'm sure it's not what it looks like."

I don't answer. Instead, I spin in a slow circle, taking in all the TVs in the airport. There are a lot of them, one at every gate and in every restaurant and store. All are watched by travelers who stare with unwavering attention. The same image is displayed on each screen, over and over and over again.

It's a picture of my fiancé kissing his ex-girlfriend.

♥

The click of the hotel door closing wakes me up. I scoot up onto my elbows and stare blearily at the clock on the nightstand. Eleven forty-five p.m. I've been asleep for a little over an hour. We had a late dinner at a nearby restaurant. Turns out Helen is staying here as well, so we invited her to join us. She was a nice addition to our group. Quiet but kind.

Since registration for the conference opens early tomorrow, we'd gone to bed shortly after we ate. Alvina's sharing a room with me, two queen beds with a nightstand between them. Wayne's right across the hall. I yawn and stretch, then snuggle back under the soft, white covers, still tired. I had a hard time falling asleep.

The image of Caleb and Lola kissing kept me awake, even though Alvina repeatedly assured me that Caleb would have a good explanation once I talked with him. I'd called him twice before I fell asleep, but no answer, a fact that only added to my unease.

The thought of Alvina makes me sit up again. I peer through the darkness, trying to make out her shape in the bed across the room, but the blankets lie flat against the mattress. She isn't there.

That's odd.

I rise and pad to the bathroom. She isn't in there either. The murmur of voices from the hallway draws my attention. I move to the peephole in our door. Rising onto my toes, I can barely see out.

The scene before me rocks my world. It's Alvina…and Wayne. They're embracing and are they kissing?!

Yes. Yes, they are.

Not just any casual smooch. This is a passion-filled kiss, like they're trying to suck the air right out of each other. They pull apart and—wait—they're beaming. I've never seen either of them look so happy.

What the heck is happening?

Wayne holds his door open, and Alvina walks into his hotel room.

I think I might puke.

It's not that I don't want to see them in a relationship. They deserve love, but I never thought it would be with each other.

On the nightstand, my phone rings with Caleb's name on the screen. A tremor of apprehension runs through me as I accept the call.

Caleb greets me, his voice deep and raspy. "Hey, I'm glad you're up. Sorry I missed your message earlier. I stayed late at rehearsals, helping orient Justin. He's still settling in."

"Oh yeah. How's he doing?" I had almost forgotten. Caleb's old understudy for his Broadway musical, *Crazy for You*, had gotten a starring role in a different production down the street. Justin was hired a few weeks ago to replace him.

"He's fine. Super-grateful. He said as soon as he got this understudy position, he quit his old job, which he hated. How about you? How was the flight?"

"Long." I climb into bed and sit cross-legged.

"Hang on," Caleb says, "let's FaceTime. I need to see you."

"Oh, good idea."

We end the call, and I redial. There's a chiming sound as our phones connect and there he is, sitting in his bed with the phone propped in his lap. The lights are turned off, leaving only moonlight and the glimmer of stars outside the window to illuminate the room. That mix of silver and gold reflects off the sharp angles of his cheekbones and adds a metallic glint to his skin. He's gorgeous, almost too handsome to be real. I drink him in. Caleb looks at me the same way, staring like he hasn't seen me in years rather than hours. My eyes drop to his full lips, and it comes back to me that earlier today that mouth was pressed to Lola's. The glow that was lit in me from seeing him fades, replaced by an inky darkness.

"How was your day?" I ask, on the hunt for the truth. I expect to have to ferret the information out of him, but I should have known better.

Caleb's not a liar.

He says, "It was okay, but I need to warn you about something."

"What?" I lean against the padded headrest, already guessing the answer.

Caleb clears his throat and says, "There was an…incident when I was leaving lunch today. I bumped into Lola." He pauses, braces himself, and plows on. "The press was there, and they took some pictures—"

"The ones where she's kissing you?"

Surprise ripples over his features. That clearly wasn't the response he was expecting. "You saw them?"

"As soon as I got off the plane." I struggle to keep my voice neutral. "They were *everywhere*. All the headlines said you two are getting back together."

Caleb's cautious, looking at me hesitantly as if I'm a bomb he needs to defuse. "Are you mad? It wasn't anything. I swear. We bumped into her and before I could stop it, she kissed me. It was over in like five seconds. I pushed her away, then left immediately."

He's telling the truth. I already knew it from the photo. I saw the stiffness in his shoulders. How he averted his face from hers. I also know because I know him. Caleb is a good man. He wouldn't cheat on me the minute my back was turned. I understand these truths, and yet it had been awful to see him in another woman's arms.

"I'm not mad," I say, working to keep my tone light. "I knew what happened right away."

He squints at me with suspicion. "Really?"

"Of course." I laugh and wave my hand in dismissal. "It's no big deal." *That your ex left her lipstick all over your face.* "It didn't bother me." *Except that it felt like someone stabbed an ice pick in my heart.*

There's a long pause where he stares at me with a doubtful expression, like he doesn't believe me. I keep my face calm, smiling pleasantly at him, while inwardly I beg him to accept my lie and move on. This is my chance to prove I can handle all the bumps that come along with his fame.

It must work because Caleb breathes out a relieved sigh. "I was worried."

"I trust you. I wouldn't marry you if I didn't." This, at least, is true. I *do* trust him to be faithful. "The most important things in a relationship are love, trust, and honesty."

"And fantastic conversation," he teasingly adds, relaxing slowly.

"That too." Tension leaks out of me, but it comes rushing back when Caleb drops his head with a sigh. He runs his fingers through his hair, mussing it.

"Something else happened today," he says in a tone that lets me know this isn't good news.

I sit up straight as my heart picks up speed. "What?"

He shifts on the bed, rearranging his legs until he finds a comfortable position. "I've mentioned it before, but I have some…overly enthusiastic fans."

"Yeah?" I draw the word out, not sure where this conversation's going.

"Stalker fans," he says with a wince.

"I remember. You showed me that website where they keep track of you.

That Secret Santa page." My heart kicks into overdrive, pounding with apprehension. "Why? Did something happen? Are you okay?"

"I'm fine." He puts his hand up, like he's testifying in court. "One of them sent me another of those gifts at the autograph signing."

"How?" I ask, tilting my head. "Did you see them?"

"No. They gave some random guy money to drop it off. He got it from another person, probably someone they also paid."

"What was it? The present?" Alarm bells ring faintly in the back of my mind. I've known Caleb has these kinds of fans. It's part of his job. Like the need for getting new headshots once a year or paying dues to the Screen Actors Guild. When you're as famous as he is, stalkers go with the territory.

He doesn't answer for a long minute. He stares out of the bedroom window with shadows in his eyes. It reminds me of when I first met him. When he came to hide out at my mom's house in L.A. because he was tired of his celebrity lifestyle, exhausted from being hunted.

He sighs. "I don't want to frighten you. Also, I don't want to scare you away. I love you."

"I'm not going anywhere, Caleb," I reassure him.

This earns me a small, sad smile. "Thanks, love." He blows out a breath and with more strength says, "It wasn't a big deal. They sent me a shirt. It…" Another pause. His eyes shift, and I get the sense Caleb's hiding something from me, but that can't be correct.

Right?

"It was a shirt with red lipstick on it. Stupid, really. I wanted to tell you, though." He stares at me through the phone screen. More urgently, he says, "Some of these people are mentally unstable. They might get jealous—especially with the wedding coming up. Please be careful, just in case. Okay?"

A knot of worry winds in my throat. I swallow past it. "Of course. I don't think they'd come after me, though. It's *you* they're fascinated by. Not me. I'm a boring regular person."

"There's nothing boring or regular about you." He sighs and shakes his head. I know he's thinking about our fight over the jet plane. There's an echo of it in this conversation. In so many of our talks recently. Is it because he's famous or do all couples have this conflict when they get married? This push and pull of how does "me" and "you" turning into an "us" fundamentally change who we are?

"How was your day?" Caleb asks, abruptly changing the subject.

"Well," I say and then hesitate, debating how much to tell him about Skylar and Hannah. "I met a couple of your fans at the airport today." I think I'm doing a good job of keeping my tone neutral, but Caleb knows me too well.

"Were they mean to you?" he asks, immediately on the defense.

"Not too bad." It's alarming how easily the lie slips out. I justify it by telling myself that I'm protecting him. Saving him from the stress of worrying about me. "They asked a couple of personal questions, but I deflected."

There's a stubborn set to his jaw. "This is what I was talking about, why I wanted you to take the jet."

"You can't protect me, Caleb. You can't lock me up in a tower like Rapunzel."

"Why not?" he argues. "Why can't I put you in emotional bubble wrap, so you don't get hurt?" A tiny hitch in his voice, so quiet most people would miss it. "I would have loved that, if someone had done it for me when I was younger."

That gets to me. I flash back to a photo that sits on the mantle in his mother's house. Seven-year-old Caleb getting his first star on the Hollywood Walk of Fame. Grinning with his front teeth missing. A gap-tooth smile that would fool most people, including his mom since she proudly displays it. It didn't trick me, though. I saw how the light didn't reach his aqua eyes. How those baby cheeks didn't fully round out.

It's merged in his mind, young him and me. He wants to save me, but there's a shadow behind me he's also protecting. That of his younger self. I understand his pain, and I empathize with it, but it's not logical. I can't live my life trying to heal hurts so deeply buried that they may never scab over.

"Because that's not sustainable," I say as gently as I can manage. "I have a life. A job. I don't want to live in your tower. No matter how fancy it is."

"What if I'm in the tower with you?" he asks, so plaintively it makes me want to cry.

"That makes it better," I tell him, further softening my voice, "but we have responsibilities. Goals we each want to accomplish."

There's an extra-long silence after that. So long that I ask, "What are you thinking about right now?"

"Nothing," he answers way too quickly.

Uncertainty sinks its teeth into me. This isn't what I'm used to. Caleb and I share everything. I can usually guess what's on his mind just by looking at him, but he's opaque to me now, and I'm hiding too. Is it because we're apart?

Unease stirs in my stomach. "What else went on today?"

He tells me about lunch, all that he learned about his grandfather and why his mom wanted to move away.

I tuck the comforter over my legs. "Your poor mother. It sounds like going to L.A. was what she needed. I'm impressed by how much she's opening up to you."

"It's better now, with her." He laughs ruefully. "It only took us 30 years, but I think we're finally figuring out how this whole mother-son relationship is supposed to work."

"Well, I'm glad. I wish my mom would work on things with me," I say, thinking about the sometimes good and sometimes contentious way my mother and I interact.

I straighten, suddenly remembering Wayne and Alvina. "Caleb! You're never going to believe what I just saw."

He hears the excitement in my voice. "What?"

"Wayne and Alvina are in a relationship!"

"Really?" His jaw unhinges, and he sputters.

I relay everything I witnessed. It's satisfying to see that his shock matches my own. "You didn't know?"

He shakes his head. "No. I had no idea. What're you going to do? Confront them?"

I twirl a lock of long, blonde hair around my finger, a habit I picked up from Jenny. "I think so? I'm not sure. Why're they keeping it a secret?"

"Probably embarrassed. Remember when they met at that karaoke bar? They both made a big deal about how they weren't interested."

"Alvina said she wasn't interested," I correct him. "Wayne was the opposite, like he was definitely into the idea."

"Guess he convinced her."

"Which is impressive, considering Alvina is rarely swayed."

We both laugh at that because it's true. Our laughter fades slowly until it settles into a silence where we stare intently at each other. The air around me thickens with longing. Even though he's far away, Caleb must feel it too.

"Hi," he says, his voice husky. There's so much contained in that small word, so much love and tenderness and happiness.

"Hey," I say, unable to hold back my grin at how his eyes trace the contours of my face.

"I miss you, Gwen. It's like my heart got ripped out of my chest and stuffed into your suitcase."

There it is. The special way he says my name.

GweN. Round G, flat N.

Each syllable vibrates with emotion.

"I know." I lift my fingers to the screen, wishing I could touch him. "I'm the same way."

"Let's never do this again. Okay?" He drags a hand through his hair, making it stick up all spiky. "I don't want to be away from you. Next time I'm coming along."

"That's nearly impossible," I say, laughing softly, secretly pleased by his earnest expression. "You have the theater, your restaurants—"

"Forget them." Caleb interrupts me, all bossy and confident. "I'm going with you, and that's final."

Happiness expands my chest, filling it until "I love you" bursts out of me.

"Love you, too. Forever and always."

There's no explaining it. The effect his words have on me. How they make me feel like the world is exactly as it should be. Like the sun and stars and moon are in perfect harmony. Like our love is a physical force, so strong it can withstand anything.

I echo back, "Always and forever."

WEDNESDAY, DECEMBER 11
13 DAYS UNTIL THE WEDDING

—JENNY—

As predicted, the day after the Lola incident photos of the kiss are everywhere. I call Gwen and am surprised to find she's handling it pretty well. Apparently, she had a good conversation with Caleb about it. I talk to her about the stalker, treading lightly because I'm not sure what details Caleb told her and what he left out. She seems to be aware enough to be careful. I add my own warnings, an urge to protect her overriding all other thoughts. I miss her, but we've been long-distance friends long enough that our near-daily phone calls feel natural. It's funny, really, how we've traded places. Now she's the one on the West Coast, and I'm here on the East Coast. A few more weeks and we'll switch again.

It's evening, and the light and the temperature are both dropping. I've just left some fabric samples for tablecloths at the wedding at Caleb's place. He needs to choose one. He'd seemed tired, dark circles under his eyes. He's probably not sleeping well with Gwen gone.

Even though he's obviously suffering from the strain of preparing for the wedding and missing his fiancée, Caleb still took the time to ask me how I'm doing, to check if I was okay.

"Let me know if you need anything, anything at all," he said, which made me feel guilty, knowing that Eddie's out there searching for dirt on him.

Should I warn Caleb? I wonder. But about what? Eddie hasn't found out about the stalker or the Secret Santa website. Besides, I don't want to add to Caleb's stress. I'll keep quiet for now. If something solid comes up, if there's a real threat, then I'll let him know. I reassure Caleb that I'm fine and say good night.

The doorman lets me out into a winter wonderland. Trees decorated with glowing white Christmas lights bow under the weight of dangling icicles. The snow is coming down harder now, piling up in drifts that cover the toes of my boots. A frigid breeze whips snowflakes into tiny tornados that rise into a spinning column and then, without warning, collapse back to the ground. The freezing temperatures are no deterrent to seasoned New Yorkers, who walk at a fast pace down the frosty sidewalk. They tuck their heads into their chins and charge against the wind like battering rams. It's past 10:00 p.m., but the streets are still busy.

A flicker of light in a car parked across the street highlights a familiar face. I wait for a taxi to race by and then cross the road with my arms out for balance. I knock loudly on the passenger window. The dark-haired man inside startles and turns toward me with a deep frown. He waves for me to go away. I point at the car door. With exaggerated facial expressions, I mouth, "*LET. ME. IN.*"

Even from the outside, I can see his shoulders move up and down as he lets out a heavy sigh. I point again. He angrily jabs at the button by his elbow, and the locks click open. I slide into the car, welcoming the warm blast of the heater.

"Hi, Dean." I smile widely, then pull off my yellow woolen mittens and raise my hands to the vent, which spills out warm air.

He gives a curt nod with thin lips and narrowed eyes. "*Jennifer.*"

"What're you doing out here?" Empty coffee cups are scattered in cup holders. The windows are partly fogged over, but he's wiped a circle clean on his side of the car. Through that clear patch, I see the front of Caleb's building.

"I'm on a stakeout."

"A stakeout?" I laugh, falling back into the seat and clutching my stomach. The word sounds so dramatic, like I'm in the middle of an NCIS episode.

Dean isn't amused. "At least I *was* until you came along and tipped off my location."

He's peeved at me.

What else is new?

"Who did I tip off? Who're we looking for?" I lean past him and squint out the window, trying to see through the snow, my shoulder brushing his.

Why is his body so hot? Temperature hot, although it's hot in the other way too.

He stiffens at our contact, but I don't pull away. It's too much fun rattling his composure, making him squirm.

"There's no 'we,' and the answer is whoever's stalking Caleb." He sinks lower in his seat, returning to his vigil. "They come here at night and take photos."

Dean takes his cell phone out of the cupholder between us and thumbs it on. The light from the screen highlights his features with broad cheeks, dark brows, and thick eyelashes. The flecks in his eyes shimmer like gold dust.

Once he's navigated to the Caleb's Secret Santa website, he swipes on the Naughty or Nice photos tab. A few scrolls, and he holds out the phone to show me a nighttime shot of the scene outside his window of the front of Caleb's building. In this picture, it's raining, and puddles on the street reflect the moon overhead. Caleb kisses a woman with long, blonde hair, leaning her back like he's about to dip her.

Gwen.

I recognize her yellow raincoat and rubber boots. Predictably, there's a big, red, "Naughty" stamp on it.

Dean flicks his finger to show me another, of Caleb stretching his arms above his head with his running shoes on and a fitness tracker strapped to his arm. The next one is of Caleb lifting a hand to wave good-bye to his mother, who is in the corner of the frame. Those two photos are labeled as "Nice." I guess even the stalker accepts that Caleb should be allowed to hang out with his mom.

The position of each photo is nearly identical, close enough to see what Caleb's doing but far enough to miss the small details, like the individual buttons on his coat or laces on his shoes.

"Judging by the angle of the shot, I think they hide over there." He points to a cluster of trees across the street, half a block away. It's lined up to be clearly visible from where we sit. "I don't know how they figured it out, but there's a blind spot there where the security cameras of all the surrounding buildings can't see. I've put up temporary cameras aimed at that location, but somehow they disable them every single time. They never show up when I'm here. It's frustrating."

I investigate the area he's staring at, searching for the culprit. All I see is tree branches dancing from the wind. Moving slowly, so Dean won't notice, I get a sugar-free strawberry candy, the kind with the soft center, from the front pocket of my jeans. I have to rise up slightly and tilt my pelvis to wrestle it out. With exaggerated care, I unwrap it as silently as I can. He turns back right after I slip the disc into my mouth. Holding my lips still, I suck on it while Dean lets out a deep yawn. He rubs his eyes with both fists, the way a small child would.

"How long have you been out here?" I ask, tucking the candy into my cheek, alarmed by the fatigue I sense in the slouch of his shoulders. He and Caleb could have a contest to see who has bigger bags under his eyes. I'm not sure which one would win.

Dean shrugs, the motion lagging. He checks his big, black wristwatch. "Since 5:00 p.m." He yawns again.

"Uh-huh, and how late do you plan on staying?"

"Dunno. Maybe 2:00 or 3:00 a.m.? That's when I left the last couple of nights."

"Wait," I say, my voice rising in volume. He winces. "How long have you been doing this? I just saw you work all day."

"I've lost track," he admits, slightly sheepish. "Four or five nights?"

I clap my hand to my forehead. "What are you thinking? Staying up all night and then working the next day? You'll be no use to Caleb if you're sleeping on the job."

His brow lowers, showing that he's offended. "I would *never* fall asleep like that. Back when I was with the Army, we trained to stay awake for days on end."

"The Army, huh?" I figured. He's got that short haircut and precise way of moving, like he's used to marching in formation. "How long were you in it?"

"From after college until about five years ago." He lets out a jaw-cracking yawn.

"Why don't I take over for tonight? You can get some shut-eye."

"You wouldn't know what to look for." He blinks slowly, as if there are heavy weights attached to his jet-black eyelashes.

"Let me guess, a scary person in a trench coat and a top hat with pockets big enough to hide a camera and maybe a weapon?" I'm joking—mostly. I punch him in the arm and smother my giggle when he jerks it away.

"Come *on*," I whine, drawing the word out. "I can do it."

"No, crazy woman. I can't let you. Can't risk it."

Of course he doesn't trust me.

He quickly changes the subject. "Did you ask them?"

"Who?"

A car passes by, momentarily bathing us in its headlights. That flash of light accentuates the square angle of Dean's jaw and the subtle bump in the middle of his nose, like it was broken once long ago.

He says impatiently, "Your friends, the reporters."

"Oh. Yeah, Ron and Bradly. I asked both of them. Ron works on the *Los Angeles Times* with me, and Bradly writes for the *Orange County Register*. Figured that way we'd have access to a wider range of intel." Look at me, using my fancy words, like I'm some kind of detective. Maybe listening to all those true-crime podcasts will finally pay off.

"Who're they? Ex-boyfriends?" Dean watches me intently.

What a weird question.

"No. The only ex-boyfriend from work I have is Eddie."

"Eddie?" He rears back. "I thought you were still dating him."

Since when does Dean know who I'm seeing? Pretty sure I've never mentioned Eddie around him.

"Not anymore." I heave a resentful sigh as I replay our breakup conversation from over two months ago. How Eddie had beaten me to the punch by dumping me. Stupid me. I'd been blindsided when he gave me the old, "It's not you. It's me. I need space. Blah, blah, blah," speech. It shouldn't have surprised me, Eddie had always been a jerk, but when he begged me to go out with him it felt good. To be wanted. I looked past his flaws and said "yes." What an idiot. Had I really been that desperate? It's so depressing that I sigh again.

"What's wrong with you?" Dean's frown deepens, and he shifts a little closer. "Why do you keep making those pathetic noises?"

"Pathetic! I'm not pathetic. I'm just…sad." Tears threaten, but I hold them back. I did all my crying right after the breakup. It's not that I cried over Eddie. He doesn't deserve that. It's more that I cried for myself. For yet another failed relationship.

"Why?" He scoots another inch closer.

"I wouldn't expect you to understand, since you lack basic human emotions, but I'm upset because it was my longest relationship, lasting over eight months."

Even though I'd never thought Eddie was "husband material," I'd held on longer than I should've, in part to prove that I could have a long-term relationship. Maybe it's time to accept that I'll never be "that" woman. The one who gets chosen for forever. I'm the fun girl. The one guys date right before they find their future wife.

"He's an idiot," Dean says dismissively.

My skin bristles at his offhand tone. "He is *not*."

Why am I defending the man who dumped me over a 10-minute phone call? The one who's currently making me miserable at work.

"A total loser," Dean declares, as if that settles the matter. "I never liked him."

"Have you even met him?" I ask, momentarily confused.

"Don't have to meet him to know he's a moron." Dean crosses his arms over his chest and leans back in his seat.

"Just because he chose to date me doesn't make him stupid." My temper flares into life.

"That's not what I said." He meets my eyes for a microsecond with an intense gaze, like he's trying to communicate through telepathy or something. Then he's back on duty, focused on Caleb's building.

"You didn't have to." I curl in on myself. I won't let him upset me. This Neanderthal of a man.

"Eight months, huh?" His back is to me. I can only see the curve of his cheek, the outline of his ear. "Why not longer?"

Silently, I mull over his question. "I don't know. Guys don't usually stick around for long. Maybe I'm too much? Too loud? Too opinionated? Too emotional? Too demanding?"

Dean scoffs. "Nonsense. You're just enough. Not too much and not too little."

Now I'm really looking at him, but it's dark and I can't make out his expression. "That was..." *What was that?* "Surprisingly kind of you." I regard him warily, wondering where this version of Dean came from.

Maybe he's so tired he's delusional?

"I *can* be nice, you know," he says, somewhat testily.

I hold up my hand, placating. "If you say so."

A moment passes. He clears his throat, straightening. His eyes flick my way. "I figured maybe it was your brothers scaring men away. Don't you have three of them? Older brothers?"

"Yeah. They're quite a bit older—36, 39, and 42 years old now. I'm the baby of the family."

"The spoiled baby?" His head turns back and forth between me and the street outside.

"More like the neglected one." I stop and correct myself. "That's too harsh. I was an 'oops' baby. No one was prepared for me, so much younger and a girl to boot. I was a rock thrown into my family's well-oiled machine. My older brothers were super-athletic. They all ended up going to college on sports scholarships.

"I grew up playing in the grass next to their baseball and soccer fields. Running wild through the stands with the younger siblings of their teammates. Always the tagalong. My brothers were so busy. They didn't want their annoying little sister around to embarrass them."

That old sting of rejection tugs at me, but I brush it aside. "It's better now that we're all grown, but back then there was one person who wanted to be with me."

"Gwen," Dean guesses correctly. The sympathy in his gaze causes my chest to constrict.

"Gwen," I confirm. "Before her dad died, her family seemed almost perfect. My parents would drop me off at her house so they could drive my brothers to their games. I'd spend all day there. She wanted to know everything about me—my favorite color, favorite food, secret crush. Being with her was like someone finally saw me." I swallow around a lump in my throat and stare at my hands, folded in my lap.

"That's why what I did, when I blew it and told Sarah about Caleb, that's why it was so bad. I betrayed my best friend. I could have ruined her chance at happiness."

There's a long silence, where I look everywhere but at him.

"Gwen's not your only friend, though. I've seen you flitting around like a social butterfly. Your phone is always lighting up with texts, emails." So sharp, his gaze, like he wants to see past all my layers. It makes me feel vulnerable, exposed.

"I have lots of friends, but they like me because I'm entertaining. Because I do zany stuff. Take me to a party, and I'll get people laughing. Everyone likes happy Jenny. Gwen's the only one who knows what to do when I'm sad." I stop, uncertain how to better explain it.

Dean opens his mouth to speak when a car driving by backfires, the sound going off like a gunshot. He flinches.

"You're so jumpy," I observe, picking a piece of white fur off my leggings. It's left over from this morning when I did yoga with goats.

His scowl is back in place. "I don't like loud noises."

"That must be why you hate me, because I'm loud." I say it like a joke, though his contempt has been bothering me. My laughter dies in my throat when he doesn't join in.

His dark brows quirk downward, like he's confused by what I just said.

Something occurs to me. "Wait. How do you know all that stuff about me? About my brothers? I've never told you." I gasp. Without thinking, I put my hand on his arm and give it a hard shake.

"Have you been snooping around?" I demand. "Is that how you learned about my family?"

Dean lifts his chin, defensive. "I background check anyone who's in close contact with Caleb."

"What? You have a file on me?" I'm practically yelling, caught between anger and disbelief.

He squares his shoulders and says, "I do."

I sputter.

"Common practice in my field," he insists.

"Oh, sure. Because that's not creepy at all," I say sarcastically, with a theatrical eye roll. "I think I found the stalker, and it's *you*."

At that, Dean throws his head back and laughs, really laughs, a deep soul-shaking sound.

I gasp, my hand flying to my chest, "Oh my gosh! Do that again."

His brow furrows, confused by my sudden change in mood. "Do what?"

"Laugh. I've never heard you do it before. You have a great laugh."

He gives me a look like I've lost my mind.

"Seriously. You should do it more often." I nod confidently.

A small shrug from him. "Not much occasion for it in my line of work."

That spikes my curiosity. "How'd you meet Caleb, anyway? Get this job? You're awfully dedicated, staying up all night."

"I met him at a bar."

My hand covers my mouth, concern softening the set of my shoulders. "I'm sorry. Do you have a drinking problem, too?"

He does another one of those deep laughs, his rich baritone filling the car. "No. That was the first time I'd been in a bar in over five years."

"Oh?" I place my elbow on my knee and rest my chin in my hand, regarding him expectantly.

He purses his lips, staring back. "You're not going to let this go until you get the story, are you?"

"Nope."

A wry smile twists his mouth. "Fine, but you can't print it."

"Understood." I grin, my anticipation almost unbearable.

Dean turns to watch out the window. "It was over four years ago in L.A. I'd been out of the Army for about six months, struggling to find work I liked. I picked up jobs here and there, but nothing felt right, like something I could do long term. Anyway, I went to the bar that night, thinking a drink might distract me from worrying.

"This man sits down next to me, wearing a baseball cap pulled down low.

I thought he was older, with the way he walked, kinda hunched over and slow. He had a southern accent, light, but definitely there. We got to talking. I guess the couple of beers I had loosened my tongue, so I told him some of what was going on."

Dean gives a lengthy pause here, and my reporter spider sense tells me he's editing the story, hiding some detail.

"The man was tipsy when he sat down and getting more drunk as the hours passed. After midnight, he lifts his cap to smooth his hair, and that's when I saw it was all an act—the accent, the walking, the mannerisms.

"I was like, 'Hey! You're Caleb Lawson. What're you doing here?' and I'll never forget what he said. He sighed and said, 'Trying to be someone else.' And I said, 'Me too, buddy.'"

Dean pauses again, sadness turning down the corners of his mouth. I resist the urge to reach out to him but restrain myself, not wanting to interrupt his story. "Then Caleb asked if I was going to stop talking to him like a normal person now that I knew who he was. Of course, I said 'no.'"

A pained hint of a smile crosses his face. "We stayed until the bartender kicked us out. Caleb was pretty sloshed by then, swaying and tripping. I demanded he let me help him home. When we got here," Dean hooks a thumb toward the building across the street, "he offered me a job. Told me to come back in the morning. I thought, "No way is this guy going to remember what he promised" but, well, I *was* looking for work. I showed up the next day, and there was Caleb, hungover, with a contract in his hands. He said, 'You're used to protecting people. I want you to protect me.'"

Understanding dawns on me. Dean's workaholic tendencies make sense now. He thinks Caleb saved him, so, in return, he saves Caleb.

I open my mouth to respond when I notice movement outside the window. I catch my breath and point. "Who's that by the front door? The woman in the trench coat?"

Dean swivels and peers through the snow. He gapes and says, "That's Mrs. Wilkins."

"Who?"

"Caleb's old housekeeper." He shoots a glance at me over his shoulder.

"We fired her once we found out she was selling Caleb's used underwear on the Internet."

"Gross." I wrinkle my nose in disgust. "People really buy that?"

"You'd be surprised. She was making a lot of money. We took away her key and changed the locks." He taps a finger against his lips, watching as the woman disappears into the building.

We wait for several minutes, staring at the door, but no one comes back out. The whole time, my brain is whirring, sifting through everything I just learned about Dean, Caleb, and the stalker.

"That's it!" I half-stand in my seat and clutch at his arm. *Why am I touching him so often tonight?* "It's Mrs. Wilkins in the conservatory with the rope!"

He squints over at me, tilting his head. "Did you make a Clue reference? Like the board game?"

I put my hand over my mouth to stifle my giggle. "Sorry. Too much?"

He must not think so, because he laughs one more time, that amazing sound, and I laugh along with him.

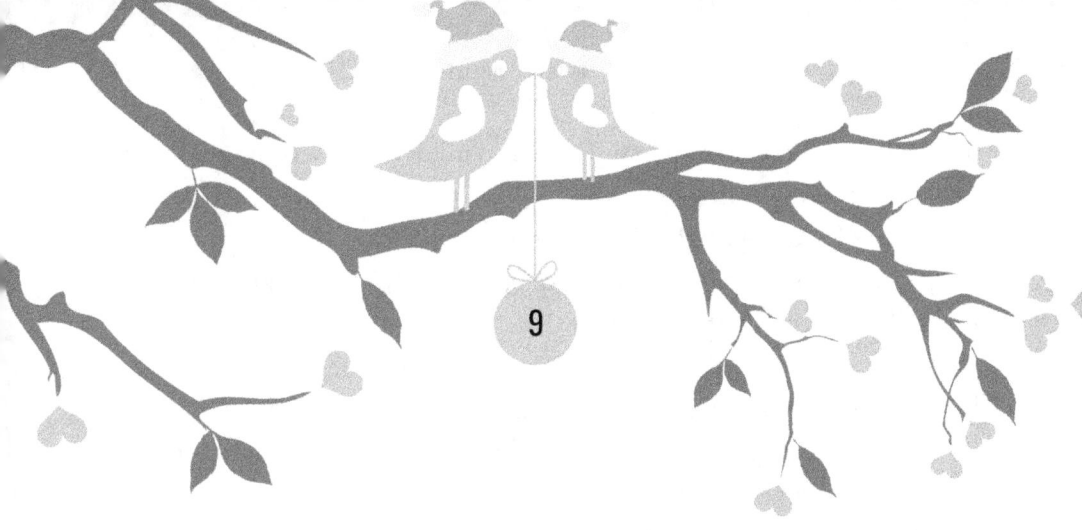

9

THURSDAY, DECEMBER 12
12 DAYS UNTIL THE WEDDING

— GWEN —

Everything is the same as the last time I was in this room. There's the couch where Caleb slept beneath my grandmother's quilt. There's the table where we put the puzzle together. The Christmas tree is in the corner by the fireplace. It's not the one that Caleb, Jenny, and I decorated, but it might as well be.

This is where I fell in love with Caleb and him with me. Is this how I'll always view things going forward? In relation to him? I hope so. I don't mind seeing the world through a Caleb-shaped lens. He makes everything seem brighter, more beautiful.

"I can't believe it's been so long," says Mom, reading my thoughts.

"I know, two years since I was here with Caleb, but it's not like we could come back before, not with the renters." The kitchen island has a light granite countertop covered in a menagerie of Christmas figurines. I pick up a jolly Santa, holding a bag of presents over his shoulder. I remember this one. It was there when Caleb and I danced on that long-ago Christmas Eve.

"They were such nice people. Those renters." Mom blows a stray piece of hair, blonde like mine but shorter and curlier, out of her eyes. The grilled cheese sandwiches sizzle when she flips them over in the skillet.

Pip leans against my leg, gazing up at me with doggy adoration. Her pink tongue lolls. I scoop her up in my arms and hold her like a baby, petting and tickling her nearly furless belly.

"Thanks for bringing Pip. I know it was a pain."

"It's fine. You want her in the wedding. Honestly, she would have hated it if we left her behind. She gets so anxious."

"How'd she do on the flight?" I ask. Pip turns her head to the side and licks my forearm, leaving a sticky, wet trail.

"Okay. The vet gave us a sleeping pill that we crushed up and put in her breakfast. She snoozed most of the trip."

"That's good." I set Pip back on the ground, but she doesn't move away, just stares up at me like she's scared I'll disappear if she blinks.

"Go put your star on the Christmas tree," Mom says, adding bacon to the skillet. It sizzles immediately, curling along the edges.

She's already placed the ladder next to the tree, so it only takes a minute to balance the battered gold star, the one we got when Teddy was a baby, on the topmost branch. When Dad was alive, he would put me on his shoulders to get the star up there. When Caleb was here with me, he had done the same thing. He'd hoisted me high on his shoulders and let me place the star. This way, with the ladder, is a lot less romantic, but it still gets the job done.

"It's perfect. Good work, honey," Mom says, gazing at the top of the tree with a sad, wistful smile. I know she's thinking about Dad too. She sighs, flips the sandwiches one last time, and announces, "Lunch is almost ready."

"Is it okay if we eat outside by the pool?"

"Of course. You could probably use the vitamin D." Mom shifts into a warmer smile, one I've missed seeing since she moved away.

I stand on my toes and reach into the cupboard, pulling out plates and cups, which I take out to the umbrella-topped table. Pip follows at my heels. It's a beautiful California day, the sky an azure blue. The weather channel in my hotel room this morning warned that a big snowstorm is building on the East Coast. Glancing around my mother's backyard, it seems unfathomable, like something that might happen on another planet.

It's bright outside, so I put on my new sunglasses, the ones Caleb gave me. I sit at the table and look at Pip by my feet. "Glasses, take picture," I order.

There's a click noise from the tiny speaker in the earpiece, and a photo of my dog materializes in front of my eyes. "Camera, text this to Caleb." A whoosh sound lets me know the image has been sent.

"How cool is that?" I tell Pip, who cocks her head, listening intently.

I check my phone, eager to see if Caleb's responded yet. We've been texting constantly, sometimes just a funny meme or a simple heart emoji. No matter how big or small, each message brings a smile to my face. It's good to know that even though we aren't together, we're still thinking about each other.

Give Pip a hug for me, Caleb texts back. I scroll through the rest of the messages. Alvina sent a photo of her eating lunch with her cousins by the marina. It doesn't surprise me to see Wayne sitting next to her. I wonder if she told her family they're dating? The thought that she confided to them before me shouldn't make me jealous, but it does. I still haven't talked to Alvina and Wayne about their relationship. The stubborn part of me is waiting for them to bring it up.

A minute later, Mom joins me with a plate of bacon grilled cheese sandwiches, my childhood favorite, in one hand and a pitcher of iced tea in the other.

"Thanks for cooking." I help her set everything on the table.

"Are you sure you're okay flying to New York tonight? I feel bad that you've been traveling so much for me."

"I'll be fine. I needed to check in on the house here, but the part of my trip I'm most excited about is your wedding. It'll be beautiful." Her eyes soften as she looks at me. "*You'll* be beautiful, Gwen. A perfect bride."

I flush, warmed by her compliment. *Why, no matter how old I am, do I still crave her approval? Will that desire ever go away?*

"I'm glad you could sneak over here for a few hours." Mom spreads a napkin over her lap. "We'll see each other at the wedding, but it'll be so busy. It's nice to have this alone time together. How's your conference going?"

"Good." Mimicking her, I take my napkin and smooth it over my legs. "I made a new friend, Helen Chu, who will be there. We met on the plane ride over. She recently joined a practice here in L.A. so she can be close to her family. She starts next month."

"Oh, really?" Mom cuts her sandwich in two and picks up one half.

"She rented an apartment in Santa Monica, by the beach."

Pip leans against my leg. I pass a piece of bacon down to her, and she gobbles it up greedily.

"A new friend? How wonderful, honey." Mom pats my hand, beaming at me the way she did when I came home in sixth grade and told her I had met a girl named Jenny.

"It's no big deal," I say casually, while inside I bask in the glow of her attention. My happiness dims when I remember Skylar and Hannah. I didn't make friends with them, that's for sure.

"I might take Helen out for a drink some night while we're in town. We could go to the club where Teddy's bartending. He said they transform the place for Christmas, make everything holiday-themed."

"That's a great idea. She'll appreciate you showing her around." Mom takes a spoonful of sugar from the bowl on the table and swirls it into her tea with a long spoon, its metal clinking rhythmically against the side of the glass.

"How's the wedding planning coming along?" she asks.

"Good, so far. Thank goodness for Marjorie. She's been an enormous help, although everyone's pitched in." I bring out my phone and pull up my Notes app, where I keep my wedding to-do list. I read off it. "The venue is ready. Catering is confirmed. So are the photographer and DJ."

I look over at Mom. "You'll join Marjorie to choose the floral arrangements tomorrow when you get to New York. The florist said don't order them too far in advance since the selection is always changing and we want the freshest ones."

She nods with understanding. "I'll go to the flower market straight from the airport."

"Perfect. That place is huge, so Jenny and Dean can help, too. Caleb needs to pick out boutonnieres." I make a note on my phone, a reminder to text my floral inspiration photos to Caleb's mom later today.

"Oh!" I exclaim. "Don't let me forget about the cufflinks." In secret, I had asked Mom to give me my dad's old cufflinks, the silver ones he wore on their wedding day. I'm planning on surprising Caleb with them the night before our wedding. Hopefully, when I see Caleb wearing them it'll be a reminder that, although he's gone, Dad's still here with me in spirit.

"I've got them all packed up for you. In their original box and everything. It's wonderful, how you want to honor your father." Mom delicately nibbles on her sandwich. After she swallows, she clasps her hands together and says, "I'm thrilled you and Caleb are getting married. Seth was right. You two are a perfect match."

Relief flows through me at her words. When Mom first heard about Caleb, she objected, but over the past couple of years she's adjusted to the idea of us being together.

Mom continues, "Some days, I look at you and all I see is a little girl on roller skates with her pigtails flying. I'm excited for this wedding, but it makes me feel like I'm handing you over to Caleb and I'll never get you back." There's moisture in her eyes when she's done talking, and in mine too.

"Oh, Mom." Sadness, grief, regret fill the space between us. "I felt the same way when you married Seth. I thought I would lose you, too."

Mom's mouth opens into an O of surprise. "Really? You never told me."

She's right. In the past, there have been things I didn't tell her because I worried it would make her sad or afraid. I used to be a person who was more concerned about other people's feelings than my own, but now I'm more confident, able to speak my mind. Being with Caleb helped with that.

"That's exactly how I felt, but here we are. I haven't lost you, and you haven't lost me."

She uses a napkin to dab at her watery eyes. "That's true. Here we are." She quietly blows her nose.

"Can you talk to Teddy when you see him? I don't like those friends he's living with." Mom drops her voice into a scandalized whisper. "I think some of them might do *drugs*." She raises her eyebrows dramatically for emphasis.

I resist an urge to snort. I've seen Teddy's housemates, and I'm pretty sure they're *all* doing drugs. Mostly, I try not to think about if Teddy's doing them, too.

"Why don't you ask him?"

She waves a hand at me. "You know how he is. Teddy never tells me anything. I need you to talk to him."

I feel sick at her words. I knew this was coming. She always puts me in the middle between her and my younger brother. I draw in a deep breath, heart pounding with apprehension, and say, "You know what, Mom? Let's not talk about Teddy. I understand it wasn't your intention, and that you were in a bad place both financially and emotionally when Dad died, but I felt responsible for Teddy—"

Mom breaks in. "We didn't have money for a babysitter. There was no life insurance and so many medical bills. I—"

"I get it, and I appreciate all the sacrifices you made for us, but if you want to know something from Teddy, ask him yourself."

Dead silence, broken only by the chirping of the birds and the buzz of a honeybee over by the flowerpot. Mom openly gapes at me, her mouth forming words, but no sound comes out.

A long awkward pause before she says, "Fine, Gwendolen. I'll talk to him."

10

FRIDAY, DECEMBER 13
11 DAYS UNTIL THE WEDDING

—JENNY—

The New York flower market has been around for over 100 years, with some shops passed down from generation to generation. It's located on 28th Street, and only early risers get the best blooms since most stores close by late morning. That's why at 7:00 a.m. I'm there with Caleb, Dean, and Marjorie.

Gwen's mom, Melinda, joins us. She blinks sleepily, tired from having just flown in on a red eye from L.A. I give her my tightest hug, happy to see the woman who partially raised me, considering how many hours I spent at her house when I was young.

"How's Gwen?" I ask her as we walk through a light sprinkle of snow into a large shop filled with shelves and bins of brightly colored flowers. I talked to my best friend last night, so I'm caught up on her activities, but I'm curious to hear her mother's opinion. Sometimes Gwen holds things in, suppresses her emotions. She does it because she wants to be strong, to not burden the rest of us with her concerns. I think it's partially from when her dad died, when she felt like she had to hold her family together. She doesn't understand that all it does is create more stress. We would all rather she expressed her real feelings.

"Fine. Excited and nervous for her presentation at the conference." A shadow flits over Melinda's expression. Her mouth tightens, and I sense that there's something more she wants to say. I wait patiently. As a reporter, I've learned that sometimes the best way to get someone to open up is not to ask questions, but to stay silent.

Finally, she says, "We had a bit of a spat. Gwen and I..."

I nod for her to go on.

Melinda shakes her head. "She thinks I put her in charge of Teddy too much. Made her the parent instead of me."

I carefully hold my expression neutral, to mask my surprise. I'm well aware of Gwen's thoughts on this subject. We've talked about it often enough, but I can't believe she actually told her mom. For years she's stayed quiet, not wanting to upset the delicate balance in her family. But Gwen has become bolder recently, especially after meeting Caleb. She's found her voice, and I've loved it, watching her come into her own.

After a moment of internal debate on how best to handle this conversation, I say, "When Mr. Wright died, you had a lot to juggle. I remember the long hours that you worked—"

"Exactly!" she cries out, nodding vigorously.

"Now things are easier, and your kids are older, so you don't need Gwen's help."

"I don't ask her for much anymore, just to check on Teddy sometimes. He talks to her more than me. I wish it was different, that we had a better relationship, but I worry about him. I don't know what to do." She wrings her hands.

"I understand," I say gently. I've seen Teddy recently. I worry about him too. He's seemed a little unsteady, a little lost, ever since he dropped out of college in Michigan and came back to California. "But that disconnect between you and Teddy isn't Gwen's fault, and she gets overwhelmed feeling like she's responsible for fixing it."

Melinda hangs her head and sighs. "I don't want that."

I reach out to give her arm a light squeeze. "Talk to Teddy. Let him know you care. Let Gwen off the hook. She worries about him too. She'll look after him whether you ask her to or not. That's her nature."

A sniffle and nod from Melinda. "I guess. I don't want to put added pressure on her. She's already got enough going on."

Marjorie calls out, asking all of us to come over. She gathers us around her in a loose semicircle. With hands on her hips, she surveys us like a general looking over her troops. "Today we need to finalize the bridal bouquet and the groomsmen's boutonnieres. Gwen sent photos of the ones she wants." Marjorie passes out a printout showing a variety of flowers accented by winter berries and boughs of pine.

"We also need coordinating flowers to place at the end of each aisle. I want each of you to go and get flowers that match this list. If you find them, take a photo and text it to me with the location of the flowers. If you see any additional flowers, ribbons, or other accents that you think will work, send those to me as well."

She holds up her phone and points to the text message icon on her screen. "At the end, I'll go through everything and put in the order. The process will go much faster with us all working together. Remember that the wedding colors are white, red, and gold. I want to keep this classy. Gwen said nothing over the top." Her mouth twists slightly, like she's disappointed she can't go all out. I picture her dressing Wayne up in a Santa's outfit to officiate and bite back a laugh.

Across the circle, Dean raises a brow at me as if he can hear my thoughts.

"Let's spread out and see what we find," Marjorie says, looking at each of us. "Remember, we're keeping the date and location of the wedding a secret from the public, so make sure no one else sees these notes or texts."

We disperse. Melinda and Marjorie go off together, chatting excitedly about the wedding. I watch as they move farther away from me. Melinda waves her hands around, and Marjorie laughs loudly at something she says. It's nice seeing them united. No mama drama for this wedding. Eddie's going to be so disappointed.

The rest of us go our separate ways. Soon I'm alone, heading deeper into the market. Since it's the holiday season, there are red poinsettias everywhere. Boughs and wreaths of fresh pine hang from the walls, releasing their warm fragrance, which merges with the enticing scent of freshly cut flowers. I stop by a bucket of delicate white tea roses, their petals lightly scalloped, and lower my nose to sniff them.

When I glance up, Dean's there, so close that I startle and take a step back, knocking into a large potted fern on a pedestal behind me. It wobbles from the impact. Dean leans around me, his shoulder brushing mine, to steady it. I jolt from the contact. My skin is instantly warmed from where we touched.

"Oh hey, how's it going?" I ask uncertainly, not sure why he sought me out.

"Fine." His expression is unreadable.

"Okay," I draw out, waiting for more, but the man just stands there. Inscrutable. I give a small shrug, deciding not to waste my brain cells wondering what's going on in that thick skull of his. I take a quick picture of the roses and send it to Marjorie. Then I turn and walk down a row of hydrangeas in colors pink, blue and white.

Dean follows.

Ignoring him, I head over to a bunch of baby's breath and then onto a basket of berries, thinking they would match the wedding's holiday theme. I capture the shiny red balls with my camera and text it to Caleb's mom. After that, I go up one aisle and down another. Dean trails along behind me, occasionally reaching out to run his fingers over a velvety leaf or to readjust a stem about to fall out of its bucket. It's unnerving having him close, so I resort to my default for all socially awkward situations.

I babble.

Anything and everything I can think of flows from my brain and out of my mouth. I talk about the weather, the wedding, the way the stargazer lilies always make me sneeze.

Dean grunts and nods, almost like he's listening.

Maybe he's following me to make sure I don't mess up? Like accidentally set the flower shop on fire?

We're in the potted plants section when I suddenly remember what I want to talk to him about. My voice low, I tell him, "I was thinking about the stalker, you know, the one after Caleb. We should check out Janice."

"Janice?" Dean echoes with a quirk of his eyebrow. "She's in her late sixties and has been Caleb's assistant since he was a teenager."

"So?" I challenge. "You think just because she's older than Caleb, she can't have romantic feelings toward a younger man?" I purse my lips with judgment. "That's rather ageist of you."

I turn the corner and start down the next aisle. "If you don't believe it's Janice, I came up with this list of possibilities." I reach deep into my pocket and pull out a crumpled piece of paper, covered in my messy scribble. "People he works with, friends, potential enemies."

Dean takes his phone from his jacket. "I have a list, too." He turns it on and holds it up for me to see. A spreadsheet with over 800 entries is displayed. "I have all his known acquaintances here. I've cross-referenced their criminal records, if they have any. I rated them on a scale of one to ten on how likely I think that they're the suspect, based on their age, gender, disposition, occupation, and economic status." He continues talking, listing statistics, half of which go over my head.

Stealthily, so he doesn't see, I shove my paper back into my pocket. My cheeks warm with embarrassment as I realize my list looks like rudimentary child's play compared to the one he's come up with.

"Honestly," Dean says, "this is probably all for nothing. The most likely scenario is that it's a fan who Caleb's never met. A stranger."

What he says makes sense. Caleb has millions of admirers. The stalker could be any one of them, but something deep in my gut says he's wrong. I'm not sure why, but I believe it's somebody Caleb knows. A person close to him.

"Can you send me that?" I ask, pointing at his phone. "To give to Ron and Bradly." I lie, not liking that I'm hiding the truth, but a plan is forming in my mind. A far-fetched one, but a plan nonetheless. It relies on my computer skills and intuition.

Dean clicks a few buttons and sends me the information.

We fall quiet again as we enter the next room full of flowers. A rose bush as tall as my hip has vibrant blossoms that draw my attention. The soft petals shatter apart when I touch them, gently raining down on my feet. I catch a couple in my palm before they tumble to the ground. Dean and I both stare at them. They're beautiful, with variegated shades of peach and a faint blush of red at the base.

"Remember the flowers in Central Park, at the zoo?" says Dean, breaking the silence.

My eyes fly up to his. His voice sounds unnaturally loud after so many minutes of not speaking. "What?" I ask, not comprehending.

"Central Park," he repeats with an intense stare.

Something tickles in the back of my mind. A memory. "Wait— What—?"

"Jenny," Caleb says as he walks over to us, breaking my train of thought. "Can you look at this? Could we use this for Gwen's bouquet?" He holds out a wide, glittering, red satin ribbon.

"Just a minute," I tell him, then swing my gaze to Dean, but he's already retreating, muttering "Forget it" as he strides away with his back rigid and his shoulders stiff.

Caleb and I turn to watch him go.

"What's up with Dean?" Caleb asks me.

"Heck if I know," I answer. The memory that was forming disintegrates, tattered wisps of recollection that fade quickly. "What do you need help with?"

He gives me the ribbon. It sparkles prettily under the overhead lights. "Gwen will like this," I say, handing it back.

"I think so too." Caleb smiles wistfully, running the fabric through his hands. "I want this wedding to be perfect for Gwen. For it to be everything she's ever dreamed of."

"It will," I tell him, sensing a sadness beneath his words.

"She's giving up a lot to be with me." There's despair in how he says it, like it pains him.

"She's getting a lot in return," I remind him gently. "She gets to be with you. That's all Gwen wants. She doesn't care about the details. She doesn't need everything to be flawless as long as she has you in the end."

"I don't want her to regret it, marrying me." He doesn't look up, but I see the droop of his shoulders.

"She won't. I've never seen Gwen like she is with you. She's light, happy. Less focused on making things okay for everyone else. She's more herself." I pause, emotional when I think back to the transformation my friend has undergone in the past few years. *Sure, she still has things to work on, but don't we all?*

"I'd do anything to keep her from suffering because of who I am." He shifts on his feet. "I wanted her to take the jet to her conference, so she could be safe. I don't want her accosted by fans or the press."

I sigh, understanding what he's referring to. Gwen told me about it. "You can't always protect her. Gwen will figure out how to deal with your fame, *if* you give her the chance. Hiding her away from the world won't help you in the long run."

"Sure, it will," he argues stubbornly. "She can avoid all the people who love to criticize me and anyone involved with me."

"No," I counter, understanding his logic but also seeing the flaw in it. "She needs exposure, time to adjust. You haven't given that to her."

That makes him pause. His jaw tightens as he considers what I said. "Maybe," Caleb says, but I don't think he believes his own words.

His eyes slide to the aisle Dean just walked down. "What's up with you and Dean?" he asks.

I notice the deliberate change of conversation, but I don't call him on it.

"What?" My voice squeaks, high-pitched.

Now Caleb's acting like the reporter. He rubs his chin and stares at me with narrowed eyes. "He talks to you."

"So?" I give a nervous laugh.

Caleb tilts his head. "He's not much of a talker."

Interesting, since I sat in a car and talked to Dean for over two hours last night. "Oh, is that so?" I pretend to not care, but a strange thrill goes through my body. "I guess I'm easy to talk with." I toss my hair and smile, to distract him from this conversation and also to lighten his mood.

It works. Caleb relaxes and grins back. "You are. I like talking to you, Jenny. Thanks for being a great friend to Gwen." He grows bashful and looks away before saying, "And to me."

Caleb lets out an "oomph" when I grab him and give him a quick hug, squeezing tight.

"Thanks for being a good friend to me, too," I say, happy Gwen chose him, of all people, to fall in love with. "This wedding's going to be amazing. Just wait and see."

FRIDAY, DECEMBER 13
11 DAYS UNTIL THE WEDDING

— JENNY —

When we all return to Marjorie, she's flipping through her text messages, poring over the photos of the flowers we found in the shop. Melinda watches over her shoulder, murmuring her approval when she sees something she likes.

"Good job," Caleb's mom says finally, looking up from her phone. "I think I have everything we need. Who wants to go to lunch?"

Melinda waves her hands excitedly and says, "Me! I could definitely go for some food and a cup of coffee."

"Sorry, Mom," says Caleb. "I've got to run home and change before rehearsal."

We don't bother asking Dean what he's going to do. It's a given that he'll stay with Caleb.

"I can't go either," I add. "I have to meet my editor from L.A."

Dean's head snaps up at that. "Who? Eddie?"

I nod affirmative. "He's here for the day to go over some work stuff. We're meeting at an Italian place a few blocks over. Ulivo, I think it's called."

The five of us say our good-byes, and I walk outside. I'm lucky that the snow has decided to take a break. It's still a dusty blanket under my feet, but it's done falling for now. I find the restaurant easily. It's small, with a glass counter near the entryway full of pastries. An éclair has been frosted like a

Christmas tree, with another one striped like a candy cane. An elaborate expresso machine sits next to the cash register.

I walk past that and into a room filled with upholstered booths and rectangular tables. Eddie is waiting for me, already seated. He doesn't bother to get up as I approach. It's hard to reconcile this version of him versus the man who would have jumped up when we first started dating.

"Eddie," I greet him and slide into the seat directly across from him.

"Jenny," he returns, raking his gaze over me in an overt way that makes me cringe. "Thanks for meeting up with me."

Like I had any choice.

"How'd the flower shopping go?" Eddie takes a sip of coffee from the cup that sits by his elbow. "Isn't Gwen's mom in town now?"

"She was there." I signal the waiter from across the room. When he looks over, I point to the coffee and then to me. I'm going to need caffeine to make it through this lunch. Talking to Eddie always makes me uneasy. He's like a spider, waiting for a bug to fly into his sticky web. "It went fine."

"No fighting between the two moms?" he asks, just as I predicted.

"None," I declare as the waiter brings a steaming coffee cup, which he places in front of me. "They're working together to make the wedding as perfect as possible."

"What about you?" Eddie leans forward, both elbows on the table.

"What do you mean?" I ask, furrowing my brow. "I'm helping too."

"No," he says. "What I meant was, does it bother you? Being the bridesmaid, but never the bride? Isn't this the third time you've been a bridesmaid?"

It's the fourth time, actually, but I won't admit that. Instead, I sputter with my jaw dropped open. I'm surprised he went there. Sure. I've had that thought over the past few weeks, but for Eddie to say it out loud, to blurt it out, is so insulting it's painful.

"Maybe it's not for you. Being the long-term girlfriend. The wife," he continues, the bastard. It's like he's seen the fear in the darkest part of my soul and has decided to give it a voice. I know he's trying to goad me. I shouldn't let him get to me, but it's too much. The back of my throat tightens, and my vision blurs as tears gather.

Before a single one falls, we're interrupted.

"I was looking for you," says a deep, familiar voice behind me. Eddie's eyes go wide as he gazes up at the man who spoke.

I turn to glance over my shoulder. There he is, 200 pounds of pure muscle paired with a stern expression, wearing his typical navy-blue suit.

Dean.

My spirits sink further. He's the last person I want to witness my humiliation. "What're you doing here?" I croak, my throat raw from unshed tears.

"I wanted to see you, sweetheart," Dean says, smiling widely in a way that shows off all his teeth. He slides into the booth next to me, bumping me aside with his hip.

Sweetheart?

My mind reels, trying to absorb what's happening. Dean ignores my speechlessness. He leans across the table with his hand out. "You must be Eddie. Pleased to meet you. I'm Jenny's boyfriend, Dean."

Excuse me? What?

I gasp, my eyes flying to his.

Dean stares back calmly with an expression that reads, *"trust me."*

The shock that is no doubt on my face is mirrored on Eddie's. His mouth has dropped open in a most unattractive way. He blinks rapidly, like he can't believe what he's seeing. The two men shake, and, judging by the wince on Eddie's face, Dean squeezes his hand hard.

"Boyfriend?" Eddie has a wrinkle between his brows as his gaze bounces from Dean to me and back again. "When did you start dating?"

"We're not," is what I say in my head, but my mouth says, "It's been, uh, about, um, a while now?" I turn to Dean for help.

He smoothly interjects, "For several months. As soon as the two of you broke up, actually."

Eddie blanches at that, his features pinched. His hand tightens on his coffee cup and a not-so-nice part of me revels in his obvious discomfort.

Dean wraps his arm around my shoulders, sending my entire body into heat stroke. He says, "The minute I heard Jenny was available, I swept in." I look at him, searching for the lie. Surely it's written all over his face, but no,

Dean meets my gaze and stares intently. "I'd been waiting forever to ask her out. When I finally saw my opportunity, you better believe I jumped at it." Then, to my absolute shock, he plants a kiss on the side of my head. Puts his lips to my hair with a loud smack.

"Oh…uh…I had no idea," stutters Eddie, anger replacing his earlier disbelief. He sends me an accusatory glare from across the table. "Jenny didn't tell me."

"She didn't want to hurt your feelings," Dean replies. He leans toward Eddie, his laser-sharp focus on my boss.

Eddie shrinks in his seat.

Dean continues, "Given how you're still single, and she's moved on. She was trying to spare you. That's *my* Jenny for you. Kind to a fault." Dean's hand lightly rubs my shoulder, and I might pass out from the sensation. "I'm sure you wouldn't ask about her personal life anyway, right, Eddie? Since your relationship is purely professional these days. Your Human Resources Department would find talk about romantic topics to be highly inappropriate. Isn't that true?"

Eddie swallows so loud that I can hear it from where I sit. "Yeah—I mean—I guess. The newspaper doesn't really encourage that."

"Good," says Dean with grim satisfaction. "No more discussions about Jenny's love life. Glad that's settled." A long pause where the two men engage in some kind of staring contest.

Eddie breaks first, glancing away with a guilty flush. "Fine," he mutters agreement.

Dean claps his hands together, so loudly that the people in the booths around us turn to see what the commotion is about.

"Great! Let's eat!" he declares and waves the server over to take our order.

Dean and Eddie shake hands again on the sidewalk outside the restaurant after lunch is over. Even though they've mostly gotten along while we ate, Dean must squeeze Eddie's hand hard again because Eddie rubs it with a grimace when they let go.

While they're distracted, I pop a hard mint in my mouth and suck on it, watching as they say good-bye. Eddie moves in like he's going to hug me, but

Dean stiffens and steps in front of me. I lean around his bulky frame and give Eddie a small wave. "See you back in L.A."

Eddie grins. The gesture sends a chill down my back. "Don't worry, Jenny. I'll be back to check up on you." With a cheery salute, he starts off down the street, winding his way through the crowd as he heads toward the subway.

Dean stays close, his arm brushing mine. Once Eddie's out of eyesight, Dean takes a large step away. I try not to take it personally, but his sudden distance stings.

I spin to confront him. "What was that?" I ask, my hands on my hips.

"What?" He blinks innocently.

The New York lunch crowd flows around us. Women in smart outfits with sensible shoes and men who wear heavy overcoats. More snow is expected later today. I motion Dean to move closer to the restaurant, so we can talk without getting jostled. He inches over until we're pressed against the large glass window. A glance inside shows they've already seated new customers at the table we just left.

"Why aren't you with Caleb?" I scan up and down the bustling street, almost expecting Caleb to be parked in his car, but he's not here.

"He went straight home," Dean says calmly. "I'll catch up to him before he leaves for the theater."

I press up onto the balls of my feet to reach eye level with Dean.

I fail. He's too tall. "That doesn't explain what you're doing here."

He shoves his hands into his pockets. "I wanted some coffee."

"Coffee? At the same restaurant where I'm having lunch?" I ask doubtfully.

He shrugs. "You mentioned an Italian place. They always have the best cappuccinos." He holds up the to-go coffee cup in his hand. He did, indeed, order a cappuccino.

Still, his story has more holes than a slice of Swiss cheese.

I tap my finger to my chin, regarding him. "So, you walked two blocks in the snow—"

"It wasn't snowing—"

"Just for a caffeine fix?"

"I was tired. We all got up early—"

"And ended up in the same restaurant where I was having lunch with my boss?"

"Your ex," he corrects me.

I tilt my head to the side. "Why'd you come over to my table then? If all you wanted was coffee?"

Dean takes a long sip of his drink, not meeting my gaze. A delaying tactic, I'm sure. Finally, he says, "I overheard what Eddie was saying to you and…"

"And?" I urge him on.

"I didn't like it," Dean says, a muscle ticking in his jaw. A quiet rage grows in his eyes. He looks scary. Dangerous. "Why do you put up with him? When he started up with that 'bridesmaid, never a bride' BS, you should have gotten up and walked away. Poured your drink over his head before you left."

"I can't do that!" My hand comes to my chest. Shocked, I say, "Eddie's my boss."

Dean takes a menacing step closer, his face reddening. "Of a department you want nothing to do with. You don't like being an entertainment reporter."

I bristle. "It's better than no reporting." I tell him the same thing I tell myself when I'm feeling disheartened about how I've stagnated in my career. How I've settled for less.

"It's a stepping stone," I say like a mantra. "A way to get to know the investigative team, so they'll consider me the next time a spot opens." I don't mention how I interviewed for a job with them months ago, only to lose the position to a more experienced reporter from Florida. The night I found out was the one when I finally allowed Eddie to take me out to dinner.

Dean's not buying it. He shakes his head at me with his lips curled.

His disgust ignites my fury. "Who are you to judge me, anyway?" I half-shout at him, drawing looks from strangers passing by on the sidewalk. "It's none of your business!"

He draws in a sharp breath at that, his expression blanking. All the rage, the indignation, that was there a minute before is erased. He's reverted to robot mode.

"You're right." His voice is flat. "I have no say in anything you do. I should have stayed out of it." Like he's some imperial prince in a grand ballroom,

Dean gives me a small bow, bending at the waist and saying a formal, "My apologies." He turns and walks away, without a single glance back.

I watch open-mouthed until he disappears, lost in a sea of strangers. My shoulders slump, and a hollow ache spreads through my chest. I replay the past two hours and see a million mistakes. Things I handled wrong with *both* Eddie and Dean. Things I should or shouldn't have said. Ways I could have done better. Regret is heavy, the tightening of a noose around my neck.

When I return to my hotel, that uneasy feeling stays with me. I think of all the people I've failed recently—Caleb, Gwen, Dean.

Myself.

No wonder no one wants me.

In an effort to shake that thought off, I open up my laptop. It's been a while since I did any hard-core coding, but the commands come back easily. I had an idea when I was with Dean in the flower shop earlier today. A way to track down Caleb's stalker. I realize it's too big a job for just me alone. Too big even for Dean. But not too big for my computer, which can work 24/7 without a break. I may be a failure in my career and love life, but I won't fail Gwen. I'll find the stalker and save her wedding.

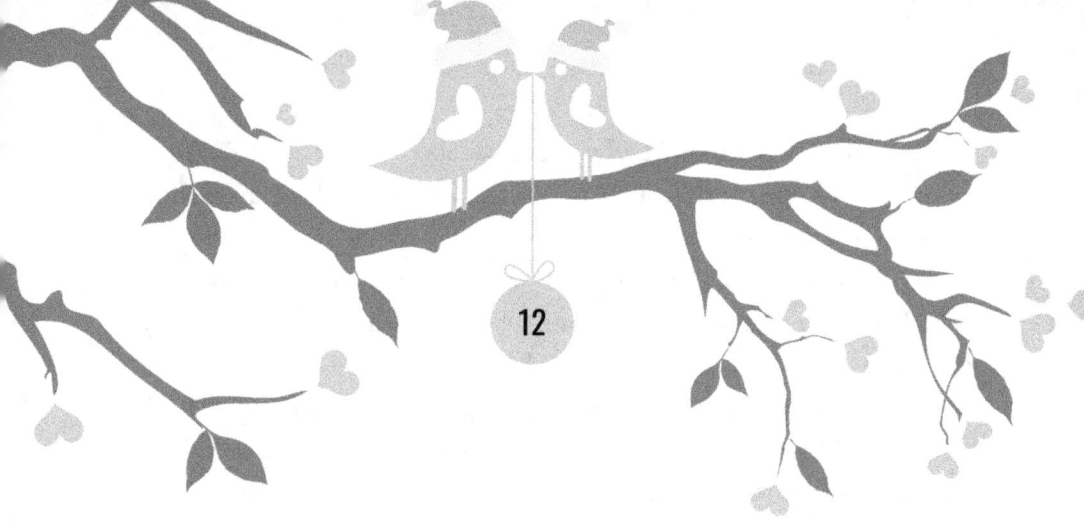

SATURDAY, DECEMBER 14
10 DAYS UNTIL THE WEDDING

GWEN

"Why hello, my beautiful future wife," Caleb says as soon as he picks up my FaceTime call the next evening. I grin at his words. He's sweaty and gorgeous in a slim fitted workout shirt with the sleeves cut off. He rubs a towel over the back of his neck as he walks out of his personal gym and up the stairs of the penthouse.

"Oh, sorry, am I interrupting?" I climb onto the bed in my hotel room. Alvina went downstairs to pick up dinner. I figured I'd get in a quick phone call to Caleb while she's gone.

"No, John just left," he says, referring to the trainer who helps him work out several times a week. Caleb takes a swig from his water bottle. For the millionth time, I'm captivated by the way his Adam's apple bobs when he swallows. Such a simple thing, but I notice everything when it comes to him.

I miss him.

"What's up with Alvina and Wayne? Any new developments?" he asks, his image on my phone screen bouncing as he walks up the steps.

"Same as the last couple of nights. Alvina creeps back into our room a few hours after she sneaks out, obviously trying not to wake me. I've been tempted to throw off my covers and yell "gotcha," but I'm worried I'll give her a heart attack."

Caleb chuckles at that. "Did you ask her about it yet?"

"No." I pull the bedsheet up to cover my legs, using the movement as an excuse to avoid making eye contact.

"Why not? It's been a couple of days." Caleb quirks his head to the side.

"I don't want to make it weird. I still have to travel with them." I sniff, not wanting to admit that my feelings are hurt.

Caleb's mouth tightens like he wants to argue, but he holds himself back. He's reached his bedroom now. He throws the towel into the laundry hamper and goes over to a yoga mat laid out on the floor in front of the large windows that overlook Central Park.

"Look," he says, holding his phone up to the view. "It's snowing. Started the day you left. I forgot to tell you."

Sure enough, outside the window, fluffy white snowflakes drift slowly through the air. I've stood at that window before and watched as the park was magically transformed, like a sugar plum fairy flew over it waving her wand. Watched trees get frosty jackets of ice to coat their bare branches. Watched snow melt into the water of the serene pond across the street. I'm sad to not be there with Caleb. To miss out on the beauty unfolding in my adopted city.

"So pretty," I croon, pressing my face to the phone.

"Yes, you are," he sings back, and we both laugh. "Oh, you meant the snow," he says with a rueful quirk of his lips. "It's nice until the cars drive through it, and it turns into a gray mush that stains the bottom of your pants."

"Shh," I tell him, my eyes locked on the picture-perfect scene. "Don't ruin this moment."

He shoots an indulgent smile my way and says, "So easy to impress my little beach baby."

I wrinkle my nose at that, which makes him laugh, that rumbly guffaw I like. I'd do anything to hear that sound.

He props the phone up on a nearby chair and starts his post-workout stretching, which is an even better view than the one outside the window.

"How're the lectures going? Are you still loving it?"

"It's great," I say, grinning, excited to tell him all about the cancer conference.

Caleb continues his routine and listens attentively as I fill him in on the presentations I attended and the interesting people I've met.

Once that's done, he says, "I'm happy for you. Sounds like you're getting a lot out of it."

I nod in agreement. "I miss you, though."

"I know. Me too."

Finished with his routine, Caleb moves to a chair in the corner of the room in front of the window. He sits perched on the edge and tells me about his day. Rehearsals, lunch with a producer friend who's trying to recruit him for an upcoming movie, a meeting with his manager, his workout.

Then he surprises me. He says, "Let's play the game."

I understand right away what he's talking about. It started after we broke up and he came to New York to win me back. I used to ask him all kinds of random questions to get to know him better. The catch was that for every question I asked him, he got one in return. We've kept it going since we reunited. It's entertained us during long walks or date nights.

"Yes," I say and beam. "We haven't played in a while."

"You start," he says.

"Okay." I screw up my face, thinking. "Oh! If you had to go the rest of your life shoeless or shirtless, which would you choose?"

He snorts. "That's easy. No shirt. I mean, have you seen my abs?"

If I were there, I'd throw a pillow at him. "So humble." I roll my eyes sarcastically.

"Next question." Caleb moves us along. "Do you ever want to move back to California, or are you happy here?" He tilts his head, regarding me intently.

I cross my knees and rock side to side as I think. This is how we play the game. We jump between lighthearted questions and serious ones. I've learned some of his deepest secrets this way.

"I'm fine in New York. It's important to me that the art therapy program is successful. It'll take a while to get it up and running." I smile, thinking about the art therapy program I instituted at my hospital last year. It has been a ton of work to set up, but now we have three full-time therapists who go to the patient rooms and use art to help the patients process their illnesses and heal.

"I miss Teddy, though." I chew on my lower lip, wondering if I could convince my baby brother to move to New York someday. I don't even bother to consider my older brother, Brandon. He'll never leave the Midwest.

"How about you? L.A. or New York? L.A. is better for movies and television."

Caleb crosses an ankle over his knee, his foot bouncing. "I'm fine with either. Working in front of a live audience has been pretty amazing. New York is great for that."

I sigh happily. I enjoy this, planning a life with Caleb. Thinking about all the things we'll do together. Sometimes I picture my heart like a house full of rooms. It used to be a tiny apartment, with just enough space for Jenny and my family. Caleb has turned it into a mansion. I've put memories of him—ones from when I first fell in love with him to last week, when he made popcorn and we watched a movie on TV—into that home. Some rooms sit empty, waiting for future Gwen and Caleb to decorate them.

"My turn," he says. "What do you think about getting a dog? Like Pip, but bigger?"

"Really?" I practically shriek. I've wanted a pet for so long but figured that with our busy schedules we wouldn't have time to give it enough attention. "Who would walk it, though? When we're gone all day? It might get lonely."

"There are tons of professional dog walkers in the city. It's a serious profession here. We'll hire one of them."

"I'd love that." We spend the next few minutes arguing over different breeds. I would love a Siberian husky. He thinks a golden retriever is better.

"Why a retriever?"

"I hear they're great with kids," Caleb says shyly.

Oh.

We've discussed this several times before and agreed that we both want children, but we haven't figured out all the details. Seems like a good conversation to have before we say, "I do."

"My question," I remind him. I drop my eyes to the white hotel bedspread and smooth out the fabric with my fingers. "I know you want more than one, but exactly how many kids are you thinking?"

He answers immediately, "Six."

"Six!" My gaze whips up to find him chuckling.

"You should see your expression right now," he wheezes out between laughs.

I mock glare at him. "You can have six when you figure out how to squeeze them out yourself."

He winces at the thought. "Ouch. I'm kidding. I'm not sure. Four?"

"Two," I counter. "A boy and a girl."

"Um, I'm not the doctor here, but last I heard, you don't get to choose." One corner of his mouth lifts.

"True." I pin him with a stare and say, "No pressure, but it's all up to you."

"Me?" His eyebrows go up.

"The sperm determines gender."

"The things I learn from you." He shakes his head and smiles, a megawatt grin. The one he's paid big bucks for, but I get it free.

"You're going to be the best mom, Gwen. I can't wait to see that." Mercurial, his emotions shift to something more serious. "There was a time I didn't think I'd be fit to be a father."

"You aren't that person anymore," I remind him gently. "Besides, it won't be for a while. I've got this last year of residency left. You have two years on your contract at the theater. We're too busy for kids right now. Let's get a dog and practice on it. It can be our furry baby. Less likely to need therapy when it's grown from all the mistakes we're sure to make."

Caleb nods. "I want to spend time with just you anyway. Not looking forward to sharing you quite yet."

As usual, we're on the same page.

Caleb looks out the window, at the softly falling snow. "If you had to choose between living in an eternal winter or an eternal summer, which would it be?"

My response comes quickly. "I'd choose whichever one you were in, because the weather means nothing to me as long as we're together."

Now I get the special smile, small and tender, that he keeps only for me. Caleb says, "That's the right answer."

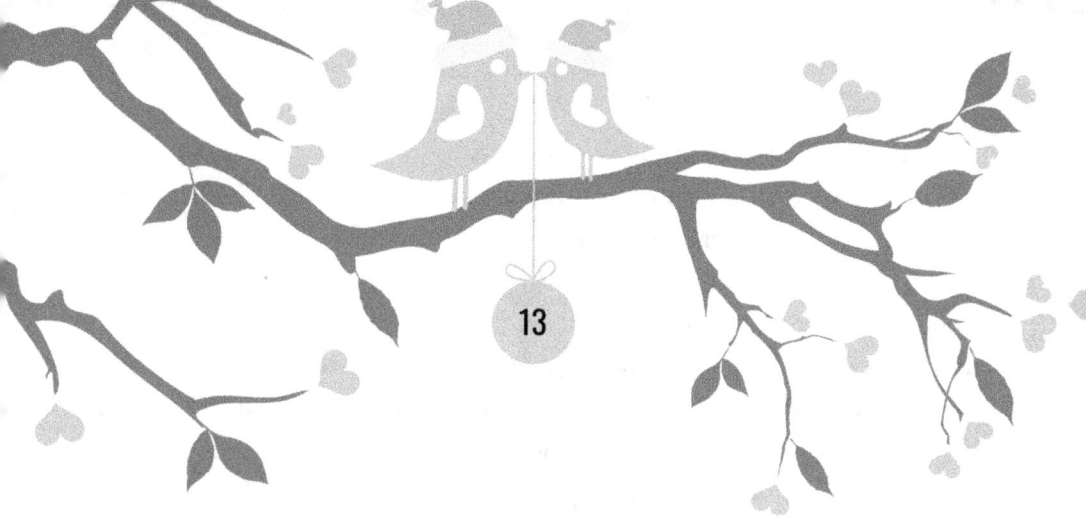

13

**SUNDAY, DECEMBER 15
9 DAYS UNTIL THE WEDDING**

— JENNY —

"You have to go cake tasting," Caleb says. It's late afternoon. He's got Dean and me lined up, sitting next to each other on the sofa. It was hard to miss how Dean scooted away from me when I first sat down. He hasn't said a word to me since our lunch with Eddie, and I haven't spoken to him either. It's the silent treatment, but I'm not sure which of us started it.

Caleb paces in front of us with his hands clasped behind his back.

"Cake tasting?" Dean repeats, sounding horrified, like he must have heard it wrong the first time.

"Cake tasting!" I repeat, clapping my hands, thrilled at the thought.

"That's right," says Caleb. "It's that new bakery, the one opened by the guy who won the Great British Baking Show. What's his name?"

I clasp my cheeks with both palms. "You don't mean Atlas Poilane? The winner of the ninth season? Magnifique Bakery?" My eyes widen in awe. "I had a cupcake from there, and it was like a party in my mouth. So good!"

"Gwen said the same thing," Caleb exclaims, stopping in front of me.

"Well, duh, because we got those cupcakes together." I look between the two men. "We had to wait in line for over an hour to buy a single $10 cupcake. It was insane."

"Ten dollars?" Dean's eyebrows shoot up.

"Totally worth it," I assure him. "It was almost as good as Alvina's cookies."

Now, even Dean appears impressed.

"I want to surprise Gwen with their wedding cake, but it's so popular I would be recognized for sure and if I used my real name to book the appointment, I'm worried someone working there would tip off the press. Then everyone would know we're getting married soon." Caleb rips his fingers through his hair. "So I used a fake name. Janice and her husband were supposed to go, but they just called and they're both sick. There's no way I can reschedule this close to the wedding."

"No problem," I'm quick to say, raising my hand. "I volunteer as tribute. I can go. It'll be a breeze to pick since I know what Gwen likes."

"I wish it were that easy." Caleb's tugging on his hair again. "They only offer the appointment to couples. The bakery said they had too many times when the bride or groom came to the tasting alone and put in an order only to find that their partner disagreed with their choice once the cake was delivered. That's why they have this couples only policy. You *both* have to go."

"Oh." I glance sideways at Dean. This is awkward.

"It's fine," says Dean with a businesslike nod.

Caleb's stopped moving. He stands before us, reminding me of a school principal, ready to lecture errant children. "I don't think you heard me. I said they only do tastings for *couples*."

Dean finally looks my way. We share a confused glance, and then it hits me. "Oh! You want us to pretend *we're* getting married?"

Caleb nods. "Exactly."

"What?" asks Dean. "Are you joking? Is this a prank?" He looks around the sunlight-filled penthouse living room, with its floor-to-ceiling windows and 103-inch flat-screen TV like he expects *Candid Camera* men to jump out at any minute.

His reaction stings.

Would it really be so awful to be fake engaged to me?

"I'm serious," Caleb answers. "I'm sorry it's an imposition, but I need your help."

"I don't know," says Dean, hesitating. "You're the actor. Not us. What if they find out we're lying?"

I turn to him and ask, "What's the worst that could happen? They ban us from their shop." As soon as the words are out of my mouth, the seriousness of that consequence hits me. I don't want to lose access to those cupcakes.

My voice pitches high as I ask Caleb, "That wouldn't happen, right? They wouldn't kick us out and tell us we could never go back?"

"Why do you sound so panicked?" asks Dean.

"You don't understand how good they are." I'm willing to do a lot of things for my friends, but giving up those cupcakes would push me to my limit.

"No one is going to take away your precious cake," Caleb reassures me. "They're not checking for a marriage license. Just act like you're getting hitched. Pretend you're in love."

Dean and I exchange a doubt-filled glance, then look quickly away. A warm flush travels up my neck.

Caleb smiles his most charming smile and clasps his hands together with a drawn-out, "Please?"

That man is one heck of an actor. He's got me convinced. Who am I kidding? He had me at "cake."

Dean, on the other hand, is still doubtful. "Really?" he asks Caleb, who nods firmly.

"Okay." Dean takes a deep breath, gathers himself, and asks me, "You ready for this?"

"Are you serious? I was born for this." I spring to my feet and head toward the door.

We enter the elevator and stand side by side, facing forward. "Hey," I say, biting the inside of my cheek. "I want to say I'm sorry about that incident with Eddie. I realize you were trying to do something nice for me and I responded by getting mad at you."

I'd talked to Gwen on the phone about that lunch and the fight on the sidewalk. She'd pointed out how Dean was being his usual protective self. She said that's what he does. Throws himself in front of any obstacles that might hurt someone else. In this case, the obstacle was Eddie, and Dean's fake boyfriend act was his way of shielding me. By the time we hung up, I'd felt like a fool for getting so upset.

Dean lets out a breath. "It's okay. I should be the one to apologize. Not everyone needs rescuing. Sometimes I forget that."

I smile at him, a wide, relieved grin. "No worries. I like your 'pour my drink on Eddie' idea, though. Wish I'd thought of it myself."

Dean's lips twitch. "I'd like to see that," he says as the elevator dings open on the first floor.

Twenty minutes later, we're in the East Village. Dean and I skirt around the long line of people waiting to order at the bakery counter and head to the back where there's a door with a bell and a sign that reads, "By Appointment Only."

Dean pushes the button. A chime faintly rings somewhere. After a minute, a young woman wearing a flour-dusted apron comes out. She wipes her hands on a towel. "Mr. Jones?" she addresses Dean, who stares at her blankly. He doesn't respond to the fake name Caleb used to book the appointment until I jab him with my elbow. Then he steps forward and hastily says, "That's me." They shake and Dean gestures my way. "This is my— er—fiancée, Jennifer."

"Hi, I'm Laura."

Her fingers are cool and slightly damp when I shake her hand. "So nice to meet you. I absolutely love your cupcakes," I gush as we follow her into the back of the bakery. We pass through a bustling kitchen that smells like my version of heaven, sugary and sweet. I inhale, savoring it.

Laura opens a door and ushers us into a small room with a round table and two seats. There's a pitcher of water on the table, along with cups, napkins, and forks.

"Please have a seat," she instructs. "I'll be right back with your cake samples."

Dean takes off his suit jacket and carefully places it over the back of the chair, smoothing the shoulders, and sits. The chairs are a delicate metal, like ones you might find in a garden. I worry that Dean's seat might collapse from that muscular body sitting on it. The room is painted a pale lavender. Framed pictures of elegantly frosted cakes hang on the walls.

The staff has decorated for Christmas. A picture of Santa eating cookies is centered over our table and a small ceramic Christmas tree with tiny lit-up ornaments is a centerpiece.

Dean's on the opposite side of the table from me. I scoot toward him, loudly scraping my chair over the stained concrete floor, making a horrible noise. Dean winces and asks, "What're you doing?"

"Getting closer to you," I grunt. This chair is heavier than it appears. "They won't believe we're in love if we're sitting far away from each other."

Now I'm so close to him that our elbows touch. "We should probably hold hands."

Dean's eyes widen in alarm, his shoulders tensing. "Really? You think that's necessary?"

I let out a peal of laughter. "No. I'm just messing with you." I bump my shoulder into his, setting him swaying.

He relaxes. "I thought you were serious," he says with a hesitant smile.

"Nope." I lean an elbow on the table. "It might be fun pretending, though. We can make up personas for ourselves. Speak in fake accents. Create cutesy pet names for each other. Stuff like that."

"Pet names?" he asks with a bemused twitch of his lips.

"What shall I call you? Let's see." I roam my gaze over him, taking in his thick dark hair, warm eyes, and broad shoulders. "Snookums? Honey bunch? Hot lips?"

"Hot lips?" Dean interjects with a laugh, the nice one, rich and deep. It echoes around the room.

Maybe I shouldn't have said that because now I'm looking at his lips, which are full and rather kissable. *Wait.* This is Dean I'm thinking about.

I don't want to kiss him.

Do I?

We hate each other.

Right?

I break off my internal monologue to find Dean staring at me. "What about you?" I ask to distract myself. "What name would you give me?"

"Sweetheart," he answers immediately, like he doesn't have to think about it. That's the second time he's said that word to me.

A warm feeling I don't want to identify washes over me. I tease, "Aww. Is that because I'm so sweet?"

"No. It's because you like to eat sweet things." He points to a picture on the wall. "Like cake and your secret stash of purse candy."

I gasp, shocked someone knows about that. I thought I'd done such a good job of hiding it.

"I can't figure you out," he continues, eyeing me shrewdly. "You work out every day. Those bizarre exercise routines Gwen's always complaining about—goat yoga, boot camps, aqua aerobics—and yet you stash candy in your purse, your pockets, your glove compartment. I once saw you take it out of your sock."

"It's because of the candy that I have to work out." My cheeks heat with embarrassment. "When did you see me get it out of my sock, anyway? I didn't think you noticed anything I do."

"I'm always paying attention to y—"

We're interrupted by Laura, who walks in bearing a platter with tiny cups filled with cake and frosting. I'm instantly salivating.

"Here we are," she sings out, placing it on the table between us. "We've got cake on this side—vanilla, chocolate, yellow, and pink champagne." She points to each one. "On this other side are the frostings—vanilla, chocolate, raspberry, and our seasonal flavor for Christmas, eggnog buttercream. You can mix and match them however you like."

I'm already picking up my fork when she says, "I'll leave you to it. Come on out if you have questions. I'll check back later."

Dean says a polite "thanks," as she leaves.

I swirl raspberry frosting on my spoon and scoop up a bit of vanilla cake, then pop the mixture into my mouth. It's so delicious that I close my eyes and let out a soft moan. When I open my eyes, Dean is staring at me with rapt fascination.

"Is it—" He clears his throat. "Is it good?"

"Good? It's divine!" I nod to his fork, laying unused on the table. "What are you waiting for? Dig in."

"I thought I'd let you pick the flavor."

I drop my hand and blink at him, uncomprehending. "Why? This cake is one of the best things I've ever eaten. You have to try." When he still doesn't reach for his fork, I cry out, frustrated, "Come on! Live a little."

His movements controlled, Dean carefully rolls back the sleeves of his pristine white dress shirt. I stop chewing, distracted by his corded forearms, which have enough muscle to crack a walnut in the crook of his elbow. Once that's done, he reluctantly reaches for the fork and picks up a bite of yellow cake mixed with eggnog buttercream frosting. When he places it in his mouth, Dean lets out a quiet, "Yum."

"See?" I take a bite. "It's amazing, isn't it?"

His eyes are bright with pleasure as he chews. "It's phenomenal."

"Here," I say, holding out my cake-laden fork, "try the pink champagne with the vanilla frosting."

Dean freezes, staring at me. I hold the fork higher, offering it to him. Slowly, his eyes never leaving mine, he leans forward and gently takes the cake between his teeth. His breath, warm and soft, brushes against my knuckles before he pulls back.

Butterflies swoop low in my stomach, fluttering their wings before I crush them. *Stop it,* I tell myself. *This is Dean. We don't like him, remember?*

I'm suddenly absorbed by the way his jaw moves as he chews, the way his throat works when he swallows, and the shallow way he's breathing, stuck in this tiny room with me. He catches me watching and stills. Brown eyes unblinking, he stares back with that intense gaze of his. There's a hint of apprehension in his expression, mixed with something intense. Tension builds, a string pulling taut that snaps when he looks away.

He clears his throat, then changes the subject. "Any updates on the wedding planning?"

Bolder now, Dean grabs a large scoop of vanilla cake with vanilla frosting.

I mix chocolate and raspberry. "The wedding?" I lick frosting off the back of my fork. Dean tracks the motion, and my cheeks burn. "Um—" I stammer, suddenly self-conscious. "I went over the to-do list with Gwen on the phone this morning. She still feels guilty for leaving."

"She shouldn't."

"I agree, but you know Gwen. She's not the best at asking for help. I told her we've got it covered. The only big thing left is the final fittings for the tuxes and my bridesmaid dress. We will go on Thursday for that. I assume you'll be there too? Getting your tuxedo altered?"

Dean nods confirmation.

"We have most of the preparations done." I drop my hands into my lap and blow out an audible breath. "Weddings are a lot of work. All this effort for an event that's going to last less than six hours."

Dean chews slowly, leaned back in his chair. He swallows. "Do you think it's not worth it?"

"Are you kidding me? For Gwen, it's definitely worth it. We've been planning imaginary marriages to our Prince Charmings since we were pre-teens. I'd do anything to give her the wedding of her dreams. She deserves it more than anyone."

Brown eyes with rings of gold observe me intently. "You really love her, don't you?"

"She's my sister from another mister." I try to say it lightheartedly, but there's a pang from deep inside because it's the truth.

A beat of silence, then he says, "I owe you an apology."

I sit up with a start. "Apology?" I repeat dumbly.

He shifts, the metal of his chair creaking alarmingly. Dean casts his gaze upward, at the ceiling, and says, "It was hard, watching Caleb fall apart when he lost Gwen, dragging him out of bars, tucking him into bed when he passed out. I know there's no one to blame but him. It was his decisions, his choices, but it's hard to be angry at someone who's already suffering so much." He visibly swallows, his voice dropping lower by an octave. "I needed to point the finger at someone, and I directed it at you. Maybe that was unfair." His eyes drift back up to meet mine. "I'm sorry."

Something inside me lightens. Dean's not looking at me like a person he hates right now. Instead, he watches me warily, like he's worried *I* might not like *him*.

Before I can respond, Laura pokes her head into the room. She says, "Just checking on you lovebirds. Do you need anything?"

I smile sweetly at Dean. "What do you think, Boo Bear? Need anything?"

His gaze narrows as my grin grows wider. Then he smirks and says, "No, Sweetheart. I've got everything I need."

Sweetheart.

"Okey-doke," Laura says cheerfully. "I've got to grab a cake out of the oven and then I'll be back to get your selection."

Once she's gone, Dean growls, "Boo Bear, really, Jennifer?"

I send him a mischievous wink. "I thought it suited you because you're big, like a bear." I grow serious, crossing my arms on the table. "We both get an honest say in which cake we like without influencing each other. I think we should speak our favorite out loud on the count of three."

Dean nods sagely. "Good idea. One…two…three."

Together, we both yell out, "chocolate with eggnog." We stare at each other in open-mouthed shock.

"Really?" My voice is small. "We want the same one?"

"We do." Dean smiles at me, amusement dancing in his expression. He moves into my personal space. "You have a bit of frosting…" His rough thumb comes out to gently swipe across my lower lip, skin dragging on skin, and I forget to breathe. I let out a soft exhale, not breaking eye contact. Dean's pupils dilate. At the same time, we both lean forward, closing the distance between us.

It's not until she speaks that I realize Laura has reentered the room. We jump back from each other when she calls out a cheerful, "What did you decide?"

"Chocolate," I say.

"With eggnog," Dean adds.

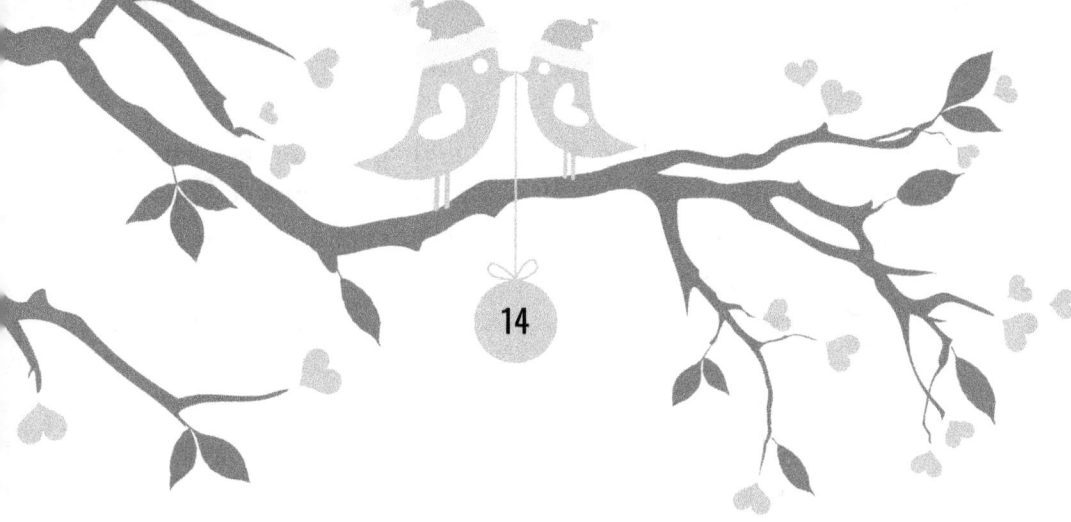

14

**MONDAY, DECEMBER 16
8 DAYS UNTIL THE WEDDING**

— GWEN —

I wipe damp palms on my thighs, hoping no one'll notice. My heart beats fast, like I've just run a race rather than sat in this stuffy hotel ballroom for the past three hours, listening to lectures on chemotherapy regimens. Helen is next to me, bathed in the pale glow of the projector from the front of the room.

When I walked into the conference on the first day, she had been sitting quietly by herself, with her eyes downcast and her fingers nervously twining in her lap. I had called her name and almost laughed at the expression of surprise on her face.

When I asked if she would like to sit with me, Helen hesitated and said, "Are you sure? I don't want to be a bother." It had taken a fair amount of convincing to get her to move to the front row with me, but eventually, after some thought, she agreed. That's when I first learned that Helen doesn't do anything willy-nilly. She's cautious, a bit of an overthinker, carefully assessing each situation.

I turn to her and admit, "I'm scared. What if the microphone stops working but I don't realize it, so I talk for the whole hour without anyone being able to hear me? What if I go over my time limit, and I don't get to finish my presentation? What if there's spinach in my teeth, but no one has the guts to tell me, and the audience doesn't hear a word I say because they're too busy staring at my mouth?" I spew out all of my worst fears in under a minute.

Helen holds up her hand, stopping me before I can spiral further. Calmly, she says, "Your teeth are fine. Your microphone just got checked by the sound crew and it works. Remember, we set the timer on your watch. Put it next to your laptop so you don't go over your limit. You won't make a mistake. You practiced this for me at the lunch break, and it was flawless."

"Okay. Okay." I nod like I heard her, when in reality I only absorbed half of what she just said.

Helen sighs indulgently. "It'll be great, Gwen."

Soon, it's my turn to walk up to the stage. As I make my way through the crowd, murmuring "Excuse me" when people pull in their chairs to let me pass, I could swear I hear Caleb's name being spoken by several different voices. When I stop and look up, no one is talking. It must be my imagination, just me wishing he was here for moral support. I reach the podium and place my watch next to the laptop waiting there for me. A click of the button on the side starts my timer.

"Hello." I smile at the crowd, feigning confidence. "My name is Gwen Wright." A murmur spreads through the audience, one I don't remember hearing when other doctors presented this morning.

The room is full, with no seats left. Some doctors stand along the walls.

Strange.

It wasn't standing room only for the other lectures.

After the rumble of the crowd dies down, I continue, projecting my voice loud and steady. "The fight against cancer is very personal to me. Eleven years ago, my father passed away from colon cancer at the age of 45. I was in high school at the time. I vowed then to become a doctor and to do anything I could to stop this devastating disease."

My heart pounds as I focus on the people in front of me. Helen is there, smiling encouragingly. I also see the head of our Oncology Department, whom I've worked with closely while developing my project. A couple of doctors from Manhattan are scattered in the audience.

My adrenaline spikes. There's an urge to perform, to not let them down.

If I mess this up, everyone at home will find out. It was bad when the truth about me and Caleb came out—the whispers and stares in the hospital hallways. It'll be worse if they're talking about me because I failed here today.

I swallow nervously and move the cursor on my screen, highlighting slides that discuss the stages of colon cancer. "As we all know, colon cancer is the third most common cause of cancer deaths. Early detection is key for improving a patient's chance of survival, which is why in medical school, and now in my ER residency, I developed a protocol for screening."

"All patients over the age of 45 who come into our Emergency Room are offered a free test. We use stool samples to determine if the patient has cancer. The test is cheap, easy to administer, and noninvasive. It scans for specific biomarkers in the stool, including methylation markers and fecal hemoglobin. If a patient is positive, then colonoscopy is used for confirmation."

"I tested over 16,000 ER patients and found 139 subjects who tested positive for cancer. Consistent with known colon cancer incidence, half of the positive cases were in women and half were in men. Colon cancer is on the rise in patients younger than 55, with this group accounting for one-third of the deaths. This was true in our patient population as well. I'm most proud of the fact that the majority of positive patients in my study had early disease, which predicts a five-year survival of over 90 percent."

I pause and gather myself for the conclusion of my lecture. This is the important part. My chance to make a difference. "Although these statistics are impressive, we must remember that behind each positive test is a patient and their family, whose life will be irrevocably changed by their cancer diagnosis. When I was compiling the results, I couldn't help but think about my own father. If he had been diagnosed earlier, could he have survived?

"If we institute free screening in not just primary care offices but also in our Emergency Rooms, I truly believe we will find more cancer and catch it sooner, leading to more lives saved. I ask that the data I've presented here today guide you in your own practices." I close the computer, relieved the most frightening part of my lecture is over. My watch says I have five minutes left.

"Are there any questions I can answer?" I ask into the microphone.

A hand shoots up in the third row. "Yes?" I point to a man, who sports a scraggly mustache.

"Did your fiancé help fund this research?" he asks.

"Excuse me?" I shake my head, certain I heard him wrong.

"Caleb Lawson?" he asks, this time louder. "Did he give you money for your study?"

"Um, no." I swallow, my throat suddenly dry. "I hadn't met Caleb when I began this project." The man nods.

Another hand is raised behind him. It's a middle-aged woman with dark brown hair streaked with silver. I call on her.

"Congratulations on your success," she begins. My shoulders, tense from the first question, slowly relax into their normal position. They tighten again as she asks, "Do you worry that your work will be discredited now that you're famous? That even if your data is valid, it will be disregarded because of who you are?"

I laugh nervously, and the sound echoes in my microphone. "I'm not sure I understand the question. Who am I? I'm an ER resident in my last year of training. I have tested thousands of people for colon cancer. That's who I am."

The woman shakes her head at me. "Speculation about your wedding is on the front page of every magazine. How do you anticipate that changing the trajectory of your career?"

"Oh, uh. . ." My mind frantically searches for an intelligent answer and comes up blank. "I'm hoping it won't change much. I mean, I'm still a doctor. I still want to help people."

The woman raises a doubtful eyebrow and frowns.

"When are you getting married, anyway?" someone shouts. A murmur of agreement follows. I bring a hand up to shade my eyes from the bright light of the projector, trying to figure out who spoke.

"Well? Do you have a date?" a new voice calls out from the back of the room. I squint but can't make out any individuals. The people merge into one demanding mass as my vision blurs.

"Uh—I—um," I stutter, completely thrown offguard.

Helen, of all people, stands up and faces the audience. She raises her arms wide and says, "No more questions. Thank you."

I stumble down the stairs of the stage, away from the podium and the crowd. Bursting through the double doors of the ballroom, I practically run out of the conference area and into the hotel lobby.

Helen follows. She points to a pair of large wingback chairs tucked in the corner of the room, next to an unlit fireplace. "Let's go over there."

I walk after her blindly, my mind whirring with the echo of the audience's questions.

Caleb.

Wedding.

Who am I?

We sit. Helen hands me a bottle of water, which I swig back, draining it quickly. I hadn't realized how parched I was. When I'm done, I screw the cap on the empty bottle and let out a bitter laugh.

Helen cocks her head at me, waiting quietly.

"For a long time, I only thought of myself as one thing," I tell her. "A doctor. That was it. All I believed I could be. Then with Caleb I became so much more—a painter, an organizer of the art therapy program at the hospital, and a better friend, sister, and daughter. But now, it's like everyone, those strangers," I hook a thumb toward the conference room, "want me to be only one thing again. Caleb's wife. That's it. It makes me feel as if I have to choose him or my career. It's not fair."

Tears choke the back of my throat. I swallow around the lump of them. "Why can't I be both? Why can't I be more? Why do we put ourselves in these boxes? Force these impossible choices? Career woman or devoted mother. The stern parent or the fun parent. The adventurer or the homebody. Aren't we all of those things at different times?" I dash away the tear that dares to trickle down my cheek. I'm heartbroken and furious all at once.

"People like to keep it simple," says Helen. "It's easier for them if they can categorize you as one thing. They'll always pick the biggest thing. For them, that's your relationship with Caleb. You're right. It's not fair." She graciously ignores my tears, directing her gaze away as I attempt to pull myself together. "If it's any consolation, I don't believe you have to choose, but you'll probably have to work harder. To prove that you're more than just a famous man's wife."

Her words depress me even more. I sniffle, a sinister doubt growing in the back of my mind. "Do you think that's why they asked me here to lecture? I'm the only resident speaking at this conference. Everyone else has already graduated from their medical training. Is Caleb why I'm here? Not because of my accomplishments?"

She shrugs. "I don't know, but you shouldn't make any assumptions. Your research is strong, and it's important. You've found another path to identifying cancer before it has a chance to spread."

I meet her eyes, trying to see if she's humoring me, but she's not that type. Helen doesn't sugarcoat what she says. "You really believe that?" I ask, relieved my message reached at least one person.

A decisive nod from her. "I do. So much that I'm going to recommend it at my hospital when I get home. We can easily replicate the program you've created."

I straighten, a little of my gloom lifting. "That'd be great."

"I doubt I'm the only one. I bet quite a few of the doctors in that room will go back and suggest cancer screening for ER patients in their institutions."

Her words help. Today didn't go as I planned. Not at all. But if I can save just a single family from what I went through when I lost my dad, then it'll all be worth it.

"I hope so," I tell her. "I really hope so."

15

TUESDAY, DECEMBER 17
7 DAYS UNTIL THE WEDDING

—JENNY—

The only part of me that's warm is my hand, from the cup of coffee steaming in it. I rap once, hard, on the car window. Dean lets me in, surprise registering on his face.

"Here." I shove the drink at him. "I brought you this."

"Um, thanks?" He stares at it like it might explode.

Are we back to this? Back to hating each other? Not trusting each other? Back to him thinking I'm crazy? I thought we had a breakthrough at the cake tasting two days ago, but maybe I was wrong.

I haven't seen him since then. Caleb's been working in his restaurant and on Broadway with no special events, giving me a rare couple of days off. I don't do well with free time. I spent it on the computer, double-checking that my code was correct. The program I created was running smoothly, filtering slowly through the over 800 suspects on Dean's list.

My mind had wandered a lot during that time, mostly to a certain stern-faced, brown-eyed man. Whenever I thought of him, I'd felt a strange urge to see him. A magnetic pull to hunt him down. I ignored it until this evening, when it finally became too much. A quick stop at the local café and now I'm sitting in the car with him.

Wondering how I got here.

Wondering if this is a good idea.

I continue to wage my internal battle while Dean takes the first sips of his drink. I'm about to give up and leave when he smiles at me and says, "Thanks for this. It's really good."

It's an open, honest kind of smile. *OHMYGOSH, is that a dimple in his cheek?* Now I'm in a quandary. I'm not sure which is better, his laugh or his smile. These thoughts are the last thing I need. On top of that, I've always been a sucker for a dimple.

"This was really nice of you. Are you all right?" Dean goes from that near-perfect smile to a frown of concern in zero to sixty.

I dig a peppermint candy out of my purse and eat it right in front of him, because who cares? My cover is blown.

"I'm fine. Why wouldn't I be?" I grumble in a very "not fine" tone. I cram the empty wrapper back into my purse, unwilling to litter in his car.

He's eying me cautiously, like a wild horse he needs to tame. "My sister once told me that when a woman says she's fine, it usually means the opposite."

And there it is. The problem. I didn't even know he had a sister. I don't know anything about this man, so I have no right to be freaking out over his fantastic laugh or dimpled smile.

UGH.

My hand goes to my shirt, pulling it down over my stomach, which I suck in instinctively.

He's staring at me, waiting for me to respond like a normal person, but all I have is frustrated silence. Finally, I ask, "You have a sister?"

"Three sisters," he chuckles. "All younger. When they started dating, it almost killed me. You can't imagine the grief I gave their boyfriends."

"What you're saying is that you've been a bodyguard for a long time?" I tease, slowly relaxing.

"I guess when you put it that way—yeah. No one's good enough for my baby sisters. Of course, they're all married now. I've got two nephews and three nieces." He says it so proudly that I almost expect him to whip out a bunch of family photos to show me.

His joy is infectious. I can't help but smile with him. "Do you spoil them? Your nieces and nephews?"

"Endlessly." He laughs, and that dimple deepens. I resist the urge to reach out and touch it, run my fingers over that divot. I don't notice my leg is bouncing until he stills it with a single finger pressed on my knee. The contact is electric, sending a tingle up my leg. I freeze, wishing we could stay like that, with him touching me.

"Is it Mrs. Wilkins? Is she the stalker?" I blurt out, desperate to regain some control over the situation. My computer algorithm hasn't ruled her out yet.

"No." Dean removes his hand and folds it in his lap, leaving a void behind. "I checked. She got a job with the Andersons on the fifth floor. They're retired university professors. I'm assuming no one wants to buy their underwear."

"You never know." My pulse has slowed now that he's not touching me. "The world's a strange place."

"That it is." He turns to stare out the window, giving me a view of the back of his head. His hair looks thick and touchable. I have an unbidden thought of running my hands through it.

He continues, "I reviewed the building's security footage. Mrs. Wilkins comes in every day at 8:00 p.m. and leaves by 1:00 a.m. Mr. Anderson has health issues. I guess she helps Mrs. Anderson get him to bed and then cleans up afterward."

"That doesn't mean she isn't taking the pictures." I almost bounce my leg again just to make him touch me but muster enough dignity to stay still. "She could take them before or after work."

It's snowing harder tonight. Mountains of snow and ice pile up along the edges of the roads now, in some places two feet high. We keep our jackets on in the car even with the heater set to full blast.

Dean pulls his phone out of his pocket and pulls up the recent photos tab on the Secret Santa website. "Lots of these were taken when I know Mrs. Wilkins was at work. See this tree right here?" He points to a stately sycamore close to Caleb's front door in the image.

I can see the real version of it from where I sit.

"When the sky is clear and the moon is full, that tree casts a shadow on the ground." His finger traces the image. "From its position, I can estimate what time the picture was taken. Like a sundial, but in this case it's a moon dial." His eyes, luminous in the darkened car, meet mine. "Make sense?"

"Yes," I confirm. "If it's not Mrs. Wilkins, then who?"

Dean scrapes a hand across his stubbled cheek. He lets out a frustrated sigh. "I'm not sure. How about your reporter friends in L.A.? Any leads from them?"

"Not yet." I crunch what's left of my candy between my teeth, the sound loud. Dean winces.

He sips his coffee, and I try not to notice how he licks his lips after he swallows. The car feels smaller than it did last time. We both stare out the window, squinting to see through the billowing snow.

"I've got it!" I cry out, a thought hitting me like a lightning bolt. "It's Lola in the library with the candlestick."

"Did you play a lot of that game when you were a kid or something?" Dean gives me an odd look, quirking one eyebrow.

I laugh. He's more correct than he knows. Gwen and I used to play Clue all the time.

"Lola's got motive," I argue. "She's still in love with Caleb."

Dean scoffs. "I doubt she was in love with him when they were together. She wasn't exactly faithful."

I think back to that encounter at Tavern on the Green. The possessive glint in Lola's eye. Certainty snaps into place. I'm right about this. I know it.

"I'm sure. She still wants him. I bet it's eating her alive—"

"Jennifer."

"Just thinking about how she's going to lose him to Gwen. I—"

"Jennifer."

"saw the way she looked at him. It's—"

"*Jennifer.*"

Dean's raised voice finally penetrates my overly excited brain. I had already been awarding myself a Pulitzer Prize for solving the case.

"Yeah?" I deliberately slow down my thoughts so I can listen.

"It's not her." He chews on the inside of his cheek. "I checked. The photos are shot during times when I can confirm that Lola's in other places. Earlier this week one picture was taken when she was at a premiere here in town, and another was taken when she was doing an interview." He shows me the images and his phone and the corresponding articles.

"No, that can't be correct," I say, fighting back but with less bluster. I had been so sure, but now doubt creeps in.

"Sorry, but…" Dean's whole hand is on my knee this time, stopping my leg from jiggling. "It's not her."

I deflate, out of steam and ideas. A sense of hopelessness rushes in. I'd wanted to solve this problem before Gwen gets home. Before the wedding. I'm not sure my computer program will find the answer in time, and, so far, Dean and I aren't any closer to an answer.

"I don't know who it is then."

"Me either," Dean says, his hand unmoving, warmth spreading from his palm through the fabric of my jeans and into my skin. Seeing my crestfallen expression, he gives my knee a gentle squeeze.

"We'll figure it out, though. Don't worry."

We.

He said we.

16

**WEDNESDAY, DECEMBER 18
6 DAYS UNTIL THE WEDDING**

GWEN

The pulse of music in the club is so loud that it reverberates in my chest. *How does Teddy work here and not get permanent hearing damage? For Christmas, I'll buy him earplugs.*

Stop it, I tell myself. Earlier today I told Mom I wouldn't parent him anymore and yet here I am, doing it again.

A few more steps inside and I see that Teddy was right. They really decorate this place for the holidays. Twinkling multicolored Christmas lights are everywhere. They hang across dark painted walls, dangle from elegant, mismatched crystal chandeliers, and are strewn among the bottles of alcohol behind the bar. Giant ornaments, taller than my head, in white, silver, and gold, are stacked into pyramids in the corners of the room. A sleigh, pulled by eight reindeer, is suspended from the high ceiling. It sways above the dance floor.

It's packed in here. People everywhere. I slip through the crowd, ducking under the flailing elbows of dancers and around a couple who embrace passionately. Seeing them brings a pang of longing for Caleb. I'd love to take him out on that dance floor. Let the music sweep us together, let our bodies move to the beat as one.

But that's a foolish dream. If Caleb were here, the crowd would mob him. Unless he was surrounded by bodyguards or in a disguise, we couldn't go dancing. It's another part of regular life I give up by being with him, like my anonymity at my medical conference. We'll never be normal Gwen and normal Caleb. We'll always be a spectacle, and I thought I was okay with that, but after the Lola kiss, the fiasco of my lecture, and now being here, the first bit of doubt trickles in.

I find a couple of open seats at the end of the bar, away from the DJ who plays music on the stage in the front of the room. He's wearing a bright red Santa hat with bulky headphones over the top of it. I sit on a swiveling stool. It's quieter here, so I don't have to yell as loud when I ask a gorgeous female bartender for the gingerbread martini I saw advertised by the club's entrance.

"Sissy!" a deep voice booms.

I lift my head and there he is, my younger brother Teddy. Almost five years separate us in age so you would think we wouldn't be close, but when Dad died I was 17 and Teddy was 12. We'd clung to each other, life rafts in a stormy sea. Mom worked all the time, and our older brother was busy with community college. We trauma bonded in a way that's unbreakable.

He comes from behind the bar to hug me. I throw my arms around him, rising up on my toes. Has he grown? That's impossible, right? He's twenty-five now. An adult. In that instant, I understand what Mom was talking about earlier. It's hard to look at Teddy and not see the skin-kneed little boy he used to be. I give my head a small shake and focus on the man in front of me.

He's gotten so handsome, my brother. Not as tall as Caleb, but still above-average height. Short, spikey, light-brown hair. Pale blue eyes, same as mine. Eyelashes long enough to make any woman jealous. He must be working out more, because his biceps strain the sleeve of his tight black T-shirt. Just like the DJ, he has on a comical holiday hat, although his is something an elf would wear.

He looks me over, grinning, then pauses, tips his head to the side, and narrows his eyes. "Is that a fanny pack you're wearing?"

"It's a waist bag," I correct, hands on my hips.

"I don't think so. That," he says decisively, pointing at it, "is a fanny pack."

Seriously? What's up with the fanny pack shaming?

Before I can argue, the bartender hands me my drink. When she passes behind Teddy, she grazes her fingers along his shoulder, giving him a flirtatious smile. He sends her a grin paired with a secretive wink. Then Teddy looks over my head with a smirk and nod of acknowledgment. I follow his gaze to a pretty brunette two tables away, who's staring at him with undisguised longing. My jaw loosens as I watch Teddy smile and wordlessly flirt with several more women in the space of five minutes.

Oh my gosh.

My brother is a player. My formerly sweet brother, who only had one girlfriend in high school, is a bona fide hottie with a harem of women.

When did this happen?

"Teddy," I grab his arm and hiss, "who are all these women?"

He grimaces, pulling out of my hands. "Ouch. Stop it, Gwen. You're going to mess up my new tattoo." His face contorted with pain, he pulls up his sleeve to show me a tattoo, so fresh it's still outlined in an angry red, slathered in shiny ointment, and bandaged with something similar to Saran Wrap. The plastic over it is clear, allowing me to see the pattern. To the untrained eye, it might look like a distorted version of Saturn. A black ball in the middle with six thin rings circling it, all crisscrossing over each other. I know what it is. It's an atom, with its central nucleus and surrounding electrons.

My throat instantly closes, my vision blurring with tears. I lift my gaze to his, which mirrors my expression, both of our faces drawn in sorrow. "For Dad?" I ask, voice trembling. Our father was a nuclear physicist. He had just gotten promoted to head his own lab when he was diagnosed with colon cancer at age 45. He was dead six months later.

Teddy nods, mouth turned down. "For you, too," he says. "Since you've always loved science so much." I smile weakly, remembering how little Teddy would help me with my experiments when we were young, patiently holding test tubes while I poured a mixture of ingredients into them and then exclaiming with wide-eyed glee when the contents of the tube would erupt like a volcano, spilling foaming liquid down the sides and over his hands.

"I love it." I point to his arm and sniffle back my tears, not wanting to cry in a crowded room.

He smiles, the gesture not quite reaching his eyes. Something metallic glints in his mouth.

"Teddy!" I grab his shirt and pull him closer, rising onto my toes to peer past his lips. "Is that…a tongue piercing?"

He brightens and sticks out his tongue, proudly displaying the long silver rod that goes through it, tipped by tiny balls on each end. "Yep. Hurt like heck when they stabbed it in."

I roll my eyes with a grimace. "Gross, Teddy. Too much information." That's a mental image of my brother I can do without.

Teddy chuckles, his shoulders lifting with the motion. Eventually, he quiets and leans an elbow on the bar. "Sorry. That was too funny. Anyway, how was lunch with Mom?"

"Fine," I answer automatically, then correct. "Actually, not fine. She's annoyed with me. I told her some truths she didn't appreciate."

"Oh, yeah?" he says, smirking. "That makes me happy."

"Teddy! Don't say that," I protest, swatting at his arm. His *other* arm, the one without the tattoo. "That's mean."

He laughs, easily fending off my ineffectual punches. "Sorry. It's just nice to not be the only black sheep in the family for once."

"Black sheep?" I drop my hands, my brow furrowing. "You're not the black sheep."

Teddy frowns and says, "Come on, Gwen. We all know I'm the wild child. The disappointing college dropout. With a brother who's a lawyer and a sister who's a doctor about to marry the most famous man in the world, it's hard to compete." His voice is breezy, his body relaxed, but I see the tightness in his jaw. He's joking, and yet there's a kernel of truth in his words.

"What?" My heart sinks, realizing this is the way he views himself. As a failure. "That's not true. You're in college."

He scoffs, "I take night classes at the local community college. At this rate, it'll take me eight years to graduate." Seeing my troubled expression, Teddy softens. "It's okay, Gwen. I don't mind who I am. I don't want you to be embarrassed, that's all."

For the second time tonight, I want to cry. "I'd never feel that way about you." I sling an arm around his narrow waist and bury my head in the side of his chest. Teddy wraps his arm around me and tucks me in tighter.

He sighs and says, "I'm just giving you a hard time." After a minute, he releases me. "What made you upset with Mom?"

"You know, stuff from the past." Teddy knows there's friction between Mom and me from when Dad died. He doesn't need the details. The last thing I want is for him to think he'd been a burden.

Teddy leans against the bar, crossing one foot over the other. "You're never going to get what you want from Mom. You understand that, don't you?"

"What do you mean?" I ask, confused.

"You want closure. You want her to admit she's wrong."

"That's not true," I argue, wondering if he remembers more than I give him credit for about that dark long-ago period of our lives.

Teddy cocks an eyebrow at me, and I flounder because he's got a point. I want acknowledgment from Mom. Maybe even an apology. But that's childish. This need to always be right.

Teddy draws my attention back to him, affectionately rubbing his knuckles on my head, messing up my hair. "You won't give up trying to convince Mom. Does Caleb know that about you—how stubborn you are?" His words take me back to before I left New York. Caleb and me laughing over that same topic, except now it's not so funny.

Take the jet.

Am I being that way with Caleb? Too stubborn? Too convinced my way is the only way? A flash of regret for how I handled that conversation back at the penthouse. So far, Caleb has been righter than I was.

"He may have figured it out." I run my fingers through my hair, smoothing it out. Quieter, I ask, "You don't think she'll ever see it my way?"

Teddy frowns, compassion in his eyes. "No. The things that happened to us with Dad. We experienced the same events, but we all processed them differently. Mom only understands it from her point of view. That won't change."

He sighs, shrugs, then asks about our older brother, "Have you talked to Brandon recently?"

"A few months ago. You know he barely ever calls. We'll see him at the wedding, though."

"At least he talks to you." Teddy's jaw tightens. "He calls me once a year at most. If it weren't for holiday get-togethers, I wouldn't even know him."

We had both looked up to our brother, but when Dad died he became angry and pulled away from all of us. It's better now that he has a wife and twin daughters, but still far from perfect.

"I miss him," I admit, eyes downcast.

Teddy squeezes my arm. "I know. Me, too. That's family for you, right? Love, affection, bitterness, resentment all wrapped up together like a Christmas present with a big bow on top. Nothing's easy, but we don't give up on each other. No matter what."

Tears threaten once more. "Stop making me cry, you brat." I breathe in through my nose, then out through my mouth, trying to soothe the ache in my chest. A newfound respect for Teddy emerges. "When did you get so smart, anyway?"

He lifts one shoulder, standing tall, acting like it's no big deal, but I see the way his chest puffs out at my words. "You know what they say about bartenders. We're untrained and underpaid therapists."

I snort with laughter. An air horn rings out, so loud it makes me startle. Everyone cheers as fake snow, the foamy kind, drifts down from the ceiling, landing on upturned faces and outstretched hands. I gasp, delightfully surprised.

Teddy grins at my reaction. "It's a holiday thing. They do it every hour on the hour."

"It's beautiful," says Helen, who's just arrived. In unison, Teddy and I turn to find her staring upward, her face lit with joy. She's lovely tonight with her straight, jet-black hair swept up into a high ponytail that bounces when she moves her head. She wears a tight red dress and has an extra earring, in the cartilage of her upper ear, that I didn't notice when we were at the medical conference. A tiny bubble of snow lands on her pert nose. She ducks, brushing it away. When she glances back up, her gaze finds Teddy and she freezes.

My hand is still on Teddy's shirt, so I feel when he stops breathing. His eyes dilate, a deer caught in the headlights.

What? My head pivots, taking in the two of them staring at each other.

Oh no. This is not good.

My brother...and Helen?

He would eat her alive.

I pull him close and whisper in his ear, "Leave her alone. She's sweet."

Teddy yanks away and scowls down at me. In a loud, offended voice, he asks, "And I'm not?"

"No! That's not what I meant." I sigh, exasperated, unable to explain what I'm thinking. Of course, I think my brother is nice. It's just that this version of him is new. I'm not sure how to interpret it. He seems...volatile. Not ready for the kind of relationship I assume Helen wants.

Teddy's scowling at me, not the happy sibling reunion I was hoping for. To appease him, I make quick introductions with Helen, explaining how she's moving to L.A. soon. She looks unblinking up at him.

Just for spite, Teddy shoots me an angry glare, takes her hand, and smoothly grazes his lips over her knuckles. He stares into her eyes, smiles innocently, and says, "It's nice to meet you. Any friend of my sister's is a friend of mine."

Helen melts under my brother's burning gaze. I kick him in the shin, moving slowly so she won't notice. Teddy grunts in pain and drops her hand. He glowers at me, and I glare right back, remembering how it feels to fight with him. We're close, but it's not like we didn't have our squabbles as kids. This interaction is as familiar as pulling on an old, worn-out T-shirt. Annoying but also weirdly comforting because I know no matter how mad we get we still love each other unconditionally.

Teddy drops her hand and asks, "What can I get you, Helen?"

"How's the Eggnog White Russian?" Helen gracefully takes a seat next to me.

"Like Santa made it himself," Teddy says, and we all laugh. He catches the eye of the female bartender and motions for her to get Helen the drink. Then he says, "I'd better go back to work. It was good to meet you, Helen. Let me know if you need help moving in." He envelops me in a tight hug.

"I'm glad I saw you, Gwen. Next time we get together, it'll be in New York for your wedding." A quick kiss to the top of my head, again messing up my hair. "I can't wait."

"Me either. Have a safe flight out tomorrow." I hug him back, saying, "Love you, Teddy Bear."

"Ditto, Sissy." Then he's gone, high-fiving people as he makes his way behind the bar.

Helen's drink gets dropped off. She tries it and licks her lips, murmuring, "Delicious."

I settle onto my seat next to her. Her eyes follow my brother as he works, flashing smiles at customers and shaking mixed drinks in chilled metal containers. I almost warn her away from him, then stop myself. They're both adults. Let them figure it out. If I butt in, how am I any different from Mom when she got upset about my dating Caleb?

Thinking of him reminds me to check my messages. I don't want to miss his call, which would be easy to do since it's loud in here. My notifications show nothing yet.

"Waiting to hear from Caleb?" Helen guesses.

I'm still staring at my phone. "Hmm. Yes." There's a picture of Caleb on my home screen, one I took when he wasn't looking. In it, he's in bookworm mode, lying on the couch in his penthouse with a novel in his hand and his white-socked feet crossed. My favorite part about the photo is the book he's reading. It's *Pride and Prejudice*. I touch the image, longing for him.

Just a few more days and I can kiss that handsome face. Our flight leaves tomorrow afternoon. I smile at the thought of seeing him, but that grin fades as I remember those comments at my lecture.

Your work will be discredited.

Change the trajectory of your career.

That's what the middle-aged lady said. Is she right? A flare of resentment strikes. It's unfair that all my hard work, my accomplishments, are eclipsed by Caleb's fame. It's not his fault, I understand that, but still, it's difficult not to feel bitter.

"What's it like? Being engaged to him?" Helen asks, leaning her elbow on the bar. She turns her stool toward me. I appreciate the question, happy she's not asking for details about Caleb but rather my experience with him.

"It's amazing—and complicated." I sigh, thinking back to Caleb when I left, how tight he held my hand during the drive to the airport. "He's wonderful.

So smart and hardworking. People don't understand how much he rehearses or how he spends hours perfecting a recipe. He's a good listener too. Lets me tell him all about my day. Every gross detail from the hospital. He likes learning about that stuff." My heart warms as I describe my fiancé. This is what I need. To remember all the great things about him.

"I'm glad for you," she says, swiveling her stool side to side and sipping her drink.

I search Helen and find only sincerity. "Thanks. It's hard sometimes, though. We can't do activities like a normal couple, and everyone treats me differently now. You saw at the lecture."

Helen listens quietly. "He's so famous. It makes you famous, too."

"It's weird to me." I shake my head. "I get why Caleb's well-known. He's accomplished a lot, but that's him. Not me. We're two separate people."

She purses her lips. "That's not how you're perceived, though. His fame rubs off on you."

"I guess you're right." I take a sip of water. "Did you know followers post marriage advice for us on Caleb's social media accounts?"

"Really? What do they say?" She leans in, like she wants to take notes, which makes me giggle.

"Most of it is nonsense. Caleb thinks I'm crazy for even reading it, but I figure there's got to be some gems of knowledge in there. The people writing him are married, so hopefully they've figured it out?"

We chuckle together. "I read a couple of good ones. One lady wrote that in marriage you fall in and out of love many times, always with the same person, which I thought was interesting. A man said to argue naked because that way you won't stay mad for long."

Helen laughs, covering her mouth with her hand. "I'll have to remember that."

An idea comes to me, a lightbulb going off over my head. "You should come to my wedding, unless you'll be with your parents?"

For a brief moment, her face lights up eagerly, but then it shifts into something cooler, more restrained. "I'm not going to California yet. I have to pack up my apartment in Manhattan, but I couldn't intrude—"

"Yes, you can," I interrupt. I like her. She's sweet and thoughtful. I've been so busy with medicine and then Caleb that I haven't had time to make a lot of friends. Inviting Helen to my wedding will help cement this new friendship. "I'm serious. Please come."

She debates with herself silently for a minute, which only makes me like her more. Most people would jump at the chance to go to the "wedding of the century," but not Helen.

Finally, she says, "Okay. If you're sure, I'd love to attend."

My phone vibrates with a message from Caleb, the one I've been waiting for. I'm happy to see his name on my screen, but there's a moment of unease when I flashback to how people asked about him during my presentation.

Still with Helen, I text. *Call you soon.*

He texts back, *Okay. Love you. Forever and always.*

Love you, too. I pause, then add. *Forever and always.*

17

THURSDAY, DECEMBER 19
5 DAYS UNTIL THE WEDDING

—JENNY—

It's our last fitting before the wedding. Caleb's on the other side of the bridal shop, in the men's section, with his dad, Dean, and his friend Nick, trying on their tuxes. Initially, I was surprised to learn that Dean was one of Caleb's groomsmen, but once I gave it some thought, it made sense. Besides Gwen, he spends the most time with Caleb. They understand each other in a way that goes beyond an employer-bodyguard relationship.

I'm on the ladies' side of the shop. Alvina and I are Gwen's bridesmaids. Luckily, Alvina and Gwen had their fittings before they left for L.A. Now, it's my turn. I stand on a round pedestal in the center of the room. I'm surrounded by mirrors, a million unsmiling images of me reflected back.

My bridesmaid dress is a beautiful deep maroon. It's red enough that you can tell it's for a holiday wedding, but not so red that I should audition for the part of Rudolph's nose. The fabric is the smoothest silk I've ever seen, shimmering when the light hits it just right. It's fitted in the bodice, waist, and hips, then flares into soft folds that flow all the way to the floor.

When Gwen showed it to me at our first fitting, I had gotten teary-eyed at how pretty it was. "I picked it out for you," Gwen told me, her eyes shining. "I want you to feel special on my big day. You should know how beautiful you are to me." That had tipped me over the edge and straight into waterworks territory. I had cried, hugging her until the staff reminded us that we only had an hour appointment and they hadn't tried on Gwen's dress yet.

Her *new* dress. Gwen had been engaged once before, but it ended before they picked out a venue. She had an old dress from that engagement, never worn, that she had donated to charity. I went with her to deliver it.

"Are you sad?" I had asked, as we stood together and watched the dress in its white garment bag get carried away.

"No," she answered, strong and steady as Gwen so often is. "I feel good knowing that gown is going to someone who will be excited to wear it. That was never going to be me." She hugged me with an arm around my waist.

"I've found my place now. Where I'm seen and loved. With Caleb."

Her words had made my heart squeeze with happiness.

Now, I'm *not* happy as the tailor flutters about, adjusting the dress. She's a petite woman, with black hair tied up messily into a bun. She talks around the pins caught between her teeth. "Can you suck in your breath a bit for me, dear?"

Cheeks burning, I bring in my stomach as much as possible. There's the metallic sound of the zipper being dragged up. The fabric constricts my abdomen and chest. It's so tight that I worry I'll split a seam. The tailor notices the way it bunches. She tugs at it, frowning. I want to tell her it's not the clothing's fault.

It's mine.

Guess I've gained a pound or two since the initial fitting. Not much, but enough to make what was already a snug dress turn downright suffocating. The tailor tsks. The sound causes a rush of humiliation that makes my cheeks glow red hot. A few more pokes, tugs, and disgruntled glares later, the woman stands.

"Okay," she says, taking the pins out of her mouth and using them to gesture down the hall, "you can go and change into your normal clothing. We're all done."

I take a long look in the mirror in front of me and hate what I see. The dress shows off every bulge and bump. When I first tried it on, I felt like Cinderella. Now I've turned into one of the evil stepsisters.

"Gotta exercise more," I tell myself. Eat better too, but that one's harder. I love sweets so much that it's hard to say no to them. Christmas is the worst time of the year, with so many delicious cookies and candy everywhere. This is a daily struggle for me, my food-loving side fighting with my harsh inner critic.

Feeling defeated, I trudge to the small changing room. Once I'm there, I deliberately avoid the mirror. Putting my back to it, I reach behind me to pull down the zipper, but it's stuck. I tug harder and feel a yank on my hair. I must've gotten some of it tangled in the zipper. The more I mess with it, the more my hair gets caught up in the dress. Soon, my head is pounding from the exertion of battling with the zipper and from all the strands that have been ripped out of my scalp.

I peek my head out, hoping I can find someone to untangle me, but no one is there. Back in the room, I work on the problem some more but only make things worse. Now big chunks of hair are caught in it. In order to not pull them out, I keep my neck tilted to the left at an awkward angle. That's when I hear a voice calling outside.

"Jennifer," Dean shouts, "are you in here?"

"I'm here," I call back, still struggling. "What do you need?"

"Do you know if Gwen put in an order for the tuxes to come with handkerchiefs? Mine and Caleb's have them, but Nick's doesn't."

"I told her to get the handkerchiefs," I say through the door. "I noticed you had one when I first met you, so I figured you'd want it."

"You remembered that?" Dean's voice is loud now, like he's close.

"Of course. That's why Gwen ordered them."

The silence lasts so long that I assume he's walked away. Another yank on the zipper pulls out my hair until I exclaim with a noisy, "Ouch," followed by a growl of frustration.

"Is something wrong?" asks Dean.

I jerk with surprise, losing more hair. My heart stops beating. I grasp at my chest in time to feel it thump back to life. "You scared me!"

"Sorry." The door rattles lightly, as if he's touching it from the outside. "What's going on in there? It sounds like you're fighting with a gorilla."

I grimace at that surprisingly accurate description. I've been trying to get this dress off for fifteen minutes with no progress. "My zipper's stuck."

A long silence broken by Dean clearing his throat. "Do you—do you need help?"

That makes me freeze. I need help, but the thought of him seeing me like this is humiliating. Still…I have to get out of this dress. That tailor lady is tiny but terrifying. I don't want her to accuse me of hogging the changing room.

"Is there any staff out there?" I move closer to the door and place my hand on it. "Anyone?"

His voice gets softer, like he's moved away. "Just me. I think they're with other customers."

Of course they are.

"I might need some help," I admit reluctantly.

With a twist of the knob, I unlock the door and inch it open. Dean's on the other side, casually leaning against the wall with both hands shoved into his pants pockets, like a model on the cover of *GQ*. When my eyes land on him, all the breath whooshes out of my body. He's stunning. He's wearing the tuxedo, a dark grey three-piece with a maroon tie—the same color as my dress—that Caleb picked out for the wedding. In it, Dean is absolute pure male perfection. A matching handkerchief is folded neatly in his jacket pocket. His slacks are tailored, hugging his muscular legs.

While my eyes have been taking a self-guided tour of his body, he's been busy staring at me with a wide-eyed, slightly shocked expression. He doesn't blink, almost like he's afraid he might miss something. We stare at each other, both breathing a bit too fast, the air crackling between us.

He breaks the silence first. "Wow. That is—you look—um, nice."

He'll never know how much I needed to hear those words, to see the admiration in his eyes. It wipes away my shame at the dress being tight, my worry about how my body might not fit the standard for classic American beauty. Moments before, I'd been convinced I wasn't attractive, but something in the way he looks at me makes me feel beautiful.

"Yeah. You, too," I say breathlessly, unable to rip my eyes away from his broad shoulders and tapered waist.

Dean shifts foot to foot, the first time I've seen him nervous. "You need help?"

"Zipper's caught. I can't get it down." I turn my back to him. I face the mirror so I can watch as he steps into the dressing room with me, closing the door behind him. We're trapped together, pressed close in this space that felt small when it was just me but seems miniscule with both of us in it.

He moves closer, his eyes focusing on the problem. "Hmm." He bites his lower lip and tips his head as he assesses the situation. "You've got yourself in quite the pickle, haven't you?"

I giggle and ask, "Pickle?"

My laughter dies the moment his hands touch me, their warmth searing through the fabric of my dress. I suck in a breath, my pulse fluttering. Over the past couple of days, I've become increasingly aware of how handsome he is, how my body tunes into his presence like it's my favorite station on the radio.

He gives an experimental pull on the zipper. "Ow!" My hand flies to my head.

"Oh, sorry." For the next five minutes, Dean painstakingly separates my hair from the dress, strand by strand. He's focused on the task, which allows me the opportunity to watch him in the mirror. There's a frown of concentration on his face, a wrinkle between his brows. He purses his full lips, the lower one sticking out. His warm breath breezes over my skin, making it prickle with goosebumps. If he notices, he doesn't comment. Several times he pauses, closes his eyes, takes in a deep inhalation, lets it out, and then goes to work. Finally, my hair is free, and I can fully extend my neck. Dean's hand stays on the zipper.

He could leave now.

I could get the zipper down by myself.

But he doesn't.

I could tell him to go.

But I don't.

Instead, we both hesitate. I hold my breath, waiting to find out what he'll do next. His brown eyes flash up to the mirror to meet mine. He holds me in that intense stare, and slowly he pulls the zipper down so my shoulders are exposed. Not low enough to see my bra, but when his gaze drops to my bare skin he swallows so loudly that it echoes in the small room.

There's a suspended moment when my imagination takes flight and I picture him pressing his lips to the back of my neck.

Dean doesn't do that. Instead, he moves a big step away, so far that he bumps into the closed door. Reaching behind, he fumbles for the doorknob and opens it, practically falling out of the room.

"Everything's fine now. You can manage the rest," he mumbles before he turns around, running straight into the tailor. She loses her balance and trips, but he catches her. She gasps, her accusing gaze bouncing between the two of us. I'm sure we look guilty as heck, with him all flustered and my dress hanging off my shoulders. Dean reaches out and swings the door shut, cutting off my view. He leaves me there.

Alone.

18

FRIDAY, DECEMBER 20
4 DAYS UNTIL THE WEDDING

—JENNY—

It's been a rough day. I spent several hours this morning trying different angles to figure out who Caleb's stalker is, with no success. My computer program glitched, and I had to restart it from the beginning. A check-in with Ron and Bradly revealed they have no leads.

I'm on my way to have lunch with Eddie, who's back in town for the day. This time there'll be no Dean to save me. He's with Caleb, who has a matinee performance. Eddie and I are supposed to meet at a local deli. I get there first and grab a booth by the window. It's snowing even harder today, with gusts of wind that blow flurries across the sidewalk.

On the corner, a man dressed up like Santa Claus rings a large brass bell rhythmically. People passing by drop cash into a bucket that hangs swinging from a pole. Even though I'm inside, I can hear that faint repetitive chiming.

Eddie's late. Bored, I pull up the list of suspects that Dean sent me. In another tab, I open Caleb's Secret Santa website. I flip back and forth between the two, trying to figure out who the stalker might be. When a voice clears loudly next to me, I jump, startled. It's Eddie, standing over me. Guiltily, I place my phone face down on the table.

"Hi," I greet him brightly, hoping this meeting will go better than the last.

He shoves a brown paper–wrapped sandwich at me. "Here, got your favorite. Grilled cheese made with marble rye." He sits down and unwraps his tuna salad on white.

I grab it and tear open the packaging. The smell of toasted bread hits me, and I close my eyes, inhaling it. "Yum. Gwen's mom is the best at making these sandwiches, but this comes in second place. I'll give you some money for it," I tell Eddie, knowing what a cheapskate he can be. When he got lunch for our department meetings in L.A., he'd make everyone pay for their own meal, down to the taxes and tip. It was always a nightmare, reporters grumbling as they opened the calculator apps on their phones. Nine times out of ten, I'd pitch in extra cash at the end because we were short.

"No need," says Eddie as I take my first bite.

I almost spit my food out. "Really?"

"It's fine." He gives me a benevolent smile, which I don't buy for one second.

"Why are you being nice?" I ask, my mouth twisting with suspicion.

He holds up his hands, like I'm about to rob him. "We can be friends, Jenny. Maybe something more?"

I put down my sandwich, quickly losing my appetite. "What?"

He swallows his food and takes a drink of soda, drawing out the silence.

"Eddie," I warn, wishing I could throw the salt shaker at him.

"It's just that seeing you with your new boyfriend got me thinking," he says with his mouth full.

I almost laugh when he calls Dean my boyfriend. What a ludicrous idea. We could never be more than friends.

Then why can't you stop obsessing over when you were in the changing room together? About how warm his hands were? My annoying inner voice asks questions.

"Well, quit it. There's nothing to think about," I say to Eddie and to myself.

Eddie leans over the table, closer to me. His expression sincere, he says, "We were good together, Jenny. It's hard for me to admit it, but I was wrong to break up with you. I want you back."

"I'm sorry. What?" I sputter.

"I mean it." He argues, "We make sense. You and this Dean guy, what're you thinking? You'll be home in L.A. in a couple of weeks."

I suck in a breath, offended he doesn't have faith in my fake relationship.

"Dean and I can do it," I tell him, with no idea where those words are coming from. He's right. I will leave New York in less than a week. A relationship with Dean would be doomed from the start.

"How?" he scoffs. "Are you going to do long-distance?"

I lift my chin. "I'm willing to try it."

Eddie crumples up his napkin and throws it angrily on the table. "You really like that guy enough to stay with him?"

"Yes. Yes, I do," I declare, half-rising from my seat. "What Dean and I have is—it's special." A detached part of myself raises her eyebrows at my theatrics, but hanging out with Caleb must have improved my acting abilities because I dramatically clutch my heart and turn away. "I won't give him up, not for anything."

"You're making a big mistake." He also half-rises, shaking his finger at me. At that moment, his phone goes off. We both stare down at it and see the name of Eddie's boss, our editor-in-chief, flash on the screen. Eddie sends me one last burning glare, rearranges his face, and picks up with a happy sounding, "Hello." He sits back down and begins a tedious conversation about the summer issue and who they should feature on the front page.

After a few minutes of this, my eyelids grow heavy. "I'm going to go get a cup of coffee," I whisper. Eddie nods, waving me away. There's a long line at the deli counter. By the time I return, Eddie's off the phone and eerily calm.

He slides a couple sheets of paper my way. It's my latest article about Caleb. The one that should run in this weekend's edition. It has red ink slashed all over it, corrections Eddie has made to my work.

"This was boring," he says. "Redo it and send it back to me later today."

I check my watch. "It's already past 2:00 p.m., and I have to do a feature on Caleb at his restaurant tonight," I protest.

Eddie pushes himself up and dusts crumbs off his shirt. "Guess you better get working on it." Without a good-bye, he turns and walks out of the door.

It's only after he's gone that I notice my phone is sitting face up on the table, though I could have sworn I left it face down.

19

FRIDAY, DECEMBER 20
4 DAYS UNTIL THE WEDDING

—JENNY—

At least Caleb cooked me a delicious meal at his restaurant. It soothed the fact that I spent all afternoon reworking the article for Eddie.

I've been on a stakeout with Dean for the past three hours. I thought he might mention the incident in the dressing room, but he's barely spoken to me, only answering my questions with one-word grunts. He keeps his expression carefully schooled, but I sense a quiet rage beneath it.

Frustration, I assume, because we haven't identified the culprit.

I think about telling him that I'm worried Eddie saw something on my phone, but I'm too intimidated. Too scared to admit that once again I've spilled my friend's secrets. Dean has started to accept me. He lets me in right away when I knock on the car window. I don't want to lose his trust, especially since I'm not *totally* sure if Eddie knows about the stalker.

After midnight, we give up on finding the Secret Santa. Dean insists on driving me back to my hotel. The weather outside has worsened, snow falling in thick blowing clouds until we can't see more than two feet in front of us. We pull up to the curb and park. Dean peers out his window, frowning with disapproval at the small four-story boutique hotel I had picked out.

"Why are you staying here?"

I bristle, leaning around him to inspect the brick building with maroon awnings. It had looked so charming online, but in reality, well, it does appear to be a bit shabby. Not that I'm going to admit that out loud.

"What? It's quaint."

"It's old."

"Everything here is old, especially to me, coming from the West Coast. Besides, that was what I was going for. This hotel was built over 100 years ago. That's why I like it. I want to embrace the history of this city."

"Yeah, typhoid was so fun back then," he says dryly.

"It's historic. It's special." I throw up my hands, frustrated.

Dean's shaking his head at me. "You're crazy. There's nothing special about small elevators and cramped closets."

Now he's making me angry. I mean, *should* I have read the reviews before I booked this place? Probably yes, but I don't own a time machine, so what's done is done.

"Like you need a big closet since you wear the same outfit every day. I'm convinced you only have three of those and you rotate them." I gesture to his standard-issue dark-blue suit and roll my eyes.

"Besides, you haven't seen the inside. I've got a four-poster bed like a princess and an original claw-foot bathtub from the 1930s." I don't mention the hard mattress or the rust stains in the bottom of the tub.

"Oh! Oh!" I grasp his forearm and bounce excitedly. "It has a tiny kitchen, too."

"All kitchens in New York are tiny," he says, not impressed.

"Yes, but this one is the teeny, tiniest. One burner and a minifridge. I'm stocked up on soup and stuff to make PB and J's."

"Wow." A sarcastic quirk of his brow. "You're really living the high life."

"I am." I sniff, lifting my chin.

"Look," he says, pointing outside the car window. "There aren't even any lights on."

"What?" I scramble forward, practically climbing into his lap, to see. "That's strange. There's always someone at the front desk."

Dean unclicks his seatbelt, sliding it off his shoulder. "Let's check it out."

"It's fine. You don't have to come in. I—"

"*Jennifer.*" One word, his eyes flashing in warning.

"Okay. Okay. Chill," I grumble as I climb out of the car and promptly slip on a patch of ice. I tumble into a drift of snow higher than my knees. Dean rushes over with a worried frown. He says something but the wind blows so hard that it rips the words away before I hear them.

"What?" I shout, holding back my hair. It whips around wildly. Curly tendrils slap my cheeks and cover my eyes until I'm blinded.

Dean leans down and yells, "I said. Are you okay?"

"Oh," I laugh, embarrassed. "I'm fine. Just slipped."

He grasps my upper arms and hauls me to my feet. With swift, efficient movements, he brushes the snow off my pants. "Let's get you inside." He keeps one hand on my arm as we struggle through the driving snow and into the lobby. The very dark lobby is lit by a single flashlight held in the trembling hand of a young night clerk whose nametag reads "Andy."

"What's going on?" Dean booms in his deep voice.

Andy, who can't be more than 19, shrinks in on himself, stuttering. "S—sorry, sir. The entire block has lost power because of the wind and snow. It's a real nor'easter."

"A nor' what?" I ask.

Dean spares a glance at me and says, "A bad storm."

"We're giving out flashlights and bottled water." Andy points to a basket on the counter, loaded high with flashlights, candles, matches, and bottles of water. In front of it a small hand-lettered sign reads, *Help yourself.*

Dean scoops up two flashlights, along with the other supplies. He stalks off, heading for the stairs, next to the now-useless elevators.

"Thanks, Andy." I give him a reassuring smile and sprint after Dean. "Hey. You don't need to stay." I'm panting from chasing him down. "I've got this."

He doesn't bother to answer. He just gives me a blistering stare, hands me a flashlight, and continues into a pitch-black stairwell that stinks of dead bodies—or maybe it's mold. I press closer to Dean, suddenly grateful for his presence. I merge the beam of my light with his so we can see what's in front of us. We climb. The only sound is our breathing, mine fast, his annoyingly even.

My room is on the third floor. The hallway leading to it is just as dark as the stairs. In the wavering light from the flashlight Dean holds, I manage to put my old-fashioned metal key into the lock. I use the weight of my body to turn it and wrench the door open. Wide curtained windows along the far wall let in enough moonlight for me to see the shadowy outlines of the queen bed and matching nightstands. A small, round table with two spindle-backed chairs sits in the corner next to the kitchen. Through another doorway, I glimpse the pedestal sink in the bathroom.

"Here it is," I say cheerfully as I sweep out a hand. "Home sweet home."

Dean scowls, casting a critical eye over the space. "What is *that?*" he asks. His flashlight plays over a small pine tree, two feet tall, in the corner of the room. The light makes the tree's shadow waver on the wall behind it. The tree is thin and crooked. I've placed ornaments on its stronger branches, but they droop under the weight of the colorful balls. A tiny gold star sits on the uppermost portion. It leans to the side, canted at an awkward angle. I picked the star out because it reminded me of the one Gwen has, back at her mom's house in California.

"It's my Christmas tree." I walk over to it and straighten the star. "I got it from the lot down the street. They were going to throw it out." I prepare myself for Dean to say something demeaning about the tree. I know it's no beauty pageant winner, but it called to me as soon as I saw it. It had seemed such a shame, to not let the little thing perform the duty it was grown for. Maybe I identified with it. It's not perfect, just like me.

He grunts and says thoughtfully, "Reminds me of that television show, *A Charlie Brown Christmas*. I watched it with my nieces."

"That's what I thought too," I exclaim, surprised by how diplomatic he's being.

Dean places the items from downstairs on the table and organizes them, putting the candles and matches together. He bends and puts the water bottles on top of the minifridge, neatly lining them up so the labels all face the same direction.

Control freak.

I place a candle on the table and light it, releasing a warm fragrance into the air. Leaning over, I sniff deeply, "Vanilla. Nice touch."

Dean reaches out and brushes back a lock of my curly hair that's fallen forward, dangerously close to the open flame. "Careful there, Tiger. Don't want you to catch fire." He tucks the strands behind my shoulder, smoothing them down with his hand. I'm suddenly in danger of combusting, but not from the candle. There was something tender about the gesture, coupled with that stupid dimple that just popped out because he's smiling at me. I feel all squishy inside, like giddy little bubbles are fizzing up from my stomach.

As if the dimple weren't bad enough, Dean has a manly smell I notice for the first time, since he's standing so close. It's not cologne, more like body wash, something earthy and spicy. It makes me envision cowboys driving luxury sports cars. That scent combined with that of the candle is intoxicating. I breathe it in, letting it flood my senses, and my knees weaken. I grab the back of the nearest chair for stability.

I need him to leave—immediately.

Candles and moonlight and dimples and yummy smells are too dangerous a combination.

"Well," I say brightly, herding him toward the door. "Thanks for the help. You've been a real gentleman. Call your mother and thank her for raising you right."

"Oh. Er—okay." Dean pauses for a second in the open doorway, concern lowering his brows. "Are you sure you'll be fine?"

"Yep. Fine. Perfectly fine."

Please leave before I do something disastrous, like kiss you.

"Have a good night. Drive safe," I sing out and, heart pounding, shut the door, even though he probably stands on the other side looking perplexed. With my back against the door, I wave a hand, fanning my heated cheeks. I hold my breath, listening to his footfalls as he retreats back to the stairs.

There. Crisis averted.

I congratulate myself on making good decisions. Something I didn't used to do, but now, after the Gwen mistake, I'm working on.

I've had just enough time to use the bathroom and brush my teeth when a loud pounding on the door makes me jump. I open it to find Dean, his hair and clothing wet. Snowflakes glitter like diamonds, melting in his eyelashes.

"I can't move the car," he says. "The snow's too high, and they haven't plowed the road." My mouth drops as he pushes past me into the room and peels off his dripping overcoat. He shakes his head, water droplets flying everywhere. "We're stuck here. Snowed in."

Well, darn.

"Are we going to freeze to death?" is the first question that flies out of my mouth.

"These old buildings have radiators that run on gas. We'll be fine." Dean sits down, taking off his shoes and wet socks. He goes over to the radiator in the corner of the room and drapes his socks over it, which is kinda gross, but whatever. There are no radiators in California, so I don't know the rules. The first time this one warmed up, it made a loud banging noise. Scared the pants right off me. Now Dean's barefoot, which he makes look attractive as he pads around.

"Didn't you say something about soup?"

"Yes, chicken noodle."

That's when I notice he's shivering, his hair still damp. I jump into action, grabbing him a towel to dry off. I put a pot on the burner. There's a minute when I wonder if the stove will work with the power out, but I turn the knob and hear the whoosh of flame. Oh, yeah, I feel a bit silly. This is gas, too. Just like the radiator.

"I'm going to call and check on Caleb," he announces. In this small room, it's impossible to not overhear his end of the conversation when he finally connects. I gather that Caleb is fine. That his fancy apartment building has a backup generator and that Tom, another bodyguard, will stay with him tonight. There are some "Hmms" and "You don't says" from Dean before he hangs up.

"Any news?" I ask.

"Caleb was worried about you. I told him you were okay. He said most of Manhattan is without power. He mentioned that it reminds him of when Hurricane Sandy hit."

"I remember reading about that. Wasn't it bad?" I get butter out of the minifridge and close the door with my foot.

His expression is sober. "The city shut down for about four days back then."

I suck in a breath. "No! That can't happen. I promised Gwen her wedding would be perfect. Said I'd personally make sure."

"I know," he says and nods. "Don't worry. We won't let this storm stop us. We'll give them the wedding they deserve."

I'm not sure where he gets his confidence from, but I like it. He makes it sound so easy, as if he can will away the chaos of this storm and create a calm, orderly wedding from nothing more than sheer determination.

A few minutes later, I've cobbled together a meal for us. Warm soup and crusty bread I got from the bakery down the street. I slather the bread with butter, reminding myself this should be the last time I open the refrigerator. Don't want the food in there to go bad. Look at me, being so responsible. So domestic and adult-ish. I snap a quick picture of the meal with my phone.

"Did you…just take a photo of your soup?" Dean cocks his head.

I sit down and spread a paper napkin over my lap, admiring the flicker of the candle in the center of the table. "Yep. I'll send it to Gwen in the morning. She'll be so proud."

"Really?"

"She's always been the practical one, while I've been the free spirit, more…" I wrinkle my brow, searching for the right word, "impulsive, I guess. I'm trying to be less that way. More like her." I put a kettle of water on the burner and set it to boil. I have tea and hot chocolate. Hopefully that'll warm Dean up.

Steam rises from the soup in his spoon. Dean blows on it. I look away from those full lips, swallowing thickly.

"Is this about your slip-up?" he asks. "Back in L.A.? When you told your friend that Caleb was staying with Gwen?"

"Maybe," I say and sigh, my gaze downcast, staring at the tabletop, which is chipped and scarred.

"Gwen's forgiven you, right? Caleb, too?"

I nod, the corners of my mouth ticking down. "*You* were mad at me as well. In case you've forgotten."

He leans back and scrubs his hand across his chin. "That was more about me than about you."

"How so?" I glance up through my lashes, taking in his pensive expression.

"I thought it would be better for both of us if I kept my distance. Staying angry made that easier."

I place my spoon on the table. "Why?"

Before he can answer, the steam kettle whistles, the sound piercing. Dean flinches. I quickly hop up to get it, stopping the noise. Dean and I both choose hot chocolate, which tickles me for some reason. I find it amusing, this strong burly man daintily sipping a drink designed for children and chewing on mini-marshmallows. A sugar-free peppermint is my dessert. I suck on it until it shrinks to half its size, then finish it off with a loud crunch.

"What's up with the candy?" Dean asks. "Why do you hide it?"

"It's silly, a leftover habit from when I was a kid." I stare down at my hands folded in my lap. "My brothers used to tease me. When I'd eat candy they'd make these noises, oinks like a pig. I learned to hide it so they would stop."

I'm surprised I told him that story. Gwen's the only other person who knows. She would get so mad on my behalf. I remember one time, when she'd had enough. Tiny Gwen had stood, hands balled into fists at her sides, and shouted at my brothers, "Leave her alone, you pricks."

Dean has grown still as a statue. Even though he doesn't move, I can sense some kind of internal storm raging under his calm exterior. In a tightly controlled voice, he asks, "Is that why you work out so much? Because of those noises your brothers would make?"

My head bent, I shrug silently.

"Give me their addresses," Dean says.

"Why?"

"Because I'm going to kill them."

I snap up my gaze at that. "It really wasn't a big deal," I rush to tell him. "It sounds worse when I say it out loud."

"Jennifer. Anytime *anyone* makes you feel like there's something wrong with you, when clearly there is *not*, it's a big deal." Each word comes out measured. If I didn't notice the tense set of his shoulders and the way he's crushed the paper napkin in his hands, I wouldn't know that Dean is enraged. "What your brothers did to you is BS. If I ever get to see them in person, I'd love to tell them that with my fists."

Something warm spreads through my chest. My breathing speeds up. I'm suddenly aware of how small the room is, of how close Dean sits next to me. Who knew that threats of violence could be so alluring?

I notice he's shivering. "You should take a shower so you're not so cold. The hot water should work, right? Isn't it gas?"

He relaxes his grip, letting the crumpled napkin fall to the table. Dean's ears turn pink. "I don't have anything to change into afterward. All my clothing got wet when I tried to dig the car out."

I glance out the window and see only white. The snow comes down so steady and hard that it looks like someone hung a sheer curtain over the glass. "There are towels in there. I have a robe that might fit. Take a shower, and I'll get it out."

He takes a candle with him since it's dark in the windowless bathroom. After I hear the water turn on, I quickly change into my pajamas, fleece with buttons and a pink plaid pattern. Very unsexy. I tuck my hair into a satin bonnet to protect it from getting tangled while I sleep. Then I grab my terry cloth robe out of the closet. It's always been huge on me, so hopefully it'll fit him. When the shower turns off, I wait by the door.

"I've got it," I say, raising my voice.

"Hang on, let me put my watch back on," he replies, muffled.

A minute later, the door cracks open. I shove the robe in, averting my eyes. "Here, try this."

Dean's fingers, damp and warm, brush mine as he murmurs, "Thanks."

I lay down in bed, under the covers, and pick up my phone. The sight of it reminds of earlier today. How I found it face up. Had Eddie seen it and the stalker information on it? Probably not. If he had, he would have brought it up at the restaurant. Knowing him, he would have blackmailed me or would have immediately issued a "breaking news" edition of the paper with all the details.

None of that's happened, so I must be overly paranoid. Maybe I moved the phone and didn't realize it? Maybe it fell to the floor while I was getting coffee, and the waiter picked it up and put it back on the table? Still, should I mention the possibility to Dean? Warn him?

That thought is quickly forgotten the minute Dean emerges. A look at him and I burst into laughter, so hard that fat tears roll down my cheeks.

"Hey," he protests, his ears bright red.

My robe comes to the top of his thick, muscular thighs. He holds it in place so it doesn't gape. He's even tied a bow into the cloth belt that goes around his waist.

"It's a little small," he says miserably.

"You think?" I'm still laughing, although softer now. I try to stifle the sound since I can tell he's embarrassed. It's just that he looks so funny.

"Come over here and get under the covers," I say.

Dean's eyes widen with horror. "Over there?" he asks slowly. "But…" his voice dropping to a whisper, like he's telling me a secret, "you're sleeping over there."

"Pftt," I say and wave my hand.

"It's fine. We can share the bed. I don't mind."

His eyes widen even more. Soon they'll swallow his whole face.

"What if *I* mind?"

I put my phone down on the nightstand and turn to fluff up my pillow before flopping back on it.

"Stop being such a baby. You're shivering again. Get in here."

He searches the room, giving serious consideration to the floor.

Now I'm mad. Is it really so bad to be in the same bed as me? *Sheesh*. You'd think I was poison ivy or something. Every time we take a step forward, we go back two. It's clear the blooming attraction I feel toward him only goes one way.

"Dean," I say, using my firm voice, the only tone that made my brothers stop and listen. "You're being ridiculous. Get in. I'll stay on my side, and you stay on yours. We're both adults here. I think I have enough self-control to keep my hands off you."

With that, he comes over, muttering, "Fine, but I'm keeping the robe on." The bed creaks when he climbs in, the white metal frame shaking. "This mattress is hard," he grumbles.

An awkward silence descends, and I'm fuming, wondering what exactly is so repulsive about me that this guy can't stand to be near me. It's another rejection. Another person who wants nothing to do with me. My brothers, Eddie, now Dean. I know I'm not perfect. Not a perfect friend. I don't have a perfect body. Still, I try to be a nice person, a good person. It doesn't matter. This is where I always end up.

In a thoroughly sour mood, I deliberately ignore him and scroll through my phone, checking my emails one last time.

The bed squeaks again as he makes himself comfortable. After a minute, he whispers a soft, "Jennifer."

"What?" I snap.

"You shouldn't use your phone. The battery will die, and we can't charge it."

"Really? That's what you wanted to tell me?" I glare over at him, anger surging through my veins.

"Well, yes," he says, all peevish, as if he has the right to be offended.

I don't bother answering, too busy imagining all the ways I'm going to murder him.

Another long silence, finally broken by a soft, "Jennifer?"

Hah. I'm not falling for that again. Whatever he has to say, I don't want to hear. I'm sick of feeling like this, like I'm not worth knowing, so I bark out a harsh, "Good night, Dean."

With more force than is necessary, I punch my pillow until it's in the shape I want. A puff of my breath to blow out the candle.

I turn away from him and fall asleep.

What was Dean going to say to Jenny before she told him good night? What was he thinking when he came out of the bathroom in that tiny robe? Read this chapter from Dean's point of view to find out! Click the link or scan the QR code below to join my newsletter and you'll receive an EXCLUSIVE bonus chapter from Dean's perspective that's only available for newsletter subscribers!

HTTPS://TINYURL.COM/DEANSWEETBONUS

20

**SATURDAY, DECEMBER 21
3 DAYS UNTIL THE WEDDING**

GWEN

"What do you mean, the flight's been canceled?" I ask the airline agent, my elbows propped on the counter.

"I'm so sorry, Dr. Wright, but a weather system on the East Coast is disrupting flight patterns. Don't worry, though. I've got you booked on the next plane out of here. You'll only be delayed by an hour."

Thank goodness.

I head back to the food court where Alvina and Wayne are eating lunch. "One-hour delay," I announce and sit across from them.

I'm tired, my eyelids heavy. Staying up every night to talk to Caleb has worn me out. I still haven't told him about my lecture or the mean girls at the airport. I haven't mentioned how I was in the restroom at the conference and overheard some female doctors talking about how hot he is. About how I don't deserve him. They'd gone silent, guiltily shifting their eyes when I came out to wash my hands. It weighs on me. I'm used to sharing everything with him. But what good would telling Caleb do, anyway? Besides make him feel guilty and potentially drive him away? I think about these things late at night. I toss and turn, worrying about the future.

Caleb.

My career.

Wondering how to balance it all.

"That's what they always say," Wayne offers, taking a large bite of his steak and bean burrito. He chews and washes it down with a slurp of coffee. "Right before all the flights get canceled."

His words strike terror in my heart. My voice pitches high, tight with anxiety. "They can't cancel. The wedding's in a few days."

"I'm sure it'll be fine," Alvina says. She jabs an elbow into Wayne's ribs.

He grunts, sending her a side-eye look, then adds a half-hearted, "Yeah, fine."

Sitting back, I assess the two of them, noting how they ignore each other and yet their legs are pressed against each other. I've given them this entire trip to tell me the truth. I thought that surely they would come to me and divulge their relationship. What did I get for my confidence in them? Nothing. Big fat nothing. They've lied to me, and it hurts.

I'm sick of waiting on them, so I look in their faces and calmly ask, "How long have you been dating each other?"

Wayne spits out his coffee across the table, choking. Some droplets land on my arm.

Gross.

An announcement overhead calls our names. Hastily, we gather our things. As we walk over, I tell them, "Don't think I've forgotten about the two of you. We *are* going to talk about this eventually."

Wayne takes a sudden interest in the tip of his shoes, refusing to look at me. He's chewing gum, probably that nicotine kind, so aggressively that I worry he'll break a tooth. Once we get to the gate, there's a long line of people waiting to speak with the agent. I want to grill Wayne and Alvina, but this doesn't seem like the place for it. Not with this many people around. After 20 minutes, we reach the front of the line.

"Your flight has been canceled," says the agent.

"I knew it," Wayne says, slamming his hand down on the counter, making us all jump.

Panic rises in me. "You don't understand," I tell her, my voice getting louder by the minute. "I have a wedding to get to. *My* wedding. I'm the bride." I want to crawl over the countertop and snatch that computer out of her hands so I can book a flight back to Caleb.

The agent keeps a wary eye on me. "I've taken the liberty of booking you on another plane to New York. It has a layover in Denver."

"What?" I wave the now-useless boarding pass in front of her. "That's the reason we picked this flight, because it's nonstop."

"Sorry, but this is your best bet to get home." She hands over new boarding passes. "It boards in 15 minutes in the terminal next door. You'll have to hurry."

I tug my backpack higher on my shoulders and tighten the strap on my fanny pack. *Darn it*, now they've got me calling it that. I mentally repeat, *waist bag, waist bag, waist bag.*

Then we're off running, shooting down escalators and past the travelers who calmly ride the moving sidewalk. We're not those people anymore. We are crazy people, desperate not to miss our flight. All I want is to see Caleb tonight.

We rush onto the small train that travels between terminals and collapse into its hard plastic chairs. It moves quickly, with drab concrete walls flashing by on either side. I have about five seconds to text Caleb and tell him of our change in plans. There's no time to wait for his response. The door slides open, and we hurry out. Then it's back up another escalator, down two hallways, and we finally reach our gate, where the last passenger has just entered the jet bridge, leaving the waiting area empty. Short of breath, we scan our tickets and board only to discover that most of the seats are taken. The flight attendant helps us each find a spot, but they're rows away from each other.

We're separated.

SATURDAY, DECEMBER 21
3 DAYS UNTIL THE WEDDING

— JENNY —

I wake to find brown eyes with hints of gold staring at me. I must have turned to face Dean sometime during the night. Our heads are at the same level, our gazes aligned. I look back, holding my breath because he's beautiful in the soft morning light filtered through the snow that still falls outside the window. There are tiny lines at the corners of his eyes and a freckle beneath his lower lip. His stubble has thickened, and there's a pillow crease in the skin of his left cheek, the one that hides that charming dimple.

I let out a small sigh. Coming fully awake, I prop myself up on an elbow, my eyebrows slashing together.

"Are you watching me sleep?" I accuse.

He rolls onto his back and stares at the ceiling. "No." The tips of his ears redden.

Liar.

I don't get him. I thought we had a moment at the cake tasting, and earlier he seemed disappointed when I kicked him out. I *know* he was feeling something in that dressing room when he pulled down my zipper. But last night, he didn't even want to be in the same bed as me, and now I wake up to this? Talk about mixed signals.

I lie back and rub my fists over my eyes. "This stinks."

"What?" He turns to me again, his cheek pressed to the white pillowcase.

Oops. Wasn't meaning to say that out loud. I scramble for a reasonable answer. "This," I say, dramatically flapping my hand at the window, which has frost in the corners, ice that clings to the glass and creates elaborate scroll-like patterns. "I had so many plans for this weekend. I was going to help with wedding preparations and then I wanted to do all the touristy winter New York stuff."

"What stuff?" One corner of his mouth lifts in amusement. His fingers twitch as if he wants to touch something, but he holds them steady.

"I don't know. Ice skating at Rockefeller Center. Um…" I trail off.

He bites back a smile. "Is that it? I'm going to be honest with you. That's pretty unimaginative."

I rack my brain for something more, something to keep him here. His mood must be rubbing off on me. I like this, lying in bed and talking with him.

"Oh! Window shopping on Fifth Avenue. I heard they have amazing displays."

"And…" he prompts.

"And…that's it." I'm sad I don't have more to contribute. "You tell me what's good for the holiday. This is your city, after all."

"Hmm," he says and scratches his chin. It sounds like sandpaper when his fingers rub over the stubble.

"The American Museum of Natural History is great. They make an entire Christmas tree out of origami. Outside the front doors, on either side, they have topiaries made of pine that look like dinosaurs. They're all lit up and hold wreaths in their hands." He smiles softly at the memory. "Then there's the music. The boys' choir at St. Thomas Church, the Philharmonic, Mariah Carey pouring out of every store and bodega." He closes his eyes and hums a tune off-key. It's familiar, but I can't quite place it.

"What's that?" I ask quietly, not wanting to break this spell. Dean's relaxed and talking to me like we're best friends. It's almost perfect.

"Handel's *Messiah*."

"It's beautiful."

The dimple makes its appearance, attached to his smile. "It's one of my favorites," he says shyly. "Then, of course, there's the Rockettes at Radio City Music Hall and *The Nutcracker* at the Lincoln Center. Traffic gets crazy when that's going on, even crazier than usual."

"That all sounds wonderful. Too bad I'll miss it. By the time the storm is over, all that stuff will have shut down."

"Not all of it. I'll take you. After the wedding. I'll show it to you."

I freeze. It hangs between us, talk of the future, of a day when we aren't snowbound together in this room. If someone had told me two weeks ago that Dean Maddox would be voluntarily offering to give me a tour of New York, I'd have laughed in their face.

He must hear it, too. His lips pull tight, and his expression shutters, cutting off the warmth in his gaze.

"Sorry," he mumbles.

What's he apologizing for? Giving me false hope that we might form a friendship? Maybe something more? It doesn't matter, anyway. As soon as the wedding's over, I'll be hitching an airplane straight back to California.

He sits up, with my robe still wrapped tightly around him. "Can you—can you turn around?" he asks out of a clenched jaw. "I want to get dressed. My clothing should be dry now."

I do as he asks, no peeking.

He clears his throat with a loud, "Done." He's put on his dress pants, but not the button-down shirt or suit jacket. He wears only a thin white V-neck undershirt, so translucent I can see whorls of inky tattoos on his chest through it. *Wow*. Who knew that was hiding under those crisp white button-downs? I look away, trying not to gape.

There's a clatter from the kitchenette. He asks, "You want peanut butter and jelly for breakfast?"

"Sure." I roll out of bed and make my way to the bathroom, ignoring the snicker I hear behind me.

"Nice PJs," Dean calls out, laughing, right before the door closes.

Jerk.

Guess we're back to this, acting out these roles, like we're frenemies. At least I know what to expect.

I think we'll be bored, but we aren't. We find a pack of cards in my suitcase and spend all morning playing them. Blackjack, hearts, crazy eights, go fish. We play it all. After lunch, I dig out a couple of romance books I brought for the plane trip here and back. I lay them on the bed, face up.

"Pick one," I tell Dean.

He takes a long time deliberating, then chooses a romantasy by Sarah J. Maas with a red cover. I'm impressed he wasn't intimidated by the thickness of the book. That thing is over 400 pages.

"Nice choice," I say, picking it up and flipping through the pages before handing it over. "Gwen and I read that together and we loved it, although the second in the series is my favorite."

We sit side by side in bed, our backs leaning against the headboard, and read in a companionable silence. I always dreamed of this. Reading next to a handsome man. In my imagination, he'd be hot, like Dean, but with glasses he'd push up his nose. When we finished each chapter, we'd kiss, nice and slow. Too bad that won't happen for me.

Dinner is by candlelight again. Chili warmed up on the stove. I have a bottle of red wine, a nice one I was going to give to Gwen the night before her wedding. I don't think she'd mind me using it tonight instead. Despite a surprisingly pleasant day, there's still a thrum of tension under my skin from being this close to Dean. It's taken strength to hide my attraction to him. To pretend I didn't notice the way he scratches his chest through his thin T-shirt when he reads or how he chews his lower lip thoughtfully before he selects a card during our games.

"Here," I say, handing him a plastic cup and pouring a generous amount of wine into it. I doubt he's stressed from having to spend the day with me, but I can't drink in front of him without sharing.

"Thanks." He takes a sip and then another.

We talk about small stuff—families, work, the gym, the upcoming wedding. "I've never seen anyone in love the way they are," Dean admits. "Caleb and Gwen. On the car ride to the airport, they held onto each other as though the world was going to fall apart if they let go."

"I know." I roll my shoulders and yawn. The wine's making me sleepy. "Relationship goals. I'm almost jealous of how affectionate they are."

He nods and gives me his dimpled smile. For a minute, I forget to breathe. The candlelight softens the normally hard angles of his face, giving him a youthful, carefree expression. It flickers, sending an undulating golden glow over his skin.

It's nice.

Seeing him here in my room, relaxed and content.

I stand to pour the last bit of wine into Dean's cup when the radiator goes off, making that sharp, pounding sound I heard the first day I checked in.

Two things happen at once.

One, Dean stands and leaps at me like he's protecting me from a drive-by shooter. He flies into me and knocks me to the floor. The bottle falls from my hand. Thankfully, it doesn't shatter, but wine spills out of it, staining the thin rug beneath us.

Two, as the knocking, rattling sound continues, Dean curls into a fetal position next to me, with his hands over his ears and his legs drawn up to his chest. I look him over, noting how tightly he's screwed up his mouth and squeezed his eyes shut. He rocks, muttering under his breath.

My heart pounds. It's scary, watching Dean spiral out of control. I stare at him—helpless. No clue what's going on besides the obvious, that he's in extreme distress. Frantic to end his pain, I wrap my arms around him, press my chest against his back, and hold him.

"It's okay," I whisper over and over. "You're safe. Everything's okay."

It seems like an eternity, but eventually he unfurls enough to look at me. There's panic in his gaze, wild and raw. He turns so that his upper body is beneath me. I'm pressed to his chest, where I can feel the rapid pounding of his heart and every ragged breath he takes.

I put a hand on each of his cheeks, forcing him to meet my eyes. "Dean, you're okay. It's okay." I repeat it, but he's trembling, his expression pure misery. It hurts me to look at him, to see him like this. I need to pull him out of it, bring him back from whatever dark place he's gone. I can only think of one thing to do.

I kiss him.

A good hard kiss, pressing my mouth to his unyielding lips. He locks up, tenses. Just when I'm about to move away and apologize profusely, he melts. His mouth falls open with a stuttering gasp, and his tongue meets mine. In a flash, he rolls us over so he's braced on one elbow above me. Wine soaks my sleeve with its cold wetness. I don't mind though, barely noticing it. I'm too distracted by the intense way he's kissing me, like he's holding nothing back.

Dean kisses the way characters kiss in books or movies. A kind of kiss I thought only existed in Hollywood, but here between the two of us, it expands into something even better. Something pure and powerful and demanding.

I wrap my arms around him and pull him closer. His lips move to my neck, where he gently scrapes his teeth over my jawline. I sigh with pleasure and turn my mouth to his. We stay like that, kissing on the floor for a few more minutes. Then Dean gives me a gentle kiss on my cheek. He says, "You know, there's a perfectly good bed right next to us."

I laugh, the sound breathless and happy. "Maybe we should move up there?"

"Definitely." He stands and holds his hand out to help me off the floor. We climb onto the hard mattress and settle against one another. I rest my head on his shoulder, my body pleasantly humming just from being close to him.

My brain isn't relaxed, though. It's busy replaying how groundbreaking those kisses were. I sigh and snuggle closer, when I realize that I haven't thought about my body all day. I haven't sucked in my stomach or adjusted my shirt like I usually would. He's seen me in my pajamas as well as in my tight-fitting jeans, and I haven't worried about it once. Somehow, lying here with Dean, feeling comfortable with myself, seems like the most natural thing in the world.

Don't get used to it, I remind myself.

There's an expiration date on my time in New York. No matter how wonderful this feels, it won't last.

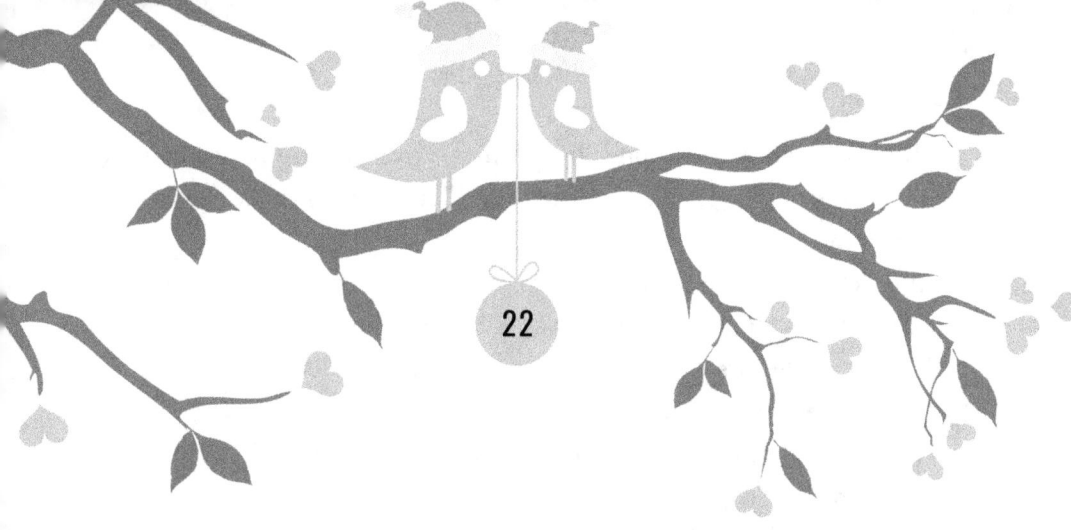

SATURDAY, DECEMBER 21
3 DAYS UNTIL THE WEDDING

— JENNY —

"What was that?" I ask Dean later, when I wake from a nap to find him propped on one elbow, staring down at me.

"I believe it's called sleep." He presses his cheek to mine, then tenderly kisses the soft spot right below my ear. The feeling of it almost makes me forget my question, which I think is what he's hoping, but I'm a reporter through and through. Asking questions is my job.

"No. Not my nap. What happened before. When you freaked out."

He sighs and rolls onto his back. "It's nothing."

"Didn't seem like nothing to me."

"I don't want to talk about it."

"Dean," I say, drawing out his name and meeting his gaze so he'll see that I won't back down.

There's a long pause. He opens his mouth, but no words escape.

"I can take whatever it is," I tell him. "I promise."

His eyes are shadowed, haunted, when he says, "What if you can't? What if it changes how you see me?"

That makes me pause, my mind spinning into overdrive. A million possibilities rise in my imagination, all of them terrible. What could scare a man as strong as Dean?

Then a thought, a bad one about why he won't open up, occurs to me. Hesitant, I tell him. "If you're worried that I'll tell someone else, I won't. You can trust me."

A quick shake of his head. "It's not that." He squeezes his eyes shut and I will myself to be patient. I don't want to badger him.

"I was…" He passes his hand over his face and rubs his eyes with his fists. "In the military for a while."

I sit up and cross my legs. "I remember that you mentioned it before. Where were you stationed?"

"Afghanistan." Another pause. Just when I think that's all I'm going to get from him, he says, "Sounds like that, loud ones, make me feel like I'm right back there."

I swallow and stare into space as I come up with my next questions. He'll shut down if I press too hard, I know that, but I need to understand what's happening. Seeing him so tortured was agony to me.

"But there's no war in Afghanistan."

His laugh is shockingly bitter. "No war? There's always war, even if reporters like *you* don't call it that."

Ouch.

He continues, "We were over there dying, just one by one rather than a thousand in a day, but no one cared about that. Who's going to cry over a couple of soldiers blown up by an IED someone forgot to defuse?" He snaps off that last part, as if he didn't mean to let it out, then clenches his jaw tight.

The silence following his outburst is deafening.

"Is that what happened?" I ask gently.

Tears well in his eyes. They gather and pool together until one breaks free to trickle down the side of his face. Dean nods mutely.

"Who?" I lower my voice to a hushed whisper, scared he'll close up and won't tell me. "Was it your squad?"

A terrifying thought occurs to me. "Were you hurt?" My eyes scan him, searching for wounds, and, sure enough, there it is. High on the side of his right arm, a gnarly scar, long, thick, and twisted, mars his beautiful skin. That's why I hadn't noticed it before. He always wears long sleeves.

He sees my gasp of horror and my hand cover my mouth. "It's nothing. Just a scratch," he tells me, dashing away his tears as if they offend him. "Nothing compared to the rest of my crew."

"That doesn't look like nothing," I say. I zero in on the last part of what he said, my reporter sense telling me this is the meat of his story.

"What happened to the rest of your crew?"

His tears have dried up. No emotion is left in him besides a simmering anger. "Dead. All of them."

I'm crying for these nameless strangers. I feel each of their passing like a blow to my chest.

"Who?" I breathe out, desperate for answers. "What happened?"

His throat works, but he doesn't make a sound. He keeps staring up, like he can avoid this conversation as long as he doesn't look at me. It's a pivotal point in our relationship. I can sense it. Either he lets me in now, or I'll be locked out forever. Dean's not a man to waver. He's decisive, driven, deliberate with every word and action.

I'd love to think that when we had kissed earlier it was because he was overcome by desire for me, but that's not true. I saw the calculation in his eye, the moment when he decided it was worth the risk. This is an even bigger chance I'm asking him to take, to let me into his memories, his mind.

He won't answer. He stays rigid and unblinking. I place my hand on his arm and squeeze. "You don't have to tell me if you don't want to or if you aren't ready, but I'm here to listen if you are. I want to know. To understand you better."

When he opens his mouth to speak, I almost weep with relief.

"Five years ago, I did two back-to-back tours in Afghanistan. It was my last week, *our* last week. We were about to head home for a break when it happened." His voice is toneless, with no change in his expression as he tells his story. "They sent us into the Kandahar Province to help train Afghan security forces. There were five of us. Me, Espinoza, McLaughlin, Gee, and Hoover."

He takes in a ragged breath. I commit those names to my memory, to be held forever. Those brave men and women who paid the ultimate sacrifice for my freedom. I imagine the people they left behind: mothers, fathers, spouses, children.

I try to stifle my tears. I can't lose it now. He hasn't even gotten to the bad part yet.

Dean drones on like he's talking about the weather. His robot face is back on, and who could blame him for it? For needing to put some distance between himself and something so horrendous. "They were supposed to have scouted our route beforehand, to get rid of mines and IEDs and assess for snipers. They told us the way was clear. We should be fine. An easy day, in and out." He swallows audibly.

"We never made it. The jeep drove over an IED about 45 minutes into the trip." His eyes lose focus, his voice dropping to a whisper. "I think about it all the time…all the time. I was at the wheel." My stomach sinks at those words and the guilt they carry. "If I had driven differently, would they still be alive? Would Gee have gotten home to see her baby? He was only two years old."

He's crying again, slow tears that roll down his cheeks, his nose. His eyes, wide with recollection, search for mine. When they find me, he holds me prisoner in that tortured gaze. "He won't remember her," Dean says, his face crumpling in on itself. "He won't remember his mom, who was like a mother to all of us. She was always scolding us, telling us to clean up after ourselves. We were a bunch of cocky, crude jerks, but she put up with us and now she's gone forever because I didn't move the car an inch to the left."

He holds up his left hand, displaying the large watch he constantly wears. The one he only took off when he showered earlier. "This was Espinoza's. His parents insisted I take it as a memento. After the funeral, they forced it on me. I couldn't believe they'd give it to me. Not after I got their only son killed."

I want him to stop. I can't take it—the pain in his voice, the anguish in his eyes—but he needs to get it out, to release this toxin before it kills him.

"It was so loud, Jenny. When the bomb went off. It was so loud. The metal of the jeep coming apart. The screams. So loud." A ragged sob from him. "Every time I hear a noise like that, I'm back there, watching them die all over again. Bright flashes of light set me off too, like the burst of white when the bomb detonated."

His eyes drift closed, tears leaking from under his lashes. "I have PTSD. I wish I didn't, but I can't stop it."

His confession doesn't surprise me, but still it's daunting to hear it said out loud.

I crawl to him and lay myself over his body like I can protect him from this pain, even though I can't. He stiffens beneath me, and I brace for yet another rejection, but his arms come up and wrap around my waist.

His voice is muffled, his lips pressed to my hair. "I told Caleb I'd be no good. What kind of bodyguard gets scared so easily? He wouldn't listen. He said it'd be fine."

"Shh," I soothe, knowing there are no words that will erase the horror he's witnessed. But still, I have to try. "I'm sorry, so sorry that happened to you. I'm sorry for your friends and their families." He shifts me in his arms so he can bury his head in the crook of my neck, shaking from the force of his tears.

"It's a terrible thing you went through, but I'm proud of you for telling me. I understand how hard that was." He nods against my collarbone, his tears slowing. "I don't know how you get over something like that."

A harsh laugh from him. "I've tried it all—therapy, pills."

I pull back to see his tear-stained face. "Did they help?"

A small shrug. "Some, but not enough." Dean reaches up and tucks my hair behind my shoulder. "This is why I wanted to stay away from you."

"What?" I roll off him and sit up, not understanding what this has to do with me.

"You're sunshine walking around on two legs, and I'm—I'm broken."

"You are *not*," I say, my voice echoing in the room. That's how loud I say it.

"Yes, I am," he argues. "I don't have a television at my place because I can't handle shows where there's shooting or scary noises or bright lights. I won't go to the movies for the same reason. Last week, a motorcycle backfired outside my building, and I barely made it inside before I had a panic attack."

I can't believe my ears. To think this is how he sees himself, something so at odds with the man before me. I tell him, "While working for a newspaper, I've heard some sad, awful stories. What you just told me, what you went through, I thought that was one of the worst, but I was wrong."

He jerks back at that, scowling, angry I'm downplaying his experience. I ignore him. What I have to say is too important to be distracted. "Of all the stories I've heard, the most awful is the one you're telling yourself. It's a lie. You are kind and brave and strong. A broken person only cares for themselves. That's not you. You always look out for others, even when you're not on the job. I don't want to hear any more of that. You need to open your eyes and see yourself how *I* see you."

"You see me like that?" he asks, so vulnerable.

"I do," I say firmly. More gently I add, "It's not your fault, what happened. Do you honestly believe that they would blame you? Your crew? That they would want *you* to blame yourself?"

"No," he says, his voice hoarse. He looks away, his throat working. "I understand that, but when the nightmares come or when I hear those loud noises, logic goes out the window. I try so hard to hold on to it. I tell myself the fear isn't real, but my body doesn't listen. My heart pounds and I can't breathe, and it feels so—so out of my control."

I don't know what to say to that. I wish I did, that there were magic words I could speak to make everything okay, but that's not real life. Some problems can't be fixed. Some hurts can never be fully healed. All I can do is hold him.

He kisses me, hesitantly, like he's not sure I'll want him anymore. I kiss him back, firmly, pouring my emotions into it, determined to prove he's worth my affection. Soon we're a tangle of lips and soft sighs. Sometimes, when you live with the shadows of the dead, you need to be reminded you're alive. I distract him from his grief with every breathless kiss. I'll heal him too, as much as I can, with talking and support, but there's time for that later. For now, there's just us and the snow outside, falling gracefully to the ground.

23

SATURDAY, DECEMBER 21
3 DAYS UNTIL THE WEDDING

— GWEN —

We're stranded in Denver.

We arrived to find gate agents waiting for us. They had clipboards and guarded expressions. "We're sorry to inform you that your connecting flight has been grounded. All flights into New York are canceled. The National Weather Service has placed the city under a winter storm warning. They're expecting blizzard conditions over the next few days."

"No!" I don't realize I've said it out loud until all eyes shift to me.

"We apologize." The agent's gaze darts to the group behind us. She'll have to repeat this same spiel to them. "We have a shuttle waiting to take you to a hotel, compliments of the airline. I have a $20 food voucher for each of you." She hands me a slip of paper, which I shove blindly into my pocket. Words are exchanged between her and Alvina, but I don't hear them. I've tuned out of the conversation.

I try calling Caleb, but it goes to voicemail.

Soon, Alvina has a hand on my elbow. She propels me through the terminal and onto the cramped shuttle, full of downtrodden travelers just like us. It's silent on the ride to the hotel. Everyone's words were used up arguing back at the airport.

Denver has snow too—not blizzard conditions, but flurries that slap against the windows and blow across the road. The driver steers through it with practiced movements, swerving around the tallest piles of snow that have accumulated between the lanes.

We check into our mid-level hotel and head up to our room. Generic beige walls and white bedspreads. Soap wrapped in waxy paper next to the sink. For an extra touch, the maids have folded the last piece of toilet paper into a triangle.

I hate it all.

I miss Caleb and my apartment and my bed.

In need of distraction from my woes, I ask, "What about you and Wayne? What's going on there?"

"It started a month ago," she says, then hesitates.

"Uh-huh. Go on."

"I was in the grocery store, getting conditioner, when I bumped into him. He saw the bottle and was all," she lowers her voice and broadens her chest, doing a comical and rather accurate impression of Wayne, "Is this why you smell so good—like coconuts?"

I halt her with a hand on her shoulder and say, "Caleb sniffs me all the time. He says I smell like strawberries from my shampoo. Is this a thing? Like all the men in the world are in a secret group chat, and they come up with these diabolical pickup lines about hair products?"

Her eyes widen at that. "I don't know, but it does make sense because it totally worked on me. Suddenly, I'm tossing my hair around, feeling flirty, thinking about how good I smell."

"That's what happened to me, too," I exclaim. "Then what?"

"I continue my shopping trip, and Wayne follows me. He says nice things and helps to reach items on the top shelves and pushes my cart without me asking."

"Wow," I say, totally serious. "That's some sexy stuff."

"I know, right?"

I nod, the movement slow and thoughtful. "Did you go home and propose to him that night? Because I would have."

She snorts a laugh. "No. We ended up going to dinner." Her features soften at the memory.

"And…" I wave my hand for her to continue.

"That meal turned into another and another. Then it was movies and day dates…and here we are."

"You like him?" I ask, a feeling of wonder lightening my sadness. I knew they were spending time together, but I wasn't sure if it was anything more. Seeing Alvina's face when she talks about Wayne, how her voice is laced with fondness, how a besotted smile lifts the corners of her mouth, I know this is more than just casual. She has that dreamy look of someone who's falling in love. I recognize that expression because I've seen it in the mirror ever since I met Caleb.

"I do," she admits. "He's different than I thought. He's caring, protective, nurturing. We have a lot of fun together. He makes me feel young. Like there's a world out there waiting for us to explore."

"Hey," I say, placing a hand on my hip, "does this new relationship of yours have anything to do with Wayne's sudden desire to stop smoking?"

She sniffs, clearly proud of herself. "I told him I didn't want to date a smoker. I saw too many of them in the ICU, hooked up to oxygen, gasping like fish out of water."

"Wow." I'm truly impressed. "He must love you to give it up."

"We haven't used that word yet. But we're talking about taking a trip together. One without *you*." She gives me a look, then runs her eyes over our hotel room with distaste. I know what she means. Threadbare carpet. Boring tan walls and dingy curtains. This definitely doesn't count as a romantic getaway. "Thought we might rent an RV, see the country. After your wedding, of course."

It's something I wouldn't have been able to picture before. City slickers Alvina and Wayne out on the open highway. However, a few years ago I wouldn't have pictured myself living in New York, engaged to a hot movie star.

That's the amazing thing about love. It opens you up to possibilities you could never imagine on your own.

I lean my chin on my hand. "I wondered about that fishing magazine Wayne was reading. It's for your trip, isn't it? To prepare?"

She nods shyly.

"Why didn't you tell me? I'm happy for you. Why hide it?" I can't keep the hurt from my voice. I've been left out. The unknowing third wheel on their bicycle.

She pinches the bridge of her nose. "At first, we thought it wouldn't mean anything, that it wouldn't last. You and Caleb might be stressed out if we broke it off. You'd feel like you had to pick sides. Later, I almost told you, but you've been so busy with work and the wedding. It never seemed like the right time."

Guilt makes her eyes skitter away from mine. "I'm sorry for how you found out."

"I get it," I say.

"You do?" She looks back at me, hopeful.

"I have a history of hiding my relationship too, you know."

She shakes her head in dismissal and says, "That was different."

"The part that bothers me the most, besides the lying and sneaking around, is that you thought I was too busy for you. It's been crazy the past couple of months, but I'll always make time for you. Whatever, whenever, I'm here for you. You're good at being there for others," I add, pinning her with a stare, "but not so great at accepting that same help."

"It's true," Alvina admits. She says, "You have the same problem. I see you struggle to adjust to Caleb's lifestyle. Does Caleb know what you're going through?"

I drop my chin. "No. I'm too used to relying on myself when things get tough. When my dad died and my mom and Brandon were always gone, I was drowning, but I didn't want Teddy to worry. He needed me to be his rock, his anchor, so I learned to push my bad feelings down. To handle everything on my own. I have no idea how to unlearn those habits. They're ingrained in me."

She pats my hand gently. "Now's the time to let that go. It really does take a village to adjust to being a wife and, someday, a mom. Ask us, Gwen. We all want to help you. Lean on us. Please don't do it all yourself."

I nod with understanding. It'll take practice to break down my walls of self-reliance, but she's right. I'll burn myself out if I do everything alone.

"I'll try," I tell her.

SATURDAY, DECEMBER 21
3 DAYS UNTIL THE WEDDING

—GWEN—

In the bathroom, with the door closed for privacy, I try Caleb one last time before going to bed. He picks up on the third ring, groggy, his voice more raspy than usual.

"Hey. Sorry to wake you," I whisper in a soft tone, feeling guilty for interrupting his sleep. He works hard, long hours.

"No. No," he says to reassure me. There's a rustling in the background, sheets and blankets being tossed aside. I assume he's sitting up. Maybe he's moved to the chair in the corner of the room. "I'm glad you did. I was waiting for you but must have fallen asleep. I see I missed your call. Sorry."

"It's fine. How are you?" I ask, my heart warming from the sound of his voice.

"Bad," he says, his tone flat.

Alarmed, I clutch the phone tighter. "Why?"

"The nightmares are back." So much anguish buried beneath those words.

I press my fingers to my temple, understanding immediately. "The drinking ones?"

"Are there any others?"

The defeat in his voice makes my heart clench. "Tell me about them," I say, like I always do.

"You already know." He's morose.

"Tell me again," I urge, surprised he's resisting. In the past he said talking to me about this helped. I've talked to him on the phone late at night when he would wake up half-sobbing.

A heavy sigh from him. "It's the same as before. I'm at a bar, not one I recognize. I drink and drink, but my glass is never empty. It tastes," here's where his words get ragged, "tastes *so* good. Like the best thing in the world. I'm thirsty. I keep going, getting more and more panicked because my mouth is so dry. I can't quench it…the thirst." Shallow breathing from Caleb echoes over the line.

"It's okay," I say gently. "Remember, the addiction specialist said this is normal. Lots of people in recovery have these dreams. That's your mind's and body's way of processing."

"It should be over by now." His words come out slowly, like he has to prod them from his mouth. "I haven't had alcohol in almost two years."

The doctor had told us the nightmares might never go away. Caleb knows that, but the crankiness in his tone tells me he doesn't want to hear it.

Abruptly, he changes the subject. "Your text says you're stuck in Denver? What happened? Last I heard you were just going to have a layover there."

I tell him about how the flights got canceled and how we were rerouted.

"That's just great," he says sarcastically. "You're gone. Dean's gone, trapped across town. Half the guests are stranded. I'm all alone. Everything is going wrong." He lets out an angry, short sigh, then says in a tightly controlled voice, "I *told* you to take the jet."

I close my eyes, stunned by the resentment in his tone. My anger flares to meet his. "What difference would that have made? All the airports in New York are closed. Even to your fancy-schmancy jet."

He doesn't like that. He spits back, "You could have gotten out before the storm hit instead of waiting at the airport for hours. Could be home right now if you hadn't been so dang stubborn."

"Wow, Caleb," I say sarcastically, "why don't you tell me how you really feel?"

He exhales sharply, muttering curses under his breath, too soft for me to make them out. I can hear his bare feet slapping the wood floors of his bedroom, and I know he's pacing. "I feel angry."

"Yeah, Captain Obvious." I'm pacing, too. I can only take four steps in the cramped bathroom before I have to turn around and go the other direction. "I got that already. Thanks."

"I feel like I've sacrificed a lot for you, and you don't appreciate it," he says. Bitterness resonates through the phone line and hits me like a punch to the gut.

My vision turns red at that. Memories of my lecture and how those girls treated me come flooding back.

"*You*? You've sacrificed? Really, tell me what you gave up."

"My movie career. I gave that up to be with you. To stay home with you."

I gape at the phone, totally thrown off by his answer. "What're you talking about? You said you wanted out of the film industry. That you were sick of it."

A frustrated groan from him. "I was, but now that I've had time away—I don't know—maybe I miss it. The producer I met for lunch, my old friend, he has a project that might be good for me."

"You want to do that kind of work again?" Emergency bells clang in the back of my mind. I see a future where Caleb's off making movies while I'm at home with 10 screaming babies. A future where I give up medicine, where I subjugate my needs to his.

It's a picture that terrifies me.

I sit on the closed toilet. The porcelain is cold and hard against my legs. "What about me? Where do I fit into these plans?"

"I don't know. I'm not even saying I'll take the job. It's just something that I would have considered before…"

My heart thuds painfully as I complete that sentence. "Before what? *Me*?" I inhale a shuddering breath and swallow down the tears that threaten.

"Forget I mentioned it," Caleb says, cutting me off. Heedless of my emotions, he pours out all his anger and frustration. "It's not just that. It's all the stress I'm under." I picture him tearing his hands through his hair. "I'm trying to keep everything together here. The wedding. Our families. The theater. The restaurants. All while you're off gallivanting around the country."

"Gallivanting!" I gasp, shocked he used that word. "Are you serious right now? *You* told me to go to this conference. You said it would be fine."

"I said to go away for a week. Not two."

His exaggeration makes me even more enraged. "I'll be home tomorrow!"

"No, you won't," he argues. "It's a blizzard here. I can't see out the window. Half the city has lost power. It'll take days to clean this up."

My stomach drops, sinking down into my feet. "Days? We don't have days."

"Why do you think I'm freaking out? Our families have flown in. My cousins came all the way from Ireland. They're here, and you're not. Do you understand what a disaster this is?"

"It's not my fault. I can't control the weather." I'm gripping the edge of the toilet lid, my knuckles white. I try to calm my racing heart, but my emotions are difficult to rein in. Maybe it's the stress of traveling or the impending wedding. This is all too much. I want to hang up on him. Go back to a time when this conversation never happened.

"This is pointless to argue about," I say, unable to admit he might be right about all of it. "I'll be at the airport in the morning and be home by nightfall." If I believe it with enough conviction, surely it will happen.

"You won't, but whatever." Bitterness leaks out of the phone.

I dig in my heels. I'll make that plane fly me home tomorrow even if I have to pilot it myself. Just to prove him wrong.

"I guess we'll see."

"Guess so," he says, sullen. "Listen, I have to be at the restaurant early to take a delivery. I've got to get some sleep."

"Fine. Well, good night then," I snap.

"Yeah, good night." There's a long pause where I hold my breath, waiting. Finally, more softly, he says, "I love you."

I relax my grip. We haven't gone a single evening without saying that to each other since we reunited. It's a talisman, those three little words. They weave a magic spell of protection over our relationship. Holds it together so we don't break apart, but tonight I'm not sure it's enough.

I tell him, "Love you, too."

It's not until after I've hung up that I realize neither of us said our usual "forever and always."

I lean against the bathroom wall and then slide down it until I'm sitting on the floor with my phone held loosely in my hand. I stare at nothing for several minutes.

Caleb and I rarely fight, never anything like the conversation we just had.

After a minute, I dial a number I memorized years ago. It rings for so long that I almost hang up, but finally Mom answers.

"Gwen?"

"Hey, did I wake you? Sorry, I know it's late on the East Coast." I rub my eyes, tired.

"No, honey, I'm up. I'm still on California time," she says, with concern in her voice. I rarely call past bedtime. "What's going on?"

I hesitate, deliberating. My mother and I don't have a perfect relationship, but at the end of the day, when I'm sad or scared, I want my mom. "I had a fight with Caleb."

"Oh no. I'm so sorry, honey. Can you tell me about it?"

Again, I pause. Complaining about Caleb feels like a betrayal, but the truth is, I'm struggling. Alvina said to lean on my support system, so that's what I'm going to do.

"He's upset that I'm stranded and not able to help with the wedding." I stand up. Sitting on the hard tiled floor is uncomfortable.

"I think everything's shaping up fine," Mom reassures me. "We got all the flowers and tuxes done."

"I know, but he's worried I won't make it home in time." I tuck the phone under my chin and wash my hands. They're sticky from the chocolate ice cream Alvina and I ordered for comfort food earlier tonight.

"If you're stuck at the airport, then so is everyone else. All of our families. This storm is affecting the entire country," she reminds me.

"What should we do? Reschedule it?" Panic stirs when I think how hard it would be to move the wedding date. We'd have to rebook all the vendors. Most of our guests are from out of town. How many of them would make a second trip?

"That's not necessary. If there's any chance of you making it, I say we keep everything as is."

I let out a sigh, glad she isn't urging me to change the date. "I'm still hoping we get in on time."

"Everyone understands the situation. Your guests are more flexible than you give them credit for—hang on a minute." There's the rustle of her speaking to someone and the sound of a door closing. "Seth's going to bed. I wanted to let him know I was talking to you. Was it just the wedding that's got Caleb upset?"

"No. He says he might want to do movies again." I move back to the toilet and sit down on its closed lid.

"Is that a bad thing?" she asks.

"It means he'll potentially spend months on location."

Time away from me.

"If you hold him back, he'll grow resentful," she warns.

"What about me? *I'm* growing resentful." I shift into the same position I was in earlier, with my feet on the toilet seat and my knees pulled up to my chin. Quickly, I fill her in on what happened with Skylar, Lola, and my presentation.

"None of that's Caleb's fault," Mom says. "He can't control how other people act."

"I know, but still it feels like there's so much I have to sacrifice to make this relationship work. Things Caleb has to give up too, like how I don't fit into the typical celebrity wife mold."

Mom surprises me by laughing. "Did you expect it to be different? *All relationships require sacrifice and compromise.* That's what happens when two people come together and agree to share their lives. There's no way they'll both want the same things at the same time."

"You and Dad weren't like that," I'm quick to point out. "I don't remember you ever arguing."

She laughs again, even louder. "Of course we fought, Gwen. We just did it at night after you kids were in bed."

My jaw drops.

"Your father was a wonderful man, but you romanticize him, honey. He was so smart that sometimes it made him overconfident, hard-headed. He was certain he knew the best path for our family. When I didn't agree, it could take hours of debate for him to see my point. The good thing was that, once I explained myself well enough, he took what I had to say into consideration. We both compromised a ton. Gave up what we wanted to keep the peace."

I can't picture my dad being that way. "Really? Like what?"

"So many things. I wanted to live in Chicago close to my family, but your dad said California was better for his job. He wanted to put you all in private school, but I thought public school was fine. He wanted to bike to work, and I was worried he'd get run over."

"How'd you figure it out? What you chose?"

"Sometimes I would get what I wanted, and sometimes he would. We stayed in California. You went to public schools, and he only biked on the weekends. That's the compromise part. It wasn't easy. Some arguments spanned years. Some were never resolved, and that's okay. It's the same way with Seth. The same for all couples, at least the ones I know."

Her words settle me down. "What you're saying is that no one ever wins? Someone's always giving in?"

"Basically," she says in a cheery voice. "It's so worth it though, Gwen. For all the times that you and Caleb disagree, there'll be far more when you see eye to eye. That's because you've picked wisely. You've selected a partner with similar values and goals. Together you'll build a family. When the years have passed and you look back at all you've accomplished, you won't remember the fights—you'll only think about your triumphs."

She takes in a breath. Emotion makes her voice waver. "At least that's how your father and I felt when we thought about you kids and the life we built. For all our bickering, at the end, before he died, he said the greatest thing he did was marry me and have all of you. I'm sure you'll feel the same way about Caleb."

Talking about Dad brings tears to my eyes. Those were the last words I had heard him say—that Mom and us kids were the best decisions he'd ever made.

Mom's right. When I look at my life, all the things I've done, my relationship with Caleb is what I'm most proud of, most passionate about. As much as I love medicine and will never leave it, the people in my life will always be my top priority.

"Thanks, Mom," I tell her, wiping away a few stray tears. "That was exactly what I needed to hear."

Caleb was correct. Flights are grounded the next day and the day after that. Every morning, the shuttle drives us to the airport. We watch with strained eyes as the time to board our flight lengthens, and the word "delayed" eventually turns to "canceled." Every night, the shuttle takes us back to the same hotel room so we can go to sleep and then get up and do it all over again.

At the airport, Christmas music plays in the speakers overhead. It's a pre-recorded loop. I've spent so many hours at the gate that I know which song is next. After *Little Drummer Boy*, it always goes to *Baby, It's Cold Outside*, the old Dean Martin version.

My nightly phone calls with Caleb grow progressively more strained.

We still end with "I love you," but I fear there will come a day when those words are too hard to push past our lips, when they are said out of duty rather than genuine emotion. The thought tears me apart.

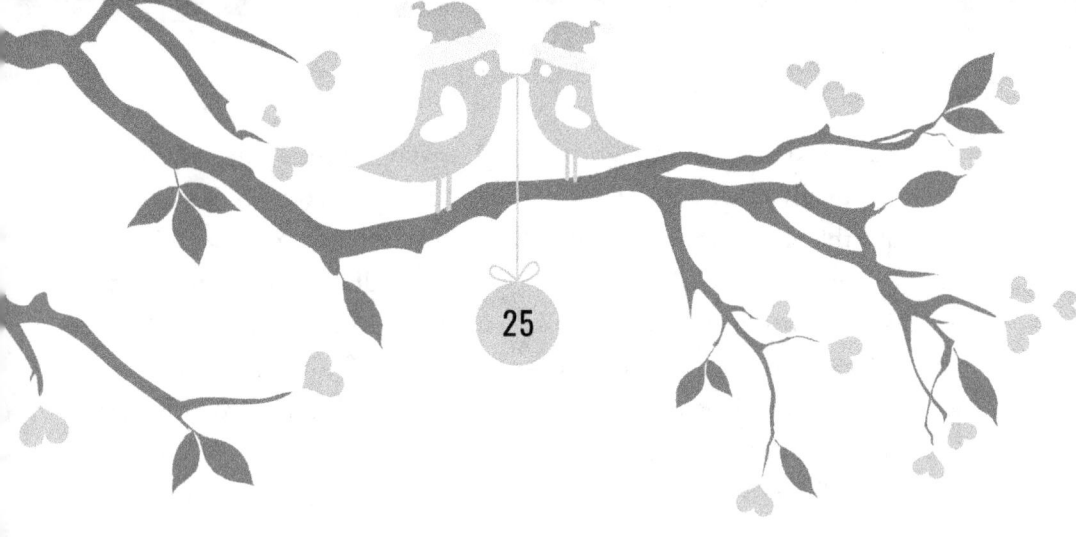

SUNDAY, DECEMBER 23
1 DAY UNTIL THE WEDDING

—JENNY—

"It's a man," Dean says excitedly, staring at the phone in his hands. I crack the hard candy, grape this time, between my teeth with a loud crunch. Dean doesn't respond to the sound, which makes me smile. He's grown familiar with my various noises over the past couple of days. I still can't believe it, can't believe I'm snowbound with Dean Maddox. It's been bliss, this time together. We've gotten to know each other better than ever before. If it weren't for Gwen's wedding, I wouldn't want the snow to ever melt.

"What man?" I swallow the candy and chase it with a sip of water.

We're sitting next to each other at the small table in my hotel room. A couple of dry pine needles have fallen onto the floor from my Charlie Brown Christmas tree. I remind myself to sweep them up later.

Dean holds out his phone to me. My cell phone died on the second day with no way to recharge it since the power's still out. He's been conserving his battery, only turning it on for 10 minutes in the morning and 10 at night. Mostly he uses it to check up on his family and on Caleb, who's in better shape than us. Caleb's also stuck in his apartment, but at least he's got power. Dean says Caleb sounds strained, though. Probably stressed about the wedding and Gwen being stranded in Denver.

Dean cackles, a triumphant sound I haven't heard from him before. "Dummy finally made a mistake."

I take the phone from his hand. It's open to the Secret Santa website, the recent photos tab. There's a picture of Caleb's building, taken from the spot we staked out before, where the photographer hides behind the trees. In this photo, Caleb has stuck his head out of the front door. He's looking around with an air of displeasure, his mouth turned down and his brows lowered, like the five feet of snow before him is a personal offense.

I'm confused by Dean's jubilant expression. "What? We already know Caleb's a man."

"Not Caleb," he says, "the stalker." He jabs at the screen, directing my attention to the left side. "He included his hand in the shot."

I bring the phone closer to my face and peer at it. Sure enough, in the bottom corner of the photo is a hand pressed against a tree trunk, like the photographer lost his balance as he took the picture and had to reach out so he didn't fall.

"You're right. That is a hand."

"A *man's* hand." Dean comes behind me and rests his chin on my shoulder so he can look at the phone too. "See? Hairy knuckles."

The pale hand braced against the tree is blocky, with short fingernails and hair across the back of it. I jerk my gaze up to Dean, my eyes widening as the implications of the photo hit me.

"This is great. We can eliminate 50 percent of the population." I think briefly about my computer program, the one I made to search for the stalker, but it still hasn't come up with any results. Apparently, my coding skills were too rusty.

I tap at the screen of Dean's phone.

"What are you doing?" he asks, watching with interest.

"Emailing Ron and Bradly, the reporters. I'm telling them to focus on men." I've kept in contact with my reporter friends. So far, they're just as clueless as Dean and I have been. I sign the email and hit send.

Dean places a whisper of a kiss in the crook of my neck. With a sigh, my eyelids flutter shut. I lean my head to the side to give him better access. My hand comes up to wrap around his head, pushing through his thick, soft hair.

He removes his lips from my skin. "Don't stop," I tell him, not opening my eyes. Strong arms slide under my legs and back, surprising me. I let out a yelp as he picks me up easily, as if I were light as a feather. Dean carries me over to the bed and tosses me high in the air. I land on the bedspread with a muffled thump, laughing.

"If you wanted to snuggle, you could have just said so."

"I always want to cuddle up with you," he says and grins, a fact he's proved repeatedly. We've spent hours holding each other, talking and kissing.

"You didn't that first night," pops out of me, so quickly that my hand flies up to cover my mouth, but it's too late.

Dean pauses and sits down next to me.

"Never mind," I tell him, mad at myself for bringing it up. "It's old news."

He frowns, quirking his mouth in a perplexed way. "What?"

I shake my head.

He sets his jaw and crosses his arms, an immovable force.

I fall back onto the pillow and stare up at the cracked paster ceiling, mentally scolding myself. "That first night. When you were wearing my too-small bathrobe. You didn't want to be in the same bed as me."

I sound insecure and pathetic. I hate it and yet I can't stop. These last few days have been like living in paradise. I keep waiting for the other shoe to drop. For the rejection to come. For him to see all my imperfections.

"I wasn't wearing anything under that robe," he says slowly, brow furrowed as if he's trying, and failing, to figure me out.

"I didn't mind," I say in a small voice, unable to look at him.

"I wanted to hide how much I like the idea of sleeping next to you." His baritone has deepened, tinged with embarrassment.

That gets my attention. I prop myself up on my elbows. "Oh?"

"You thought I didn't come to bed easily that night because I wasn't attracted to you?" he asks, like he can't understand the language I'm speaking.

I'm back to looking at anything that's not him, because he guessed correctly. That's exactly what I was thinking. It hadn't occurred to me that he could want me. With the exception of Gwen, no one wants me. At least not for long.

I turn my gaze to the window where the snow is lightening into occasional spats of flurries broken by periods of calm. The weather service on Dean's phone says the worst of the storm is over. We'll leave this room eventually. What will happen to us then? Most likely I'll go back to being Jenny, the best friend in Los Angeles, and he'll go back to being Dean, the bodyguard in New York. The idea of it sends me into a pit of despair.

"Jenny," he says in a commanding voice, one that forces me to look at him. "Is that what you thought?"

"Yes," I admit. "It never occurred to me you'd be interested in me. Why would it? We fought all the time and…" I gesture down at myself, as if that explains what I'm trying to say.

He's not touching me. He just sits and stares at me with a quizzical frown. "What are you talking about? I've been attracted to you for a long time. Years even. Do you remember when we first met?"

I scratch my forehead and think. It only takes a second because, of course, I haven't forgotten. "Gwen and Caleb had gotten back together. They were in their dating phase, when they would get dressed up in disguises and go out. I came here to New York to visit Gwen that summer."

I'd stumbled over my words the first time I saw Dean. One look at his stern yet handsome features and muscular body had me tongue-tied. I don't think I even said a proper "hello," just nodded mutely when we were introduced. He had his professional robot face on then, remote and icy.

"We all went to the Central Park Zoo to see the seals." I grow wistful as the memory takes hold. "They kept swimming right up to the edge of the tank. They would splash us. Gwen got soaked, and Caleb lent her his jacket." It all comes back to me vividly. The chemical smell of the seal's water, how sticky my wet shirt felt, the sun's warmth on my bare arms and legs.

"You wore a red dress with white polka dots," Dean says so quietly it barely registers.

Lost in the memory, I continue, "I recall thinking how nice that would be, to have someone take care of me like that. To choose *me* out of the millions of women in the world."

"What about the flowers? Do you remember those?" he asks in a way that tells me this is important.

"The petunias?"

"The flowers over by the water fountain," he prompts.

I pull up the image. A sun-faded ceramic planter as tall as my waist, full of flowers. Bright purples, red, and blue. Tiny, white-edged vines trailing over the side. How the blossoms bobbed when I touched them. Their fragrance, organic and earthy. The slick feeling of sap on my fingertips. It all comes back to me.

I sit up and glare at him, offended from reliving the day. "I smelled them, and you made fun of me. That was when I started to dislike you."

"You stuffed your nose so far into them that you got pollen all over it. Looked like you'd been sniffing yellow paint." Laughter bubbles up from his chest.

Just like he laughed at me back then. I'd been so embarrassed. I wanted to impress him, but instead I was caught making a mess like a toddler. Pollen all over my face, hands, and dress.

"You were rude. You made fun of me."

"*I* was rude?" His voice rises an octave. "I lent you my handkerchief, and you called me a grandpa."

My lower lip juts out. "It was a fabric handkerchief. Who even uses those anymore?"

"You asked me if I was wearing Depends, the adult underwear. I'm only 34!"

My mouth twitches. "You have to admit—that was kind of funny."

"It was funny. I thought *you* were funny and beautiful and smart. I watched you all day, skipping through that park like a kid with your skirt swishing and those long legs of yours. All that gorgeous skin. I had to remind myself constantly that I was supposed to keep track of Caleb, not you." He tilts his head, his gaze sharpening. "You still haven't remembered the flowers."

I squeeze my eyes shut and cast my mind back. "You mean after the pollen incident? You put a flower in my hair, behind my ear." I can picture that blossom now. Its delicate petals were peach with a faint blush of red at the base, exactly like the ones at the flower market.

"What did I say to you about that?" His hand gently cups my calf. I glance down, enjoying the way his pale fingers contrast against my skin. Dean drags his thumb over me. His touch distracts me.

Think, I tell myself. *Think*.

After a minute, it comes to me. "You said something about how women in Hawaii put the flower over one ear if they're taken and the other if they're single, but you never told me which ear was which."

He smiles, pleased I got it right. "A flower behind the right ear means the woman is available. Behind the left ear means they're dating, engaged, or married. I spent a year stationed on Oahu after boot camp."

"You tucked the flower behind my ear." I lift my hand, mimicking what he did that day. My heart had stuttered when he brushed back my hair and stuck the blossom in. I didn't know it then, but it was the closest I would get to him for years.

"Which ear?"

I can almost feel it, that phantom bloom, and how his breath had ghosted over my face.

"Which ear did I place the flower behind?" Dean breathes out, his eyes locked on mine.

I gasp when I realize it's my left hand I'm holding to my ear.

He nods and says, "It was your left side. I claimed you back then, even though I had no right." His eyes drop to my leg, where his fingers are so long they can wrap around my ankle and still overlap.

"As for the rest, I already told you. After that day, I knew you were a weakness I couldn't afford, more for your sake than mine. I found reasons to be mad at you, to keep us apart."

I'm stunned, my heart at his feet. Any reservations I have melt away by that story of long-ago Dean pining after long-ago me.

"I wanted you then, Jenny. I want you now." There are flames in his eyes, the steady glow of a bonfire at night.

"You said my name. Jenny. You've been saying it the past few days." I twist my fingers together in my lap, overcome by all the confessions from this last hour, but even more overcome by the idea that someone might want me. Choose me just as I am.

"Did I?" His smile solidifies, becomes brighter.

"Yes. The first time was when we…um…" I'm awkward, cheeks flushing at the memory of our first kiss.

"We what?" he teases.

"You know," I can't look at him. If I see that dimple, I'll lose it.

"Kissed?" A husky chuckle.

I nod, blushing furiously.

"Jenny's not what I want to call you."

My head swings his way. It's been such a blissful couple of days. I swear if he says something aggravating right now… With trepidation, I ask, "What do you want to call me?"

"Mine," Dean says.

"I want to call you mine."

26

TUESDAY, DECEMBER 24
WEDDING DAY

— GWEN —

On the morning of my wedding day, Christmas Eve, we finally get the go-ahead to board. Cheers erupt from the travelers at Gate 14. They clap, high-five, and hug like their favorite team just won the Super Bowl. Even the gate agents and flight attendants are grinning as they scan our boarding passes and welcome us onto the plane.

I made it. About to take off. I text Caleb and our mothers. I won't arrive until 2:00 p.m. Our wedding starts at 6:00 p.m. There's barely enough time to get home, have my hair and make-up done, and drive to the ceremony.

I'm returning to my fiancé, to my wedding, but I have no idea what reception I'll receive.

Will Caleb be happy to see me?

I'm restless during the flight, only sleeping fitfully. I chew on my nails, worrying about everything.

Caleb. The wedding.

The descent is turbulent. Wind buffets the plane. It dips and bounces, which makes me nauseous to the point where I'm clutching my stomach. Wayne gives me a worried side-eye and slides an air-sickness bag my way.

A bumpy landing jostles my already full bladder. "Hey," I tell my friends as we walk off the plane. "I need to stop by the bathroom."

"There's one over there," Alvina says, pointing. "You go, and I'll help Wayne with the bags."

I don't take long. When I come back out, a handsome young man is waiting for me. "Dr. Wright?"

"Yes, that's me." I pull my phone out of my waist bag and turn it on. It pings repeatedly, alerts notifying me that I've missed a bunch of text messages.

"Your friends have your luggage." The man smiles, showing off straight, overly white teeth. "They asked me to take you to them."

I'm distracted, scrolling through my texts. One is from Caleb, saying, *Okay, sounds good.* My head down, I follow the man. We walk through a door and into a dim room. I've just looked up when something cold and wet is placed over my mouth and nose. I have a second to register that it smells awful before the world goes dark.

27

TUESDAY, DECEMBER 24
WEDDING DAY

—JENNY—

"I can't be yours," I answer Dean, my heart clenching at that unpleasant truth.

"Why not?" His dark brow quirks downward.

"I'm leaving. After the wedding, I'll go back to L.A. I'll move on to the next assignment."

Move on from you.

I don't say it, but it's implied.

His hands twitch. A frown settles so deeply into the lines of his face that it looks like it's permanently etched there.

Guilt weighs me down, an empty hollow feeling. I've hurt him. It's in the squint of his eyes. In the twist of his lips.

"I'm sorry," I say, rushing to fill the awkward silence, my heart aching. "I thought you understood. This is only temporary. That's all it can be. I'm leaving, and you're staying."

This is for the best. Say it before he does. Leave him before, days or months from now, he leaves me.

His face smooths into the blank expression I know so well.

"Of course," he says mechanically. "I knew that." A brittle laugh. "I got carried away for a minute. Sorry."

I fumble, lost. That ache expands until it's a swirling black hole I could drown in.

What am I doing?

I open my mouth to apologize, to beg for forgiveness, to say I made a mistake and this isn't what I want.

The phone rings so jarringly loud that we both jump.

When he answers, Dean turns his back to me, and it feels symbolic of what's happening between us. He's done with me. Cutting me out of his life. *But that was inevitable, right? This was always where we would end up?*

It's Caleb on the phone. They talk for a few minutes, Dean speaking so quietly that I only catch half of what he says. He hangs up and stands there, not facing me. I stare at the rise and fall of his shoulders as he breathes like it's Morse code. A pattern to tell me what he's thinking.

Finally, after a deep exhale, he turns to me. Devoid of emotion, he tells me, "The electricity is back on. The snow has melted. Gwen's on an airplane heading home, much to Caleb's relief. She's going to land and then go to the penthouse to get dressed for the wedding."

"Oh, that's—that's great," I stutter, caught between despair for myself and happiness for my best friend. Today is Gwen's wedding. I should put my issues aside and focus on her. She doesn't need a teary bridesmaid ruining her special day.

"I'm going to Caleb's now." He brushes past me, careful to not make contact, on his way to get his shoes. They sit beside the door, neatly lined up next to my boots like they're best friends. The sight breaks my heart.

"I'll go with you, so I can get ready with Gwen." I say, not wanting to stand in the leftover snow and hail a taxi. I need to reach Gwen. Help her out.

A flicker of anguish darkens his face, quickly extinguished. "Fine. Let's go."

We're quiet as we gather our things, each lost in our own thoughts.

The snowplows have been busy. It doesn't take long before we arrive at Caleb's penthouse. The elevator whisks us to the top floor, and we walk in to see Caleb pacing in the living room. He looks awful, hollow-eyed and tight-jawed. His hair is messy, and not in his usual tousled movie star way. This is more like he's run his hands through it a hundred times.

What's going on?

He's supposed to marry my best friend today, but he radiates more stress than excitement.

I open my mouth to say "hello." The word doesn't make it past my lips before Caleb asks, "Jenny, can you explain this?" He holds up a newspaper, the *Los Angeles Times*. There, on the front page, is an article, "Will Stalker Ruin Caleb Lawson's Wedding?" Under the title are photos of the Secret Santa website. My stomach clenches when I read the name of the author, Eddie Rulanski.

My ex. My boss.

Caleb shakes the paper open and reads out loud. "According to sources close to the couple…" He stops and gives me a sharp-eyed glare before continuing. "Lawson has been stalked for years by the alleged 'Secret Santa,' who tracks his every movement. This reporter has discovered a list of over 800 suspects, including the bride-to-be's friends and family. Could it be that Lawson doesn't trust his own fiancée?"

"What!" I exclaim. "Gwen's not the stalker!"

"Of course not," Caleb spits out. He reads, "Will there be an unhinged wedding crasher when the couple gets married on Christmas Eve?" He angrily throws the paper onto the coffee table. "It goes on to give the exact time and location of the ceremony."

"Oh, no." My hands cover my gaping mouth. This is the worst thing that could happen. We've all worked hard to keep it a secret, but now the whole world knows when and where the wedding will be. My heart hurts to see how upset Caleb is, but it absolutely shatters when I see the betrayed expression on Dean's face.

Caleb crosses his arms over his chest, his gaze fixed on me. "I don't understand. How could this have happened?"

I hold my hands up. "I—I can explain. I had lunch with Eddie, and I think he may have seen something on my phone—"

"You think?" interrupts Caleb, his voice rising.

Dean rubs his forehead, muttering, "We're going to have to up security at the wedding. I'll need to coordinate with the police." Flat brown eyes narrow at me. "We told you to keep this a secret. You promised."

"I kept my word. I swear! I didn't tell Eddie anything."

Dean doesn't respond. He looks at me like he's never seen me before. The man who kissed me so fervently this morning has vanished. It makes sense. Of course, he'll side with Caleb, who he's known for years, who he respects. He would never choose me, the person who rejected him, who he used to hate.

Shame burns from my chest to my cheeks. I want to curl up into a ball. To fade away. Anything to escape from the judgment I see in their expressions. It's too much. To lose *both* Dean and Caleb on the same day.

"You must have said something to Eddie," Caleb insists. "He wouldn't have just randomly looked at your phone."

"You don't know Eddie." I let out a humorless laugh.

"We'll have to figure this out later." Caleb rips his hand through his hair and squeezes his eyes shut. "Gwen's going to land soon. Our families and I are going to surprise her at the airport. The twins made Welcome Home signs and everything. I want Gwen to know how happy we are that she's home." There's something fragile about how he adds, "*I'll* be so happy she's home."

Caleb opens his eyes and looks my way. "I was going to ask you to join us, Jenny, but maybe that's not the best idea right now…"

This is it.

I've broken his trust, Gwen's and Dean's as well, too many times. I've been a poor guardian of their secrets, of their privacy, and this is what I deserve.

To be left behind yet again.

My head drops, and my gaze falls to the floor. I feel small and useless. Sadness swells, rising up so big I can't even cry. I just stand there, dry-eyed, with my heart so heavy I wonder how it's still beating.

"I believe her," Dean says, his voice breaking through my cloud of misery. I snap my eyes up to see he's addressing Caleb, not me. "If Jenny says this article isn't her fault, that the information was stolen from her, then I believe her."

Caleb still looks doubtful. "I don't know…"

"Come on," argues Dean. "Jenny loves Gwen. She's known her far longer than you have, Caleb. Do you really think she'd do anything to hurt her best friend?"

Shifting his weight, Caleb turns to me. "Not on purpose, but—"

"No buts." Dean steps closer, the heat of his body radiating through my clothing. It warms me. "Jenny's family to Gwen—and to you, Caleb. She put her career on the line for you. She could have had her dream job if she sold you out, but she hasn't. Every day she's proven she can be trusted."

Butterflies that had their wings broken years ago flutter to life at Dean's words. They rise and take flight, straightening my spine, filling me with a sense of belonging and confidence I thought was lost forever.

She can be trusted.

I'm trustworthy.

I'm worthy.

My chest swells with gratitude and something I'm not ready to name as I sway toward Dean, wanting to express my thanks, but he pulls back, subtly angling his body away from me. It hurts, knowing he defended me out of a sense of justice rather than affection.

Caleb opens his mouth to argue, but his phone on the table rings, interrupting him. He stalks over and answers it with a barked, "Hello?" He cocks his head, listening. His expression changes from anger to disbelief to terror.

He asks, "What do you mean, Gwen's missing?"

28

TUESDAY, DECEMBER 24
WEDDING DAY

— GWEN —

I can't figure out why my limbs feel so heavy, why they won't move. My eyelids are heavy too. It takes me forever to drag them open. When I do, I find I'm in semidarkness, surrounded by suitcases and bags stacked so high they make a wall around me, like a fortress made of luggage.

My arms are tied behind my back. The bindings are tight, with nylon rope that digs into my skin. My feet are spread and tied to the legs of the cold metal chair I sit in. I blink once, twice, and slip into unconsciousness.

29

TUESDAY, DECEMBER 24
WEDDING DAY

—JENNY—

Dean drives the Aston Martin to the airport, breaking the speed limit and swerving around corners. Caleb takes the passenger seat, and I'm in the back like a child. There's a tense silence between the three of us.

I'm fuming. Mad at myself. If I hadn't made the mistake I did years ago, when I leaked Caleb's location, when he was hiding out in California with Gwen, then none of this would have happened. Caleb would have taken my side, not Eddie's. But I messed up back then, and that one error is going to haunt me forever.

It's not fair.

I've tried to make amends. I've worked on myself. More responsible now, I think before I speak. Maybe it's hopeless, though. Once I've been branded as an irresponsible gossip, that label is irrevocable. It'll stick to me, like a sale sticker adhered to the cover of my favorite book. I sigh, depressed by the thought of it.

My phone dings. An alert I set up weeks ago sounds off, buzzing loudly. I peer at the screen, my thumb rapidly scrolling through data from the computer program I coded. By the end, my hand's shaking.

Quickly, I fire off an email to my reporter friend, Wes. I know he has inside contacts at the police department. I label the subject: *SOS ASAP*.

A wild-eyed Alvina meets us at the airport, with Gwen's family right behind her. They're all present—Gwen's mom, stepdad, two brothers, and twin nieces. Even her tiny chihuahua, Pip, is there on a leash held by Megan, the smaller of the twins. Caleb's mom and dad are there, too.

"Gwen's gone," Alvina tells us, her voice tight with panic. "Wayne's out looking for her. She went to the bathroom down by baggage claim and never came back. Airport security is checking the camera footage. The police are on their way." I'm so frightened by her words that I feel lightheaded.

Airport security shuffles us all into a large private conference room, one they use for departmental meetings and debriefings. The walls are frosted glass and there's a long oval table in the middle of the room surrounded by black office chairs with armrests and sliding caster wheels. The twins sit at one end of the table coloring on construction paper someone scrounged up. At the other end blueprints of the airport are spread out. Caleb, Dean, the police, and airport security pore over them. Hours pass as they use walkie talkies to cross check locations with search parties who roam the airport's terminals and back corridors.

By my own choice, I sit on one of the chairs in the middle of the table. Not part of the family group at one end or part of the investigative team at the other. I'm in literal No Man's Land. Hopelessness is setting in when my phone buzzes loudly. It's an alert I set up weeks ago. I peer down at the screen, rapidly sorting through data from the computer program I coded. Then I switch over to my social media accounts, double checking that my suspicions are correct. By the end of my scrolling, my hand's shaking. I fire off a text to my reporter friend Wes, subject line SOS ASAP. I know he has inside contacts at the NYPD. He responds within minutes and gives me the information I was dreading. This changes everything. I have to tell Dean and Caleb, but I can't afford to make another mistake, not with Caleb still doubting me.

"I figured out who runs the Secret Santa website and who's been taking pictures outside Caleb's apartment."

He squints down at me. "What're you talking about?"

"Do you understand how social media works?"

He gives a small shake of his head. "Excuse me?"

"TikTok. Facebook. Instagram. All of them. They know where you are using your location settings."

"What?" His brow puckers with confusion.

Frustration rises in me. I'm not explaining this well. "Think about it, Dean. When a 13-year-old girl in Alabama posts something, it wouldn't make any sense to show it to some middle-aged guy in Japan. Social media is too smart for that. Instead, first the post is shown to followers geographically close to the girl. Subscribers with demographics similar to hers. The post spreads out in a ring around her. If it gets engagement, that ring widens and it's sent to more and more people, until eventually it might go viral and spread across the world."

"Jenny," Dean says softly, as if he's concerned for my sanity. "What does this have to do with Gwen?"

"Everything!" I shout, and he flinches. I grab his upper arm, lowering my voice. "Social media posts are geotagged. Each one of them. Sometimes it's obvious, like in the corner it'll say where it's from, but often it's embedded in the code."

Swallowing, I will myself to meet his eyes. "I made a computer program to decipher the social media geotags of all Caleb's known contacts, the ones from that list you gave me. I had it crossmatch their locations with Caleb's over the past couple of years. It was a lot of data to filter through, so it took a long time. Honestly, I didn't think it was going to work, but just now it came up with results."

"Dean," I say, squeezing his bicep, hard enough to hurt. "I know who the stalker is."

Dean asks urgently, "Who? Who is he?"

My stomach churns from the information I'm about to reveal. "It's not a *he*. It's a *they*."

"They?" His voice rises with the question.

"That's the reason we couldn't figure out who was behind everything. The pictures. The website. It's not just one person."

Dread settles deep in my bones. "There's two of them."

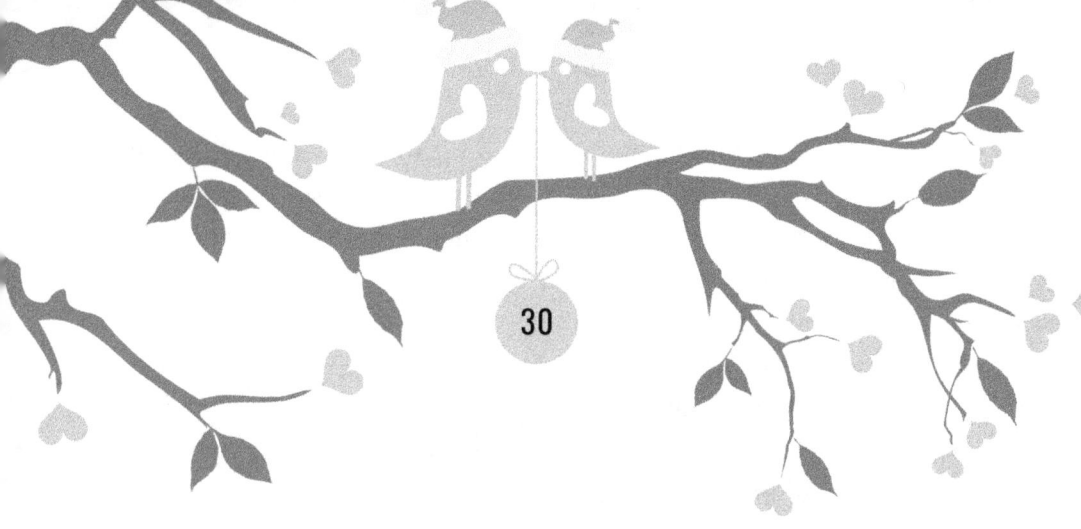

30

TUESDAY, DECEMBER 24
WEDDING DAY

—GWEN—

t was all a bad dream. That's what I tell myself the next time I wake up. I keep my eyes pressed tightly closed, desperately wishing I'll open them to find Caleb before me. When I finally pry my eyelids apart, my spirits plummet.

The nightmare is real.

I'm tied to a chair in what looks like a storage area. The gray concrete floors beneath me are cracked and uneven. The ceiling soars high above my head, metal rafters with sporadic industrial lighting. Mounds of luggage are all around me. They're piled on top of one another, creating a wall of black and gray with the occasional burst of color from a floral duffle bag or a maroon suitcase. Dust coats the canvas and hard-shell sides of the bags in the lowest portions of the stack. They've been here a long time, the luggage in this room. Forgotten things, lost and abandoned.

Have I joined them? Never to be found again?

My hands and feet have gone numb. My neck aches. It must have hung forward when I was unconscious.

I'm not alone. A man separates from the shadows and steps in front of me. It's *him*.

The guy who promised to reunite me with my friends.

Lies.

This man has knocked me out and tied me to this uncomfortable chair. The scary thing is that he seems so normal. He's better-looking than most men, with dark blond hair, sharp cheekbones, and full lips. There's something familiar about him. It takes me a few minutes to figure it out. When I do, a pit forms in my stomach. He's weirdly similar to Caleb, like a poor man's version of my fiancé.

"What's happening? Who are you?" My words come out slurred. The effects of whatever drug he pressed to my mouth, chloroform maybe, linger in my system. I blink my eyes, trying to clear the blur from them. My head is pounding.

"Quiet!" he commands, his face twisting with anger. "You don't get to speak. Not after the things you did."

"What?" I'm bewildered. "What are you talking about?"

"I think you know," he sneers. "How you and your boyfriend like to go around sabotaging other people's careers."

"I have no idea what you mean." I swallow with difficulty, my mouth parched. "Can I—can I get something to drink?"

He shakes his head, about to refuse, when a female voice, full of authority, speaks up from behind me. "Justin, get me a water."

The man transforms. His rage vanishes, replaced by a look of adoration. He moves off to the side. I hear him rummaging around. I crane my neck, trying to follow his movements and to see the woman who spoke, but they remain out of sight. The woman's voice was sultry and melodic—vaguely familiar—but I can't place it.

Justin.

I know that name. Where have I heard it before? Sometime recently. I rack my brain. Something to do with Caleb? The answer is there in my mind, wispy and ethereal—just out of reach.

High heels tap on the concrete floor, and she stands in front of me. If I weren't strapped to this chair, I surely would have fallen out of it.

Lola.

Lola Monroe, in the flesh, stands before me. She's dressed in red, like Santa, but a distorted, sexy version. Tight dress with white fur at the neck and hemline. A wide, black belt. Tall, spiked heels. Christmas ornament earrings, similar to the ones that I have, hang from her ears, swinging with the movement of her head.

I've never met her in person, but I remember all too well the time I caved to insecurity and Googled Caleb, when we first got together. I had scrolled through pages and pages of photos of them with their arms around each other. Back then, those images had made me feel physically sick. I have the same sensation now.

"Lola, what's going on?" Anger seeps into my voice. I tug my wrists and am rewarded by a sharp pain that shoots out to my fingers.

"You know my name," she says with an amused quirk of her lips. "But do you know all the things you've stolen from me?"

She's talking gibberish. I keep silent, staring at her stonily.

"Cat got your tongue, eh?" She comes closer and bends down until we're eye to eye. She inspects me as if I'm a bug she's about to squish with her stiletto heel.

"What is it about you?" she muses, her gaze traveling over me. "What does he see in you? For the life of me, I can't figure it out. You're a plain little thing. So mousey. Not worth his attention, or mine for that matter."

She stands and stares down her nose at me. A scowl carves lines in her forehead, marring her near-flawless skin. "I thought at first you were a rebound from me. It made sense to go from someone like *me* to someone like *you*. Men do that when they get hurt. They run to something different, totally opposite from what they had before. But now he's going to marry you, on Christmas Eve, of all days."

Her beautiful face contorts with anger, turning it into something ugly. "I could have forgiven the rest of it, how you took Caleb and my career, but you went too far when you put the wedding on Christmas Eve." She practically shrieks, "I won't let you ruin my favorite holiday. Christmas is *mine*!"

Her hands turn into fists, and I'm sure she'll lash out and hit me. She wants to do it so badly. I can sense it. Fear stirs low in my belly. I turn my head to the side, bracing myself. But she reels herself back in, slowly calming her panting breaths.

Once she's under control, she gives me a satisfied, red-lipped smirk and says, "No. No wedding for you. It's too late for that now."

I suck in my breath. My head swings around wildly, looking for a window or a clock, something to tell me the time.

Lola laughs, the sound light and airy. She waggles her finger in front of my face, taunting. "Oh no, little mouse. You've been out for hours. Your wedding has come and gone. It's past 7:00 p.m. Santa will be here soon, and all you'll get is a lump of coal, you naughty creature."

I want to believe she's lying, trying to upset me, but the way she says it, with so much glee, tells me it's true. I've missed my wedding. A sorrow I haven't felt since my dad died descends on me. My head drops, and silent tears fill my eyes, but I don't let them fall. An image of Caleb waiting for me at the end of the aisle fills my mind. The hurt and confusion on his face when I failed to show up is vivid in my imagination. It's agony to wonder what he must have thought. Things have been strained between us. Did he assume I abandoned him?

These dark thoughts lead to ones that are even worse. What is Lola planning? Is she going to ransom me? Kill me? I want to sink into despair, but I can't give up. I need to find a way out.

"I haven't taken anything from you. You broke up with Caleb." I'm proud the words come out strong, even though I'm quaking inside.

"That's true, but it was temporary." She looks at me with disgust. "He wasn't supposed to fall in love with *you*."

"How did you do it? How do you know where Caleb is? Do you have a tracker on him?" I ignore her rambling and ask the questions that have been on my mind since I first heard about the Secret Santa website.

Her laughter is chilling. "Caleb? Why would I do that when it's so much easier to monitor his bodyguard? They're always together, those two. Back when I was dating Caleb, it wasn't hard to put a tracker in Dean's watch when he was in the shower." She turns to Justin, who stands behind her, and takes a bottle of water out of his hands.

So that's how she did it.

It all makes sense now. I decide to keep Lola talking. If I stall long enough, Caleb will realize I'm missing. He'll send help.

"Everything you said proves I didn't steal him from you." I straighten my shoulders, pulling as tall as the ropes allow.

"You stole Caleb, and, even worse, you stole my career." She twists open the water bottle and pauses dramatically.

My eyes are glued to that drink. I'm so thirsty I almost beg for it, but that's what she wants.

"I might have miscalculated," she continues. She casually takes a long drink.

Hearing her swallow makes me want to cry.

"Since we broke up, I've gotten fewer callbacks, not as many roles. You know Hollywood, they always side with the man."

She screws the lid on the water bottle and hands it back to Justin. She smiles at him, slow and sensuous. He can't glance away from her. He stares at her with a rapt, cult-like look of worship.

I frown, confused. "You still love Caleb though, right? I've seen the website. You write 'naughty' on every photo where he's with another woman."

Lola lets out a tinkling laugh. "Love? Oh, no. Not me. That was all Justin with the 'naughty or nice' and the lipstick on the clothing. The only reason I wanted that website was to make money. Got to replace those lost wages."

"What?" My head swivels between the two of them.

Justin takes a step toward me. He snorts like he can't understand why I'm so dense. "I wasn't saying *Caleb* was naughty or nice. I meant the women he was with."

His face reddens with anger. "It made me *so* mad how they would fawn all over him when I'm standing right there. They're all so naughty! I'm better looking than Caleb, more talented. Why does he get all the attention? Those women should throw themselves at me." Using both thumbs, he points to himself.

Lola sidles up to him and breathes into his ear, saying, "Absolutely, Justin. You deserve it all."

Justin!

In a flash, it comes back to me. Caleb had mentioned that name as his understudy at the theater.

"Justin," I call out. His attention snaps to me. "What are you getting out of this?"

"Me?" He steps closer. A glint of light reflects off something tucked into the waistband of his pants. Terror turns my blood to ice when I see it's a gun, a small revolver.

"I get everything Caleb Freaking Lawson was too dumb to keep. I get his job." He wraps his arm around Lola's waist, the motion tentative. When Lola allows him to draw her close, his features turn into a smug smirk. "And I get his girl. He'll be so upset after losing you, he'll step down, and they'll all be mine."

"Lose me?" My gaze pivots between the two of them. "I would never leave Caleb."

"You'll have no choice." There's an unhinged satisfaction in the way Lola says it.

"You're going on a trip, Gwen." Lola turns to Justin and strokes a single red-tipped fingernail down his cheek. Justin purrs under her caress. "A trip you won't be coming back from."

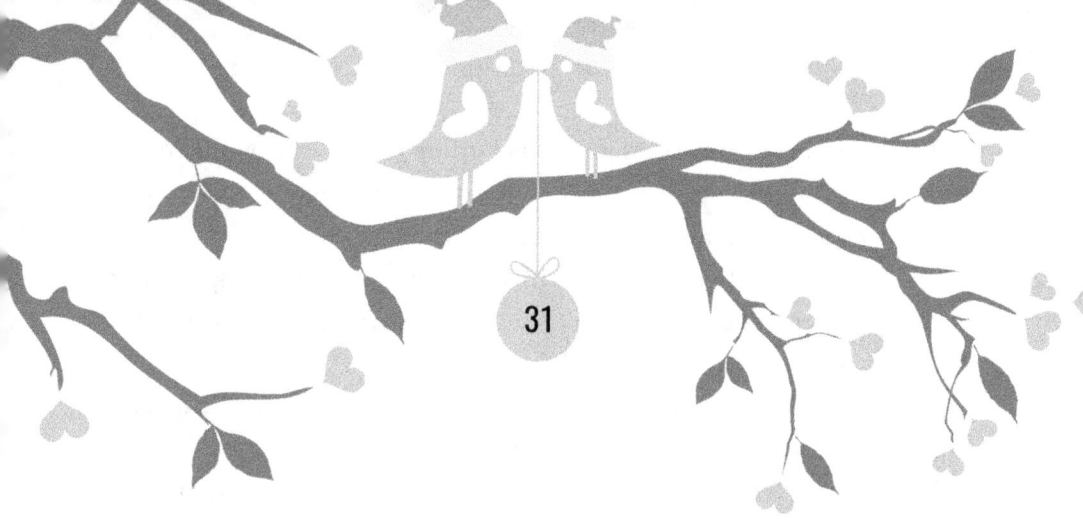

TUESDAY, DECEMBER 24
WEDDING DAY

— JENNY —

I hold my phone up to Dean. It's set on an Instagram post from a month ago.

He says, peering at the tiny screen, "That's Lola."

"I know. It's from Tokyo. She was there at the same time as Gwen and Caleb." I tell him. "Look at the background. See that man back there? In the shadows?" I scroll to a TikTok post from six months earlier and then to another from last week. "Here too. The same guy is behind Lola in each picture."

"Justin," says Dean, sounding stunned.

I nod. "*Both* Justin and Lola's social media posts correspond to Caleb's trips in and out of L.A., and these photos prove they're together. In this one, Justin has his hand around her waist."

Dean bows his head and scrubs his hands over his eyes. "We have to tell Caleb."

As we walk, I give my phone to Dean. "Read that email," I tell him. He pales when he sees what Wes has written.

Caleb's hair sticks up when we approach him. He's been running his hands through it again. Dean and I exchange a worry-filled glance.

"You know Justin Barnes?" I ask Caleb.

His eyes ping-pong between Dean and me, searching, "He's my understudy at the theater."

221

"Do you have any idea what job he had before he started working in your show?" I try to keep my tone calm, not wanting to frighten Caleb more than he already is, but internally I'm panicking. Based on the email from my reporter friend Wes, Lola's secret boyfriend Justin has an alarming criminal history that includes extortion and assault. Wes's investigation also touched on Justin's previous occupations.

"No." Caleb's mouth draws into a tight line. "He mentioned he hated it, wherever he worked, but that was it. Why?"

Dean takes over. "He was a baggage handler here, in this airport. He's been working with Lola—"

Shock drops Caleb's jaw. "Lola?"

"Lola and Justin. They're the ones who have been taking pictures of you and posting them to that Secret Santa website." Dean hangs his head. "I'm so sorry. I background-checked Justin, but he used an alias and I fell for it. This is all my fault."

A pang of sympathy for Dean. I can feel him take on this burden, the blame for Gwen's disappearance. He's adding it to his list of failures, along with the explosion that killed his friends. I want to comfort him. To tell him this had nothing to do with him, but there's no time.

Dean continues. "If something happened to Gwen at this airport, Lola and Justin must be behind it. It's too much of a coincidence."

"No." Desperation and fear tighten Caleb's voice. He looks from Dean to me. He pleads, "I can't lose Gwen. I just can't. She's everything to me."

"I know." My chin quivers. "I feel the same way. We have to find her—"

The color drains from his face. "If they hurt her—"

I finish my sentence. "Before it's too late."

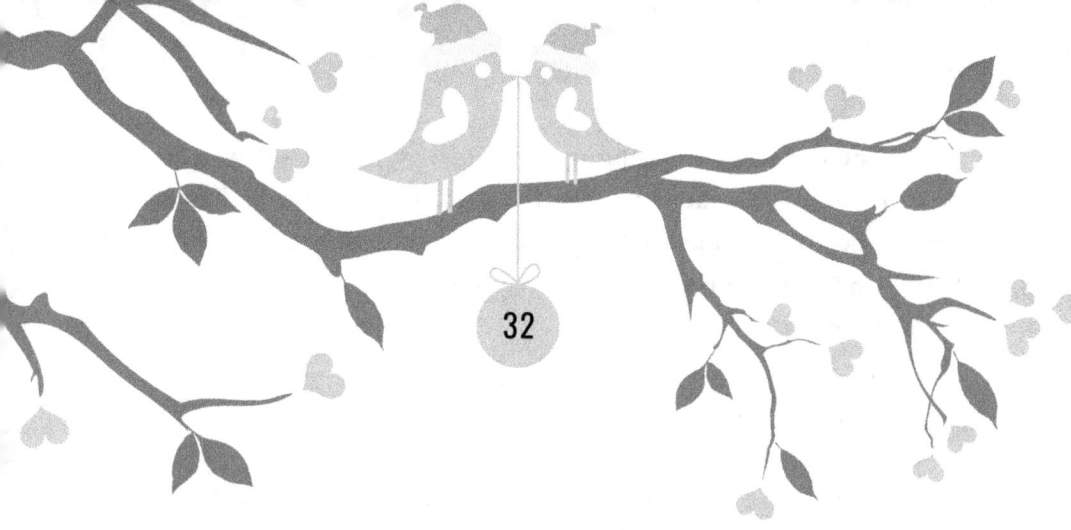

32

**TUESDAY, DECEMBER 24
WEDDING DAY**

—GWEN—

They put me in a box, steel with chipped yellow paint and broad metal cross beams. Some sort of storage container, about six feet tall by eight feet wide. Stacks of boxes are in with me, strapped to the side. There are gaps, small holes in the sides, enough that I won't suffocate. Earlier, I pressed my eye to one of the openings and watched Justin hop onto a forklift. Shifting gears so fast that his hands blurred, he expertly drove it over and lifted the container, jostling me in the process so that I fell over onto my side.

After I regained my balance and looked out the peephole, I saw that Justin had placed me onto a conveyor belt in a long line of containers identical to this one. I can't see where the belt leads, but I don't need to. Lola was more than happy to explain my fate in graphic detail. I'll be loaded into the belly of a large airplane. Not the kind used for carrying people, but the kind that carries cargo.

"The thing about those kinds of planes," Lola had said with a maniacal grin, "is that they have no oxygen or temperature control."

Meaning that once the plane gains enough altitude, I'll die from hypoxia or hypothermia. Whichever kills me first. Justin started up the conveyer belt. The engine running it is loud and rumbling. It slowly rolls me forward, sending me to my doom.

My mind races, sorting through possibilities. My hands sweep over my body. I wince when they pass over the welts on my wrists and ankles. I've been untied, but it does me no good. This box is locked from the outside. Finally, my fingers brush over a bulge at my waist.

My fanny pack!

I mean waist bag.

Ah, heck, I might as well admit it.

It's a fanny pack.

Lola and Justin must have overlooked it, since it's not a purse or a backpack. Elation turns to dust when I open it to find my cell phone missing. Of course, they wouldn't let me keep that.

In the dimness of my cage, I can only use the sensation of touch to search the remaining contents of the bag. My hands fumble over my dad's cufflinks, which I had put in for safekeeping, not wanting to part with them in case the airline lost my luggage. How I yearn for that time, less than 24 hours ago, when that was my biggest concern. Beautiful as they are, cufflinks won't help me now. I continue to ransack the fanny pack. I graze ChapStick, sunglasses, hand sanitizer, Kleenex, spare change, and keys.

Wait…

Sunglasses!

My hand closes around them. The smart sunglasses Caleb gave me. They look exactly like regular sunglasses, so there was no reason to take them away. With shaking hands, I get them out and slide them over my eyes. My vision goes from dim to pitch black once they're on. I won't be able to see Justin or Lola if they approach. I can only hope I'll hear if they come back.

In a soft whisper, I command, "Glasses, call Caleb."

My lower lip trembles when ringing sounds from the tiny speaker in the earpiece. I had worried that I was so deep in the storage area that I wouldn't get cell reception, but Caleb answers before the first chime is complete.

"Gwen? Gwen? Where are you?" I've never heard him so distressed.

"I'm not sure exactly." Quickly, I fill him in on everything that's happened and what I know about my location. Sadly, it's not much. The room I'm in is nondescript, probably one of many in an airport this large.

"I'll find you," Caleb says. "The police are here. Our families, too. We'll bring you back." He speaks with such confidence that for the first time during this entire ordeal I start crying.

"I love you. Forever and always," I say, sobbing, part of me convinced they won't get to me in time. If I'm going to die, I need him to understand how I feel. I want those to be my last words.

Caleb knows me too well. He hears my unspoken good-bye.

"Don't you give up," he replies, his voice stern. "Don't you dare give up. You're Gwen, the bravest person I've ever met."

I'm crying harder now, unable to stifle my sobs.

There's shouting from his end of the line. Rustling sounds follow, as if he's on the move. Caleb is breathing faster.

"You have the heart of a lion. I've heard it beating." Panting like he's running, he says, "Hang on. I love you. I'm coming for you."

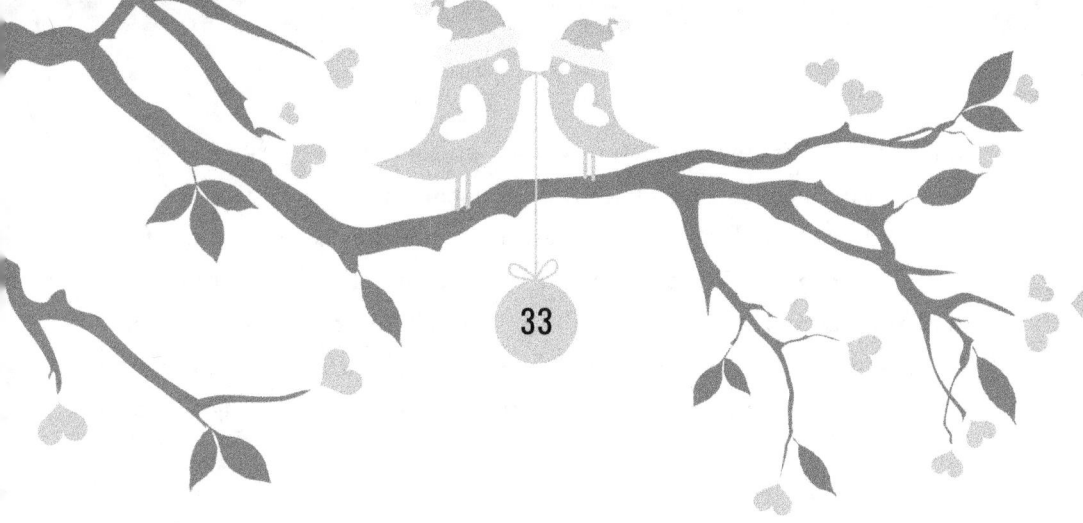

33

**TUESDAY, DECEMBER 24
WEDDING DAY**

— JENNY —

Gwen's alive, thank God. Caleb is talking to her now. He grasps the phone so tight I'm worried it'll snap in two. We're sprinting through the airport accompanied by the police, security, and the rest of Caleb's bodyguards, who Dean has called in. Without hesitation, I run along with them. Over my shoulder, I see Caleb and Gwen's families trailing behind us. I debate telling them to wait in the gate area, but who am I to say that? They have as much right to search for Gwen as I do.

Down one corridor we run, and then another. We pass through swinging doors labeled "employees only." Now, we're in the back portion of the airport, the part that normal travelers never see. Out of open doors that flash by, I get glimpses of the tarmac and planes waiting there. Some airplanes are so large that their tires are as tall as I am. Small carts driven by workers in orange vests and bulky ear protectors zip along, delivering luggage and cargo. There's a deafening whoosh as a plane taxis down the runway, its engines roaring as it gains enough speed to lift into the sky.

We take a sharp left and move away from the airplanes. The hallway we're in now is wide, with scuffed olive-green walls and linoleum flooring. Pools of light from metal caged light bulbs flash under me as I run.

"Over here," shouts an airport security officer. He holds open a set of large double doors. We enter a cavernous space, stacked high with boxes and rectangular containers. It smells like grease and gasoline.

"She's in one of these," the man exclaims, pointing to the center of the room where a long conveyor belt slowly carries containers into a waiting plane. It's enormous, with wide wings and the back half lowered to make a ramp.

We skid to a stop. Dismay opens a hole in my chest right where my heart should be. There must be at least 50 of those containers trundling along, all identical.

"Which one?" I shout.

The grinding noise of the machinery that operates the conveyor equipment is so loud that I doubt we would hear Gwen, even if she's yelling for help.

"We'll go turn it off," says the security guard.

The police, Caleb, and Dean follow him, moving deeper into the room. They call out Gwen's name, but the sound of their voices is quickly lost, swallowed by the racket of the machinery.

The door slams open as the rest of the family catches up. A small tan blur flashes by my feet, accompanied by a loud, excited yipping.

"Pip!" shrieks Megan, her hand outstretched to the tiny dog, who runs ahead with her red leash trailing along behind her. Megan's crying, holding onto her mother's leg. "Pip pulled too hard," she sobs. "It hurt my hands. I had to let go."

Her mother, Liv, drops to her knees to comfort the child.

I look back in time to see the tail end of the leash disappear behind a container. The little dog's yapping loses volume as she gets farther away. Before I can think it through, I chase after Pip, my legs pumping, my heart pounding. I turn the corner so sharply that I almost fall over. Only the wild flailing of my arms keeps me upright.

There she is!

Pip is right ahead of me, moving faster than I've ever seen. Her pink tongue hangs out of the side of her mouth. She's barking, her sides heaving. She flies along like she's been shot out of a cannon.

I've just caught up to her, close enough to grab her leash, when she stops in front of one of the containers. It's slowly rolling forward. Pip stands on her hind legs, prancing next to it. She barks repeatedly. Breathless from my mad dash after the dog, I bend over with my hands on my knees. The loud grinding noise is replaced by silence as the conveyor belt comes to a shuddering stop.

A voice, high-pitched with fear, cries out from the container directly in front of me. "Over here! I'm in here."

"Gwen? Gwen? Are you okay?" I frantically search the container, looking for a way to open it. The door is locked with a large metal padlock, the kind you can only unlock with a key.

A muffled shout pleads, "Get me out of here." It comes from air slots in the side of the container. "Please help!"

That plea turns into a shriek of terror as gunshots ring out.

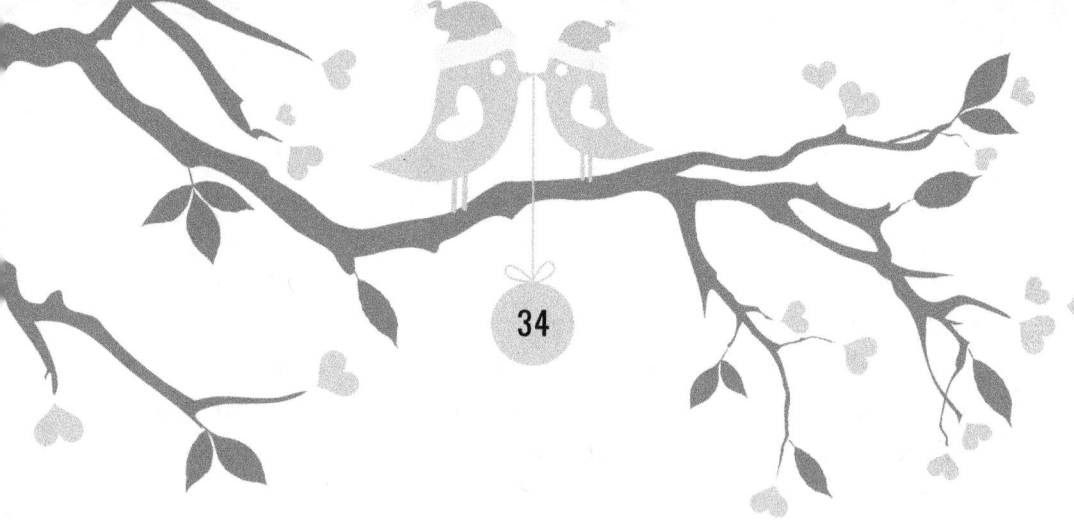

TUESDAY, DECEMBER 24
WEDDING DAY

—JENNY—

I veer off, around the container that holds Gwen and toward the sound of the gun firing. Some tiny part of my mind is screaming, "Run away from the bullets, not toward them, you dummy." I ignore it because, as loud as that voice is, another voice is yelling even louder. It only says one word, and that word is "DEAN!"

If he's in trouble, I need to help him.

As I round the corner, I see a ghastly tableau in front of me. Justin holds a pistol in his outstretched hand with a tendril of smoke curling from its tip. Lola stands behind him, cowering. She has her hands over her ears, like the sound of the gun shooting was too loud.

Caleb and a couple of police have taken shelter by a stack of metal containers on the other side of Lola and Justin. They poke their heads out, then draw them back when Justin wildly swings the muzzle their way.

The worst thing I see is Dean, crumpled on the ground not far from me.

I'm sure he's dead.

Shot by Justin.

I notice he's breathing with shallow pants. He has his hands over his ears, like he and Lola are playing some deranged game of Simon Says.

I duck behind the nearest container, a few feet away from him. "Dean," I hiss, trying to get his attention. "Dean!" I say louder this time.

No response.

Caleb and the police are shouting at Justin, telling him to put down the weapon. He's distracted, looking their way.

I take the opportunity to scoot toward Dean. I crawl over to him and tug on his arm, but he doesn't respond. His eyes are shut tight. His hands remain clamped over his ears. I pull harder, trying to drag him back to safety.

It's no use.

He's too heavy.

Once, a long time ago, Gwen told me how they rouse unconscious patients in the ER. People who have overdosed or had a seizure, for example. She said in that situation you rub your knuckles as hard as you can on the patient's sternum. I have no idea why that particular conversation occurs to me at this moment, but I decide to try it. I push my knuckles into Dean's chest and move them back and forth, pressing on his breastbone.

The result is instantaneous. Dean's eyes fly wide open, and he jerks up into a sitting position.

"Dean," I whisper, "we have to go."

His expression is glazed, but he must hear because he moves with me over to safety behind a pile of wooden pallets. There he curls into a ball.

"Jenny," he gets out through clenched teeth, "leave me. Get Gwen. Help Caleb."

"What? No!" I protest.

His words make me look back at the container that holds Gwen. She's gone silent. Pip sits at the base of the container, staring up at it. I mentally will the tiny dog to stay quiet.

Holding my breath, I lean around Dean to peek out from our hiding spot. Across from me, the police continue to argue with an armed and angry Justin. Caleb moves away from them, creeping along the back of the container where they hide. Instantly, I see his plan, just from the direction he's heading. He's going to go behind Justin and Lola and try to surprise attack them from that angle. If I went that way, I could do the same thing. The two of us could flank them from the rear, each coming from opposite sides.

More gunfire breaks out, the sound reverberating through the large space. I whip my head toward Justin in time to watch the police scramble back to their container. They must have tried to sneak up on him, and he caught them. Luckily, there's no blood—no one appears to be hurt.

"Go!" Dean cracks an eye open. The agony I see in it almost brings me to my knees. This is literally his worst nightmare.

"Please, Jenny," he begs. "Please go."

"Okay." I rise, trying to be quiet. "Don't move," I command, pointing my finger at him. "Stay put."

He nods miserably. I double-check that he's out of eyesight from where Justin and Lola stand.

With an aching heart, I leave him and make my way behind the stacks of metal containers. Once I've gone a few feet, I turn to see Dean drag himself toward the container where Gwen is imprisoned.

35

TUESDAY, DECEMBER 24
WEDDING DAY

—GWEN—

The open slots on the side of my metal cage are large enough for me to see everything.

With my heart in my throat, I watch Jenny rescue a fear-stricken Dean. I see the police almost get shot.

The scariest thing I witness is Caleb making his way *toward* Justin and Lola. Crouching low, hidden by containers like the one I'm trapped in, Caleb slowly moves to the back of the room. He approaches from the left.

A minute later, Jenny goes the same direction, but she comes from the right.

I want to shout at them. To tell them to stop. To say I love them, and I can't stand to lose anyone else close to me. But I don't yell. I won't risk revealing their locations. If Justin sees them, he'll shoot them. Earlier, when he fired at those police, it wasn't in warning. He was trying to kill them.

I rise on my toes and press my eye to the opening. The cool metal indents my cheek, but I barely notice. Caleb's seen Jenny now. They have a wordless exchange, trading nods and hand gestures, right behind Justin's and Lola's backs.

"Gwen," whispers a deep voice from outside of where I'm trapped.

"Dean? Is that you?"

"Hold on. I'll get you out." His words fade as he moves away. I want to cry for him to stay, to not leave me. I'm so frightened. I'm shaking. My hands tremble like fall leaves when the wind sweeps in.

I move along the edge of the container, peering through the open slots until I find him. Dean's rummaging through a set of tools. He makes a triumphant sound as he pulls a crowbar out of the pile.

We're lucky. The locked door of my prison is on the opposite side of Lola and Justin. They can't see Dean apply the crowbar to the lock and try to pry it off, his muscles bulging.

Shouts from the other side send me running away from Dean and his work. I return to the spot where I can best watch what's happening with Caleb and Jenny.

Caleb must've told the police to distract Justin, because the blue uniformed men poke their heads out from their hiding place. They shout threats, and Justin screams back at them, spittle flying from his lips. He's so focused on them that he doesn't notice Lola shuffling backward, away from him. I narrow my eyes when I see what she's up to.

The coward.

She's going to abandon her secret boyfriend.

Once she's gained some freedom, Lola turns and runs smack dab into Jenny, who's moved to intercept her. Jenny grabs Lola's arms, pinning them to her sides. The two women struggle, wrestling with each other. Lola has at least a foot of height on Jenny, but Jenny works out every day. All those hours spent hauling tire tractors in boot camp and lifting weights in aqua aerobics pay off. Jenny spins Lola around and slams her against the nearest container. Lola's head hits the metal wall with a loud thunk. Her eyelids sag like she might pass out.

The sound of the women's struggle draws Justin's attention. He turns his back on the cops and faces Lola. Caleb jumps behind a nearby box to hide.

"Lola?" Justin calls out, confusion making his voice rise higher at the end of the sentence.

"Help me!" exclaims Lola as she fights to peel Jenny's hands off her arms.

Justin raises his gun just as Jenny turns around. Now Lola is in front of Jenny, acting as a human shield.

"She was running away!" Jenny cries out to Justin. "Lola was going to leave you."

Justin gasps, the gun in his hand wavering. He points it at Lola, who places her hand over her heart and says, "Don't listen to her. She's a liar."

"It's true," Jenny shouts. "She's been using you."

Justin trembles with rage. "Shut up!" he screams at Jenny, his face turning red.

Lola squirms in Jenny's arms, then brings her high heel down on the instep of Jenny's sneaker-clad foot.

"Ow!" Jenny exclaims, hopping on her uninjured foot.

Lola takes advantage of Jenny's imbalance and shoves her hard. Jenny's hands slip. Lola twists and breaks free, exposing Jenny to Justin, who lifts his gun.

"No!" I scream without thinking.

Justin cocks the gun and aims as I watch helplessly, my heart in my throat. Jenny looks around desperately, searching for a place to hide, but her fight with Lola has her trapped between the back wall of the room and a large metal container. There's nowhere for her to go.

She's going to die.

Caleb comes out swinging. He emerges from where he's been inching closer and closer to Justin. He raises his arms with his hands tucked into tight fists. Once, years ago, my ex-boyfriend grabbed me in a parking lot. Caleb saved me back then. He told my ex-boyfriend that Olympic boxers had trained him for one of his movie roles. He'd said, "I don't think you want to see what my right hook can do."

My ex had backed down and run away. As a result, I never got to see that punch, but I witness it now. Caleb brings his fist back like a cobra about to strike. So quick it's hard to follow, his hand lashes out and pistons into the side of Justin's head. Justin's entire body rocks backward from the blow. Justin stumbles, and the gun goes off. A bullet flies out of its smoking muzzle straight at Jenny, but Caleb has thrown off the aim. With a pinging sound, the bullet punctures the container next to Jenny instead of hitting her. She throws her hand up to shield herself from the tiny fragments that ricochet from the punctured steel.

Behind me is the sound of banging and metal wrenching from where Dean works on the lock, but I can't take my eyes off the scene in front of me.

Before Justin can aim again, Caleb is on him, raining blows to his head, chest, and belly. The gun clatters to the floor as Justin raises his hands to defend himself. Caleb kicks it away with his foot, sending it spinning toward Jenny, who bends down and scoops it up. Now that Justin's unarmed, the police come rushing over.

Jenny raises the pistol. She points it at Justin and shouts, "Stop! Don't make me shoot you."

When Justin sees that Jenny has the gun trained on him, his shoulders slump in defeat. The cops are on him in a flash, pulling out their handcuffs. They read him his rights.

Justin's not listening to them, though. His head swings wildly.

"Lola?" he calls out, panicked. "Lola?"

Jenny, Caleb, and the officers stop what they're doing. They look around as well, but Lola's not there.

The dim container suddenly floods with light. I cry out and throw my arm over my stunned eyes. I'm falling, crumpling to my knees, but strong arms are there to catch me.

"I've got you," says Dean. "You're safe."

TUESDAY, DECEMBER 24
WEDDING DAY

—JENNY—

The police have taken Justin away. They're still searching for Lola, but they worry that she's found a flight out of the country. Gwen's off getting a quick medical check-up, with Pip in her arms. That little dog has growled and bared her teeth whenever we've tried to separate her from Gwen. Finally, we gave up. I'm talking to Gwen's and Caleb's families, going over everything that happened for the third time. When the shooting started, they had wisely grabbed the twins and fled the room.

Out of the corner of my eye, I see a muscular brown-haired man stride past without a glance my way. He heads for the elevators that lead to the buses and taxi stand.

Dean.

Caleb comes over with a stormy expression. His glare shoots daggers at Dean, who's entered the elevator.

"What's going on?" I ask Caleb.

"Dean just quit. Said he'd turn in the formal resignation letter later today." Caleb directs his furious gaze at me. "I can't deal with this right now. I need to make sure Gwen's okay."

The elevator doors begin to close. I get a glimpse of Dean facing forward, his face smooth, expressionless. Mr. Roboto is back.

"I'll handle Dean," I tell Caleb. "You go take care of Gwen." Without waiting for Caleb to respond, I run to the elevator. I stick my foot between its closing double doors. They hit the edge of my sneaker and spring open.

Dean doesn't say a word when I step inside. He doesn't look at me or acknowledge my presence.

I wait for the door to close before I turn to him. The elevator shudders and begins its descent.

"What was that?" I demand, my lips pressed tight.

Nothing. No response. It's like I'm not even there.

My brothers had this game they would play when I was a kid. They would ignore me and pretend I didn't exist. I would shout in their faces, pinch their arms, and they wouldn't flinch. They were so good at it that sometimes I almost believed them. I wondered if I was real or maybe I was a ghost? The leftover memory of someone who used to be alive. My brothers would continue that game for days, always when my parents weren't looking. Eventually, when their silence got to be too much, I'd go to my room and, all alone, cry myself to sleep.

This, how Dean won't respond to me, feels like that. Tears gather in the corners of my eyes. That old sadness, the feeling of worthlessness, rises so big it overwhelms me.

Forget this.

I reach for the elevator button, ready to give up on him. My plan is to stop and get out as soon as I can. The cool metal grazes my fingertips, when I notice Dean's hands. They clench and unclench by his sides, full of restless energy. The rest of him is still, unmoving.

I pause, uncertain what my next move should be. Get off the elevator or stay on. Risk another failure or walk away. All my life, I've waited for someone to choose me. To pick me out from the crowd and give me their love. In that moment, I realize I've got it backward. I can't control who decides to love me, but I can control who I love. I choose who to be with, who I let into my life. I take a deep breath, and…

I choose him.

A step closer and I slide my hand into his. Dean stiffens but doesn't pull away. It's a little thing, him standing there with his warm palm in mine, but it feels big.

Like maybe we have a chance.

"What are you doing?" I ask quietly. I stare straight ahead, not looking at him.

"Quitting." His voice is rough, sandpaper scraping against my soul.

I squeeze his fingers, the gentlest of pressure. "Why?"

He turns to me, and the despair I see in him rips a hole in my heart. So much pain in his troubled gaze.

"What kind of bodyguard am I, what kind of man, if I can't protect the people I care about?"

"You're human. That's the kind of man you are. Not perfect, just like the rest of us. We're all made up of strengths and weaknesses. I fidget and am insecure about my body. You get scared by loud noises. Those are our flaws. That doesn't mean we don't have strengths, too. I'm loyal, if given the chance. You're caring, always looking out for others before yourself."

"It's not the same," he says, morose. "I'm a failure. I didn't avoid that IED. I didn't figure out the stalker in time."

"You're the one who saved Gwen. You got her out of that cage," I say, insistently.

"It's not just what happened today. It's *every* day of my life." He watches me, solemn. "I told you before. I'm not good enough." He drags in a breath, then warns, "I'm worthless."

"I can tell you a bunch of things I'm bad at, things I can't do, but would you call me worthless?"

His thumb strokes over the inside of my wrist, running over the spot where my pulse pounds for him. "I'd never say that about you."

"Give yourself that same grace." I sigh, wondering why we're always harsher with ourselves than we are with others. Dean would forgive weakness in me, but not in himself.

He wavers, and hope lights up in me, but it goes dark when he pulls his hand from mine. "You should leave me alone." He stares blankly before him.

"No," I say firmly, committed to pulling him out of the pit he's crawled into.

After the craziness of today, I'm a mess of emotions—sorrow, despair, anger. I decide to focus on anger. I can already tell where he's going with this. The "it's not you, it's me" speech. I just got that from Eddie. I'm not taking it from Dean.

Moving in front of him, I point a finger in his face, which makes him blink in surprise. I lean forward into his space and hiss, "Listen, buddy, if you think you're shaking me off with your issues, you have another thing coming. I'm not going anywhere. You can stay as messed up as you want for as long as you want. I'll handle it. I've got my problems, too. You'll have to deal with that." I pause, thinking over the hours I spent snowbound with Dean. "What happened between us in my hotel room is not over."

His ears go pink, and I know he was heading that direction. That was going to be his next suggestion, not because he's not into me—you don't stare at someone sleeping if it's a casual relationship—but because he's revealed all his weaknesses and now he wants to run, to avoid. If he doesn't get close to me, he can pretend we never had this connection. It's a scary thing, to bare your soul to someone else, and this man before me…he's terrified.

I can relate. This morning, when I rejected him, I was frightened too. But seeing Dean on the ground while Justin waved his gun was the worst moment of my life. That was when I understood how, in a short amount of time, he has become important to me.

"This is a thing, a real thing, between you and me. I have no idea where it's going. Could be a train to Disasterville, but we're on it." I jab him in the chest, once, for good measure. "So choo-choo. Climb aboard Dean, because we're riding it until the end of the line." Glaring up at him, I cross my arms and impatiently tap my foot.

I expect him to argue, the stubborn fool, but he doesn't. Instead, his mouth twitches. "Disasterville?"

I pull myself tall, nod once, and settle back down. More softly, I say, "I know we have things to figure out, with me being in L.A. and you in New York, but I'm willing to work on it."

"Okay," he says, surprising me. He smiles, a sad smile, but still, it's something.

"Okay?" I echo, confused. I hadn't dared to hope I could convince him.

"We'll try it." He softens. "I'm tired of finding excuses to stay away from you."

I shyly shift closer, then let out a shriek when he drags me to him.

He crushes me to his chest. "What do you think about that?" he asks. Anxious brown eyes with hints of gold scan my face, looking for clues.

"I think…" I drag it out because I still like to make him squirm. He glares down at me, mock angry. "I think it sounds pretty decent, maybe better than decent."

A flash of a smile, then his lips are on mine.

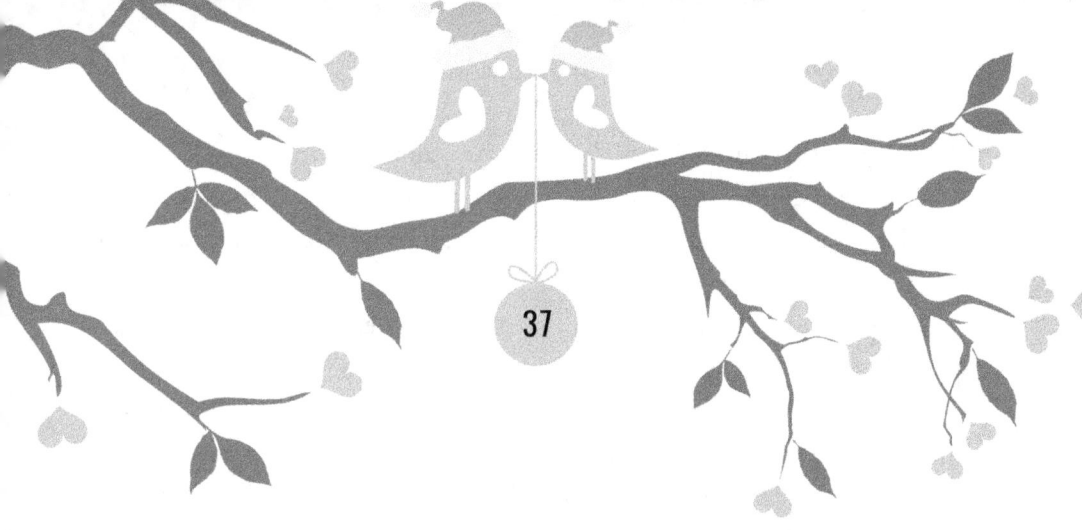

37

**TUESDAY, DECEMBER 24
WEDDING DAY**

— GWEN —

"Way to steal my thunder, Jenny. I was supposed to find Gwen, not you," Caleb jokes. The hand that's wrapped tightly around my waist is unsteady. Except for when the EMTs checked me out, he hasn't let go since I climbed out of that tomb of a box.

"Sorry, dude. You may play a superhero in the movies, but it turns out I'm the real deal." Jenny playfully socks him on the shoulder. "Although Pip's really the hero. She's the one who figured out where Gwen was." She points over to Pip, who snores softly, asleep on Megan's lap. After the EMTs said I was okay, it had taken almost an hour of coaxing to convince Pip that she could leave me, and I'd still be safe.

I glance around Gate B14, where all the seats are empty, except those occupied by Caleb's and my family, plus a couple of his bodyguards stationed along the perimeter. Airport staff had assured us that no more planes would be leaving from this gate tonight. They told us we could stay here as long as we wanted. We're currently waiting on Dean, who is the last of us to be interviewed by the police.

Boarding is called over the loudspeaker for the gate next to us, B13. I watch the passengers line up and wait patiently for their turn to scan their boarding passes. One by one they disappear into the jet bridge. I have no desire to join them in their travels. After the trauma of tonight, all I want is to stay close to home.

Caleb's tense next to me. He coughs into his hand. "Jenny, I'm sorry for what I said back at the penthouse."

Strained lines deepen around his mouth. I tighten my grip on his waist, wondering what's going on.

Caleb responds to my touch. He gazes sadly at me and says, "I had a hard time without you, Gwen. Lost my head. I accused Jenny of things I shouldn't have, and I feel awful about it." He pulls away from me. I follow with my hand on his back. He's not the only one who needs the reassurance of physical contact right now.

He takes a step toward Jenny. "I'm sorry. You would never hurt Gwen or me. You're one of our best friends, and I treated you worse than a stranger. Please forgive me?"

Jenny doesn't hesitate. She throws herself into his arms and gives him a hug that I know from experience is rib-crushing. "Forgiven!" she cries loudly, with such an expression of relief and joy that it makes me grin.

I reach up and touch my cheeks with wonder. There were moments in that container when I thought I'd never smile again. Moments when I thought I wouldn't get out, yet here I am. Gratitude isn't a big enough word. There's a settling of my bones, a loosening of my limbs, to know I'm here safe and sound with the ones I love.

As if he can hear my thoughts, Caleb reaches back for me. He grabs me and pulls me close. Jenny's still hugging him, so I join in. The three of us stand there quietly for a minute, with our arms wrapped around each other.

Dean walks up behind Jenny and splays his large hand over her shoulder. She breaks out of our embrace and turns to face him.

"You okay?" he asks her, which is odd considering *I'm* the one who was kidnapped. Jenny stares up at him, her eyes dreamy.

Out of the corner of my mouth, not moving my lips like I'm a ventriloquist, I whisper to Caleb, "What's happening right now? Why aren't they trying to murder each other?"

His laugh is a low rumble in my ear. The familiarity of it sends a shiver dancing down my spine. "A lot has changed since you've been gone." Those words turn my shiver into one of dread. I push against him, slowly inching him backward, away from our friends and family. Far enough that we can talk without them overhearing.

He goes willingly.

"Those things that have changed," I say, staring at the floor, unable to look him in the eye. "Are any of them how you feel about me? About the wedding?"

"Of course not. Nothing could ever change my love for you. We're getting married." Caleb removes his iron grip from my waist. Now he's the hesitant one, avoiding my gaze. "If you still want me?"

Words aren't enough to answer that question, so I let my body do the talking. I wind my arms around his neck, rise on my toes, and kiss him with everything I've got. I pour all of my fear, my insecurities, and my love into him and he gives it back ounce for ounce. Caleb tilts his head, his fingers on my chin, adjusting me as we refamiliarize ourselves with each other. By the time we pull away, my heart is racing from his touch.

I bite my lower lip, his darkened eyes tracking the movement. "I can't believe I went so long without touching you."

He sets his forehead against mine and squeezes his eyes shut, but not before I see the tears glistening in them. "I was so scared," he rasps. "Scared you were mad at me. That you were going to leave me. Then when you were missing, I was terrified."

He rips his hand through his hair. "This is all my fault. I should have warned you better, been honest about the danger. You would never have been in this situation if it weren't for me. Lola wouldn't have targeted you. She's still out there. The police can't find her."

"Shh," I say, placing a finger over his lips. "Stop. This isn't your fault. I don't blame you, and you can't blame yourself either." I wrap my arms around him and bury my head in his firm chest, inhaling his spicy cinnamon scent.

"Lola's on the run. She won't be able to come after me again. Not with the police after her and the fact that our bodyguards know to look out for her. Plus, she's so recognizable, someone's bound to find her."

Caleb lets out a breath. "I hate how things have been strained between us the last few days. If I'd lost you before I got a chance to tell you that I'm sorry for not being more patient, more understanding, I never would have forgiven myself."

"It's not just you. I've been stubborn, too. The truth is, I've struggled while we were apart. You warned me that it would be difficult dealing with your fame, but I was naïve, in denial. You were right. People recognized me, my lecture didn't go well, and I hid my feelings from you. I don't know how to handle being secondhand famous." It takes a minute to break old habits, to find the bravery to say, "Please help me? I can't do this on my own."

He tenderly cups my cheek. "Gwen, no one expects you to be an expert on this. I've been a celebrity my entire life, and I still have no idea what I'm doing. It's not an easy path, to walk beside me. No one would blame you for bailing."

I lock my eyes to his and say vehemently, "I'm not walking away from you. *Never*. I understand this will be hard and there will be days, weeks even, like the past couple of ones, where I'll fail. I used to be terrified of that. Of letting people down, not having everything under control. I'm learning more and more how unpredictable the future is. Losing my dad, meeting you, Lola and Justin, so many things change the direction of life without warning. I'm ready to let go of needing to be perfect and strong. Instead, I'll roll with the punches and adapt. I'll ask for help when I need it. I promise. I can do this with you. Forever and always. Please don't give up on me?"

"Give up?" He shakes his head, incredulous, like he can't believe what he's hearing. Caleb leans his forehead to mine. He closes his eyes and says fervently, "Don't you know, don't you understand that when I walk into a room, you're the one I see? When I sleep at night, it's you dancing through my dreams. You are my past and my future. You're the *only* one for me."

We stay like that for a minute, leaning against each other. Our foreheads pressed together. Our breath mingling between us.

Finally, Caleb pulls away. There's still a hint of hesitation when he asks, "We're still getting married?"

I nod, grinning up at him. "We're getting married."

Caleb whoops so loudly I swear the entire airport looks over. If all the random tourists hadn't noticed that Caleb Lawson was in their midst before, they certainly notice him now. He picks me up by the waist and spins me around until I'm dizzy. Then he places me on the ground and kisses me, quick and hard. He says, "Thank you. Thank you for giving me this life. It's better than anything I ever dreamed. I wish I could marry you right now. Right here. No more waiting."

"I can help with that," says a rough voice next to us.

Surprised, Caleb and I jump apart. We were so consumed with each other that we didn't notice Wayne has come up to us.

Wayne repeats, "I can help. If you want, I can marry you right now."

DECEMBER 24
WEDDING DAY

—GWEN—

That's how I ended up marrying Caleb Freaking Lawson on Christmas Eve at Gate B-14 in LaGuardia Airport.

First, we tell everyone the plan. Caleb's mom cries again but reassures us that they're happy tears. Jenny runs to the nearby gift shop, where she swears they sell flowers even though Dean says they don't. The two of them go off, holding hands and arguing. When they return, Jenny triumphantly holds out a dozen slightly wilted red roses. A "Welcome Home" balloon is tied to the bouquet. It floats behind her, bumping into the side of Dean's head. He bats it away with an irritated scowl.

We assemble by the large windows that look over the runway. In the background, planes take off and land, the roar of their engines dampened by the thick glass. Wayne stands with his back to the window. Caleb and I move in front of him. Jenny and Alvina flank me as my bridesmaids. Dean takes his place next to Caleb. Our families form a loose semicircle around us.

Behind them, a crowd has formed. It grows bigger with every passing minute. Strangers hold up cameras. They take photos and videos, some even livestream. A month ago, all these fans would have intimidated me, but now I notice how happy they are for us, how they chatter excitedly with each other.

Disjointed comments float to me.

"Isn't it wonderful?" asks a young woman to another.

"So romantic," her friend replies.

"I remember when he was a child," says a white-haired woman to her husband. "He was on that show—I can't remember the name. You know, the one set in San Francisco."

"I heard she's done some great things for her hospital," a man in a suit says to a woman who wears a pilot's outfit. She nods in agreement, then adds, "Just think what they can do together. With his fame and her brains, they can raise all kinds of money."

I tune the crowd out and step up to Caleb.

"Oh!" I press a hand to my cheek. "I was going to give you my dad's cufflinks. The ones he wore to his wedding."

"Give them to me," says Caleb.

"I can't. You're not wearing that kind of shirt." I gesture to the long-sleeved athletic T-shirt that he wears. Caleb brings his wrist to his mouth. There's a loud tearing sound as he uses his teeth to rip a hole in his sleeve. He repeats the same process on the other side. "I've got room for them now."

My fanny pack is still at my waist. I hand Jenny my bouquet of roses and dig out the cufflinks. I push them through the holes that Caleb's torn in his sleeves. Their weight makes the fabric hang unevenly, but I don't care. It makes me happy to see them here, sparkling, a physical reminder of my father.

I imagine what it would be like if Dad were here. He would walk me over to Caleb, with his hand on my elbow. He would brush his lips across my temple and wish me good luck. A whispered reminder that love is easy, but marriage is hard. He would say that it's not just about saying "yes" to your partner on this day, but on every day after, even the times when "no" would be easier.

Wayne pulls himself tall, preening with his self-importance. "Quick version or the slow one?" he asks under his breath so only Caleb and I can hear. Caleb eyes the fans and says, "Let's go quick this time. I still want the full wedding later." He directs his gaze at me with a twinkle in his eyes. "I need to see Gwen in her dress."

"You got it." Wayne clears his throat. All our family hushes. Even the shuffling crowd stills.

He's about to speak when the gate agent interrupts. "Here." She thrusts the small microphone she uses to make announcements at Wayne. "Use this so everyone can hear."

Wayne takes it from her and holds it up to us. "Is this okay with you?"

Caleb and I glance at each other, and I shrug.

"It's fine," answers Caleb.

There's a minute of fumbling while Wayne attaches the microphone to his shirt. When he speaks again, his voice is amplified.

"Dearly beloved," he intones, "we are gathered here today to witness the union of Caleb Augustus Lawson and Gwendolen Jane Wright. Let us support them on this day as they enter into sacred matrimony."

I hear loud sobbing from behind me. I turn to see my mother and Marjorie crying as they cling together, their arms wrapped around each other. Jenny and Alvina are misty-eyed as well. Even Dean is choked up.

"For the sake of brevity, we will skip the longer vows today," Wayne says, giving a wary glance at the crowd, but the fans and strangers keep their distance and stay quiet. Their focus is on us.

Caleb steps closer and takes my hands in his. His thumb strokes lightly across my skin. The touch is comforting as my nerves kick in, anxious but in an excited way. I want to savor this moment, but I also want it to speed ahead. To see what the rest of our lives will be like. All the things we'll accomplish together.

This is it.

We're really doing this.

Surprising me, Wayne's voice holds a slight quaver as he asks, "Do you, Caleb, take Gwen to be your lawfully wedded wife? To have and to hold from this day forward, forsaking all others, 'til death do you part?"

Caleb looks at me, and the love I see shining there so brightly in his eyes is overwhelming in the very best way. It consumes me, surrounds me, assures me that no matter what happens, we will face life together.

Caleb says a loud and firm, "I do. Forever and always."

Wayne beams at Caleb with pride. He turns his attention to me. "Do you, Gwen, take Caleb to be your lawfully wedded husband? To have and to hold from this day forward, forsaking all others, 'til death do you part?"

In my loudest voice, so all the world can hear my commitment, I answer, "I do. With my whole heart, I do."

Caleb squeezes my hand, his eyes glowing with pride and love.

"With the authority given to me by the state of New York," Wayne takes in a breath and proclaims, "I now pronounce you husband and wife. Caleb, you may kiss your bride."

Cheers ring through the airport, from our families and from the fans, so loud that it drowns out flight announcements from the overhead speakers. Caleb's grinning, his biggest smile, as he brings his lips to mine in a passionate kiss.

I keep my eyes open until the last minute, wanting to etch his happiness into my memory. I take this moment and place it into one of the many rooms in my heart.

To be held there forever.

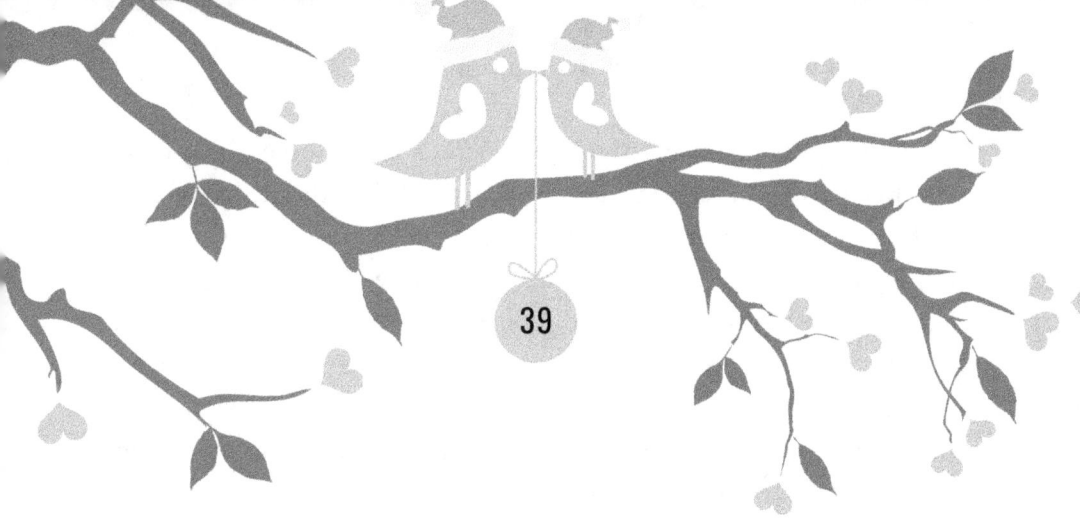

39

**WEDNESDAY, DECEMBER 25
WEDDING DAY (AGAIN)**

GWEN

Our wedding ceremony, the fancy one, happens the next day, Christmas Day, in the Broadway theater where Caleb performs. It's the place he brought me to years ago to win me back.

Even though it's a holiday, the vendors and most of the guests still agreed to attend. Once they heard the circumstances of our delay—which was all over the news thanks to the onlookers at the airport—everyone had been sympathetic. It helped that most of the people attending are close friends and family.

The staff spent the late afternoon transforming this place and the hotel where the reception will be into our dream wedding. Our mothers had been there to supervise, while Caleb and I stayed at our respective apartments, getting ready.

Now, when I peek through the double doors that lead into the theater, I realize I should never have doubted the combined power of my mom, Marjorie, and an inspired work force. They've layered sheer white fabric in swooping bunting between the seats. Deep red roses, glossy berries, and boughs of pine cluster together in vases around the room and on the end of each row. Shining gold ribbons are tied into bows at the base of the flowers. The gold matches the elaborate gilded scrollwork that sits high on the theater walls and surrounds the stage where soon I'll exchange vows with Caleb.

Even more stunning than the flowers and fabric are the thousands of lit candles on the stage. They glow and twinkle in every shape and size, giving the space an eclectic, romantic feeling. Candles have also been placed on balconies that line the walls, rising high over our heads. The theater has taken on a sophisticated winter vibe that perfectly matches the vision I had.

"What's it look like?" asks Jenny, raising her voice over the jazz that Caleb selected. The orchestra had insisted on being here today. They told us they would be honored to perform our wedding music live. Many times, Caleb has felt isolated. Apart from everyone around him. Seeing his co-workers support him on this has touched him deeply. It was a reminder that the relationships he forged here are lasting. That he was no longer alone.

"It's like a fairytale brought to life." Answering Jenny's question, I'm amazed at the decorations.

Jenny leans a hand on my shoulder and jumps, trying to see over me.

"Is Dean there yet?"

I giggle at her eager expression.

"I'm not sure who's more excited to walk down the aisle, me or you."

That makes her laugh, a light pealing sound.

I grin at her. "I've never seen you so smitten."

"I know. I can't stop smiling," she admits and impulsively hugs me, too tight like she always does, crushing the white tulle of my dress, but I don't mind. After almost losing my life at the airport, I have a newfound appreciation for my friends and family.

If it weren't for them, I wouldn't be standing here today, dressed like a princess. Jenny pulls away, and I straighten the gauzy folds of my wide skirt, which brushes the floor. The bodice of my gown is off the shoulder. Sparkling seed pearls and rhinestones hand-sewn onto the fabric create flowers and vines. My favorite part, the thing that made this dress stand out from all the others, is that some beads form tiny pine cones. I loved how that detail fit with our wedding theme.

"You and the theater are both beautiful," says Jenny.

I take in my best friend. She's glowing in her maroon bridesmaid's dress. I tell her, "You're gorgeous, too."

She smiles, ducking her chin shyly. "Normally, I'd think you were just saying that to be nice—"

"What?" I interrupt. "I mean it. You look lovely, Jenny, like you always do."

She straightens, standing tall. "You used to say things like that, and I'd dismiss them. I couldn't see it in myself."

Sadness tugs at my heart. I know this about my best friend, all her insecurities.

She continues, saying, "Now when you tell me I'm pretty, I'm starting to believe you. It's partly because of Dean, because he makes me feel beautiful, but recently I've been working on myself. I don't want to only feel good because some guy likes me. I need to do it alone. To realize I might not be perfect, but I'm perfect enough."

I grab her hand and squeeze it between mine. "That's wonderful. I want you to view yourself the way I see you, as the kindest, most beautiful inside and out, person I know."

We share another too-tight hug, grinning at each other. I peer through the door and watch as our guests enter and settle into their seats.

"Everything's worked out." Jenny adjusts the wide, glittering, scarlet ribbon that holds her bouquet together. It matches mine, glossy berries with pine and snow-white roses.

"Not everything," I say and sigh. "Lola's still out there. No one's found her."

"They will," Jenny reassures me. With a grimace, she says, "I've got news."

"What's that?"

"Eddie got fired. I guess Caleb's lawyers contacted the newspaper about him obtaining that list of suspects unlawfully, since he stole it from me." She scuffs her foot on the ground. "There's more. I found out he gave me a bad review, as my supervisor. That's why I got passed over for the investigative team."

"What?" Anger bristles and races through my veins. Murderous thoughts surface, all directed toward Eddie, that little weasel.

Jenny smiles sadly at me, her shoulders slumping. "Sorry to dump that on you right before your wedding, but I didn't want to hide it."

I calm myself, not wanting to add to her worry. After a couple of deep breaths, I say, "It's okay. Last night, Caleb told me he was getting his legal team involved. I'm glad Eddie got what he deserved.

"I have news too. Justin's being held without bail. They think he's too much of a flight risk since he's already changed his identity once. The police called this morning and asked if I would press full charges. I said 'yes.'" I sigh shakily, nervous about the trial and all the drama that will surround it. Before I left for California, I had wanted to stay out of the limelight, but now I'll be thrust into the middle of it. I know I'm strong enough, though, especially with Caleb by my side.

"I'm sorry." The sympathy in Jenny's gaze tightens my throat. "That's a lot to deal with right before you get married."

"It's not what's really bothering me, though." Waves of grief wash over me, a swirling vortex that threatens to pull me under. "I wish my dad was here to walk me down the aisle."

Jenny frowns deeply. "Oh, Gwen. Of course, you miss him today. We all do." A sorrowful pause and then she brightens. "Hang on, I have an idea." She leaves the room but is back seconds later with a pen in her hand.

"Give me your shoes," she commands.

"Why?" I laugh. "I'm not Cinderella."

She doesn't budge. "Trust me."

"I do. I trust you," I say.

Jenny flashes a brilliant smile at that. So big it makes me think I haven't told her that often enough. One at a time, I pass my white satin pumps over to her. She quickly writes on the bottom of each heel. She shoves the cap back on and hands over my footwear.

"What'd you write?" I ask, inspecting where she's scribbled the letters RW.

"Your dad's initials, Robert Wright," she answers. "Now when you walk down the aisle, he'll be with you in spirit, every step of the way."

My vision blurs as tears fill my eyes. I flap my hand in front of my face, willing them away.

"Thank you. I love the idea."

"I'm glad." Her breath is minty from the hard peppermint candy in her mouth.

A deep voice behind us says, "Excuse me."

Jenny lets out a squeal when we turn to find Dean, looking sharp in his three-piece dark gray tuxedo and red bow tie. A small boutonniere is pinned on his lapel. It has a sprig of pine and delicate white rosebuds.

"What are you doing here?" She flies over to him.

Dean holds out his arms to catch her. They're laughing as the two of them collide in an embrace.

"I'm here to escort you down the aisle, sweetheart," Dean rumbles. The tender way he gazes at her makes my chest fill with happiness.

Jenny casts a glance back at me.

I mouth, *sweetheart?* and quirk my brow, teasing her.

She giggles again. Because she's the sister of my heart, I can read that's she's already in love with him, even though she might not know it yet. She raises her eyebrows in a *crazy, right?* motion. Her giddy expression has me laughing along with her.

"Hey, now," Dean says and narrows his eyes suspiciously, interrupting our moment. "What're you two talking about?"

That makes us laugh harder. Gasping, holding her sides, Jenny says to him, "Nothing! Who, us?" Her high pitch gives us away.

Dean pretends to glare at us, suppressing a smile.

I'm grateful for them, my friends. Grateful for Jenny distracting me from my pre-wedding jitters. Grateful that they stand beside me when I'm right and also when I'm wrong.

"Remember to save some energy for tomorrow," Dean tells Jenny.

"Why? What are you guys up to?" I ask.

Jenny lights up as bright as the sun. "Dean got us tickets to *The Nutcracker.* Then we're going ice skating. He wants to show me all the holiday things to do in New York."

"That sounds fun," I exclaim, glad to see my friend so happy.

"Wayne's ready," announces Alvina as she sweeps up to us. Megan and Maddie enter the room, adorable in their matching dresses with pure white ruffles and dark ruby sashes. They're my flower girls, and Pip is my ring bearer. Maddie will hold her leash as they walk down the aisle. The rings are tied around his neck with a wide ribbon that matches the girls' dresses and my bouquet. I made sure to double knot it, so it won't fall off.

My heart beats erratically as my mother and stepfather, Seth, enter the room. They line up on either side of me.

"You look beautiful." Seth takes my left hand and gives it a gentle squeeze.

"You really do," my mom agrees. She adjusts my veil, straightening it, and then loops her arm through mine. "I'm so proud of you, Gwen. I couldn't ask for a better daughter. You're everything your father and I dreamed of. If he could be here today, he would say the same thing."

Her words make my chest swell, like my heart has grown too big for it. "Thanks."

The wedding march sounds from the orchestra. All the bridesmaids, groomsmen, flower girls, and ring dog take their positions. I attempt to calm my racing nerves as they walk out in pairs. Jenny goes with Dean, her hand tucked into his elbow. Alvina leaves with Nick, Caleb's partner in his restaurant business. The twins, Maddie and Megan, exit with nervous giggles. Pip trots along behind them on her leash. Each time the door swings open, the music swells louder.

Eventually it's only me, Mom, and Seth.

"Are you ready?" asks Seth. I release a shaky breath and nod. He says, "Caleb loves you, like I've never seen him love before. He'll be a good husband."

"I know," I tell him, thinking of how Caleb's always supported me. How we've overcome so many hurdles. "He's already proven he's prepared for this."

Seth gives me a last squeeze, and the doors open.

The music rises louder. The wedding guests rise too. They all stand and stare at me, but I don't notice them. There's only one person I see. He's standing at the end of the aisle, up on the stage, looking more handsome than I've ever seen.

Caleb.

In his gray tux, with his hair perfectly styled, he's giving me my special smile, small and tender. It's so sweet, so charming, that I almost trip over my feet.

Alvina had coached me to walk slowly down the aisle. "Draw it out, be demure," she had instructed. I don't do any of that. I practically run to Caleb, my shoes barely touching the ground. All I want is to be with him. To feel his hand in mine.

At the end of the aisle, Mom and Seth give me over to Caleb. He takes both of my hands in his. Wayne says a more detailed version of what he said before at the airport. I don't hear him. I'm too focused on the man I'm marrying.

My husband.

The time comes to recite our vows. The ones we wrote for each other.

"Caleb," I say into the microphone that Wayne holds. I brace myself for feedback, like I got at my mom and Seth's wedding when I first met Caleb, but it doesn't happen. My voice rings out true and clear. "Caleb, I love you. You've shown me pieces of myself that I thought were gone, buried under grief over losing my dad. You've shown me pieces of myself that I thought would never exist. Brave parts of me that demand the best from myself and from those around me. You've taught me to speak up and not be afraid. You've shown me pieces of yourself that you don't allow most others to see, and I'm eternally honored to have that privilege. To get to know you, love you, build a life with you. I'll never take that for granted. Today, I choose you. For the rest of my life, it's going to be me and you."

The guests clap, the sound loud. Teddy sits in front, with Helen two rows behind him. He whoops, his fist in the air. "Go, Sissy," he cries out, and the crowd laughs.

When everyone settles down, Dean hands me Caleb's ring, which he got from a sleeping Pip. The tiny dog barely opened one eye when the ribbon was untied from her collar. Taking my time, I push the band onto Caleb's left hand. It fits perfectly.

It's Caleb's turn. He addresses the theater. "When I need to express my emotions, I find I do it best with music, so that's what I'm going to do now." He directs his aqua blue gaze my way. "Gwen, this is for you."

My heart is too full to speak. With unshed tears in my eyes, I nod, wondering what kind of song he's crafted for me. Whatever it is, I'll love it, just like I love him.

Caleb pulls a wooden stool and a microphone on a stand from behind the curtain, where he must have hidden it earlier. He sits with one leg outstretched and the other bent with his acoustic guitar, my dad's old guitar, resting on it.

"This song is called *Angel* because that's what Gwen is to me." There's a pause as he closes his eyes. Even though he's a successful Broadway and radio singer, he still gets stage fright. I know that's what he's overcoming at this moment. He pushes through and sings, his voice husky and deep and beautiful. It resonates through my body like he's a tuning fork set to my frequency.

He sings,

> Angel
> Can I borrow your wings?
> I'm made of broken things.
> A puzzle you put back together.
> You picked out the best pieces.
> In you I see happily ever after.
> So, give me your finger and I'll put on a band.
> A golden circle with no beginning or end.
>
> Angel
> Can I borrow your wings?
> Together we'll build a house, a home.
> We'll grow a family, nice and strong.
> Babies who'll fall asleep in our arms.
> Children with eyes of blue.
> And every time it storms outside.
> I promise to reach for you.
>
> Angel
> Can I borrow your wings?
> I want to offer you so many things.
> A Christmas Day that lasts forever.
> A promise to always be together.
> I'd offer you the moon, but it's too high to reach.
> So instead, I offer you imperfect me.
> To faithfully, gratefully
> Your husband be.

Caleb's looking right at me as the last lines of his song fade into the air. I'm crying, teardrops that wash away my makeup. I couldn't stop them if I wanted to. It's not because I'm sad. It's from feeling so loved, so safe, so *seen*.

Back at the airport, Marjorie had talked about happy tears. I hadn't understood what she meant, but now I do. These are tears of joy. Of a happiness that's too big to fit in my body, so it rolls out from my eyes.

Caleb gently places the guitar on the ground and comes to me. Careful not to drop it, he takes my diamond encrusted wedding band from Dean and places it on my finger. His touch lingers there, a gentle brush of his fingers over the ring, like he's sealing it to my skin.

I offer him a smile, my chin quivering. "Thank you," I tell him sincerely. "Thank you for being you and for loving me."

He lights up at that. He cups my cheeks in his hands.

As soon as Wayne pronounces us husband and wife, Caleb doesn't wait for Wayne to add his "kiss the bride" line. In front of all our friends and family, he dips me backward, bending me so low that I can feel my veil sweep the ground. He brings his lips to mine and gives me a long, deep kiss.

Our guests go wild. They give us a standing ovation, clapping, whistling, and cheering. When we finally break apart, Caleb tells me, "I love you, Gwen. My wife. Every part of me loves every part of you. Forever."

I answer back, "and always."

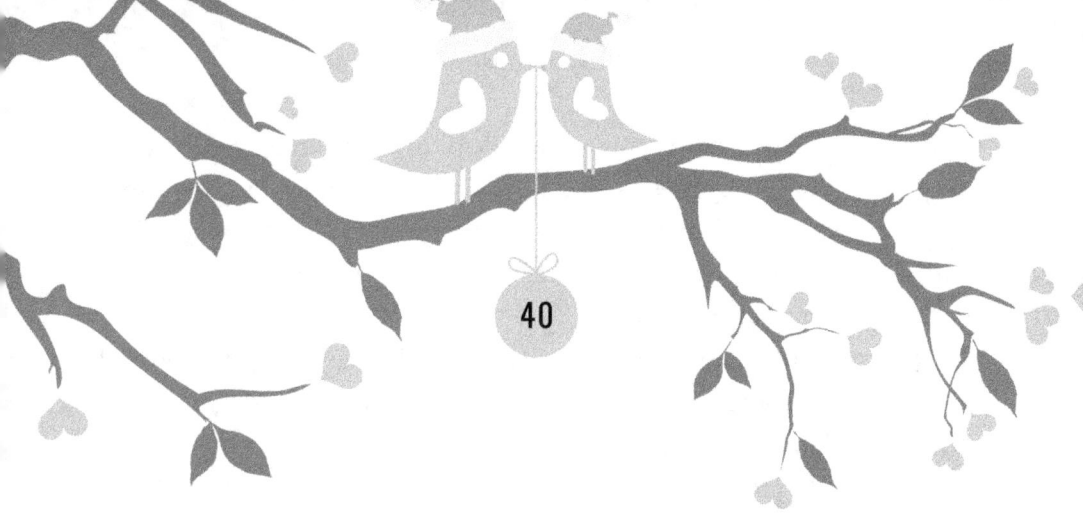

40

TEN MONTHS LATER

— GWEN —

"Mrs. Lawson! Mrs. Lawson! Over here." The reporters crowd the velvet rope that separates them from the red carpet. I release Caleb's hand, but he holds onto my fingers. He's got that worried line between his brows. If we weren't in front of all these people, I would run my lips over it and smooth it out with a kiss.

"Are you sure?" he asks, keeping his grip tight on me.

I move close and whisper, "I'm fine."

A quick peck on his cheek has all the cameras flashing, from paparazzi who want the shot for tomorrow's cover. Caleb releases me, and I walk over to the horde of microphones. Walk might be too generous of a term—at nine months pregnant, it's more of a waddle.

Apparently, we had a little too much fun on our honeymoon, because a couple of weeks after we returned I started to feel sick. Alvina took one look at me and declared that I was pregnant. I took a test just to prove her wrong, but, much to my surprise, there were two pink lines. When I told Caleb we were pregnant, he was thrilled, happier than I've ever seen.

"Mrs. Lawson," shouts a female reporter with Ariel hair, long and red. She yells louder than the rest of them. "What do you think about your husband's return to the big screen?"

"First of all, it's Dr. Wright, not Mrs. Lawson," I correct, softening the words with a smile. I don't want to be rude or pretentious. As much as I've accepted that there are times when Caleb's fame overshadows our day-to-day life, I've learned that it's still important for me to hold on to the pieces of me that are distinct from him. My name is symbolic of that.

"Sorry about that," the reporter says.

"No problem," I answer smoothly. "I'm proud of anything my husband does, whether it's acting in a movie, performing on Broadway, singing on the radio, or cooking me a meal. He does it all well."

"Will there be more movies?" a gray-haired man who reminds me of Wayne asks.

My mind drifts to Wayne and Alvina. They're off on their RV adventure, going wherever the wind takes them. They send us postcards from each stop, a tradition that's got me running to the mailbox every day. Caleb and I have a map at home, where we track their progress with a yellow highlighter. It's fun to live vicariously through them since I won't be traveling anytime soon. Not with the baby due any day now.

"Caleb's decided to do one movie a year, if our schedule allows it," I say to the man.

After the wedding, I sat Caleb down and forced him to tell me more about the project his producer friend was offering him. After a long conversation, he admitted that he wants to make movies again, but only if it works in our lives. He made this film during my second trimester but doesn't want to do more until the baby is at least a year old.

Caleb refuses to miss out on time with this child. He's been working on his relationship with his dad. They've been doing more activities alone together, but still, he wants to be a different kind of father than the one he had. More hands-on, more involved, and I love him for that.

"What designer are you wearing tonight?" asks another reporter, shoving her microphone at me.

I glance at the glittery red, wrap-style dress that flows over my bulging stomach and hangs down, brushing the floor. It's deep cut, revealing a tantalizing flash of cleavage. When I had come down the penthouse stairs earlier, Caleb's eyes had snapped wide. He had whistled and said, "Pregnancy looks good on you."

I respond to the reporter, saying, "I'm not sure about the designer. I got it at the mall."

There's a stunned silence from the press, which I use as my excuse to retreat. I kindly thank them for their time and walk away.

Dean shadows me, chuckling. "You love to surprise them, don't you?"

My hand covers my mouth as I giggle. "I can't help it. It's too fun reminding them that there are a lot more people who shop at local stores than on Rodeo Drive." I understand what's expected of me—to be a well-behaved princess, married to Hollywood royalty. For Caleb's sake, I play that role, but on my own terms. That's how I've learned to live with his fame. To allow it into our lives without it consuming who we are as individuals and as a couple.

I'm lucky. Caleb doesn't want me to be the picture-perfect celebrity wife. He just wants me, the *real* me, and I want the real him. It's what he was looking for when he came to my mother's house in L.A. all those years ago.

Surprisingly, the public has embraced my irreverent responses to the press. After events like these, social media comments discuss how "down to earth" and "relatable" I am. Caleb teases me that soon I'll be a bigger celebrity than he is.

Dean laughs along with me.

"Are you seeing Jenny after this?" I ask him.

I swear his steps get more bounce as he answers, "She's coming over when she's finished here."

Jenny's also on the red carpet tonight, but farther down on the other side of the rope. She and Dean had done long distance for six months, getting to know one another, before Jenny made the move to New York. Now she works for *The New York Times,* still in the entertainment department, but she has an interview with the investigative team next week. There's a good shot she'll get the job. They've already told her they're impressed by her computer skills and by her part in cracking the case of Caleb's stalker.

Dean lowers his voice and confesses, "I'm thinking about telling Jenny I love her. Do you think she'll say it back?"

I swallow my grin, knowing for a fact that Jenny loves him because she's been complaining to me for the past month, wondering when he'll say the words. Can't make it too easy for Dean, though. I scrunch my nose and tap a finger against my lip, pretending to ponder. "Not sure. I guess you'll have to see what she says."

He sets his jaw and nods once, the motion resolute. "I'll do that."

We've reached Caleb, who winds an arm around my waist and draws me close. He presses a kiss to my temple amid the flashing of cameras.

"How'd it go?" he asks, still nervous about letting me handle the press on my own.

"She did fine," answers Dean with a note of pride.

We pose for a couple more pictures, then follow the rest of the cast into the movie theater where the premiere will be held.

I pick a long piece of gray dog hair off the bodice of my dress. "Hope those photos don't include this little detail." I shake it off my hand, laughing.

Caleb watches as it flutters to the ground. "Was that from Harry or Sally?" he asks, referring to the two puppies he surprised me with a month after we got married.

"Definitely Harry," I say. "That was husky dog fur, not retriever like Sally." Thinking about our goofy dogs makes me grin. At first, I felt overwhelmed when he brought them home.

"Is it a good idea?" I had asked him. "Having baby dogs and a baby human at the same time?"

Caleb had been confident. "It's a great idea. This way, they can grow up together." His words reminded me of Pip, who was so often my best friend during my childhood. That was all it took to convince me to keep the pups. Now, I hardly remember what life was like before them, with their joyful barks, slobbery dog kisses, and wagging tails. This baby will be so lucky to be raised with two furry siblings.

We start down the stairs to our seats. I watch my feet, careful not to trip in my tall heels. Right before we sit, I gasp from a sharp pain that ripples across my belly. I press a hand to my abdomen. A tiny foot kicks against my rib cage, followed by a tightening sensation.

"Are you okay?" Caleb says at my side, with his hand pressed over mine. This is his new favorite pastime—to feel the baby moving.

I take a cleansing breath. "I'm fine. It's nothin—*ow!*" The pain is back, even sharper. I reach out blindly and end up with one hand on Caleb's arm and the other on Dean's. The two men crowd me, alarm written all over their faces.

"We need to get her out of here," Caleb tells Dean.

"No. We'll miss your show," I protest, then suck in a breath as another wave of agony roars through me. It leaves me dizzy, gasping.

"Who cares?" Caleb cries out. "What if you're in labor?"

Unable to argue, I pant through the pain. It's like an iron vise is clamped around my belly, tightening more with each passing minute. Together, Dean and Caleb hustle me back up the stairs and outside. Luckily, most of the reporters have left now that the red-carpet portion of the evening is over. I try to keep a calm façade, but I can't hide the bead of sweat that runs from my hairline down to my jaw.

Dean's talking on his phone, his body turned away so I can't hear him. He must have called Jenny because she pulls up in her compact four-door sedan.

"You look pretty," I get out when she rushes over, her eyes wide with alarm.

I hadn't seen her yet tonight, so this is the first glimpse I get of the long gold dress she wears. It hugs her curves in all the right places. Jenny doesn't pull at her clothing the way she used to. She doesn't frown in the mirror like she did when we were growing up. Even in the haze of my pain, I can appreciate that my friend is finally comfortable in her own skin.

"Thanks," Jenny says distractedly. She holds onto the side of the car and balances as she unstraps her shoes from her feet.

"What're you doing?" Dean pulls the passenger door open and climbs in.

"Have you seen these things?" She lifts them up, showing off six-inch spike heels. "I can't drive over five miles an hour in them."

A sharp jab in my belly has me hissing through my teeth.

Caleb rubs my back, making soothing noises. "We need to get her to the hospital," he says urgently.

"Hurry, get in." Jenny waves her arm frantically, as if she's on a runway trying to land an airplane.

There's an awkward moment where Caleb has to shove from behind to fit me through the small doorway. Like a cork coming loose from a champagne bottle, I pop into the car and struggle into the back seat. Caleb sits next to me with his hand on my belly. Jenny looks over her shoulder at the advancing traffic. She guns the engine and merges into the closest lane.

"I'm not ready," I tell Caleb as I grip his arm. Panic is setting in. "I need more time. What if I'm a bad mom? What if the baby hates me? What if—I—"

"Shh," Caleb says, brushing a sweaty tangle of hair back from my face. "You're going to be a great mom, Gwen. The best. This child and I are lucky to have you." His voice is gentle, soothing.

I relax at the sound of it.

At least until the next contraction hits.

I hiss in pain. My fingers dig into his arm so hard I know I'll leave bruises.

"Sorry. Ow! It hurts," I exclaim, curling around my swollen belly.

With an edge of panic, Caleb shouts, "Jenny, drive faster!"

"I am," she snaps, equally stressed.

"She's going as fast as she can," Dean tells Caleb, his protective side coming out to defend his girlfriend.

"I think I might puke," I moan, the lurching of the car adding to my growing nausea.

"Drive faster. Gwen's turning green," Dean tells Jenny. His head swivels from me to her and back again.

"Please don't throw up," begs Caleb. He swallows rapidly and says, "If you do, I'll vomit too."

"Not in my car. No puking in my car." Jenny takes a turn so fast that my butt slides across the seat. I plow into Caleb, who catches me in his arms.

I gag, which makes Caleb gag, which makes Dean gag.

"Seriously Jenny, we need to get to the hospital *now*." Dean pinches the bridge of his nose, breathing in shallow gasps.

Through gritted teeth, Jenny says, "Will you stop already? I'm going as fast as I can."

My eyes water from the nausea and pain.

"We took those prenatal classes," Caleb says, holding me tight

I love him so much, but the feeling of it is too constricting. I push him away.

"Sorry," I pant, "need," pant, "space," pant.

"You're supposed to do that special breathing," he tells me.

"I don't remember how." I clap one hand over my mouth and the other on my belly. It feels like the baby is trying to burrow out through my back. That's where my pain is.

Caleb makes weird panting and hissing noises. Not at all how the Lamaze instructor did it.

Desperate for relief, I mimic him. Quickly, I lose my train of thought. "I can't," I whine. "Oh no. It hurts."

"Come on, Gwen. You can do it," Jenny encourages from the front seat.

I remember the breathing and try it again, Caleb doing it with me. Soon Dean and Jenny join in. All four of us are taking sharp, deep breaths. The car is filled with the sound of it, broken by my low moans when the contractions hit.

We swerve around cars. Horns honk. A cabbie cusses us out, waving his hand threateningly. I'm only half-aware of it. All my concentration is focused on what's happening inside my body.

With a screech of tires, Jenny pulls up to the Maternity Department. It has a separate entrance for situations like this. Caleb, Dean, and Jenny jump out. Dean grabs a wheelchair from the lobby. Caleb and Jenny help me out of the car.

I'm bent over, my hands clasping my belly. As soon as Dean brings the wheelchair, I collapse into it. A feeling of wetness spreads under me.

"Caleb," I say, tears of embarrassment gather in my eyes. He comes closer, leaning down. I whisper, "I think I just peed myself."

A voice from a few feet away says, "That's your water breaking." I look up to find an older lady with navy blue scrubs. "I'm Mary. The head nurse here."

Simultaneously, we all breathe a sigh of relief. Help has arrived.

Mary surveys our now-disheveled group, all in formal wear. I'm a sweaty mess. Caleb's bow tie has come undone. Dean's taken off his jacket. Jenny stands barefoot on the sidewalk. Mary doesn't even blink. I have a feeling she's seen worse things than us.

Caleb steps forward. "This is Gwen, my wife. I think she's in labor."

Right as he says it, the biggest contraction yet hits me like a freight train. I screech, gripping the arms of the wheelchair for dear life.

Jenny, Dean, and Caleb crowd me, all of them asking if I'm okay at the same time.

Mary shoos them away. She comes behind and takes the handles of the wheelchair. "Looks like labor to me. Who's ready to have a baby?" Without waiting for an answer, she pushes me into the hospital. My husband and friends follow.

JENNY

"What's taking so long?" I ask for the twentieth time. I pace back and forth in the maternity waiting room. It's crowded in here. Others wait anxiously. I'm not the only one wearing a groove in the scuffed linoleum floor.

"I'm sure they're fine," Dean tries to reassure me. He sits in a plastic upholstered chair with his legs spread and his hands loosely braced on his knees. A table full of magazines sits next to him, with perfect families in color-coordinated outfits grinning from the covers.

I pick up a magazine, flip through it, and toss it back into the pile. "It's been hours and hours," I complain.

"This is lasting forever," Marjorie agrees. "We should ask them what's going on." She stands, but Caleb's dad places a hand on her arm and pulls her down.

"We checked 10 minutes ago," he reminds her. "If they have news, they'll come tell us."

I shoot a quick text to Gwen's mom, who's back in Japan, letting her know there's no change in the situation here. She'll pass the message along to Gwen's brothers. Once the baby is born, they all plan on coming to New York to visit.

After another excruciating half-hour, Caleb comes bursting into the room. His jacket and bow tie are gone. His sleeves are rolled up. He's got the biggest, goofiest grin I've ever seen on his face.

"A boy," he announces.

Surprising no one, Marjorie bursts into tears. Her husband pats her shoulder. They go to their son and share a family hug. Then it's my turn and Dean's to embrace Caleb. He babbles through all our congratulations, like he can't help himself. The joy inside him radiates outward and is infectious.

"A boy," he repeats with wonder. "Seven pounds, four ounces. He's so small I can hold him with one hand. We're naming him Carter. Robert is his middle name, for Gwen's dad." Tears shine in Caleb's eyes and in mine, too.

"You should have seen Gwen," he tells me. "She was so brave. I've always known how strong she is, but it was amazing." He shakes his head with admiration. "I can't believe it. I'm so lucky. The luckiest person alive."

We talk for a while longer. Caleb lets us know he's already called Gwen's mom and Seth to tell them the news. He says the baby and Gwen are sleeping now, both of them tired from the birth. Once they wake up, we can go see them. He answers our questions about what the baby looks like—*adorable*—and if Gwen is happy—*ecstatic*—then exits to check on his wife and newborn.

Marjorie and her husband head to the cafeteria to get coffee, leaving Dean and me alone. For the first time since we arrived, I collapse into the seat next to him. I allow myself to slump down and rest my head on his shoulder. He runs a gentle hand over my curls. I lean into his touch and take comfort from it. He has a way of evening me out, soothing me.

"That was exhausting, and all I did was drive here," I tell him.

He murmurs his agreement.

I sit up straight and turn to him. "I can't wait to meet my godson."

Dean smiles at me, the beautiful, unguarded smile that he only releases when he's truly happy. It melts me every time I see it.

"He's my godson, too, you know," he reminds me, as if I could forget. We had both been so honored when Gwen and Caleb asked us to be godparents.

After they had told us, I had cried, big hitching sobs.

Gwen had come and sat down by me. "This is good news. Why are you sad?"

"It's just that I didn't expect it. You really have forgiven me for telling your secret, for revealing that Caleb was at your mom's house, haven't you?" I had inhaled, my shoulders heaving.

"Of course, I have." Gwen had hugged me lightly. "I never think about it, and you shouldn't either."

Her words had healed a rift deep inside of me. With effort, I released my guilt and embraced my new role in her life. Best friend and godmother. It was a big commitment to help guide this child, but I was ready for it.

I look at Dean, so strong and handsome. "Do you ever worry," I ask, dropping my eyes, "about if we break up. How awkward it will be, seeing each other at baby Carter's birthdays and graduations?"

"Not really." Dean stretches his muscular legs.

My head whips up, brows lifted with surprise. "You don't?"

He chuckles at my expression. "Sweetheart. I know it hasn't been that long, but only a fool would let you go. I told you before, you're mine, and I intend to keep it that way. As a matter of fact, there's something I've been meaning to tell you."

My heart leaps.

"Jenny," Dean says, his brown eyes warm, the gold in the center sparkling, "I've been on my own for a very long time. I honestly thought it would be that way forever, but then you came into my life like an exercising, fast-talking, fidgeting, candy-eating tornado. You turned my world upside down in the best possible way. I'm in love with you, and I'm hoping you feel the same."

"I love you, too." Those words taste sweet on my lips. I've waited so long to say them. "I'm going to keep on loving you, going to drive you crazy, for as long as you'll let me."

He kisses me right there in the waiting room. A no-holding-back kiss, with his hands on my cheeks. When he pulls away, his dimple is on full display. He brushes my curls behind my shoulder and says, "I like your kind of crazy."

42

GWEN

My lashes flutter open. There's a second of panic as my wild gaze searches for Carter, but he's there, pulled up next to my bed. Mary, the nurse, has taped a sign to his see-through bassinet.

It reads, "Welcome to the world, Carter Robert Lawson." Underneath that, in her neat handwriting, are all of his pertinent statistics—birth weight, length, and APGAR scores.

His numbers are good. Even though he's a few days early, he's fully grown. Ready to be out of my belly and into the world.

Out in the world that could hurt him, disappoint him. The thought of him ever being in pain makes my stomach clench. I want to fight anyone who threatens him. I want to lock him away to keep him safe. I want to tuck his blankets tight around him, so he never gets cold or lonely or scared. I love him in a way that's completely new. In an all-consuming "I would jump in front of a train for you" kind of way. They're good and frightening, the feelings I have for him.

Carter sleeps on, oblivious to my overprotective mom thoughts. I'm biased, but he really is a gorgeous baby. Rosy-cheeked with fair hair that glints from the overhead lights. His eyes have only opened a couple of times. When they did, I got flashes of aqua blue, the same color as Caleb's. I love that, knowing my husband's gorgeous eyes have been passed down to a future generation.

I shift my gaze to Caleb. He's asleep in a chair next to me. Of all the beautiful things I've seen in my life, none of them prepared me to watch Caleb hold our child for the first time. He'd taken Carter into his arms and cradled him against his chest so naturally, like he handled babies every day. As he rocked our baby, he thanked me about a million times. He thanked me until I interrupted and said, "You contributed, too. That child is half yours."

Caleb had laughed and said, "I got to do the easy part."

My aching body agreed with that. It was no simple task carrying a baby for nine months and then pushing him out. I feel as weak as a newborn kitten, sapped of my energy.

Caleb must feel the weight of my gaze. He lifts his head, blinking slowly until his eyes land on me.

"You're awake." Stretching and yawning, he rises from the chair.

I hold my hands out to him, beckoning. "Come here and hold me."

He gives me my special smile and responds, "With pleasure."

The bed creaks when he climbs in. I scoot over to make more room. We're probably not supposed to do this, lay together in this narrow hospital bed, but I don't care if we get caught. I need to touch him, to feel him solidly in my arms. Caleb settles against me with a contented sigh. He slings one leg over me and rests his cheek on my temple. Quietly, we stare at our baby.

"He's perfect," says Caleb. "He has your hair. I hope he has your strength, too."

"He's got your eyes," I return. "And I bet he's got your big heart."

"Wouldn't it be amazing," muses Caleb, "if he gets the best of both of us? I wonder what his future holds? What great things will he do for this world?"

"I don't know, but I can't wait to find out." Shifting, I wiggle in Caleb's embrace until I'm facing him. "I do know he has the best daddy in the world, the best husband I could ask for." Caleb kisses me, his lips soft as silk.

"I love you," I tell him. "And I love this life we've created."

"I love you and Carter, too." Caleb kisses me again, delicately, like after the trials of the day he's scared to break me. "I'm going to keep loving you and all of our future children—"

"Future children!?" I sit up. "Let's get through this next year before we start to think about more babies."

He's laughing as I sink back against his firm chest. "Okay, we don't have to talk about future children…*yet*. What I was saying is that I'll love you and any of our children. That I'll do my best to protect and teach them. I'll be your equal partner as we raise them. I want you to know that I'm here with you. That we're doing this together."

"Good." I snuggle deeper into him, taking comfort from the familiar warmth of his body, his spicy cinnamon scent. "I wouldn't want to create a family with anyone else. You're it for me, Caleb."

He presses a kiss to the top of my head. "Forever and always, my love. You and me."

I tuck this memory into a room in my heart, along with those of my father, my family, and Jenny.

"Forever," I whisper to my husband, to my slumbering baby, "and always."

BONUS EPILOGUE

WEDNESDAY, DECEMBER 25
GWEN'S AND CALEB'S WEDDING

HELEN

Is there anything more awkward than being at a wedding where the only person you know is the bride or groom? They're enjoying their big day while also being gracious hosts. They're circulating to each table to say hello to their guests.

I was lucky. Gwen spent an extra 10 minutes talking to me in the bathroom. She asked how packing was going and if I was excited about my new job in California. I answered "good" and "yes" to her questions.

Now I sit in the corner of the room, idly swirling my glass of red wine. Droplets cling to the sides and then slide down like rain on a window. The wedding reception is at the Mandarin Oriental, just off Columbus Circle. We're in a ballroom at the top of the building, on the 89th floor. Crystal chandeliers gleam over an Asian-inspired carpet so plush that my high heels sank into it when I first walked in.

Dinner was delicious, the food provided by Caleb's restaurant. Tender, flaky salmon and thick steaks paired with thinly sliced scalloped potatoes in a buttery cream sauce. After we ate, Gwen and Caleb together held the knife to cut their three-tiered wedding cake. It sparkled with edible glitter designed to look like snowflakes, each one unique.

Now the guests are up, wandering around to talk with each other. A crowd steadily grows on the dance floor, which is flanked by a DJ with spinning turntables and an open laptop.

I watch as Gwen floats across the room, breathtaking in her princess-style white dress. The ceremony earlier was the most touching I've ever seen. The way Caleb serenaded her, his words brimming with emotion. It almost made me believe that love is a real thing. Something that can be captured, shared for eternity, *if* you find the right partner. Since I haven't dated for over a year, it's highly unlikely I'll find a soulmate, but I was gratified to see that my new friend has hers.

Gwen pauses by her brother Teddy, whom I've met once, a week ago. He's dancing with a large group of young people. I've already noticed him several times tonight. He wears a black suit. Earlier he'd had on a red bow tie, a nod to the color scheme of his sister's wedding, but now it's gone along with his jacket. The top three buttons of his shirt, also black, are undone, revealing a fine sheen of sweat across well-defined pectoralis muscles.

When I first met him, an uncharacteristic zing flowed through my body. Like I'd stuck my finger into an electrical outlet. That night I'd watched him work and flirt his way through the bar. I'd been oddly enchanted by his mischievous grin and lighthearted laugh.

I'm not lighthearted about anything. I'm measured and ambitious. Responsible to a fault.

Gwen tugs on his sleeve until he bends his ear down to her. She rises onto her tiptoes and whispers. Teddy glances my way. I flush, suspicious they're talking about me. Sure enough, he gives her a nod and saunters over to where I sit.

"Hey." He's breathing fast, and a wicked grin lifts his lips. "Do you want to dance?"

"Oh no," I tell him. I'm embarrassed that he's obviously been sent on a mission by his sister. I can just imagine what kind Gwen said to him. "Go get Helen from her sad corner and make her dance. I want everyone to have fun at my wedding." This is a pity visit. Not something he would have thought of on his own.

"Thanks for the offer, though."

My eyes widen in surprise when he responds by flopping down in the seat next to me. I expected my refusal to be met with relief. That he would be happy to move on, knowing he'd fulfilled his brotherly duty, but that's not what he does. Instead, he slouches in the chair and tips his face to the ceiling, closing his eyes with a weary sigh.

"Mind if I hang out with you for a couple of minutes?" he asks.

"Uh, sure." With his eyes shut, I can stare as much as I want. This close, I see how long his eyelashes are. How the angle of his jaw is sharp and straight, like it was drawn with a ruler.

We sit together in silence, which is another surprise. Usually, with someone you don't know, there's this pressure, this urgency to fill the air with chatter. A comfortable silence is earned from knowing the other person well enough to not default to idle chit-chat. But this quiet between us is calm and oddly familiar, as if we've sat like this many times before, which we definitely have not.

Finally, his eyes flutter open and slide my way. "I love my sister," he says, "and this wedding is the best I've ever been to, but I still can't wait to leave." Then he flinches, as if injured by his own words. "Don't tell Gwen I said that, please," he begs, regretting his candor.

"I won't say a word," I assure him, then tilt my head to the side. "You seemed like you were having a good time out there."

He waves a languid hand in the air. "Old friends from high school. Haven't seen them in years. You'd think it would be fun catching up, but the truth is, I already know what they've been up to. With social media, I've watched them grow up, get married, and have a kid. I even saw how they just got back from a trip to Orlando."

He rolls his head without moving the rest of his body to look at me. "Reunions stink these days. There's no mystery. No wondering how Bobby from Spanish class turned out." He sticks out his bottom lip in a pout that makes me laugh.

"I guess I never thought about it that way," I admit.

"You're lucky," he says. "You don't have to pretend that you don't already know how little Ricky won the All-Stars baseball game last summer."

I think back to him laughing and dancing with abandon. "You didn't look too miserable."

He angles his entire body my direction. "Why? Were you watching me?" Teddy purrs, teasing and flirting all at once.

I'm glad it's dark in this corner, so he can't see my cheeks flush.

His smile falls away. "I'm a good actor," he says with downcast eyes. His morose expression makes my heart pinch. "Maybe I should give Caleb a run for his money. I could be the one to win an Academy Award."

I don't often try to change the mood of people around me. I believe we are each responsible for our own emotions. It's not my job to make someone else happy. But seeing Teddy like this feels wrong. It's like looking at a lightbulb that's been turned off. I have an urge to flick his switch. To make him shine again.

"You know what? I would like to dance, after all."

His head whips my way, surprise opening his mouth. "Oh, okay." He scrambles to his feet and stretches his hand out to me. When my fingers touch his and he folds his warm palm into mine, I feel that jolt of electricity again. It travels up my arm and burrows into my chest. I wonder if Teddy feels it too, because his body jerks and he sends me a perplexed look, his arched eyebrows drawing downward.

Hand in hand, we wind our way onto the dance floor. A slow song plays, the melody filled with longing. Across from me, Gwen rests her head on Caleb's chest as they sway together. He rubs small circles on her back, the gesture so tender that there's a sudden stinging in the back of my throat and a yearning for someone to caress me that way, which is silly. I'm an independent woman. I don't need a relationship to make my life complete.

Teddy hesitantly puts his hands on my waist, his touch feather-light. I place my palms on his broad shoulders. We're awkward, pulling closer until my chest brushes his and then we both jump back.

Just this one dance. I steel myself to get it over with, uncomfortable with how my fingers tingle from where they contact him.

I can already picture leaving after this, going home to my half-packed apartment on the Upper East Side and reading through the stack of medical journals by my bedside until I fall asleep alone in my king-sized bed. My idea of a perfect evening.

The song ends, and music with a techno beat starts up. I drop my hands from Teddy, about to excuse myself, when he flashes that devilish smile at me again. He dances, his movements fast, almost frantic, but he's not doing the usual moves for a song like this. Instead, he breaks out every cliché '80s dance you can think of. He does the running man, the cabbage patch, the sprinkler, grinning at me the entire time. It's so unexpected and goofy and funny that I laugh, delighted. That makes him laugh too. He reaches for me and spins me around, twirling together.

"Your turn," he calls once we stop turning. He points at my feet and gives me a look of challenge.

"What? Like a dance off?" I shout over the music, which has gotten louder as more wedding guests flood the dance floor, eager to join in.

"Exactly." He sways his hips, with his hands over his head in a way that draws his shirt tight across his chest. My eyes dip, taking in the ripple of his muscles and trailing down to his narrow waist.

Teddy steps into my space and leans down. He says right into my ear, "Unless you're scared." He dances away, light on his feet.

Oh. That was the *wrong* thing to say to me. My competitive streak flares to life. I pride myself on being the best at anything I do—otherwise I don't bother doing it. My eyes narrow at him, which elicits another of his carefree laughs.

"Uh, no. Have I made her mad?" he taunts. "Helen is fired up."

I lift my head and straighten my spine. "Step back." I flick my hand at him, urging him away.

He lifts his hands in mock surrender. "I can't wait to see this." His smile stretches wider. I don't miss the long look he sends over my body, his eyes trailing me from head to toe like he's really seeing me for the first time.

Dramatically, I throw my arms out. What Teddy doesn't know is that I've taken dance classes my whole life, beginning at three years old. Mostly I've done ballet, but I also had jazz, hip-hop, and tap lessons. I close my eyes, calling back the ability to find the rhythm in the music, a little worried because I haven't done this type of dance in a long time. It comes to me instantly. The beat flows through my body like it's a physical thing, like it's in my bloodstream.

It spreads to each limb, and they come to life. I lift my arms high over my head and let my hips move, undulating almost like a belly dancer.

Teddy freezes, his eyes wide.

A tiny smirk touches my lips. That was exactly the reaction I was going for. Slowly, I spin in a circle, my arms dropping to slide along the back of my head, my neck, my shoulders, the sides of my body, and finally to my hips, which have stayed in constant motion. Teddy tracks each brush of my fingertips against my body like he can't tear his gaze away. I suppress a chuckle.

Men.

So predictable.

My eyes close. I focus on my body and the way it responds to the music. Soon I'm enjoying dancing for myself, not even thinking about the man across from me. I'd forgotten this sensation of freedom, of giving myself up to movement. Living only in this moment where I become one with the notes and the lyrics.

A favorite song comes on, and I sing along with it, whispering the words under my breath, humming the tune. I'm energized, lit up from the inside, like the power of the universe is at my fingertips, like I can sense the secret magnetic vibrations that run through the world.

I'm so lost in the moment that I let out a squeak when strong hands grab my waist and pull me close. Teddy's there, holding me to him tightly, letting his hips bump up against mine. His gaze runs admiringly over my face and then down at my body. My cheeks heat. No one's looked at me like this in a while, years even.

It's…nice.

Maybe those medical journals can wait. I wrap my arms around Teddy, and together we dance, every touch electric. Teddy does a break dance move, spinning on his knees. He points to my feet, and I tap dance, my shoes moving so fast they blur. I'm having so much fun that I barely notice the crowd that grows around us. They form a circle and chant our names. The wedding photographer takes a couple of shots, which makes me laugh, thinking how inadvertently I've ended up in Gwen's wedding album.

Teddy pulls me close for a dramatic tango, his cheek against mine as he whisks me back and forth over the dance floor. The crowd parts when we swing dance, Teddy twirling me again and again. I lose track of time. Minutes, hours, fly by and my inhibitions with them. Normally I'd be put off by a near-stranger dancing with me, but not with him. I sink down to my knees before him, bounce once on my heels, and then rise up with his hands on my arms guiding me. He drops to one knee, spins on the ground, and then springs up, grinning. I throw my head back and let out a laugh, so big it makes my eyes water. Sweat beads on my forehead. I'm panting from the exertion of dancing harder than ever before.

After many songs have passed, Teddy grips my shoulder. "Let's get a drink." He plucks at his shirt, which clings to him in an alluring way. "I'm overheated."

The crowd groans its disappointment when we walk away. Teddy raises his hand and waves to them like he's exiting from a televised dance competition. *Dancing with the Stars* would be appropriate, I guess, since Caleb's here.

We stop by the bar. Teddy gets a long-necked bottle of beer while I grab an icy water, the cup slippery with condensation. Without discussing it, we push through swinging doors to the expansive balcony that overlooks the city. New York spreads out in front of us, a tapestry of lights and sound. Even from so high up, I can make out the faint noise of sirens and cars honking.

"Wow, it's beautiful." I wave my hand at the view and stroll down to the far end of the balcony. Teddy follows. It's secluded here. Large ferns in golden planters are highlighted by illuminated scones set high on the wall. The plants cast spiky shadows on the floor. Music from the wedding fades as we move farther from the door. We're alone, the only people who've ventured out to enjoy the night air.

Teddy turns to me, his eyes gleaming. The spaghetti strap on my dress has fallen off my shoulder. With a single long finger, he slides it back into place and then rests his hand there, caressing my skin lightly with his thumb. I'm exhilarated by the dancing, the music, the enchantment of the evening. I want more of this, more feeling alive, more of *him*.

Operating purely on impulse, I surge up onto my toes and kiss him. I slam my body into his with such force that he stumbles backward into the metal railing behind him. Teddy lets out a startled "oomph" and his mouth opens, probably in shock that I've just attacked him. A dim part of my mind warns this may not be a good idea, but it shuts up when his lips instantly respond to mine.

Teddy kisses me back, and this time I'm the one surprised. Something warm and metallic is in my mouth, something foreign. I explore it with my tongue and realize he has a piercing. The sensation of it is unexpected. I suck it into my mouth, and the kiss deepens. Teddy presses closer. He kisses me harder, using his whole body. Each brush of his lips and tongue matches his hands, which draw me close, circling my waist.

"You're stunning," he whispers against the skin of my throat. "So gorgeous," he murmurs into my ear.

I pull away to stare into his eyes, which swim with longing.

Now that we're not touching, a worried crease appears between Teddy's brows.

"I'm sorry," he says. "We can stop."

I consider his words.

We could stop kissing, but is that what I want?

There's a recklessness in Teddy that calls to me. It awakens a long-suppressed urge to leave my normal self behind.

Just for tonight.

"Kiss me some more," I tell him.

I hold my breath and wait for his response…

The End

(To be continued in *Holiday Love,* coming next fall/winter.)

ANOTHER BONUS EPILOGUE

Would you like to see the wedding scene from Caleb's perspective? What was he thinking when he watched Gwen walk down the aisle? Use this link/QR code to get access to this EXCLUSIVE bonus content and to join my newsletter, where I give you FREE chapters of my upcoming novels, writing updates, giveaways, and more.

HTTPS://TINYURL.COM/CALEBSWEETBONUS

THANKS FOR READING!

Can I please ask you, dear reader, for a BIG favor? If you enjoyed this book, pretty please leave a review.

I know that your time is precious, but reviews are what make or break an author's career. They influence everything from reaching new readers to training Amazon's algorithms to put this book on the top of the page when you search for it.

It doesn't take much, even just a line or two on Amazon and GoodReads is enough for a helpful review. I personally read every one, and your feedback helps me write the books YOU want to read. We are in this together, you and I.

Thank you a million times over for reading this book and for leaving a review. You are literally making dreams come true.

XOXO, Melissa

Here's the link and QR code to review.
HTTPS://TINYURL.COM/HOLIDAYWEDDINGSWEET

DO YOU LIKE GAMES?

Me, too!

I'm a BIG Disney fan.

In this story, I mention THREE Disney princesses.

Can you find one or more of them?

Email me if you do! hello@melissadymondauthor.com

I have special prizes that I'm ONLY sharing
with winners of this challenge, so email me your answer.
If you get it right, I'll send you a prize! Let's play!

BONUS: FREE FIRST CHAPTER OF
PAGING DR. HART BY DR. MELISSA DYMOND.

Have you read this swoony best-selling medical romance with suspense yet?

Available on Amazon and at most major book sellers. FREE to read on Kindle Unlimited!

Get it now!
HTTPS://TINYURL.COM/PAGINGDRHARTSWEET

Loving him might give her a heart attack.

CHAPTER 1

PRESENT, COLUMBUS, OHIO

Everyone's staring at me when I get the first mysterious text message. Because of course that's when it would happen. Not when I'm home alone or in my car or studying at the library.

Nope.

It has to be right then, when I'm about to start my presentation. The Mercy Hospital medical staff gathers in our auditorium every day at 8:00 a.m. for our morning educational conference. We take turns giving lectures about interesting cases, using them to teach the medical students and younger residents about disease processes and how to treat them.

Today it's my turn—my very first time. I'm not nervous, though. I mean, sure, my mouth is the Sahara Desert and my heart has crawled up into my throat, but I'm fine. *Totally fine.* At least that's what I tell myself as I gaze out into the sea of doctors. They look back with expressions that range from vague interest to frank boredom.

"Ladies and gentlemen," I begin. Heads swing my way, and conversation hushes. I've set my phone to silent. It sits on the podium, next to my laptop. I take a deep breath, about to continue my lecture, when the phone screen flashes and the phone vibrates so hard it skitters across the wooden surface. The noise startles me. I jolt and drop the microphone, which falls to the ground and lets out a squeal of feedback, like it's crying about its rough treatment.

Shoot.

Heat warms my cheeks. I let out a shaky, apologetic smile. The audience stares back, waiting for me to get on with the show. While I'm on my hands and knees, fetching the microphone, I wonder who the message could be from. Hardly anyone ever calls or texts me. The phone is still vibrating rhythmically when I stand. Acutely aware of the crowd, I peer at the tiny screen. The text is from an unfamiliar number, but the image is all-too-familiar. It's a photo of the iconic Las Vegas sign. The one you see when you first drive into town, right before you reach the southern end of the neon-lit Strip.

"Welcome to fabulous Las Vegas, Nevada," it proclaims in bold, blood-red letters.

That's...odd.

I grew up in Las Vegas, but everyone I knew there is long gone. I scroll down. There's no message, no name. Nothing to explain who sent the picture or why. A chill shivers through me, the icy fingers of the past walking down my spine. I inhale a shaky breath and glance around, searching the shadows of the room, but find them empty. Nothing lurking. Still, foreboding settles low in my stomach, weighing me down.

With the audience watching, I can't react, so I carefully school my features. I need to nail this lecture. Hopefully, if I do well, it'll win me the

Resident of the Month award. I've wanted that certificate, with its shiny gold seal, since I first started working here three years ago. It's physical proof that I've transformed. More importantly, I need it for the $1,000 bonus that comes along with it. I'll give this same presentation at a medical conference in a couple of months. It's an honor to speak there, one not usually given to residents. The money will let me stay at the swanky hotel at Disney World, where the conference is being held, instead of a cheap motel 30 miles down the road.

Another glance at the text stirs dark memories, which I bury. With a sigh, I set the phone aside, refusing to think of it again. It's time to focus. Luckily, or rather unluckily, I'm good at compartmentalizing.

I've had *lots* of practice.

"A 56-year-old male presents to the emergency department with blood in his urine," I begin. Methodically clicking through my slides one-by-one, I outline how the patient was diagnosed with renal cancer. A CAT scan appears on the screen. With my pointer, I demonstrate how cancerous tendrils extend from the kidney and worm their way up into the biggest vein in the body, the inferior vena cava.

"For renal cancer," I explain, "we use tumor staging to help define the extent of disease and prognosis. Because the tumor extends outside the kidney, this patient is stage T3c." A click later shows photos from the surgery when the kidney was removed. Nearing the end of my talk, I discuss the patient's treatment and what imaging we will use for follow-up. This man will get repeat CAT scans every six months to make sure he remains cancer-free.

I pause to catch my breath, since I've been talking nonstop, and survey the audience. Everyone's still alert, and most are paying attention, which is all I can ask for. These early-morning presentations are often dry. Even I've had to fight to stay awake in this dark room when it was someone else up here lecturing.

"I'd like to open the floor to questions now," I say. There are a few raised hands from the crowd, asking about the man's long-term chance of reoccurrence and treatment options, which I answer easily. Relief floods through me. The finish line is in sight. There've been no technical difficulties. I haven't stuttered or said anything embarrassing. I give myself a mental pat on the back and prepare to end the presentation.

That's when a hand shoots up into the air.

It's a man, about my age, with ruffled brown hair, dark straight brows, and a square jaw. He sits next to Dr. Washburn, my residency director and boss. There's something mesmerizing about him. Something difficult to define but hard to look away from. It's partly his eyes, which are stunning, an unusually light color, warm amber like a glass of whiskey when the sunlight filters through it.

I've never seen him before.

I'd remember a face like that.

I nod politely. "You have a question?"

The man's voice is deep, carrying easily through the auditorium. "Yes. It's about the tumor staging. You said it was stage T3c?"

"That's correct." I frown, wondering where he's going with this.

"I think it's actually T3b. T3c is when the cancer is in the inferior vena cava but goes *above* the diaphragm. T3b is when it stays *below* the diaphragm. In those images you showed, the tumor was below."

Flustered, my normally orderly mind reels.

"Um—give me a minute." Time stretches out as I frantically search through the notebook where I wrote my research to prepare for this lecture.

Someone in the crowd coughs. Chairs squeak as people shift. The projector overhead whirs, its fan turning on. My breath comes in brief spurts. Hands shaking, I flip through the pages.

Where is it? Where is it?

Ah. It's there in my handwriting.

T3b.

The handsome stranger is right.

Darn it. There goes my award.

Heat rushes up my neck to splash across my cheeks. Humiliation gives way to fury. I'm mad at myself for making the error, but I'm also angry at *him*. Why would he correct me in front of everyone? Who even does that? I should have known. No man can be that pretty without also being cruel. Every eye is trained on me, waiting to see how I'll respond.

I swallow around the boulder in my throat. "It is T3b. I must have typed it wrong. I apologize."

"No problem," he says graciously.

Now, I hate him. First for pointing out my mistake and second for acting like it's not a big deal.

To me, it's a *very* big deal indeed.

Available on Amazon and at most major book sellers. FREE to read on Kindle Unlimited!

Get it now!
HTTPS://TINYURL.COM/PAGINGDRHARTSWEET

MEET MELISSA!

Melissa Dymond is a mom, doctor, and best-selling author.

Born and raised in California, she did her medical school and training in the Midwest. Now she lives in the Southwest surrounded by boys, including her doctor husband, three amazing sons, and an adorable Siberian husky, Buddy.

When she's not working, you can find her drinking an iced white chocolate mocha while voraciously reading, scrolling social media, and planning her family's next Disney vacation.

She would love to connect with you on her website, www.melissadymondauthor.com, where you can sign up for her newsletter, get free chapters and writing updates, see character art, get the best deals on bookish merchandise, and share book related–memes.

Also, she would love to chat with you on social media, where she spends WAY too much time. Join her at:

Instagram: https://www.instagram.com/melissadymondauthor
Facebook: https://www.facebook.com/melissadymondauthor
Tiktok: https://www.tiktok.com/@melissadymond6

ACKNOWLEDGMENTS

Hello, Dear Reader,

I never meant to write this book. When I finished my debut novel, *Holiday Star*, I thought it was done. Gwen and Caleb had found their happily ever after. As much as I loved them, it was time to move on.

That's when the emails, DMs, and comments started rolling in. Turns out you loved them too, and you weren't done.

You had questions. What's going on with Teddy? We're worried about him.

You had suggestions. Jenny should get her own book. Wayne and Alvina need to get together.

You had unresolved issues. Caleb's and Gwen's moms have unresolved conflicts with their children. Maybe a redemption arc?

Most of all, you wanted TO SEE THE WEDDING!

After reading through your thoughtful reviews, comments, and suggestions (thank you for them all!), I realized I wanted to see the wedding, too.

So, I took a mental trip back to California and to New York to spend time with some of my favorite characters. Can I tell you, I had the best time finding out what they'd been up to!

I would never have known those details without you, dear reader, asking me to revisit these old friends. I truly enjoyed seeing how they'd grown and how relationships old and new had developed. My favorite part was watching Gwen and Caleb get married and start a family of their own. I hope you found that as satisfying as I did.

Okay, on to the acknowledgments. The most important person I want to thank is YOU, dear reader. There would be no book without you. Please know how much I appreciate your taking a chance on an indie author like me. Thanks also to those of you who leave a review, post on social media, reach out with an email or a DM, and recommend my books to your friends and family. Those extra steps make all the difference.

If I can be known for one thing as an author, it's that I write for you, my readers. It's your happiness I'm after. The ability to entertain you. Make you laugh, cry, or swoon. That's what I want, and I'll do anything to make sure you're smiling by the time you read the words, "The End."

I'm fortunate that I have a talented team who help make this book a hundred times better. Thank you to my editor, Caroline Acebo, for your insightful critique and suggestions. Thank you to my mother, Lura Dymond, who is also my editor. I couldn't do this without you.

Thank you for being patient while formatting this book, Steve Kuhn. Thank you to my book cover designers at Qamber Design. Thank you to my character artists; Hungrydamyart (Etsy), Lorena@Chocological.art, lulybot, and moondraw_s. Thank you for creating and maintaining my gorgeous website, Katharine Bolin. Seriously, this website is so pretty! www.melissadymondauthor.com

Thank you to my personal assistant, Hayley Faryna, who has completely transformed my Instagram page into something gorgeous. Beyond that, she beta reads, strategizes, and occasionally talks me off a ledge. Thanks to Maude Levesque, who also helps with social media and is just about the nicest person ever. Thanks to Tina Marshall, who is so generous with her knowledge about social media and publishing and who doesn't mind that I DM her anytime anything exciting happens.

For this book I had more beta readers than ever before. They spoiled me with their useful insights and critiques. I told them that now they've done it, because they all have to keep beta reading until eternity. They are in no particular order, Diza Parker, Nicole Rempfer, Jackie Hernandez, Amber Butler, Jenn Trocine, Daisy Hernandez, Celina Lyles, and Sara Kleinschrodt. Thank you to author Layna James for being a sensitivity reader. You helped me understand Jenny and Alvina better than ever before. Thanks to Crissi VanderWoude, who gave me the idea of writing Gwen's dad's initials on the bottom of her wedding shoes. Crissi, who lost her mother Annie to colon cancer, did this at her real-life wedding. Thanks also to my street team. Somehow, I ended up with the best, most amazing group of people to help cheer and champion these books. I'm so grateful to them.

Thank you to all the wonderful and supportive friends I have had through the years: Michelle Center, Judy Fann, Karen Fann, Tricia Verhoeven, Charity Yarnal, Pam Noll, Janelle McGough, Nicole Danner, Jen Julian, Jenn Hamilton, Marcie Lane, Nicole Rempfer, Julie Sallquist, Liz Martin, Jill Rother, Jackie Hernandez, Camila Parris, Maren Umlauf, Collin Zaffery, Stephanie Horton, Parris Maxwell, Darren Todd, Dorene McLaughlin, Jenna Price, Laura Weiss Ross, and so many more.

Thanks to my mom and dad, the best parents in the world. Love to my beautiful sister-in-law Amelia and her awesome husband Steven.

Thank you to my husband and three sons who have been (mostly) patient when I take forever to answer their questions (No, I don't know what's for dinner.) because I'm too busy daydreaming up stories. Like Gwen's mom said, when I look back on my life, marrying my husband Andrew and having our sons are the things I'm most proud of, the most passionate about. It's an honor to be a part of their lives.

Check out my website and join my newsletter for exciting updates about writing, book releases, great book deals, freebies, and more.

WWW.MELISSADYMONDAUTHOR.COM

www.ingramcontent.com/pod-product-compliance
Lightning Source LLC
LaVergne TN
LVHW010309070526
838199LV00065B/5503